Praise for the Wildlands Series

DARK ALCHEMY

"This fun adventure in modern-day Wyoming introduces Petra Dee, a geologist looking for her missing father and trying to make peace with her past. Bickle (*Rogue Oracle*) adds a dash of romance to the charming adventure, wrapped up with a perfect ending."

—*Publishers Weekly* (starred review)

"Mix in some Native lore, great characterizations, a gift for bringing a setting to life, and a plot that eschews any hint of the tiredness of too much contemporary fantasy, and *Dark Alchemy*'s a winner on all fronts for this reader. Bickle writes with an individual clarity and style, leaving the reader to appreciate a dark sense of wonder that's all her own. Highly recommended."

—Charles de Lint, *Fantasy & Science Fiction*

"*Dark Alchemy* reads like a stand-alone work, but Petra is such a likable protagonist and the slightly off-balance world in which the town of Temperance exists is so well drawn that it's hard not to hope we'll see more of Petra's adventures . . . More, please."

—RT Book Reviews (4 1/2 stars)

"If *Dark Alchemy* was a movie, it'd pass the Bechdel Test and more than passes equity tests . . . *Dark Alchemy* was a compelling read with a satisfying conclusion promising more Petra Dee stories set around Temperance. I'm hooked."

—Dark Matter Zine

MERCURY RETROGRADE

"This wonderfully unusual Weird West novel combines the best of contemporary fantasy with metaphysical magic and mayhem, and even a bit of romance. Bickle has a knack for creating atmosphere, and she fills the fast-paced narrative with vivid scenes of wonder and a poignant story of death and rebirth. Fans of the first book will be enthralled, and new readers will easily fall into the quirky, dusty land that Petra and her unusual friends inhabit."

—*Publishers Weekly* (starred review)

"Petra's adventures in a magic-choked version of Yellowstone continue to balance nicely with a sense of fun, well-done and subtle worldbuilding and characterization, plus some serious stakes . . . The series feels like it's building splendidly, and there's certainly room for expansion."

—RT Book Reviews (4 1/2 stars)

"Bickle's world and characters are enjoyably complex, sinking the reader happily into this contemporary fantasy landscape."

—Omnivoracious

NINE OF STARS

"Bickle is well on her way to establishing her work as a cornerstone of her genre."

—Publishers Weekly (starred review)

"Following the prequels *Dark Alchemy* and *Mercury Retrograde*, Bickle's series launch mixes alchemy, folklore, and Native American traditions with a wintry Western landscape that will intrigue fans of the Weird West subgenre."

—Library Journal

"*Nine of Stars* is an outstanding entry Weird Western, and I can't wait for the next installment. If you're looking for a series that will hook you from the first page, this one hits the target with dead-eye accuracy."

—Shana DuBois, B&N Sci-Fi and Fantasy Blog

". . . Laura Bickle's latest hits that sweet spot."

—John DeNardo, *Kirkus Reviews*

WITCH CREEK

"Bickle's story is a rich, surreal, alchemical brew, as wondrous as the magic that infuses her fascinating weird west setting."

—*Publishers Weekly*

"Bickle has a good sense of how to blend existing and new story elements to come up with resolutions that don't feel inevitable or out of left field. By the end of the novel, more intriguing changes are afoot, and maybe Petra's biggest challenge yet."

—RT Book Reviews (4 stars)

PHOENIX FALLING

By Laura Bickle

Wildlands Novels

NINE OF STARS
WITCH CREEK
PHOENIX FALLING

Dark Alchemy Prequel Novels

DARK ALCHEMY
MERCURY RETROGRADE

Anya Kalinczyk Series

EMBERS
SPARKS

Delphic Oracle Series (written as Alayna Williams)

DARK ORACLE
ROGUE ORACLE

For Young Adult Readers

THE HALLOWED ONES
THE OUTSIDE

PHOENIX FALLING

A WILDLANDS NOVEL

LAURA BICKLE

HARPER Voyager
An Imprint of HarperCollinsPublishers

PHOENIX FALLING. Copyright © 2019 by Laura Bickle. All rights reserved. Printed in the United States of America. No part of this book may be used or reproduced in any manner whatsoever without written permission except in the case of brief quotations embodied in critical articles and reviews. For information, address HarperCollins Publishers, 195 Broadway, New York, NY 10007.

First Harper Voyager mass market printing: March 2019

Print Edition ISBN: 978-0-06-256735-2
Digital Edition ISBN: 978-0-06-256733-8

Cover design by Amy Halperin
Cover images © David Glen Larson/KHIUS/AlohaHawaii/Shutterstock
Chapter spot art by Shutterstock

Harper Voyager and the Harper Voyager logo are trademarks of HarperCollins Publishers in the United States of America and other countries.

HarperCollins is a registered trademark of HarperCollins Publishers in the United States of America and other countries.

FIRST EDITION

19 20 21 22 23   QGM   10 9 8 7 6 5 4 3 2 1

To my husband, Jason, who has consigned himself to the destiny of having the moon forever parked on his chest and the sun lolling on his feet, both purring their heads off.

CONTENTS

CHAPTER 1

Murmuration

The world was on fire.

The ravens knew it. Heat slipped through their glossy feathers, so much more blistering than the usual wrathful scorch of summer. They flew north, over the burning forest. The acrid taste of smoke was bitter in the backs of throats. Still, they charged toward the fire, dozens and dozens of them. Their heartbeats thundered through their light bones as they flew.

They did not fly as ravens usually flew. They flew as unquiet starlings did, in a tight, seething cloud over the charred trees. They turned right, left, in a curling formation, determined that none of their number should be left behind in the smoke and char. A hundred black eyes peered through dust and ash at the blackened timbers standing straight, like black fingers reaching through the ruined land.

They flew farther, toward the line of brightest heat and the light, twisting, turning. The sound of feathers flapping was deafening, churning over the crackle of fire as they banked and turned. The birds moved with one mind, their hearts hammering in singular thunder, wings fanning the smoke and the fire, sparks slipping in the spaces between them.

They were legion.

Movement glittered in the corner of one raven's eye. It cawed an alarm, a raucous cry soon echoed in the shrieks of its fellows. The ravens spiraled down, down, into a patch of lodgepole pine, a tightening vortex of black that pulled together at the last instant. Feathers collided into flesh, falling into a black hole that seemed to turn inside itself in a flurry of cawing . . .

. . . and coalesced into the shape of a dark-haired man. A man with one heartbeat.

Gabriel covered his nose with his hand against the smoke that had begun to drift his way. He could feel the fire approaching this part of the forest; the heat was intense on his naked skin. He wasn't much for casual nudity, but modesty was the least of anyone's worries. The fire was sweeping north and would be here within minutes.

He ran to the east, the pine needles prickling the soles of his feet. He could hear the crackle of the blaze in the distance and the crashes of pinecones, opened by the heat, landing on the forest floor. The pinecones were adapted to fire—in some ways, they *needed* it now; they'd seed and grow a new forest.

But warm-blooded creatures were not so fortunate.

He climbed over a rise to see what had snagged

his attention from far above: a pickup truck stuck in a ditch, its back wheel spewing loose dirt. A woman sat in the bed of the truck with her arms wrapped around a blanket-shrouded lump, and he realized they were animal wranglers. The man in the cab was gunning the engine, trying to get the truck moving, but it was going nowhere.

Gabriel climbed down the slope to the truck. The woman in the back of the truck turned her head and looked at him in horror. The man in the cab let up on the gas and fumbled in the glove box, likely for a gun.

Gabe lifted his hands. "I'm here to help." He paused by the driver's side window.

"What are you doing out here?" the man in the pickup asked. The unspoken question was: *What the hell are you doing out here stark naked?*

"Swimming." That was plausible. Much more plausible than: *I flew here in a cloud of ravens. Like one does when the roads are closed.* Instead, he said: "The fire's about five minutes southwest of here, coming fast. Your only way out is that way." He pointed east.

The man in the truck popped the door open.

Gabriel shook his head again, pushing the door gently closed. "You can't outrun it on foot. Let me work on that tire."

The man nodded. Gabe could see his eyes in the rearview mirror, the fear and distrust evident.

Gabe walked to the back of the truck, where the wheel was stuck. The woman watched him with frightened eyes. Her burden squirmed, and a blanket fell away from the face of a fawn. It was young, likely not more than a day old. Late in the season for such a creature to be born. Late and unlucky. Gabe knew plenty about bad luck.

Gabe inspected the tire. The tire itself was intact; it had just sunk into a rut dug deeper by the attempts to move it out. He motioned for the driver to hit the gas. Gabe pushed on the back bumper with all his might. The engine howled, and the woman covered the deer with her body. Heat shimmered behind Gabe, and he struggled to keep his sweaty hands on the bumper. Dust and dirt kicked up, coating him in a film of yellow clay, small rocks tearing tiny cuts into his legs. Sparks began to rain down from the sky.

He felt the tire tread grasping, gave the truck a final shove . . .

. . . and the pickup lurched forward twenty feet, narrowly missing a tree before the driver wrestled the truck under control. Gabe landed facedown in the dirt.

He picked himself up, wincing as embers landed on his back.

"Get in!" the driver shouted, motioning for him to jump in.

Gabe shook his head. "I've got a ride."

The man paused, his eyes wide in the rearview mirror, this time fear mixed with gratitude. The woman looked at Gabe then and gave him a tight-lipped nod.

The truck sped away, east, bumping over the cracked dirt.

Gabe looked behind him, at the fire licking over the crest of the slope.

He inhaled, summoning all his will into his body.

When he exhaled, he shattered into hundreds of ravens, exploding like ink in water. The ravens rushed up, up into the black layer of smoke, then through to the hazy shade of white.

They climbed higher, higher, in a thick murmuration, seeking cooler air above. The birds began a slow turn, skimming east to look for more stragglers, be they man or beast. The birds had herded some Canada geese away from a shallow creek an hour ago; he hoped they hadn't tried to return, but they *were* notoriously stupid.

A brilliant light, bright and hot as a meteor, sliced down through the sky, through the heart of the murmuration of ravens like a blazing sword. It came from above the fire, not spit up like a flare from the ground below. Gabe sent the birds scattering in all directions, like rings from a stone cast in water. Still, he wasn't fast enough, and he smelled charred feathers.

The murmuration turned away and dove to the earth, toward ground untouched by the fire. Gabe could taste ash and feel sparks lighting feathers as the air fed the fire. They flew down as quickly as they could.

The birds skidded to land in a cawing mass of confusion, beside his truck parked in a field. Gabe drew all the burning pieces of his consciousness to himself, reforming his body . . .

. . . and he realized that his arm was on fire.

Gabe swore and reached into the open truck window for his hat. He beat out the flames, feeling his arm hair disintegrating as he did so. His flesh was pink, but not yet blistering.

He reached into the truck for his clothes—jeans, flannel shirt, boots—and dressed quickly. He frowned at the soot on his hat but parked it on his head anyway. He realized then that he was missing part of an eyebrow and rubbed at it with his palm. It itched.

When he was reasonably satisfied there was no serious harm done, he looked back to the sky. Smoke churned over a line of trees. In the distance, he saw the animal rescuers in the pickup heading safely east, toward the main road.

There was no sign of the streak of fire that had come from above. His first guess was that it was a meteorite, and that it had little to do with the fire already blazing out of control on the ground. And it might be exactly that—a meteorite. Or it might have been an unlucky goose that caught fire, or a bit of hot debris from a helicopter hauling water. It could be any number of ordinary things that produced a freakish result.

But this wasn't an ordinary place, and there were no coincidences here. This was Yellowstone National Park, in the backyard of Temperance, Wyoming. An alchemist once prowled this land, centuries ago, eventually founding the town. And while Lascaris was long dead, Gabe knew some of his magic still survived, just beneath the dull senses of the humans who lived and worked in the backcountry. He'd seen things over his unnaturally long life that curdled his blood and froze his marrow. And he was part of it, too.

Gabe knew he could bank on the extraordinary gaining a toehold in the ordinary here, in this darkly enchanted land.

* * *

"THAT SURE ISN'T normal."

Petra Dee Manget rocked back on her heels. She stared into the hole in the ground yawning open before her, as if the earth were frozen in midscream. A deep dusting of ash that had precipitated from the fire covered the ground. It had been dubbed the Magpie Fire, as it had first been noticed near a creek of the same name. Nearby ash and lodgepole pine trees had been flattened, like black matchsticks, in a circular pattern around this crater. The small vegetation immediately surrounding the hole had been vaporized entirely. The wildfire that had been sweeping through Yellowstone for the last week had long since passed through this place, leaving behind dust and silt. The ground still felt warm to touch. Petra didn't know if she imagined that it was more than ordinary summer heat, but it radiated through the soles of her boots, as if she stood on the skin of some sleeping, living thing.

She adjusted the respirator mask over her face. She wasn't keen to inhale more of this ash than she had to. She'd been recently given the gift of a new set of lungs—and pretty much everything else in her body—and she was determined not to ruin them prematurely.

Initially, she had thought this was a sinkhole. Or maybe a shallow paint pot, a brilliantly colored acidic hot spring that had the water and noxious fluids boiled off in the fire as it passed through. This may have predated the fire—something flammable under pressure that was set off by a spark that may have ignited this whole nightmare. She'd originally spied this anomaly from the air days ago, when she'd been helping the Park Service decide where to dig firebreaks to curb the blaze. The fire was long since gone in this area. Now, though, there was no harm in digging at the edges of what remained. She really wasn't supposed to be here, and she knew it. But if this was the now-cold ignition point of the fire that had begun last week, perhaps she could loop in the investigators with the Park Service, and they might be able to keep this from happening again . . .

Maybe. She peered into the hole. It was about nine feet wide from edge to edge, with slightly irregular borders. Yellowstone National Park was a playground for geologists like her, and she considered that it might be a new geologic feature forming. Maybe there was a hot spring, mud pot, or buildup of flammable gases at this site that had blown a hole that deep and wide?

Only one way to find out.

Petra tied a rope around a burned tree stump. The skin of the pine was blistered and black, but it felt solid enough underneath to hold her weight. Loosening the rope slowly, she climbed down into the hole, her gloves digging for earth beneath the ash.

She swept away ash with her fingers, revealing charred black dirt. Beneath it was solid basalt. Runnels had formed in it, as if it had liquefied and refrozen. It still felt hot to the touch, like the handle of a cast-iron cooking pot. The heat wasn't her imagination, nor the work of the distant sun trying to burn through the haze. Her filthy brow wrinkled.

That was odd. A gas dispersal event would probably have leaked around such heavy stone, rather than gone right through it. And most gas dispersal events would have been unlikely to get this hot.

She slipped off her backpack and dug for her tool set. With a small shovel, she scraped at the bottom of the crater. She frowned as she cleared away a yellow dust that she could smell even through her respirator. It smelled like rotten eggs . . . It was sulfur; she would bet a hot twenty-dollar bill on it. But if it was, it should have burned up in the conflagration. She scraped away a sample into a collection jar to confirm later.

She continued to dig, and her shovel blade rang against black stone. More basalt, still warm and frozen in smooth eddies around deep fractures with dull edges. It would take great heat, at least a thousand degrees, to cause basalt to melt. Forest fires could burn several hundred degrees hotter, but a fast-moving fire wouldn't have enough sustained time to cause this degree of melting, and not all the trees surrounding the hole were obliterated by the heat. A dynamite blast would be too short-lived to produce this kind of molten effect.

As always, geologists feared what would happen if the super volcano beneath Yellowstone were to awaken. She hoped against hope that this was not a sign of that dreaded scenario coming to pass. If it happened, they were all toast. Not just her and the Park Service trying to manage this fire, but everyone, everywhere. Humanity would go the way of the dinosaurs if and when Yellowstone ever woke up. She scratched the point of the shovel against the stone, leaving behind a bright white mark. It didn't make much sense, unless . . .

. . . she moved to the edges of the crater. With her hands, she brushed away ash, revealing blast marks. Her heart hammered. Maybe . . . Maybe a meteorite had hit here.

A big one.

She smiled. Such a find was a geologist's pot of gold. It would explain the intense heat and these scorch marks . . . She ran her hand across a now cold stream of liquefied basalt, streaking up like the ray of a black sun. A meteorite could get up to three thousand degrees Fahrenheit, streaking through the earth's atmosphere. It would be a short event, but intense enough to cause this kind of damage. And the fallen trees . . . They reminded her of the pictures she'd seen of the Tunguska event in Siberia.

She sucked in her breath and began to look at the burn pattern more closely. It was regular, though, almost too regular to be explained by a meteorite strike. As she worked her way around the crater, she found a black tentacle of a blast mark every three feet or so. They were nearly all the same depth and size, reaching up over her head. It looked almost man-made. Almost.

She stood back, turning on her heel and surveying the crater. If she were an artist, she might say she was at the center of a carefully constructed mandala. There was no sign of melted meteorite materials—moissanite, or anything else foreign to the area—just this crypt with the seven black rays extending from the heart of it. The meteorite in Tunguska exploded before it hit ground. Maybe the same had happened here, but on a much-smaller scale.

"Did you find anything?"

Petra looked up. Gabe squatted at the edge of the crater and peered down.

"You look . . . crispy." Her husband's left eyebrow was gone, and his hat was covered in soot.

"It's warm out," he said noncommittally.

"This," she said, sketching the circle of the crater around her. "This is not normal. It might be a meteorite impact. A miniature version of Tunguska or something."

Gabe cocked his head like an inquisitive bird. "Tunguska?"

"Yeah. In Siberia, around 1908, a meteoroid vaporized in the atmosphere. It had the effect of an atmospheric nuclear detonation. But tremors were noted, and there was no crater, like there is here. It was thought that the meteoroid experienced an 'air burst,' and the meteoroid didn't hit the ground. There was just a scorch mark on the earth, with the trees fallen around it. Maybe this was a much-smaller meteorite that did actually hit ground. There haven't been any reports of seismic disturbances . . ." She was thinking aloud now, talking herself into the idea.

Gabe's eyes narrowed fractionally. She saw that the pupils were still in the shape of a bird's, small black dots in amber. He'd been in the sky. "Could be."

Petra blew a strand of sweaty strawberry blond hair out of her face. "What did you see up there?"

"Something burning in the sky. Almost hit some of my ravens."

Petra clapped ash from her gloved hands in a puff. "It's the right time of year for the Perseids meteor shower. I can check to see if sky watchers have been reporting more activity than usual. Not that they can see much through the smoke haze." That meteor shower could generate up to a hundred meteors an hour under peak viewing conditions. Any meteoroids striking the ground were improbable, though. But that was the most rational explanation she could come up with.

Gabe frowned. He dug into his pocket and chucked an object down into the hole. Petra caught it. It was a gold compass, as big as her palm, and she grimaced to see it.

"We should ask the Locus. Just to be sure," he said.

She blew out her breath, disturbing ash. The Venificus Locus was a magic detector, inscribed with alchemical symbols and forged by Lascaris long ago. It couldn't tell her what kind of magic it sensed, whether it was good or bad, but it could tell her if something supernatural was afoot. It was useful.

But it ran on human blood.

Gabe looked away. Petra knew that he would run the Locus if he could. But he was no longer human. Humans didn't break apart into ravens. Humans didn't sleep underneath the alchemical Tree of Life at night. Humans . . . Humans got married. She'd married him over the winter, when he'd been human. When he had blood and a pulse and slept beside her at night, snoring softly. There was no alchemy between them then, but it was magical just the same, and things had been good. At least, they had been for her.

Then, she'd been human, too. And she clung to the idea that she still was. She wasn't really certain, though. Her consciousness had been moved from her failing old body to a new vessel—to a homunculus. It seemed to work like a perfected version of her old body, but she didn't fully know what it meant to have taken it over. She hadn't admitted it to anyone else, but the idea of leaving humanity behind scared her. She knew she should be grateful to be alive and to be healthy and whole, but she was terrified of what this transition meant. Would she wake up some evening with a relentless taste for human blood or something? Would she live a normal life span of eighty years or so and then rot quietly underground without waking? And if so, what did it mean for her afterlife—if there was a heaven, was she barred from it? Hell, she didn't even know if she could donate her organs, if she was fortunate enough to die a mundane death. She looked real, felt real, but what was she, truly?

She'd been putting off this test, using the Locus. It would tell her for certain if she was still human— still *Petra*. She'd shut the artifact away in a kitchen drawer, buried it among plastic silverware and orphaned restaurant napkins, and hoped that she could go back to normal. Without knowing the truth for certain, she could go around dressed in this skin and pretend for as long as she wanted to that everything was fine. Maybe if she went on acting *as if*, she would someday believe it.

Gabe offered no comment. He just looked at her sidelong with a coldly assessing eye. What did he think—that she had become something other than human? At the very least, he had to think her a coward. And if that was the case . . .

"Fine."

She ripped her glove off with her teeth, exposing her pale left hand where her wedding ring glinted. She spat out the glove and gnawed at a hangnail on her ring finger, looking at her impassive husband as she did so. He sure was ready to delve back into the world of magic, starved by being apart from it for a couple of seasons. He changed into birds each second he got, slept later and later beneath the Tree of Life.

He didn't seem to understand that she wanted to be as far away from magic as possible.

She'd gambled more times than she cared to admit, won, and knew not to push her luck. And this— she didn't really want to know. She had a right not to ask, didn't she? To count her blessings and move on? She wanted to confront him with this, to yell at him that she was ordinary, because she had decided to be, dammit. And that this was the end of it. He could find his damn magic elsewhere.

Yet she still ripped off the hangnail and let her finger ooze out a nice fat droplet of blood. She held the Locus in her right hand and prepared to drop the blood into the groove surrounding its edge.

But she stopped. She stared at the blurry compass. The cardinal directions were circumscribed by inscrutable symbols. The directions were marked, and through them cut the seven rays of alchemy . . .

. . . seven rays. She looked at the black scorch marks surrounding her.

She closed her hand over her bleeding finger and dropped the compass into her pocket. She turned away, from the magic and from him. She rubbed her nose. She wouldn't let him see her cry.

"Petra?" Gabe asked softly.

She shook her head. "I just . . . I don't want to know." The words burned on her tongue. She had always prided herself on her scientific curiosity, on wanting to know the truth. But not about this. "Not yet. Maybe not ever."

There was silence, and she wondered what went through his head. If he thought she was weak, in denial . . .

There was a thud on the rock behind her as something landed in the crater, then footsteps. Arms circled her shoulders, and she smelled something burned. Gabe's arms radiated cold beneath the flannel.

An ordinary-tasting tear slipped down her cheek and landed on her lip. Only humans could cry— right?

That would have to be enough for him—and her.

"We'll find out some other way," he said quietly. "It's okay."

But she knew that it really wasn't.

CHAPTER 2

The Separation Process

"Did you find anything?"

Park ranger Mike Hollander leaned in the pickup window to peer at Petra. Gabe had obediently stopped his truck at a Park Service checkpoint; parts of Yellowstone had been cordoned off from visitors. From the West Entrance to the Northeast Entrance, only authorized personnel were permitted. Mike wasn't too fond of anyone wandering into the fire zone, but he'd trusted the two of them to check out the crater, since the main fire was nearly five miles away from that point. Gabe had no intention of mentioning his extracurricular activities at the fire line.

Petra frowned. "As weird as it sounds, what we saw from the air a few days ago could be a meteorite impact crater. It's cold now, but it meets all the geologic criteria. Under the right conditions, it could have sparked the fire. I need to do some more research. But this may not be a man-made problem created by campers who didn't properly douse their campfires. It could be some kind of a celestial fluke."

Mike looked skyward, as if imploring a sympathetic supernatural source for patience. "Do not tell me about weird. I just got a report that a naked guy was wandering around helping stranded motorists."

Gabe was suddenly very interested in picking a piece of lint from the dashboard.

Petra raised an eyebrow. "Triple-A for the clothing-optional crowd?"

"I guess. Helos haven't seen him, so I hope that he doesn't get crispy." Mike made a face. "No casualties yet, but I'm not sure it's gonna stay that way. The Magpie is angry. And she's hatching little magpies that are crawling all over the place."

"The fire crews aren't able to contain it?" Petra asked.

"They're trying. But the wind is shifting constantly, and it's been consistently strong wind. Rain isn't coming for another week, according to the weather geeks. Normally, we'd expect something like this just to burn itself out and we'd keep people out of the way. Help the animals. But the fire crews say that this is different. The Magpie Fire is faster, hotter than what they've seen, and it's jumping over creeks and roads without stopping. And little magpies keep flaring up in the most unexpected spots."

"I know it's supposed to be a normal part of the ecosystem, the fire—" Petra said.

"Yeah, well, this isn't," he answered shortly. And she could hear his exhaustion and frustration. "And if what you say about the meteorite pans out . . . that's even less normal. Most fires around here are caused by dumb human activity. Sometimes lightning, but more often than not, someone didn't put out a campfire correctly or chucked a cigarette butt into the brush." Mike's jaw had hardened. They both knew that the ex–military policeman had little patience for those who didn't follow the rules in his jurisdiction, even if the offender was something as elemental and unpredictable as fire itself.

"I took pictures and grabbed some samples," Petra said. "I'll do some work on my end. But, right now, my money's on a meteorite as your original ignition point. But there might not just be one meteorite to worry about. This could be an ongoing problem if there's a meteor shower that's still feeding the fire." She glanced at Gabe.

Gabe nodded. "I saw a fireball in the sky about three hours ago. Didn't look like any kind of lightning that I've ever seen, so it makes sense that it was another meteorite." He wasn't sure what to think about the event that had crisped his ravens. Not yet. But it didn't hurt to advance a mundane, if unlikely, explanation to Mike. Mike was a decent man and a good ally, but neither Gabe nor his wife trusted Mike with the magical secrets they knew about the backcountry. Mike had enough on his plate with ordinary problems.

But Gabe thought Mike was beginning to suspect that things were off, at least where Gabe and Petra were concerned. He looked at the two of them with an investigator's stare. Gabe caught him looking at his left eye. He'd been blinded in that eye last winter, but he was now able to see. His limp was gone. Mike's gaze roved casually over Gabe's burned wrist and the back of his hand. That had been careless of him; it was too late now to pull down his sleeve.

Mike gestured at him with his chin. "You run into a flare-up? We thought that area was cool . . ."

"It was," Gabe said evenly. "I just kicked over a pile of ash. Wind swept up, and there were still live embers."

"You should get that looked at."

"It'll be okay." And it would. By tomorrow morning, the shallow burn would have healed—a small miracle. Gabe would have to remember to bandage it for a few days to make sure that Mike wasn't suspicious.

But Mike wasn't just suspicious of him. As Mike discussed the new road closings with Petra, Gabe watched how Mike looked at her. He didn't look at her in the way that men often looked at women, with a sense of covetousness. This was an objective evaluation. Less than six months ago, she'd been dying of leukemia. Now she inhabited a body that was smoothly perfect, as if she'd been hatched from an egg. Her accumulated scars were gone, and even the sun-freckles had vanished on her face. The soft lines at the corners of her eyes had been wiped away. Petra had tried to minimize the change; she'd cut her hair, let her friend Maria add a few freckles with henna on her face and body. For the first couple of months after she'd gained the body of the homunculus, she'd learned to add shadows under her eyes with makeup. But something was imperceptibly off. It was as if a soap opera had become real and a twin had taken over her life. Something uncanny. It was weird, and Mike had a nose for weird.

". . . and your little buddy has been waiting for you," Mike was saying. He turned to a Park Service Jeep parked beside them and popped open the door. A flurry of grey and gold fur bounded out and launched itself through Petra's open window. Gabe wound up staring at the ass-end of a coyote, tail slapping his face while the canine's front end slathered Petra's face with slobber.

"Jesus, Sig, that's cold!" Petra giggled and twisted away to grin at Mike. "I see you kept the AC cranked up for him. Thank you."

Mike chuckled. "He howled piteously when you left. To distract the little guy, we unwisely put him in charge of guarding our cooler full of sandwiches."

Gabe glanced at the Jeep. A piece of wet bread was stuck to the windshield, and a bit of lettuce draped over the steering wheel. "Sorry. We owe you—"

Mike waved him off. "I'll catch up with you guys later. You can buy me a beer. Or three." He glanced past them, at a rental Winnebago that had pulled up behind them, and gestured for it to pull over.

Gabe tipped his hat and put the truck into gear. He nosed the pickup past the barricades to the main road.

Petra sat with her arms around Sig. Sig had jammed his head under her chin and was leaning against her chest in adoration. Her fingers stroked his back. "I'm worried about him," she said.

"His appetite is fine." Sig leaned back to stare at Gabe and emitted a belch that smelled like salami.

"He's gotten awfully clingy," she observed, frowning. "Since . . . since . . ."

"Since you died," Gabe finished.

"Yeah." She looked out the window. "But I'm alive now."

"He loves you," Gabe said simply. And it was the only truth he knew about the situation. Or any other, really.

They rode in silence, through shadows drawn long by the setting sun. The sky was a red haze, and Gabe kept the windows up and the decrepit air-conditioning running. They rolled through the tiny town of Temperance's single stoplight, and Gabe parked before the church. Well, it had once been a church, and Gabe had never fully forgotten that. The Compostela had been reincarnated as a bar in modern times. Usually well populated by the local denizens of Temperance, there were only two filthy cars sitting outside this evening.

Gabe popped the door and stepped out on the pavement. A thin layer of pale dust saturated everything, darkening the brilliant color of Compostela's stained-glass windows. Ash from the fire had been blowing toward the tiny town for days. It swirled in eddies on the street, summoning up miniature dust devils.

Petra seemed to hesitate before climbing out with Sig. Sig inhaled some of the grey dust, smearing his nose with a pale smudge. She wiped it away with her sleeve and squared her shoulders before walking into the bar.

Dust motes drifted in orange sunshine inside.

The interior of the Compostela felt cool as a cave and nearly as quiet; only three patrons sprawled in a booth made of church pews, playing cards. They glanced up as Petra, Sig, and Gabe passed, and quickly looked back down at their cards again. Gabe scanned the room, taking in the pieces of obsidian perched on top of the door and window frames. Bits of magic from the owner, no doubt, and recently installed.

Petra led Sig to a booth at the back, sinking into shadow and the thin striations of smoke that seemed to have settled into the place. Sig scuttled underneath the table, where he promptly found a stray French fry to gobble down. A canine normally wouldn't be allowed in a bar—that likely violated all kinds of health regulations—but Temperance was, in its way, beyond the reach of most conventional law.

And Sig wasn't a conventional "dog," either.

Gabe slid into the booth opposite Petra. She plucked a menu from the basket at the end of the table, not making eye contact. Nothing had changed on the dog-eared, stained menus for years. He just waited for her to speak.

"Do you know anything about that naked guy roaming the backcountry?" She glanced up then, a smile quirking at the corner of her mouth.

Gabe gave a small shrug. "Maybe."

She nodded. "Just *maybe*."

Sig, having exhausted the crumbs below the table, flopped down on Gabe's feet with a huff.

"It'll be a story someone tells around a campfire. Then it'll fade. I promise." Gabe leaned back in his seat. "I'm more worried about what's up there." He pointed skyward.

Petra frowned, and she put the menu away. "You think it could be something . . . alchemical?"

"Maybe. In his day, Lascaris made a great many experiments. Not all of them were successful. Some were buried. This might be something that he buried."

"Lascaris," she said, wincing slightly at the name. "Have you seen any sign of him?"

Gabe pulled out the alchemist's pocket watch and set it on the table. Its hands were frozen at noon. It stopped and started in fits, as if it were ticking away a pulse from some distant beast. Gabe did not dare wind it up, and simply watched it shudder to life and still again.

"I was sure he was dead. Dead in the fire that burned his house to the ground." Gabe ran his thumb over the face. "Now I'm not so sure." The watch had belonged to Lascaris, allowing him to keep track of the most powerful times to perform magic, noon and midnight. It had appeared in Gabe's dreams, and then in reality, when one of his dark creations had recently found it. Deep in Gabe's gut, it was a bad omen, if not something worse than that.

A shadow crossed the table. Gabe looked up. "Hello, Lev."

The owner of the Compostela nodded coolly at them. "Haven't seen you folks in a while."

"Been busy."

"Yeah. Those fires are gathering strength." Lev's storm-colored eyes flicked to the door and the hazy landscape beyond. "I don't remember one quite this unpredictable. Not even in 1988, when the park turned into a postapocalyptic hellscape. How about you?"

Gabe's mouth flattened. "Not since then. That was the worst I've ever seen." And for Gabe, *ever* was a very long time. He could be frank with Lev. They weren't friends, but they knew too many of each other's secrets. Lev was longer-lived than Gabe, but he was still a relative newcomer to Temperance by Gabe's reckoning.

Lev nodded. "I've been battening down the hatches."

"Saw your obsidian over the door."

"The fire won't touch this place." Lev said it with confidence. Gabe had no idea how far the old *domovoi*'s household magicks went, but he figured that the guy knew how to keep a house from harm.

Petra sank down farther into her seat as Lev placed two beers before them.

"How's that body wearing?" Lev asked, with forced casualness.

Petra sucked in her breath. "Good. It's good. I mean, it's . . . perfect." She lifted her hand before her and curled her fingers. Wonder still lighted her eyes. In the middle of the night, Gabe would sometimes wake to see her, sitting up in bed, staring at her hands.

Lev nodded. "I knew it would be," he said quietly. His eyes had turned the dark color of a bruise. Gabe knew that he mourned the loss of the son he had intended to inhabit the homunculus he'd created. In a way, Petra was now his magical progeny, though neither of them were ready to admit it anytime soon.

"Lev." Petra looked up at him. "I'm sorry," she

blurted. "I know you didn't intend to save me, but I am thankful that—"

Lev cut her off with a dismissive gesture. "It's done and over. We're all good." But this was something that would never be good, a debt that could not ever be repaid. Gabe knew about debts, and this one—this one was forever.

Despite that—or maybe because of that—Lev changed the subject, away from magic and back to something normal. There seemed to be a lot of that going around lately "The special tonight is the pulled pork sandwich with baked potato and slaw."

"That sounds good," Petra said. "I'd like that and an extra order of pork for the little guy."

Gabe nodded. "I'll have one, too."

"Coming right up." Lev drifted away, back behind the bar.

Gabe wasn't willing to let the discussion of magic go. He reached across the table for Petra's hand. "You know that I love you, whether you're human or not."

She yanked her hand back and made a fist. She shook her head, wisps of hair slapping her cheeks. Her eyes were squeezed shut, and it looked like she was trying not to cry. "Can we not talk about this right now?"

Gabe's brow furrowed. "No matter what, okay? You loved me when I was ordinary, and when I was magic."

She rubbed her brow and steadied her breath. "You would love me for whatever I've become. But I'm not sure I can love myself."

Gabe didn't know what to say at that. To him, love and magic were intertwined. He loved her, and he did love magic. There was no conflict in that, was there?

"Do you love me less now that . . . now that I'm a Hanged Man, again? Did you love me more when I was human?" His brow creased.

Her fingers pressed to her mouth. "I loved you on both sides of the veil. Truly. But this isn't about us. It's about me. I mean, I don't even know if I'm really me. I think so, but . . . what if I'm just a copy and this"— she ran her fingers down her arms—"isn't real?"

"I think you're real," Gabe said. She smelled and tasted the same, and the way her eyes changed color in the light was exactly as it was before. But she needed more than that, so he offered: "And reality is, at best, a subjective thing."

She gave him a sad smile. It was clear she was done with this discussion. He'd fucked up somewhere, but he wasn't sure what exactly he'd said.

She jerked her chin toward the television over the bar. "Look."

Gabe glanced up at the television. Images of wildfire raced across the screen. A map showed the area of the Magpie wildfire contained within the park for now, but the projected path was anyone's guess. Some phone video showed a fire whirl advancing across a field at night. It looked for all the world like a tiny tornado of flame, twisting and churning before the wind sucked it back up into the sky again.

"At least the tourists are mostly gone," Petra said. "I can't imagine what it would be like to try and herd large numbers of people out of the park. Mike's colleagues did a good job of playing bouncer."

"There are always stragglers, though," Gabe said, thinking of the man and woman rescuing the deer.

Petra just nodded.

Lev reappeared with a tray full of plates. He set one before Petra, one before Gabe, and slid a plate piled high with pulled pork underneath the table. Sig made snorkeling noises of delight as he slurped the meat. Lev vanished again, and Petra picked at her sandwich.

Finally, she gave up the pretense of eating and said, "Tell me about the fire that killed Lascaris."

Gabe took a bite of his sandwich and chewed slowly as he dredged his memory. "It was in summer when it happened. August 12, 1862. The Hanged Men had been sent by Lascaris to acquire some . . . tools for his experiments. He'd been working some distillation rituals at the time."

"That's the sixth stage of alchemy?"

"Yes. Distillation serves to purify, to remove what is no longer needed and leave the essential spirit behind. Lascaris felt that he was close to completing the Great Work, to achieving the Philosopher's Stone and all the power of immortality that came with such a discovery. He had ordered many exotic things shipped in by train—myrrh, spikenard, cinnamon, peacock feathers. Most of these things wound up ruined in his laboratory workings, but he persisted. He felt that he was close to something, a breakthrough that would lead him to his goal of eternal life.

"His basement laboratory at that time was full of various cruelties. He had a man stuck in amber.

There were jars of ox blood, doves' hearts, and powdered human livers lining his shelves. Even the salamanders that lived in the athanor fire would not touch the Hand of Glory that he kept on his table."

At Petra's questioning glance, he explained: "A severed hand of a murderer, desiccated and coated with the criminal's own fat, burned like a candle to paralyze all who witness it."

She squinted doubtfully. "Did it work?"

"I never saw it lit, though I think it was a precursor to the project of the man in amber." Gabe shrugged. "If it didn't work, he likely kept it around for psychological effect."

Petra stabbed her potato with her fork. "It would certainly shock most people into paralysis, anyway."

Gabe didn't disagree, but he was pretty much inured to the shock factor of Lascaris's workings. "The night of the fire, Lascaris had sent us out to harvest souls."

Petra's fork stilled. "Is that a particular way of saying that you were sent out to kill his enemies?"

Gabriel didn't much like discussing his past misdeeds with Petra. Though he had been under Lascaris's magical sway, he was not proud of what he'd done. And he was aware that those deeds created space between him and his wife. But so would lies. "Sort of. Lascaris had created a set of mirrors. They looked ordinary, the kind a lady would use to check her reflection. But these held more . . . they held souls.

"We were sent to slip into the houses of Lascaris's enemies with these soul mirrors under cover of darkness. We were told never to look into them until we had forced the enemy to gaze into the glass. Then, the devices were safe, the particular cantrip expended. We would creep into the bedchambers of his slumbering adversaries and turn the mirrors to their unaware eyes. The victims would awaken and catch themselves staring back. There was a sound like a sharp inhalation. Sometimes the target would thrash once or twice . . . but then they lay still. The mirror would be put away, and the enemy would move no more. In town, it was thought that a dread disease stalked the upper echelons of society. They called it 'the sleeping sickness.' There was a sickness," he said bitterly. "But its name was Lascaris.

"We would return the mirrors to him, where they would be labeled and set upon a shelf. It seemed to me that a fine mist roiled within, and that a shadow of a man moved inside each one. Was that the ephemeral soul, separated from the body? I didn't know for certain. But the cold bodies would be discovered in the morning and buried soon after.

"The night of the fire, Lascaris had sent us to take the soul of Father Adrian, the then-priest of this church." Gabe sketched his hand around the room. "We were to take him and two of his deacons who were causing trouble for Lascaris. The Church had heard rumors that Lascaris was dabbling in the dark arts. Though the Church enjoyed his money, they could not let this stand. There were murmurings of driving Lascaris from town and taking over his gold mining operation . . . problem was, no one knew where his mine was. They just knew that the gold kept coming, and had no idea that it had been created by alchemy. Summer heat fed the discontent, and things soon boiled over.

"The climate had reached a fever pitch only days before, when one of the streams near town had run black with stinking toads and black ichor. The fish had leaped from the inky water and suffocated themselves on the banks, rather than swim through that seething noxiousness. Father Adrian declared it the result of witchcraft, and the church was crowded that Sunday. Even Lascaris attended. Father Adrian very nearly called him out publicly but settled on giving all witches three days to repent, or he would conduct an inquisition."

Petra grimaced. "No independent woman would be safe from that."

"Exactly. An inquisition would not only target Lascaris and the Hanged Men, but it would also have the convenient effect of clearing out the brothel next door. Several women of means took the next train out of town. The daughter of the innkeeper who suffered what we would now think of as schizophrenia was packed up to live with an aunt out East. The atmosphere was tense, to say the least.

"Lascaris didn't need to wait three days. He decided to cut the head off the snake that August night. The Hanged Men split up before midnight. Some kept watch. Others took soul mirrors to the deacons' houses. As the leader of the Hanged Men, it was my responsibility to take Father Adrian's soul.

"At that time, the priest of the church had no rectory. He had his quarters in the church itself. I let myself in the back door." Gabe's eyes trailed to the shadows behind the bar. "I was able to pick the lock without any difficulty. I found him sleeping in his spartan quarters, his hands wrapped around a pillow as if it were a neck he wrung in his sleep.

"I leaned over him and turned the mirror to his face. His eyes snapped open, and he gasped. He did not go quickly . . . he convulsed, even tried to knock the mirror from my grip. But he, like all the others, succumbed to it. His eyelids flickered shut, and he fell back against his pillow. I arranged his arms in a peaceful, natural way, noting that he did not breathe, and his heart made no movement in his chest any longer.

"When I left the church, I saw a glow on the horizon, in the direction of Lascaris's house. I ran, thinking that one of Lascaris's experiments had failed spectacularly, thinking I needed to help. By the time I got there, however, the grand house was in flames. Only salamanders escaped, slipping out into the grass. Townspeople ringed the house, holding torches, and I knew immediately that the townsfolk had taken it upon themselves to drive the evil out of their midst.

"I knew, too, that they would likely turn their ire on me. So I retreated to the Rutherford Ranch, intending to lie low until the dust had settled. I thought that perhaps Lascaris might have found a way to escape, and would find us there. We had nowhere else to go, and we would wait for him underground.

"We learned later that Lascaris had been inside before the house was torched. The arson had been a disaster, and many townspeople who invaded the house were said to have been killed in the fire. Lascaris didn't emerge during the burning, and Rutherford assumed that the alchemist was dead. The ranch owner quickly moved to take control of Lascaris's assets, while the townsfolk discovered the dead priest and deacons. They assumed that this was Lascaris's revenge from beyond the grave, and the town was fearful and subdued as they buried the churchmen. Rutherford took power easily, promising law and order to those who stayed. That would later prove to be difficult, as the alchemist was no longer around to conjure gold. Many men searched the backcountry for his secret mine, but no one ever found it. People left the town in search of greener pastures.

"After a couple of weeks in hiding, the Hanged Men began to emerge. Rutherford sent us to the graveyard to set stones for the priest and the deacons. Rutherford's doing so was seen as a magnanimous act to heal the town. The Hanged Men and I had come to the graveyard, but we had brought something else with us—the soul mirrors.

"I had the intent of discreetly burying the mirrors with the bodies. I didn't know what lay in the afterlife, but it seemed like the decent thing to do. Rutherford had no idea we had them, and I was fast learning that keeping secrets from whichever Rutherford held the ranch was for the good of the Hanged Men.

"When we were setting the stones, though, some men from the town arrived. One of them recognized me as a man who had done Lascaris's dirty work. He took a swing at me over the priest's tombstone.

We fought, and the mirror in my jacket pocket was shattered on the ground. I felt it break against my hip, felt a shocking coldness, like ice water, when it happened.

"The fight broke off when there was a sound from the ground moments later. It was thumping . . . screaming . . . coming from Father Adrian's grave. My attacker moved away to stare at the ground and before I knew what was happening, he was on his knees, praying.

"I noticed then that the Hanged Men were discreetly breaking their mirrors behind the townsmen's backs. The terrible grave-sound was echoed by the deacons' graves—howling, scratching.

"The townsfolk grabbed shovels. We feigned shock and helped them dig up the coffins. I glanced at the stones and figured that the men had been three weeks in the ground in hot summer. I did not relish what we would find.

"They opened the coffin of Father Adrian. Inside was the corpse, bloated and red and putrid. The nails on its blackened hands were gone, and teeth rattled from its gaping mouth. The body had begun to liquefy, staining the clerical collar.

"Yet the thing that had been Father Adrian moved. It howled. I realized that the breaking of the mirror had caused the reinstallation of his soul in his body. I knew that it could not survive long in this state, but for this moment, it was self-aware . . . and in agony.

"Horrified, the townspeople cut off its head. They did the same to the deacons. The men of Temperance decided that Lascaris had not been the root of the evil in the town, after all. They decided that it had to be Father Adrian and his deacons. There was no other rational explanation for living corpses. The graves were heavily salted, and a new priest was brought in to reconsecrate the ground.

"After that, there was nothing new coming up from underground. Nothing that the town knew about, anyway." Gabe took a shuddering breath, the story taking more out of him than he anticipated. He swigged the last of his beer.

Petra peered into her bottle, as if it might provide some answer to the horrors that haunted Temperance. "I am sorry you had to go through that."

"It was a long time ago."

"Probably not long enough, though."

He had no response for that.

"No one ever saw Lascaris again?"

"No. Not that I know for certain." He wondered about Muirenn, though. Months ago, one of Lascaris's creations, the Mermaid, had resurfaced with the pocket watch Gabe now had in his hand. She was dead now, and there was no way to question her.

Petra shook her head and pushed her plate away. "I'll be back." She stood and headed to the ladies' room.

Gabe disentangled his feet from a snoring coyote and carried his beer bottle up to the bar. He pulled out his wallet to settle the bill.

Lev appeared, wiping his hands on a dish towel. "It's thirty, even."

Gabe put two twenties on the glossy surface of the bar. Lev scooped them up.

"Lev?"

"Yeah?" Lev turned away from the register.

"About Petra." Gabe didn't shy away from the facts. He'd seen too many horrors in his hundred and fifty years on earth, and scraping up against them had made him a man of unvarnished truth. "Is she still human? Or is she something else now?"

Lev paused. He shook his head. "I never made a homunculus before. Only saw it done just the once. Those people who made one long ago . . . understand that I didn't follow them afterward."

"You don't know."

The bartender gave an enigmatic shrug. "Your guess is as good as mine."

CHAPTER 3

The Dream Beyond the Body

The Eye of the World saw everything.

Nine knelt beside the water, the pool that the people of the reservation called the Eye of the World. She tied her silver hair back so that she could peer into the water without distraction. The sun had set a little while ago, leaving behind a streak of red on the horizon. Wind pushed through the grasses of the surrounding field studded with white yarrow blossoms and red fireweed. The movement inspired continuing ripples on the surface of the water. A black toad hopped out of the pool, further disrupting the surface, and scuttled away under a rock. As the water settled, the Eye reflected the violet sky, a spangled handful of stars shivering on the surface. Even the brightest stars burned more dimly than they should.

Nine reached into the warm water with a cupped hand. She brought the water to her lips and drank. It tasted sweet and heavy. Her fingers lingered on her lips as the liquid slid down her throat.

This was a ritual she undertook almost every night. She'd slip from her bed back at Maria's house, cross the field behind it. The mountains were silent and lightless in the distance, the sky stretching out infinitely above her. She'd drink from the pool and hope that the sweet water of this spring, the Eye of the World, would take her back to her family.

"Take me to the pack," she breathed.

Her eyes slipped shut, and she had the sensation of falling, falling into a reality that smelled like pine needles and ash. When she opened them again, she was still wrapped in darkness, but a different darkness. No stars glittered overhead, and brittle pine needles crunched under her feet. She was in a wooded thicket, surrounded by sentinels of lodgepole pine. Red glowed on the horizon, gleaming through the branches.

Nine threw back her head and howled. She howled not with the voice of a woman, but with the voice of a wolf. Her human body had sloughed away in the reflection of the Eye, stripping her back to her very essence. Her paws paced in the pine needles and her nose twitched. She couldn't smell the rest of the pack, all she could smell was the acrid stink of sap burning.

An answering howl emerged from her left. She lowered her head and ran toward it, slipping around the pines like a phantom. Nine truly missed this, this freedom of running, unencumbered. She was faster as a wolf than anything she encountered, not slow and vulnerable as she was as a woman on two feet.

Not *diminished*.

The pack was just ahead; she could hear their yips and barks. Nine plunged into a thicket, and was immediately surrounded by wet noses and wagging tails. The wolves tumbled over her, whining and nipping. Nine had always been the omega of the pack, but they still held affection for her on her nighttime sojourns that brought her back into their fold.

For all their joy, there was also a high hum, a panic about them, their yips and nips. They had descended into lower lands after prey, and the fire had pushed them far from their home range. They knew the fire was growing close, and they were being forced to flee their hard-won territory. They were trapped between the push of the flames and the pull of longing for the lost territory.

Ghost, the leader, barked shortly. The wolves followed him at a brisk trot, sliding through the darkness. Nine heaved a sigh of relief as the wolves moved away from the glow on the horizon.

She followed the pack as far as she dared, until she felt her body begin to fade, and her sadness increased. This wolf-form wasn't a real, solid form, only a projection of the spirit world assisted by the Eye. It was constructed of her memory and her hopes, and it faded more and more quickly with each passing day.

Nine opened her eyes. She found herself kneeling by the pool, and her silhouette in the water was that of a woman. Her knees had fallen asleep, and her fingers were knotted together.

She swallowed, longing and fear surging up in her throat. She missed the pack more than she'd ever missed anything in her life. They had always been her world. She rubbed her nose and wiped her eyes. Even as she felt the pain of self-pity, her tears came more because she was afraid for them. They were safe for now, she reminded herself. Ghost was a good leader and was wise enough to lead them away from the fire. But for how long could they evade it? This was not their first fire. But this fire felt sharp, viciously unreal. It felt like something that saw wolves as prey.

The black toad hopped out from beneath the rock, regarding her with a dour expression. Nine leaned down to look at it. The toad opened its mouth and spoke in a hiss:

"The sky is falling."

She gasped, and the toad jumped into the Eye, vanishing in the dark depths.

Nine blinked up at the sky, and her brow furrowed.

A streak of brilliant orange light swept from one bank of the river of stars to the other. It was brighter and fiercer than any comet that Nine had seen in her long life, and more transient. It faded quickly, leaving behind a bright streak that burned her night vision.

Nine sucked in her breath. She climbed to her feet and ran back to the house as fast as two feet could carry her.

GABE PULLED HIS pickup truck up before Petra's trailer. The sun had set, lending an orange cast to the field in which it sat. The silver skin of the Airstream seemed to glow, as if reflecting the distant light. The shadows of dry summer grasses swept long over the field, contrasting with pockets of blue lupine.

He turned off the ignition and stared at the door. Petra glanced at him. "Are you staying?"

His chest ached at the simple request. They were married. They should be able to spend every night tangled in each other's embrace, with a coyote drowsing at the foot of the bed. But this was not to be. Not for them.

He shook his head. "Not tonight."

She nodded and looked away, turning to open the door.

He reached for her, turned her face to his, and kissed her soundly. It was wistful, longing, and tasted like tears.

She broke away first, gathered his face in her hands, and kissed his forehead. She opened her door and slid out with the coyote, walking to her front door and a cold bed. She did not look back at him, not once.

Gabe watched them go inside and a light go on. He put the truck in reverse and turned back down the gravel road, headed back through town, and followed the two-lane road into the gathering darkness.

It was night by the time he reached the Rutherford Ranch. Gabe didn't bother to turn on the headlights as he turned off the main road and down a dirt road cutting through a field. In the distance, there were lights on in the main house. Owen Rutherford, county sheriff and current king of the Rutherford Ranch, was home. Gabe had no desire to speak to him, nor have the man know anything about his movements.

He drove into the fields he knew by rote, crossing pastures speckled with sleeping cattle, blue flax, and purple penstemon in the shadow of the mountains. He paused for a moment when he skirted the edge of the field where the Hanged Men were buried. He missed them, more than he would admit to anyone, even Petra. Though they were largely silent and flawed, he had grown used to their presence. They were his shadows, and he felt unmoored to the world without their darkness behind him. These men had been closer to him than any brothers could have been, as tangled as they were in each other's destinies and dreams. Since Sal had killed them, a deeper silence than any other he'd known rang in his ears.

He passed the rill in the land that marked their grave site and a sapling tree. His gaze lingered there, and his foot faltered on the gas. It was no more than a dirt-filled ditch, with bones slumbering beneath, he reminded himself. He tore his gaze away and moved on, south, to the alchemical Tree of Life.

The Lunaria, the Tree of Life, stood on a hillock in the center of a field studded with wild white geranium. Gabe parked the pickup beside it and grabbed his hat from the dashboard. He climbed out to stare up at the tree in the darkness. Leaves rustled above him. He swore the span of the oak's branches grew every day. It had only stood here for a few months, but it had the appearance of a two-hundred-year-old tree. Its branches swept up to heaven, while great tangled roots dug into the earth.

As above, so below.

Gabe walked to the west side of the hill. A creek pierced the foot of it. Tree roots were exposed, winding into a rusted iron grate. At his approach, the grip of the roots loosened, just enough for him to pull the grate open. He stepped inside, up to his knees in water. The roots wound around the iron, sealing it behind him. This place smelled like dirt and petrichor and something sinister.

It was one of the most comforting smells he'd ever known.

In darkness, he walked along the bank of the creek that widened into an underground river. He needed no light to see by. When he glanced to the black water, his gleaming amber eyes were reflected. The burn injury to his arm glowed golden, shining through his sleeve. In daylight, his blood looked like blood. But darkness revealed how inhuman he truly was.

He walked until he reached a veil of roots, corresponding to where the trunk of the tree stood topside. The roots twitched, and then a golden glow slipped through them, as bright and warm as sunshine. The tendrils reached down and picked him up, as effortlessly as if he weighed nothing. He sighed as the roots wrapped around him, winced as an overaggressive tendril dug into his back.

He had been made a Hanged Man under a different tree. That Lunaria had been gentle with its fruit, treating the men under its care as if they were its children. This Lunaria was more impatient, impetuous. Perhaps it was because it had no more children. Perhaps it was another work of magic entirely, and not a reincarnation of the old one, as he had hoped.

Nevertheless, the roots tangled in a cocoon around him, taking him in. It sought Lascaris's watch in his pocket, stroking the chain and probing at the case.

Gabe closed his eyes. He felt his skin softening, the golden light churning in filaments around him. This was the curse of the Hanged Men—to return to the tree, to rot and be reborn each night. His muscles loosened from his bones while the contents of his guts liquefied. He could stay away perhaps a night or two, but he was driven to return, to regenerate, to become whole again in this place.

To become something other than the husband of his beloved Petra Dee.

And he mourned that loss, that widening chasm between them.

In the grip of the Lunaria, he dreamed. He often dreamed in the Lunaria's embrace. And sometimes the tree dreamed, too, and he glimpsed fragments of its alien consciousness. The tree would dream of lightning, and he would feel a visceral fear in his marrow at the sound of thunder rumbling across the sky. The tree would dream of spring, of soft rains that fed it and the birds that lived in its branches. Gabe would dream of perching in the tree then, feeling that warmth and the life under raven's talons. One or the other of them would dream of the Hanged Men, and they would remember how the Hanged Men hung underground, like glowing fruit, digested and regenerated by the tree. These were symbiotic dreams. It was often hard to remember where one began and the other ended.

Lately, since the fires began, the tree had been afraid. It shuddered under the memory of fire, how its first incarnation had been burned to a stump. Gabe could feel it hiding itself, cloaking itself, drawing up water from the underground river for fortification.

The tree had dreamed of fire for many nights now, shuddering in its sleep.

But tonight, Gabe dreamed of Petra. He dreamed of what he wished he had.

He dreamed that they built a cabin in the backcountry, on a plot of land bought and paid for with alchemical gold. He had envisioned the dimensions of this cabin perfectly in his many nocturnal adventures. He knew that he could build it himself, with an ax and time.

This cabin, on a ridge overlooking a valley, was far from the Rutherford Ranch. He knew that the tree sensed this. In this dream, Gabe no longer kept a shroud of skin over raven feathers. He was a man, and only a man. In the dream, Gabe and Petra lived together as a married couple should. They read books before a fire with a coyote sleeping on his back with all four feet in the air. They hiked in the backcountry and watched the eagles hunt. They slept together in the same bed, with no fear of magical creatures or human threats. There was no need for the Venificus Locus. Petra was human, too, in this place. Her skin had become freckled once more in the sun, and she no longer wore the gold necklace that her father had given her. That jewelry, a lion devouring the sun, was gone, replaced by a necklace he'd given her with a green stone. Sun and moon passed overhead, stars spun, and they grew older. As people should.

In that dream, they lay dozing in bed after making love. A coyote climbed into bed at their feet, yawning. Gabe smiled and gazed drowsily into the dwindling fire in a fireplace.

But then the crackling of the fire changed in pitch. It changed to a ticking. Gabe glanced at the nightstand, where Lascaris's pocket watch lay, case open, hands moving closer and closer to midnight.

He sat upright in bed, alarmed. The blanket fell away, and he snatched up the watch. It ticked with the staccato rhythm of a heartbeat.

There was a bark and a whine behind him. Sig had jumped out of bed and was pawing at a floor-length mirror pinned to the wall. He quickly turned to look at the bed, and Gabe realized with a sickening feeling that Petra was gone.

He ran to the mirror. The mirror was cloudy, like Father Adrian's had become. The shape of a woman churned behind it, like smoke trapped behind glass.

He reached for a lamp and flung it at the mirror to break it, to release the soul that was trapped there. The glass fractured, spilling shards out on the floor in a crystalline roar. He reached in, trying to retrieve the soul behind it.

An arm reached for him, but the arm withered and transformed into a tree root. The root wrapped around his wrist and hauled him in, into darkness, leaving the barking of a coyote behind.

THERE WAS NO sleeping in this empty bed.

Petra rolled over on her futon in the tiny Airstream trailer, fussing with her blanket. In doing so, she disturbed Sig at the foot of the bed. Sig grumbled and crawled up to her chest, where he promptly flopped on his side and made himself the little spoon against the curve of her body. Petra tangled her fingers in his ruff and pressed her cheek to the top of his head, which quickly grew damp.

"I miss him," she confessed.

Sig gave a deep sigh, and she felt his tail thump against her belly.

"But there's nothing to be done for it. I know. I'm being selfish, really. It's not like he's been shipped overseas for years on end or something. I see him often enough. But . . . I think that what bothers me the most is . . ." She forced herself to say it aloud, and the terrible words tasted like poison. "The thing that bothers me the most is that there is no end to this. He will always, always sleep beneath the tree. And the more he does . . . the less human he seems. And I wonder if he will eventually become like the rest of the Hanged Men were. Silent. Automaton-like."

She could feel Sig's eyebrows working against her cheek.

"I mean, don't get me wrong. Immortality is a wonderful thing for him. I'd rather have him in this state than not at all. It's just that I married a man. And I don't know what he is now, or even if he wants to find his way back to being that. Every time he becomes the ravens, I feel like he becomes a little less human, you know?"

Petra sniffled for a moment and rubbed her nose. She wasn't given much to feeling sorry for herself, but something about tonight chewed at her. Maybe it was her trying to cling to humanity and him pushing it away. "It's like . . . he's married to that tree, and I'm the mistress." She laughed aloud. "Listen to me . . . jealous of a damn tree."

Sig didn't laugh at her. He did, as always, take her

very seriously. He turned over, collar jingling. He looked at her with deeply serious eyes, leaned forward, and licked her nose.

She laughed in spite of herself. "Yes, my dear Sig, I know I have you. And I will always love you. I'm a lucky woman."

She turned her gaze to the window over the futon and looked out at the dark sky. She was lucky. Very lucky. Lucky to have Sig and Gabe, in whatever form he took, and lucky to be alive. But there was a sorrow that was creeping into her mind, and she knew that if she didn't shake it, it could contaminate her relationship. And maybe more than that.

It could poison her whole life, if she let it.

She shook her head to clear it, then climbed out of bed and found her boots. She slept in a T-shirt and sweats, good enough to wander outside in. She jammed her feet in her boots and unlocked the front door of the trailer.

Sig hopped down from the futon, yawning in an exaggerated fashion. It was clear that he did not approve of the idea of going out. But he would follow her anywhere. Funny how he was turning out to be the great love of her life. Maybe she needed to be okay with that, make peace with the knowledge that human love wasn't really eternal and didn't conquer all. Maybe, if she did that, she could accept whatever came without trying to possess it. Maybe that's what she was trying to do with Gabe. Possess him. And she knew, deep in her gut, that was unjust. She wanted to be a better person, to be able to love selflessly and without demand. That was what true love was supposed to be all about, right? Unconditional love. She wanted to give it unconditionally, but if she was being honest, she was having to force herself. She just felt like she was grasping at someone who was slipping away, and that she was going to be alone.

Not that being alone was a bad thing. She'd been alone for most of her adult life, and had shocked herself by getting married at all. But meeting Gabe had been something she hadn't been able to predict. He was everything she hadn't realized that she'd ever wanted. She pressed a hand to her aching chest. Maybe this loss she was feeling was the loss of something true and beautiful, and she was managing to fuck it all up. She was clumsy enough to break almost anything, she felt, and manage to cut herself on the pieces.

She rubbed at her blurry eyes, stepped down the wooden steps, and walked around to the back side of the trailer. The summer grasses in the field beyond were pale and brittle, scraping against her sweatpants. Once Sig had awoken himself, he plunged into the field, vanishing in the tall grass. She could only gauge his position by the movement of the tassels.

The distant horizon was vermilion, a lurid red that illuminated the crest of the distant mountains. It was disturbing to see that at night. The wind had turned, blowing ash. Dark smoke billowed skyward, swallowing the stars overhead. She could taste it in the back of her throat, like unseasoned firewood.

Sig returned to her side, leaning against her leg. Petra reached down to rub his ears. "The fire's a long distance away. Many, many miles." But she still wouldn't leave Sig home alone during the day at the trailer. She'd never forgive herself if the fire turned toward Temperance and something happened to him.

And she wanted him close for other reasons. Gabe's story chilled her. It was possible that Lascaris—in some form—was somehow still out there, roaming the backcountry in search of power and magic. She was fully aware that this place, the site of the trailer, was where Lascaris's house had once stood. That fact had crept into her nightmares more than once. She didn't *think* it was haunted. But she sure didn't want to find out. Nor did she want to find out, if Lascaris had returned somehow, that he was homesick.

The fire beyond swirled, almost like a distant solar flare. She couldn't hear it at this distance, but she imagined the roar and popping sound it made as it consumed everything in its path. Despite the summer heat, she shuddered. She had rarely felt at the mercy of the elements like this. She'd experienced storms at sea before when she'd been working as a geologist on an oil rig, but this was different. This was something creeping irresistibly across the land, something that felt so much more alive than a storm that blew over in a matter of hours. Storms ended. This firestorm seemed inexorable.

She turned to leave, to go and get back into bed, but something crunched beneath her boot. She paused, peering downward. Something glittered at her feet, so she knelt to inspect it. Pieces of broken glass sprouted up from the ground like claws. Conscious of Sig's bare paws, she carefully plucked up the shards to discard them safely inside.

CHAPTER 4

The Dark Side of the Mirror

There was no life on the other side of the mirror. The dark side of the mirror was cold, featureless, and still. Aldus Lascaris had remained pinned to the other side of the magical glass for an eternity. He didn't know how long this eternity was—there was no way of measuring time in this place. But hells are always, always eternal.

The mirror hadn't been his first choice. The townsfolk had come for him that night in August, having concluded that he was the root of all evil in Temperance. He *was* the root of evil; he didn't delude himself about that. But he was the root of *everything* in the town—good, bad, and indifferent. Without him, without the gold he conjured, the town would have been dust. No trains would have churned through the station three times a week. There wouldn't have *been* a station. No brothel or church would flourish.

He had created this place, supported it with his magic, and it had turned on him.

He wasn't naive, though. He knew that they'd come for him eventually. From the view of his second-floor window, he saw the men walking down the long road to his house with torches. They had turned on him, after all he'd given them—livelihoods, houses, and this little oasis in the wilderness. How quickly they forgot. How quickly they wanted to destroy him and the home that he had built so carefully. They were invading his sanctuary, likely to loot the priceless treasures in his laboratory. In truth, they were the ones who were naive. Because there was no way he would let them have what he built.

If he were driven out, he would take it all with him.

It wasn't as if he hadn't considered running. He might have been able to flee into the wilderness, to begin again elsewhere. But Lascaris intended to play the long game. And, he would admit, he was stubborn. Why should they take what was his? He would not let his enemies gain his treasure. And he would return, one way or another, to avenge himself.

He moved down the stairs to the first floor. All the lights were out in his house, and the human servants had disappeared. Maybe they'd even been in on it. He checked that the doors were locked and moved on to the door to the basement. He barricaded the basement door behind him and faced his alchemical laboratory for the last time.

The athanor, the alchemical furnace, glowed red in the corner. That fire, tended by salamanders, never went out. It cast just enough light for him to see by, though he knew every feature of this place by touch.

He sucked in his breath as he descended. He had, indeed, been betrayed. Some of his materials had been moved. Some items were missing. He snarled, thinking of his servants vanishing into the night with his potions and notes. Furious, he slammed his hands down on the experiment table.

If they wanted war, he would bring war to them.

Though some of his equipment was gone, his most recent project was fresh in his mind, his pursuit of the Great Work. He snatched a fistful of peacock feathers from a jar on a shelf and threw them in an iron bucket with a handful of raven claws. He cast in an eagle's beak, sulfur, a nugget of gold the size and shape of a human heart, two silver coins, and thirteen fire agates. Muttering dark incantations, he added the contents of a jar of myrrh, spikenard, cinnamon, salt, quicksilver, and a capped flask he'd hidden back on a shelf. The flask had been his best effort at conjuring quintessence, the ether that moved all the unseen things in the world. He dumped the silvery contents of the flask into the bucket.

He yanked open the door of the athanor. An unhappy salamander scuttled out and hissed at him. Looking at the fire lizard in scorn, Lascaris placed the bucket in the belly of the athanor, closed the door, and drew the symbol of quintessence on the floor before the athanor in chalk: a circle on the floor, then a triangle within it, then a square within the triangle, and another circle within the square. At the corners of the triangle, he hastily scribbled the alchemical symbols for salt, mercury, and fire. The phoenix he summoned would be drawn to magic, and he knew that he was the most magical thing in Temperance.

"I call all the elements—air, fire, water, and earth. I summon the sylphs of the east, the salamanders of the south, the undines in the west, and the gnomes of the north. I call upon all the elemental doors to open, to bring forth the creature of quintessence, the phoenix, into this world."

He was conscious of the sounds of men pounding on his door upstairs. Something splintered, and boots clomped on the floors above. Something heavy was flung on the basement door, and he knew that they were coming for him—that they would get through soon. But all that sound receded behind the pounding of his heart.

The contents of the bucket boiled over, spilling into the fire. Where it met the flame, the concoction flashed, like dynamite. The suggestion of a wing sparked into being, stretching in the heart of the athanor.

Sweat prickled Lascaris's brow and his heart thundered. The phoenix. It was coming. He lifted his hand to the furnace. The light was so bright he could see the bones underneath his red flesh.

So close so close so close so . . .

Men flooded into his basement, into his sanctuary. They grasped his arms, dragged him out of the symbol of quintessence. He fought and struggled. The bucket in the athanor spilled, pouring liquid fire on the floor in a pool of lava that ignited everything it touched. Bookshelves, papers, his table—they all began to go up in flames. But the phoenix that was nearly pulled into form was gone. The magic was spilled and ruined.

The men surrounding him shouted at the flames.

One had caught fire, and they were beating the flames out on his shirt. They began to retreat, back up the stairs, barely beyond the fire's touch. Jars on the shelves exploded under the heat.

Lascaris moved to crawl up the stairs, but the door was slammed shut before him, something heavy dragged before it. He slid back down the steps, crawling beneath the smoke. The basement walls were pierced by tiny windows near the ceiling, but they were too small for a man to crawl through. Fire washed up and blanketed the ceiling. There was no escape from this place. This house was going up, with him in it.

He was going to die.

No. He would not let them win. He could not. He crawled to a shelf and dug through its contents, coughing. The fire was climbing up, up, but that wasn't his concern. It would not be the fire that killed him, but the smoke. A salamander basked in the fire devouring his laboratory table, and he glared at it with murderous rage. He knew that he'd lost control over the elementals in the spell, that there was no recovering it.

He opened a box that contained a spell that he had never imagined using on himself, only his enemies: the dark mirror.

He turned the mirror on himself as the smoke bore down on him.

The roar of the fire and the shouts of men fell away, as if an iron door had been closed on them, shutting them out.

And Lascaris was in darkness, a grey darkness that seethed indistinctly around him. He had no body anymore, no sense of separation of his form from the darkness. He was nothing. He could see and hear nothing, not even his own voice. He dissolved into the back of the mirror, into a limbo, accompanied by only his thoughts.

He guessed that time passed, though he didn't know how much. That darkness stretched forever, an infinite unwinding. He passed through periods—perhaps *decades*—of madness that slipped into lucidity. During those times, he hoped that the Hanged Men would return, that they would excavate the site, find the mirror. Gabriel might guess at what he'd done, if he found the mirror. If no one else came to look, then the mirror might remain in the debris of his ruined laboratory, to be filled in by rain and dirt and time. His sentence might be forever.

The weight of time pressed down on him, and on the mirror. He imagined that the ruins of his house compacted, decomposed. Maybe someone filled it in, creating smooth land again. Water trickled through, and the earth churned, as it sometimes does. Things worked free, moving up, sideways, as holes were dug and the earth shivered. Roots of plants reached down, turning, licking water from the face of the mirror.

At some point, he knew that the pressure of earth on the mirror caused it to fracture. He felt it like a thunderclap. He felt the shards crackling upward, toward the sky as water pushed them up, through gravel. With the thunderclap came a flash of light . . .

. . . his spirit cast about, searching for his body. But his body was long gone, burned to ash. There was nothing to return to.

And so, he was catapulted into the spirit world. He'd been released, but to a different hell. He found himself digging himself out of a field, surrounded by shards of mirror. His form felt insubstantial and shadowy. It took him great effort to move the clods of dirt, and when he looked at his hands, they looked like black smoke trapped under glass, the suggestion of hands, churning and transparent.

As he stood, muddy in that familiar-looking field, he realized that he was standing at the spirit world's reflection of his home. They were tenuously connected, through all the magic he'd worked in the physical world. And the spirit world remembered all his efforts.

His house stood here, before him, behind the iron fence. The house loomed in all its former glory, exactly as he'd built it. Which, in turn, was an exact replica of his childhood home. He had told no one this secret. He had simply made it as exquisitely perfect as he could.

He walked through the open iron gate to the house, transfixed, his heart hammering in his chest. The cedar shingles looked freshly whitewashed. The slate roof even had the same green color that he recalled, and the ironwork the same scrolling, with roses vining around the posts. The gate closed softly behind him. He gazed in wonder at this, amazed that the spirit world remembered it as well as he had.

He climbed the porch to find the front door ajar. He stepped inside, unsure whether he'd find his childhood home or his alchemist's lair.

Something moved in the parlor, to his right. He rounded the corner, and his gut twisted.

A coffin lay in the center of the room, on a table. In the open box, his oldest sister, Addy, lay, her hands wrapped over her chest and fingers tangled in wilting violets. Her face was pale and sunken, the appearance of a corpse that had lain in a box for three days in summer. But he knew that she had just been put in, that she'd been ill for a year.

A priest stood at the head of the coffin, reading from his Bible. His remaining family stood around the coffin. His father, his younger sister, Beth. His older brother, Dyer, had fallen ill with the consumption a month before Addy died. He was the favorite boy, and had been sent to Colorado for fresh air. The girls in his family were not so lucky. Beth coughed into her hand, and their father glared at her. She tucked her hand, covered in blood, behind her back.

He gazed in resentment at his father, the improbably named Pleasant Lascaris, standing there with his stupid hat over his heart as if it were broken. He stepped up to his father and tried to slap the hat from his hands. But his father's gaze didn't register on him, and his hand slid through the felt of the hat.

He reached for Addy in her coffin, remembering the violets he'd picked for her. His shadow-hand passed through hers. He was no more than a ghost here, in this world. Were these truly his family, or some shadows the spirit world had conjured up to punish him?

He retreated to the front door. He found it locked. He couldn't open it. His hands passed through the ornate doorknob. He turned to the windows. Perhaps one of them was open . . .

. . . but they were shut. Shut and painted black. No light from outside shone within.

It was a trap. Lascaris snarled and murmured some incantations that he thought might break the window seals, but they remained stubbornly closed. He was a fly caught in the honey of memory. He could not escape it, even as the honey rotted.

He faced the staircase. Screwing up his courage, he climbed the steps. His gaze lingered on the scratches the coffin made on the wall, going downstairs. He shook his head and ascended the stairs, to his mother's room.

His parents' bedroom stood at the end of a short hall. Feeling the trepidation of a small child, Lascaris moved over the fine carpets to his mother's bedside.

His mother was exactly as he remembered her. Patience Lascaris lay in her bed, eyes closed, her face glossed in sweat. Lascaris sank into a chair beside her.

"Mother, it's Aldus. I don't think you can hear me," he said. Or maybe he thought it. In this form, as a shade, he wasn't certain. "But I remember you. I remember all of this."

His mother made no move. Her lips were speckled with red, and so was the handkerchief knotted in her fingers. At the bedside were some noxious concoctions that the doctor had prescribed for her. Given what Lascaris knew now about herbs and tinctures, he knew that they were useless. They were used mostly to quiet her cough and allow his father to get some sleep. In those last weeks, his mother never really woke up. She wasted away, and his father let her.

"After I left, I searched . . . I searched for the key to eternal life," he told her. "I was so close. So close." He ran his shaking hands over his head. "I thought I could keep this from happening again. I thought I could complete the Great Work and conjure the Philosopher's Stone, that magic could succeed where prayer and medicine failed."

He leaned forward, so close that his breath should have disturbed her hair. "And it will. It will."

He turned at the sound of footsteps. His father stood in the doorway, without his hat. He was reading a letter. He looked at Patience, his face showing the first signs of distress that Aldus had ever seen on his father's face.

His father stood over his mother's bed. "A letter came from Colorado. Dyer . . . Dyer is dead."

He let the letter drop to the quilt. Patience's fingers scrabbled weakly toward it. Pleasant walked away, down the hallway, a broken man.

"Was it worth it?" Lascaris snarled. "You sold everything to save him. And it didn't work!"

Lascaris turned back to his mother. She was still, cold in her bed. Her chest no longer rose and fell.

Anger bubbled up in him, and he walked down the hallway, after his father, but his father had vanished.

He paused before his sister Beth's room. Beth was as he had found her one early May morning. She'd fallen facedown on the floor, tangled in her bedspread, covered in blood. A small puddle leaked from her mouth. She was not yet fifteen, had not even had the chance to have her own household and marriage.

Beth was dead, dead, and his father hadn't called the doctor. That had been up to Aldus. His father had done nothing after Dyer died. He couldn't even be bothered to have a grave dug for his own wife. Aldus had done that, paid the diggers with the family silver and the priest with his mother's wedding ring. He had kept himself and Beth fed after that, existing as quiet ghosts around the simmering wrath of their father. When Beth would cough around him, he would slap her. Aldus tended Beth for the months until she died, boiling broth from bones and wiping sweat from her brow. But it was for naught. All of it.

When Beth died. Lascaris buried her himself. There was nothing left to pay the gravediggers. The priest, feeling sorry for Aldus, came by for free to offer a blessing. There was no one else at that grave.

Coated in mud, Aldus returned to the house late at night. It was as he saw now, his father staring out of a black window, wordless in his fury at losing his favored son.

Aldus was alone. He knew this. He knew that life was fleeting, and it was only him and his father.

He wanted to be more alone than that.

Aldus reached for the small kerosene lamp on the table, the only light in the house. He reached for it and flung it as hard as he could at Pleasant.

The glass shattered, and lamp oil spattered all over his father and the wall. Pleasant went up like a wad of ephemeral paper, flailing and howling. His struggles caught everything he touched on fire—the drapes, the settee, his paintings.

Lascaris watched. He watched his father die and then walked out of the house.

He studied alchemy, in search of the key to eternal life, the Great Work. He knew that, somehow, there had to be a way to defeat the monster of consumption. He thought he'd found it in the texts of the old alchemical masters, in his own experiments.

But that was at an end. Now, in the spirit world, he could not kill his father and walk away. He was trapped, bound to these images of his family, playing over and over in this cursed house. His father simply gazed out the window, into the black, with his hands behind his back, burning slowly. Soon, he fell into a puddle of ash and a stain on the carpet.

Lascaris turned away, to the basement. There had to be a way out of the spirit world, out of his private hell. He spied on the physical world, peering into his teacup, where pale images of the physical world moved if he concentrated hard enough. He glimpsed the passage of time, the wonders the modern world had conjured without magic, with only the tools offered by science. Imagine what the world could be if magic were invoked again! He knew that there must be ways to reach it, at certain times of year and under certain moon phases, with certain artifacts, ways to touch it. He would discover them; he would find his way back.

And when he found his way back, he would complete the Great Work.

He would master the terrible art of immortality, no matter the cost.

CHAPTER 5

Off to See the Wizard

"This is something like going to see the wizard, isn't it, Sig?"

Petra opened the door to the nursing home for the coyote. He trotted inside, wrinkling his nose at the smell of bleach. Sporting a collar, Sig was often purposefully ignored here and assumed to be a service dog. The staff had come to know him and turned a blind eye. Mostly. As Petra reached the front desk, the night nurse behind the desk whistled for him. It was 6:00 a.m., too early for the front office staff to arrive. Sig trotted up to him and sat down, head cocked in an adorably manipulative fashion, tail wagging. The nurse grinned back at him and gave him a dog treat. Sig took it delicately from his hand and chewed it thoughtfully.

"Thank you," Petra said to him, pausing to sign in. It was early for official visiting hours, but the staff were fine with Petra visiting her father as often as she could, as long as she wasn't interrupting treatment.

"I brought you folks a little something." Petra placed a paper bag on the desk.

The nurse peered inside and grinned. "Chocolate muffins! Awesome!"

"They're from Bear's Gas 'n' Go. They're amazing. I had one on the way over, and I can die happy now."

The nurse leaned around a flower arrangement to speak with her in a low voice. "It's good that you're here for your dad. He's been having a tough time lately."

Petra felt her brow furrow, and she set the pen down. "What's going on with him?"

The nurse shook his head. "He hasn't been sleeping well. He's been having some hallucinations. Sometimes, it's like he's not even here."

Petra felt her gut clench. "His Alzheimer's is progressing."

"It seems like it. The doctor will be by on rounds later, and I know she'll want to talk with you about his treatment. Maybe switching up his meds. It's okay for you and Sig to go back, though. He's been awake for several hours."

Petra nodded slowly. "Thanks. I appreciate the heads-up."

She and Sig walked slowly down the green-glazed tile hallway. She always had a knot in her belly every time she visited. She feared opening the door to his room to find an empty bed, and being told that her father had died without her at his side. They'd had, at times, a contentious and distant relationship. But he was her father. And the only alchemist she knew.

Petra knocked softly on the door to his room.

A snarl emanated from inside. "What now?"

Petra opened the door hesitantly. Her father sat in his wheelchair, still dressed in his pajamas, with a blanket spread over his lap. His arms were crossed over his thin chest, and his face was screwed up in a scowl. Beside his unmade bed, on the nightstand, Petra took in a collection of geegaws: a dismantled cigarette with the tobacco arranged in an intricate circular design around the paper, a silver dollar, a handful of pennies, and what looked like a dried-out apple with toothpicks jammed into its desiccated flesh.

His face cleared immediately when he saw her. "I thought you were the damn night nurse with a cup of pills."

Petra shook her head. She came to sit on the edge of the bed opposite him. Sig slithered around her legs and put his front paws on her dad's knee. The old man grinned and chuckled as he bent close for Sig to wash his face with his tongue.

She was, truth be told, glad to see him lucid. Such times seemed to be dwindling. A couple of days ago, she'd come by to find him in bed muttering about suns and lions. Alchemy. He had seemed not to see her, then, and called her by both her name and her mother's, even as he reached out to touch the pendant around her neck. But she was relieved that he recognized her clearly today.

"I brought you something," she said. She pulled a muffin out of her jacket pocket and gave it to him. It was the reverse of when she was a child and he would bring her a candy bar from the vending machine at work. Then, he'd been a respected chemist, and she'd been seven years old.

Her father snatched the muffin away and tore into it greedily with liver-spotted fingers. Crumbs fell into his lap.

"How've you been?" she asked cautiously.

His shoulders stiffened, then sagged. "I can't sleep. No matter what pills and shots they give me, I just can't. I wake up ten times a night."

"Is there something waking you up?"

He leaned forward. "I hear things. Sometimes, it's voices, voices coming up from the drains in the bathroom. Laughter. Sometimes it's a bell. I don't know." His watery eyes turned to the window. "I wonder what it means. If it means anything."

"I don't know." When she'd found him in the nursing home, she'd sworn to herself that she would always be honest with him. "Did you tell the doctor?"

He shook his head vigorously. "No. They'd decide I was crazy." He looked at her and then amended: "Well, crazier."

Petra leaned forward to hug him. He seemed thinner than he'd been since her last visit. She'd have to bring him more muffins.

"You look good." Her father patted her cheek when she sat back down on the bed. "That new body is doing good things for you. You look strong."

She looked away, down at her hands. Hands that were hers somehow, but that she hadn't worn for the past few decades. "It's taking some getting used to."

"You'll just have to break it in. It will come." He said it with such certainty.

But she didn't want to talk about the body. *Her* body. It was still hard to think of it as hers. She changed the subject clumsily. "Have you been following the fires on TV?"

Her father nodded vigorously. "Yes. Terrible thing. All those animals and all that wilderness affected."

She took a deep breath and told her father what Gabe had seen in the sky and the meteorite crater she'd discovered on the ground. When she finished, he was leaning forward in his wheelchair with his elbows on his knees, eyes glittering in interest.

"My gut says it's some kind of fire elemental at the root of this. Too big to be a salamander. Those little critters are subtler in their mischief. But it could be the work of a drake, dragon, phoenix . . . something on that order. Something big." He spread his hands out. "Something with wings, so that would rule out the drake. Probably a dragon, too . . . a dragon would den up and not be gadding about in the sky in broad daylight. They're cagier than that."

"You don't think it was a meteorite? I mean, it is time for the Perseids . . ."

He chuckled. "If you really thought it was a meteorite, you wouldn't be here."

Petra pressed her mouth into a thin line. He was right.

He continued: "The phoenix, if that's what it is . . . it's a symbol of a completed cycle. The old myth is that the phoenix burns and is reborn in its ashes. In alchemy, it's a sign of transition from the physical to the spiritual, of freeing one's spiritual force from earthly bonds. It's both completion and beginning anew, the ultimate purification. Alchemists would associate its presence with sulfur and gold. It's a sign that the Great Work is close to completion."

Petra frowned. "I found something that looked like sulfur there. I have to test it to confirm. And basalt. There was melted basalt, sluicing off in a pattern of seven rays . . . sort of like what's depicted on the Venificus Locus."

"It seems like it would be the hallmark of a phoenix, evidence of an alchemical operation. It's likely that it slept there, and then rose automatically, as part of its cyclical programming." Her dad tapped the side of his head, seeming deep in thought.

"Awesome. Just awesome." Her shoulders slumped. She had been so hoping for a meteorite. That would have been something she could have written a paper on, a mystery that she could have unraveled using scientific methods. There was no writing a paper on a rogue phoenix or putting it in a test tube. And such a creature would be just as difficult to wrangle as rogue meteorites.

"Sorry. I am often the bearer of bad tidings." Her dad spread his hands helplessly.

"Not your fault. I asked." She took a deep breath. "I just hope that this doesn't have anything to do with Lascaris. But it probably does . . . it's probably something he got involved with in his time on earth. So I guess what I really hope is that it's not a sign that he's back, somehow." She wrapped her arms around herself. "Gabe has his watch. And it's trying to start keeping time."

"I've been looking for clues about his whereabouts," her dad offered. "I've taken a few trips into the spirit world, and . . ."

"Dad. No." She shook her head, slinging hair into her face. "I don't want you risking yourself." The spirit world was a dangerous place, and given her father's fragile mental health, she feared losing him in it.

The old alchemist's shoulders drew up around his ears. "I do what I want, dammit."

And that was true. All the time that she'd known him, no one could dissuade him from taking off on quests. Being bound to a wheelchair was no obstacle to him.

"Yeah, Dad." She pinched the bridge of her nose. "I know."

"The good news is that I haven't seen any signs of Lascaris there. Yet. But things are unsettled in the spirit world. Lots of energy moving around, creatures hiding." He frowned. "I haven't gotten to the bottom of it yet, but I will."

"Dad, please." She reached forward and took his lined hands in hers. "This isn't good for you. Just leave it to Gabe and me. If he shows up in the physical world, Gabe will know about it. And if he's in the spirit world, and he stays there, he can't hurt us. Okay?"

He looked away, his mouth stubbornly taut. She knew that she couldn't force him to stay on this plane. She couldn't force him to do anything, any more than her mother had been able to force him to stay home and be a dutiful husband and father.

She let go of his hands. "So what does a phoenix

want? How do we get it to stop torching the backcountry and . . . I dunno . . . go to sleep again?"

Her dad looked her straight in the eye then. "I
have no idea. But I can look—"

"No. No!" she said, regretting even bringing any
of these issues up with him. "You stay. Stay here
and . . ."

Her phone rang in her pocket, and she thumbed
the button to answer. "Hello?"

Her friend Maria's voice came over the end of the
line: "It's Maria. Is it a good time?"

"Sure. What's up?"

"It's Nine. She needs to see you, as soon as possible."

"Is she okay?" Petra blurted.

"Yes, yes. She's fine. But she needs to talk to you
about something she saw in the Eye of the World."
Petra imagined that she could hear Maria's lips
pursing at the end of that. Maria had as much concern about Nine wandering into the spirit world as
Petra had for her father.

"Understood. I'm at the nursing home now, but
I'll be there as soon as I can."

Petra hung up and turned to her father. "I've got
to go. Will you . . . will you stay here . . . and out
of the spirit world if I bring you more muffins?" It
seemed ridiculous to bribe a grown man this way,
but she was desperate.

Her father screwed up his face in thought. "Hmm.
What kind?"

"Any kind you want."

"More chocolate?"

"Yes. I'll bring you more chocolate muffins."

He nodded. "Okay, then."

"Great." She leaned forward to kiss him on the top of his shaved head, resolving to bring lots of muffins and not bring up supernatural things with him when she returned. "I'll see you soon."

Sig stood up from where he'd been draped over her father's feet and stretched. Her dad scratched his ears before Sig followed Petra to the door. Petra slid out into the hallway, Sig tangled at her feet, and she closed the door.

"Ms. Manget?"

She turned. A woman with a stethoscope draped around her neck was holding a clipboard. Petra swore in the back of her head, knowing she'd been busted by someone with serious authority for having what looked like a dog in the nursing home.

Sig was not worried. He cocked his head in his best "cute puppy" expression and perked up his ears. Damn. He was getting good at that manipulation.

Petra cleared her throat. "Yes?"

"I'm Dr. Vaughn. Can I speak with you?" No mention of Sig. The doctor was deliberately not looking at Sig, so Petra nodded.

"Of course."

Petra followed the woman down another hallway to a small office. The office smelled like lavender. Behind a scratched metal desk stood a wall of files and a chair. Dr. Vaughn slid into the chair and gestured for Petra to sit on a sofa opposite the desk.

Petra sat down, sinking deep into the chenille sofa. Sig wound around her feet and sat down, pretending to be a good service animal.

Dr. Vaughn clasped her hands. They were spotted

with freckles and the fingers decorated with rings. "I wanted to talk with you about your father's condition."

"I am hearing that he's not doing very well."

"Your father's chart shows a lot of ups and downs. When he first came here, as you know, he was catatonic. He stayed in that state for years. He made a stunning improvement, against all odds, shortly after you found him a year ago. He had a good several months in which he was lucid for more days than not. He was generally aware of his surroundings, alert, and responsive. Even though he refused all therapy."

"Yeah. He's not the most compliant guy. Getting him to talk to a therapist would be a tough sell."

"It's not just behavioral therapy. He rejected physical therapy, too." The doctor's mouth turned down. "Despite rejecting physical therapy, we think he can walk. He just doesn't want anyone to know. One of the orderlies has been leaving his favorite socks on a top shelf in his closet as a test. He seems to be able to get them down and on with no problem. And there's lint on the bottom of the socks, like he's been shuffling around."

"He's a stubborn man." This, Petra knew, was an immutable law of the universe. Like gravity. But her heart lifted at the idea that his physical health, at least, was improving.

"Yes. In the last few months, though, we've seen a gradual decline in the amount of time he's lucid. He has good days and bad days, but the bad days are outnumbering the good ones."

Petra leaned forward with her elbows on her knees. "I've seen him when he's not all there. He's a handful."

"Sometimes, yes. Sometimes, he's very quiet, almost like the catatonic state he was in before. Other times, he's grown violent. Last week, he took a swing at an orderly who was trying to wake him up for breakfast."

Petra frowned. "I didn't know."

"Most of these incidents have centered around sleep, and they happen at night or early in the morning. The majority of the things that get moved around in his room move at night, too. I'm suspecting a sleep disorder of some kind. Possibly more than one. I'd like to run a sleep study on him, but he won't allow monitors to be attached. He even tears off a heart monitor. We haven't been able to get a good EKG for him for months."

Petra's thoughts scraped against what she knew of her father. Perhaps he was dipping into the spirit world as he slept, and was coming back disoriented. But who knew? Maybe the old alchemist had figured out a way to levitate his socks to him from the top of the closet.

"I've seen in his file that you have health care power of attorney over him," Dr. Vaughn said. "We need to run some tests on him, like the sleep study and some brain imaging, to give us some information that will help us treat him and hopefully reduce the speed of his decline."

Petra flinched. "You didn't say 'reduce his decline.' You said 'reduce the *speed* of his decline.'"

"Yes. Your father, sadly, *is* going to decline. It's inevitable. We are honestly just trying to reduce the speed of it, to give him—and you—more time."

Petra didn't want to lie to her father, and it seemed as if the doctor wasn't going to lie to her. Petra stared down at her hands. She and her father had had little time together. He'd vanished when she was a teenager, and Petra had not found him again until a year ago. It wasn't fair. There was just too little time. She sucked in a breath. "Regardless of whether I give you permission or not, he's not going to submit to those tests."

"That's why we want your permission to do so. We would have to restrain or sedate him in order to accomplish some of them. But, in consultation with my colleagues, we do agree that's in his best interest."

Petra's stomach churned. Allowing them to do this could very well sever the fragile bond she had with her father. "I don't know."

"At the very least, we would like to set up a camera in your father's room, so that we can more accurately gauge his sleep patterns and physical abilities."

"You want to . . . spy on my dad without him knowing?" It seemed like such an affront to what little dignity her dad had left.

Dr. Vaughn made a little moue with her mouth. "Yes. That's the least invasive way we can think of to figure out what he's up to."

And what her father was up to . . . might involve things that should remain hidden. What if her father really had figured out a way to levitate his socks? What arcane rituals was he conducting with the tobacco mandala and coins at his bedside? What if he was talking to spirits at night? Having a party with them? Her dad, at the very least, deserved privacy as a human being. If he was dabbling in alchemy, they couldn't find out about that. Not ever.

She shook her head. "No. No surveillance. I will talk to him, see if there are any tests he might willingly submit to. But I won't force him."

Dr. Vaughn sighed and laced her glittering fingers together. "At least, think about it. What we learn about him could extend his life."

And that was the rub, wasn't it? They might gain a few months, even years, by strapping him down and poking at him . . .

. . . but her dad was going to die anyway. And she wasn't ready for that.

CHAPTER 6

The Rattler Spills His Guts

Nobody ever confessed their secrets without motivation.

There were lots of motivations, to be certain. Sometimes secrets were disclosed for money. They could be told to impress or intimidate someone else, to gain unfair leverage. Sometimes people vomited them up to avoid punishment or to cut a deal with the law. Once in a while, they spilled their guts just to be able to sleep at night. When a secret came out, there was always a reason. And if there was one thing that Sheriff Owen Rutherford had learned in twenty years in law enforcement, it was just as important to know the reason behind spilling the beans as the secret itself. Knowing the light of one showed the shadow in the other, and the truth usually lay somewhere between the secret and the reason. And a secret was what had called him to the jail today.

He had something else on his mind, to be certain. And that something was the Magpie Fire. The fire was out of his jurisdiction, burning on parkland. But that could change at any time. Owen had canceled all leave requests and sent as many deputies as he could spare to the border of his county and Yellowstone to close off roads, ferry supplies, and maintain order with the Park Service. He'd been spending his days developing evacuation plans in case the fire crept beyond the roadblocks and threatened civilians. Parkland was relatively easy to clear; people didn't have homes and property that they would stay to defend. Enforcing an evacuation got tougher when a person's whole life was in the path of the fire. And there were a whole lot of cantankerous old dudes in his county who felt like they were God with a fucking garden hose, able to start a Great Flood around the foundations of their houses.

This errand to the jail was an unwelcome distraction. Owen didn't spend a lot of time at the jail anymore. Sure, it was his domain and his jurisdiction as county sheriff, and he kept an office in the building. Every person who pissed in an alley or who spat on a deputy and got arrested wound up here, for at least a little while. He thought of his domain as having two sides. There was the upper world of the open road and sunshine, driving in a cruiser and feeling the wind tickle his mustache. He liked that one, the feeling of being free in the world. This, though, was the underworld, the lightless place where unlucky souls waited for the gears of justice to grind them down or open the door to let them out. This one, he avoided when he could. He knew that strange things happened when men were given power over other men, and he knew that he was just as susceptible to abuses of power as the next guy with a badge. So he stayed the hell away. Or as much as he could.

Today, though, the underworld had dialed him up and asked him to come on down.

Owen opened the heavy metal door leading to the jail. He used his left hand; his right was missing. Not that a casual observer would see that. He'd had a prosthetic made. But he was still getting used to it; it felt clunky and annoying and in the way. He was right-handed, and he was still figuring out how to shoot and fiddle with his cell phone with his left. In his dreams, he still had two hands, and if he wasn't paying attention, he swore his phantom fingers could feel things. Even in the summertime, he wore gloves on both his real hand and the prosthetic one. The rumor that went around town was that he wore gloves so that he wouldn't leave fingerprints behind on whatever shady business he was dabbling in. Owen didn't address those rumors at all.

The door closed behind him, leaving him in a tiny vestibule with a locked door before him. To his right stood a wall-mounted line of small lockers, resembling a stand of PO boxes at the post office.

A little blonde girl at his side stared up at him, chewing on the drawstring of her pink hoodie. "What's in there?"

"Guns. Mace. Tasers. Whatever weapons that cops carry." Owen was mindful to turn his back to the camera perched in a dome over the locked door. Wouldn't do for anyone to see him talking to himself. Because Anna, the little girl beside him, was a ghost. A ghost no one else could see. There were enough rumors swirling about him; he didn't need to add madness to the stew.

Owen unholstered his sidearm and secured it in a lockbox, pocketing the key. Though no one would challenge him if he strode through his jail with a bazooka on his shoulder, Owen was careful about which rules he decided to break and which he didn't.

Anna poked at the empty boxes on the bottom row. "Why would you give up your gun?"

"Because this is a place with bad men behind that door, and we don't want to take a chance that the bad men would get my gun." Owen tipped his head to the second heavy metal door. It had been painted many times, and the most recent beige color had been chipped away in spots to reveal black and grey underneath. There was a bar to his left, which suspects could be cuffed to while arresting officers surrendered their guns. Sort of like tying up one's horse outside a saloon.

Anna's pale face twisted in a grimace. "Bad men?"

"Lots and lots of bad men. I'm going to talk to one of them today."

She shook her head vigorously. "Yuck. I'm going to go play with the puppy."

"Good idea."

Anna walked through the exterior wall of the little chamber without opening the door and vanished. In a few seconds, Owen heard barking. He peered through the tiny bulletproof glass window at the top of the door to see Anna standing beside a patrol car from a nearby city, tapping on the glass of the backseat window. A police dog was going nuts, pawing at the window. Owen took this as some small evidence that he wasn't entirely guanopsychotic. Maybe the dog could see her, too.

He had been told by folks with their fingers in the supernatural that Anna wasn't real, that he was, in fact, insane. But he'd seen enough creepy shit in his jurisdiction to believe a lot of screwed-up things. Anna, the ghost of a murdered girl, was the most benign supernatural thing he'd encountered, certainly more pleasant than carnivorous mermaids, undead cowboys, and the alchemical Tree of Life. And Anna had been with him for years.

He had, after he'd been told she wasn't real, tried to ignore her for about a week. He tried to act like a sane guy. But that was hard to do with the ghost of a kid demanding that he turn on the cartoon channel on the television or chattering at him about the wildflowers growing near the mailbox. He finally decided that Anna was real. He may be batshit crazy, but he knew what he saw, and in a world of ever-shifting reality, he decided to believe in her.

Owen smacked a red button beside the interior door. Within seconds, an intercom crackled to life. "Good afternoon, Sheriff."

Without any explanation required on his behalf, a loud buzzer sounded. The door to the outside locked behind him, and the interior door unlocked with a thick *thunk*. Owen pushed it open and strode into the intake area.

There were no windows here, only buzzing fluorescent lights overhead. The area had been painted a sickly pink, the color of calamine lotion. The entire interior of the jail was painted in this color, from bars to walls, ever since the time Owen's father had been sheriff. Owen's father had read in a law enforcement magazine that pink was supposed to be a calming color. Owen had no idea if it worked or not, but knowing his father, he suspected it had more to do with his father's odd sense of humor.

Owen's skeleton staff was running the jail without complaint. Probably because nobody really wanted to get sent to direct traffic on hot asphalt all day. Behind a Plexiglas wall in a tiny control room, a deputy's face was glued to security cameras and computer monitors, a stack of paper court orders printed out beside him. Another deputy was searching a row of molded plastic benches for left-behind contraband, keeping one eye on an orange-clad prisoner talking into the wall-mounted telephone. The prisoner was hunched over, clasping the phone in handcuffed hands. The place smelled like piss. No matter how much cleaning happened, it always did. One got used to it, of course, and the deputy supervising the inmate caller had marinated in enough fragranced body spray to make flowers wilt.

Owen nodded at the deputy. He moved to another door and swiped his keycard at a lighted panel beside it. The door crunched open, and he entered the men's cell block.

No matter how often he ordered the plastic-covered lights overhead changed, the light had a dim, amber cast. This was where male inmates who weren't considered too sick or dangerous were kept. Four inmates crowded a steel cage with a lidless toilet piercing the floor. Beds were bolted to the concrete, with thin plastic-covered mattresses arranged on them. The inmates, dressed in orange suits and plastic molded sandals, watched him as he passed the pod. Some stared, some snickered. One rushed up to the bars and howled at him, like he was Lon Chaney under a full moon. Owen was very glad that Anna had stayed outside. This wasn't a place for children, and so far Anna had never followed him in.

Owen didn't look directly at the inmates. He'd cultivated a thousand-yard stare that could look right through a person. He didn't quicken his pace, either—that was a sign of fear, and this was his backyard. He just kept moving toward the end of the hall. The handful of solitary cells the jail had were there, featureless rooms with solid doors and mattresses on the floor.

The interview room was here, as well, at the end of the hall. It had once been a utility closet, but space was limited. This was where attorney visits took place. Today, Owen would be conducting another type of interview.

Owen keyed the radio pinned on his uniform shoulder. "L2, this is S1. I'll be awaiting our guest in interview room one."

His radio crackled back: "S1, this is L2. I'm en route." The lieutenant on the other end sounded frazzled. Owen wondered if his interviewee was giving the lieutenant some shit.

No matter. Owen parked himself in the first tiny interview room. He sat down in a molded plastic chair in front of a desk bolted to the floor. There was nothing else in the room except another chair.

A dull, grinding noise echoed in this area, sounding like excavation equipment. It came from the basement, and Owen could feel the vibration of it in his feet. The jail had a machine that ground up all the materials that inmates flushed, like a giant garbage disposal the size of a closet. It destroyed everything from plastic forks to contraband, chewing it all up and spitting out sludge. It was an irritating sound, and was not always helpful for interviews. Owen had hated the expense, but having plumbers out every week to retrieve shredded shoes and bedsheets from pipes was more expensive.

The door to the interview room opened. The shift lieutenant ordered an inmate to enter. The man in the orange jumpsuit looked to be in his late forties, but it was hard to tell. Grey mingled with stringy brown hair. The guy was skinny, in the way that guys who did far too much meth were. His face was covered with stubble and red marks. Whatever he was on, it was causing him to pick at his skin something awful.

The lieutenant pulled out the plastic chair on the other side of the desk and asked the inmate to sit, then lean forward. The inmate obediently extended his hands to the metal bar welded to the desk. The lieutenant quickly unfastened his cuffs and recuffed them around the bar.

Owen sat back, watching, rocking on the back legs of the chair. "What's his story?" he asked the lieutenant.

The lieutenant nodded at the inmate. "This is Luke Timothy Rogers. He goes by 'Rattler.'"

Owen covered a snort. *Of course he did.* He addressed the inmate: "You in a biker gang or what?"

Rattler leaned forward and pulled his lips back

on a grin of loose and missing teeth. "They call me Rattler on account of my superior dental hygiene." His tongue wiggled one of his front teeth.

Owen looked at his lieutenant. "Wonderful."

The lieutenant continued, reading from a folded-up paper that she removed from her pocket: "Rattler has a lengthy history in this and nearby counties. Grand theft auto, domestic violence, possession of criminal tools, assault and battery, possession of narcotics with intent to distribute, burglary, and"—she paused for a moment, a perfectly shaped eyebrow creeping up her forehead—"using a firearm to fish."

"I was drunk," Rattler said by way of explanation. "Fish got away."

"As it happens when one goes fishing with a firearm." Owen rubbed his mustache. "What's he in for now?"

"He was pulled over with a trunk full of stolen collectible bowling balls. Twenty-six of them. Their value is enough to make it grand larceny, and Rattler's least favorite judge is not sympathetic to his protestations of innocence."

Owen did some quick math in his head. "That's over four hundred pounds of bowling ball . . . How was his bumper not dragging the pavement?"

"That was how he was discovered. The bumper of his vintage Caddy scraping the road generated enough sparks to catch the attention of the arresting officer. It was likened to Fourth of July sparklers."

The corner of Owen's mouth crept up beneath his mustache. "Thank you. You can leave us now, Lieutenant."

The lieutenant nodded. "I'll be outside when you're finished."

Owen waited for the door to shut and turned his attention back to the scraggly guy chained to the table before him.

"I don't know how those balls got in my—"

"I didn't come down here about that. You insisted that you had information about a murder. And that you would speak only to me."

"Right—yeah. I know some things about a murder that happened twenty years ago." Rattler's tongue poked at his tooth.

"And I imagine that you want to tell me now out of the goodness of your heart?"

"Nope. Got no goodness left in my heart." Rattler grinned. "But I'm willing to make a trade in exchange for shaving some time off my sentence."

Owen knew he sounded bored. "I'm guessing you spent as much time behind bars as out on the street. Why make a deal this time, after twenty years? And why not go through your attorney?"

Rattler chuffed dismissively. "My attorney is useless. Hence all the time I spent on the inside. It's better to get an audience with a man with clout, go direct."

Owen shrugged. He wasn't impressed.

"Look, I know I'm looking at hard time . . . a fifteen-year minimum on this stupid bowling ball charge. All the small shit adds up, since I guess I'm what they call a repeat offender." The Rattler's face soured, and he looked spooked. "Judge said that if she ever saw me in her courtroom again, she'd make sure it was my last. My attorney ain't gonna do nothing to stop that. But I think that you've got enough pull to maybe get it done."

Owen was wary. "How about you tell me what you know, and I'll tell you if it's worth anything?" Likely, the guy had made something up or had something insignificant on a case that had already been put to bed.

Rattler grunted and shrugged. "I understand. A man's time's limited. I'll cut to the chase. Twenty years ago, I spent some time here while I was waiting for trial."

"Which time was that?"

"The time I stole a hearse."

"Oh yeah. The auto theft. Go on."

"I shared a cell with a guy for three days. A guy who was in for misdemeanor possession. Robin Wayne Cuthbert."

The name meant nothing to Owen. "Go on."

"After a couple days, the guy's girlfriend came in to visit him. She slipped him some pills. We crushed 'em up and snorted 'em. He had more than I did, since his girlfriend was the one that brought 'em, and when he was lit, he talked about a little girl who had gone missing." Rattler paused for dramatic effect. He'd been around the block a few times. The dude knew how to work a story and the system. "Would what he said about that girl be worth something?"

Owen slowly lowered the chair so that all four legs sat on the floor again. He reached into his pocket for a pack of cigarettes, the lingua franca of the jail. He tapped out a cig and offered it to Rattler.

Rattler leaned forward, and Owen stuck it in his mouth, successfully resisting the urge to grimace at

Rattler's complete and utter lack of familiarity with a toothbrush. Owen plucked his own cigarette out of the pack. He lit his cigarette first, and then Rattler's. Rattler sat back in his chair, sucking on the cancer stick like he hadn't had one in days. Which was probably the truth. Dude had to be experiencing withdrawal from God-knew-what.

"Anyway, this was some strong shit that the girlfriend brought. Robin went on a bad trip. Said he was being haunted by a Toad God named Pigin." The lit end of the cigarette bobbed as Rattler talked. "I dunno if the acid sent him to another dimension, or what."

"A Toad God. Named Pigin." Owen was beginning to regret wasting a cigarette.

"He said it was a really profound experience. Spiritual. Described a toad the size of Jabba the Hutt."

"Um. Far out?" Owen hoped he was describing it properly.

"Totally. This Pigin promised to grant him the power of persuasion . . . the ultimate silver tongue. Like, Robin would be able to talk anyone into anything. As you can imagine, Robin really dug the concept. The number of scams he could do, the amount of shit he could rip off . . . it would be staggering."

"Staggering," Owen repeated. Owen had the sensation of falling down a rabbit hole of psychedelic weird. Trying to get this over with, he said, "So what did Robin say about the girl?"

"He said he went over to a dude's house to crash for the night. Dude was a regular customer, and Robin was lying low from the fuzz. He'd gotten in some trouble and he wanted not to be at home if anyone came knocking." Rattler sucked on the cigarette deeply. "He got there to find his customer passed out on the couch. Robin began looking for some drugs to keep him entertained for the evening."

"As one does?"

"As one does. Robin discovered, however, a little girl sleeping in her back bedroom. And he swears that Pigin told him to kill the girl."

"And did he?" Owen's heart was hammering.

"Yeah. He did. He took her and killed her for the giant toad." Rattler nodded, ash trailing from the cigarette.

Owen tried to keep his tone neutral. He reminded himself that this was a weird yarn, but there was no evidence behind it. Nothing concrete. "Rattler. This is gonna be hard to take to the judge . . ."

"Robin said he wrapped the body up in a blanket, took her to his car, and ditched her in a well."

Owen's heart stopped clunking around in his chest like the transmission of an old car. Twenty years ago, he had found a body at the bottom of a well. That detail was not public knowledge; the news had reported that the body in question was found in the woods.

Rattler sucked on his cigarette for a moment with his wrinkly lips before he spoke again. "So there it is. I hope it's worth something. The guy confessed to murdering that little girl."

"It's worth something," Owen said softly, before taking a deep drag on his own cigarette. "It's worth something if you knew the killer of Anna Jean Sawarski."

* * *

THERE MIGHT HAVE been sun if there wasn't so much smoke in the sky. The fire turned the sky overhead a storm-like violet as Petra drove. The sun broke through once in a while, streaming through the smoke, not with summer's full invincible wrath, but with a pale, sickly light. It reminded her of the sun in February. Petra had the windows down against the heat that clung to the land, winding down two-lane roads toward Maria's house. The air-conditioning didn't work on the Bronco, and Petra had never bothered to get it fixed, a decision she was now second-guessing. Sig sat on the passenger side, leaning his head out the window. His eyes were slitted in joy and ears flapping in the breeze. Some things about canines were universal, she thought.

She flipped on the radio for news about the fire. It was still within the park, but seemed to be pushing toward its borders, sweeping south and east. Depending on the way the wind moved, it could push toward Temperance, the reservation, or the Rutherford Ranch . . . The weathercaster was unwilling to make any predictions. Never mind trying to guess at the motives of a phoenix.

She gripped the wheel tightly as she dropped off the paved road onto gravel when she crossed into the reservation, transmitting her frustration to the pleather steering wheel cover. Because guessing the motives of a phoenix was *exactly* what she needed to do. Once she figured that out, maybe then she would have the mental space to figure out what was best for her father. At least, he was well out of harm's way on the other side of the county.

Maria's house soon came into view, bathed in sultry summer. The cheerful white cottage house shone like its own sun under a dim sky. Ripe tomatoes cascaded from cages in the garden, and squash vines snaked up to the porch, where a grey and white cat sat behind a pot of marigolds.

Petra parked in front of the house and opened the door. Sig scrambled through the open window and ran to the cat.

"Sig!" she scolded.

Sig stopped right before the cat, leaned over, and gave her a slurp on the top of her head that bent one grey feline ear backward. Pearl gave Sig a murderous look and stiffly walked away with as much dignity as she could muster with her ear turned back and dripping coyote spit. Petra swore that Sig smirked as she retreated.

Petra stepped up on the porch and knocked at the screen door. It opened almost immediately, and Maria beckoned her inside. Her friend, a social worker, had the day off. Instead of her usual business casual gear, she was dressed in a blue sundress with her dark hair loose over her shoulders.

Indoors felt immeasurably cooler than outside. All the lights were off, the drapes were drawn, and a ceiling fan spun lazily overhead. The bright colors of the quilts and afghans piled on the furniture inside seemed muted somehow, as if some somber spell had been cast inside.

Maria grasped Petra's elbow and hissed in her ear. "Nine came home late last night and shut herself in her room. She keeps saying that something's coming, and that she has to talk to you. She won't say anything else."

As Maria was speaking, Sig trotted past Petra and down the hallway. Gently pulling away from Maria's grip, Petra followed him. He nosed the door to one of the bedrooms open five inches and squeezed through.

Petra paused before the door and knocked on the door frame. "Nine? It's Petra. Can I come in?"

An answer came from behind the door: "Yes."

Petra pushed the door open. The curtains were drawn in this room, too, but it was even darker than the other rooms. Petra saw that a quilt had been hung over the window, as if it could block out the scorch of the day. She saw a perfectly made bed. On top of the bed was a full backpack. There was no sign of Nine or Sig. It was as if someone were preparing for the apocalypse and already had one foot out the door.

"Nine?" Petra asked softly.

A soft canine whine emanated from under the bed. Petra dropped to her knees and lifted the lace bed skirt. Eyes gleamed back at her, two pairs of reflective canine eyes.

"Nine?"

One pair of eyes blinked, and they looked more human than before. "You came," Nine said.

"Yes. Of course. What . . . what are you doing under the bed?"

Nine sighed. "It really seems like the safest place to be." She sounded a little embarrassed when she said it, though. But she also didn't come out.

So Petra flattened herself and backed under the bed. She got herself arranged so that she was on Sig's other side and all three faced the door. She thought it remarkable that there were no dust bunnies under the bed, a testament to Maria's meticulous house-keeping. Petra knew that there was likely enough coyote fur underneath her futon to manufacture an entirely new canine.

"What are you doing?" Nine asked.

Petra tried to shrug, but she didn't have room. "Well, if you guys are hiding under the bed, I figured that I should be, too."

Nine chuckled darkly.

Sig put his head on his paws. Petra looked over his ears at Nine. "So what's up?"

"I went to the Eye of the World last night," she said softly. "As I always do."

Petra rested her head on her arm. "Checking up on the pack?"

"Yes. With the fires, I've grown concerned. I stepped into the spirit world and followed them as they avoided the fire. When I came back here, came back to myself, I heard a warning from a toad. And I saw something in the sky. Something I had not seen for more than a hundred years."

Petra's gut clenched. "What did you see?"

"I saw the end of everything."

CHAPTER 7

Waking the Dead

When I was a little girl," Nine began, "a traveler crossed paths with our tribe. He was a magnificent storyteller, a collector of tales. He told many stories, stories of white buffalo, of the Thunders and Spider Woman. He had traveled all over, gathering legends from all the people he spoke to. The pack he carried was light, but his head was heavy with lore.

"He told us a tale of a firebird. The firebird came to earth during the time before fire, when the world was damp and cold and the people ate their food raw. The firebird swept down to earth and offered fire to a virtuous soul who could catch the flames on its tail with pitch and wood. The people chased the firebird across the land, through forests, over mountains, and across plains. Once or twice, a fast runner would get close and profess their good deeds, but was unable to hold the fire because their heart was impure.

"The firebird eventually came to the home of a widow. The woman had heard of the firebird's bargain. The firebird asked her about the good deeds she had accomplished in her life.

"The woman shook her head. She said she had no time for good deeds, as she was busy caring for her ailing father and children and their animals. The firebird landed on earth and offered fire from its tail feathers to the woman. Professing good deeds meant nothing to the phoenix—it was the work itself that mattered.

"The woman gratefully accepted the fire, and the firebird flew away. The woman summoned all the other women she knew, and the fire was shared among them far and wide. No one saw the firebird again."

Petra's brow wrinkled. "That sounds like a good thing? The firebird bringing fire to the world?"

"That's what I thought, as a little girl. Then, I thought of the firebird as a benevolent spirit that brought light and blessings to humankind. I asked for that story to be told to me over and over. I felt safe in the darkness, knowing that a creature of great light and generosity watched over us, that something magical loved us and saw the goodness in us enough to give us part of itself. We were beloved people.

"But that changed years later, when a flaming bird appeared from the sky. It swept low over the land, its wings setting fire to the dry grasses of the fields, to trees, to our possessions. People, horses, deer . . . were burned as it flew. Lightning flashed from its eyes. Nothing and no one was safe from its wrath. My sisters and I huddled in a creek as it passed, and we were terrified. The phoenix seemed determined not to give us the blessing of fire, but to force fire upon us and destroy us. We were . . . unloved. My childhood stories were lies.

"My father, as strong as his magic was, was powerless to stop it. He cast spell after spell, and the people made fine offerings to placate it, but the firebird was not deterred. It burned the earth for days, reducing trees to ashen shadows and turning the sky black. I remember squatting in the creek, gazing to the sky with terror as that streak of fire blazed above.

"It is that blazing creature I am certain that I saw last night. I know this creature is to blame for the fires. It is ferocious."

Petra reached over Sig's back and stroked Nine's silvery hair. "Gabe saw it, too. I spoke to my father . . . he says it's a phoenix, a creature summoned by alchemy."

"Whatever its name, it is death in flame."

"When you saw it as a child . . . did it go away? Did your father find a way to stop it?"

Nine stared toward the door, her gaze unfocused. "My father went into a trance and said he could communicate with the creature. The creature was searching for something, something that would make it whole so that it could sleep. You see, the firebird—the phoenix, as your father calls it—is immortal. It can be woken and go back to sleep, but there is no destroying it.

"There was a woman from another tribe who arrived at the creek on the seventh day. She was well known for many miles as the most powerful shaman in the land . . . she could change night to day by plucking down the moon and could poison a man with a glare. By then, much of the water in the creek had evaporated, and we feared what another attack by the bird would bring. There was already nothing left around us but broken trees and blackened earth.

"The shaman walked across the field, barefoot, as if the heat did not bother her. She pulled my sister and me from the creek and told us not to worry. She told us that the bird was lonely, that it sought a companion.

"Suddenly, the creek became flooded with tiny black toads, thousands and thousands of them, swarming us. They reeked of decay. And a giant rotting toad emerged from the creek, large as a horse. He was a god, a god of death and rot that had come to the land ruined by fire.

"The Toad God told the shaman that she could not defeat the phoenix alone. He agreed to fight the bird, to weaken it, so that she could step in and defeat it. The shaman argued with him, knowing that this would hurt or kill him, but the toad would not listen. He was death, he told her, and she had no dominion over him.

"As they argued, I saw the fire in the sky and pointed. The firebird swept down to the ruined field. The instant it lighted to the earth, the Toad God attacked it. It took the bird's throat in its jaws, and the bird's wings beat at it, catching it on fire. The smell . . . it was like nothing I'd ever experienced. And the battle raged all afternoon and into the night.

"When the moon rose, the firebird beat away the toad, sending it smoking to the ground. The Toad

God, defeated, crawled back to the creek. The shaman stood alone before the bird, her willowy figure the only thing left standing. She opened her arms. The firebird landed before her, smoldering, and wrapped its wings around her.

"The fire . . . collapsed. It curled around her, flattened, and then there was nothing. No shaman, no phoenix. Just char on the ground and silence."

Nine sighed and turned her head toward Petra. "We gathered up what remained of the tribe, those who hid in streams and caves, and began again. But we always feared the return of the firebird."

Petra chewed on her lower lip. "The mythology I read about phoenixes suggests that they're cyclical in nature . . . that they awaken once every century or two and then self-immolate." Maybe this one wasn't on a super-regular schedule, if it woke irregularly. Hell, it might have insomnia, for all she knew.

Nine laced her fingers under her chin. "This might be the same one as before. But there is no god of rot to fight it and no shaman to offer it."

The door to the room opened, and Maria's feet appeared, bare and toes painted cerulean blue. In moments, she peered under the bed.

"Hey," Petra said.

"Hey," Maria said, sitting down on the floor in a puddle of blue calico fabric.

"I think we might be screwed," Petra said.

Beside her, Nine nodded.

Maria put her head in her hand. "Well, what else is new?"

"Do you happen to know any shamans who might submit to self-immolation? Or gods of death?"

"No. I do not know any shamans, nor do I know anyone who's keen to do the burning alive thing. I know an undertaker, though, but I'm pretty sure that's not who you're looking for."

Petra rested her chin on the floor. "Yep. I think we're fucked."

A TRIP TO the spirit world could typically only be undertaken under certain conditions. Certain phases of the moon could allow one to slip through more easily, as could disciplined meditation, a few flavors of ceremonial magic, and some earthly locations where the veil between the worlds was stretched thin. Joseph Dee didn't bother with such things, not anymore. He could slip into the spirit world with a simple wish, much like a child wishing on a dandelion. *Inhale. Focus. Exhale.*

He had been occupying his bed at the nursing home, the television volume cranked up loud enough to drown out the twittering of the stitch 'n' bitch going on next door. He slipped away from the physical world in the middle of his favorite game show—a rerun—motivated as much by the desire to search for answers to the riddle of the phoenix as the desire to get away from overheard gossip about people's grandchildren he didn't give a rat's ass about.

Inhale. Focus. Exhale.

At least the spirit world was quieter than the physical world. Joseph had spent years and years here, when he'd been in a catatonic state to all eyes monitoring his physical form. Joseph opened his eyes in a soft, misty realm. A pearly grey fog surrounded him, cool against his skin. He smelled water and trees and moss.

He climbed to his feet to survey his surroundings. Here, he had always been able to walk, and he was a good twenty years younger than he was in the nursing home. He hadn't always had a human body here, but he had acquired one in the past year, after Petra had found him. Here and now, his body felt strong and his head clear of drugs and confusion. He was wrapped in a black oilskin coat, on which water was already beginning to condense. The mist was wrapped around trees, impossibly tall, with branches that disappeared into the fog. The ground was covered in shed pine needles, muffling his footsteps. A ring of stones surrounded him, each stone as big as his fist. They were a variety of types and colors from both the upper world and the lower world: larimar from the foundations of Atlantis; limestone from the right foot of the Sphinx; quartz from Lemuria; jade from Xanadu. This simple ring had taken so many years to construct, but it was his portal to the spirit world.

He'd come here to look for the phoenix, despite his daughter's prohibitions. He didn't know where its original birthplace was, but starting here seemed as good a place as any. He kept a mental map of the spirit world, and he always chose to begin his wanderings here, in the embrace of this protective circle. Nothing could harm him here. Within the circle, he could collect his thoughts, summon, and plan with impunity.

A silver string, fine as spiderweb, was pinned by a rock to the center of the circle. Joseph reached down and tied the string around his waist. This astral cord would extend as needed, and would allow him to find his way home. He'd created this enchantment after spending many years lost here. He always wanted to find his way back, and the cord would lead him home.

A raven cawed overhead. His brow wrinkled. "You're not the bird I'm looking for. You're not bright and flaming."

The raven lit on a branch and cawed again.

"Do you know where it is?" Joseph figured that most winged creatures gossiped among themselves. The raven likely knew.

Slowly, the raven began to fly away.

Shrugging, Joseph stepped over the ring of stones to follow the raven down a pine-needle-strewn path. The raven meandered slowly, lighting on low branches, waiting for Joseph to catch up. The silver string drifted behind Joseph, pushed by the breeze.

"I suppose you know all the birds in these parts, don't you?" Joseph asked. It wasn't silly to talk to animals here. They always understood. And sometimes they talked back.

But the raven kept his silence. Joseph followed him through the mist until the path spilled into an open meadow. The grasses here were as tall as his knees, and mountains had sprung up at his back. The land looked largely undeveloped. In the distance, though, he could make out a town and the tracks of a railway.

But closest to him stood a house, about a half mile away. It was a house built in an old-fashioned style, two stories, surrounded by wrought iron fencing.

The raven flew off toward the house and perched on the chimney. Joseph waded through the grasses toward the house. The windows of the house were black, as if they'd been painted on the reverse side. Perhaps this house existed in the past, and this was the imprint of it on the spiritual ether. Whatever its origins, there was something wrong about the house.

The wind changed, and Joseph smelled it. He smelled something viscous, like mud and nightshade.

There was magic here.

Joseph reached to his side for a weapon. Weapons in the spirit world could take any shape or form. His was a bullwhip made of quicksilver, solid when he needed it to be. He loosened it from his belt and let the fall of the tail trail among the grasses, serpentine as it hissed along the ground.

He advanced on the house and paused outside the iron fence. At first glance, he thought it might be decorative. But as he held his hand above it, he felt the weight of the wards buzzing against his hands. It was like holding his hand against a beehive—vibrating with danger. The fence was likely a magic circle like the one he'd materialized in, designed to keep some things in and others out.

Something moved at the base of a fence post. A black toad the size of an apple moved into view. It stared at Joseph and spoke with a voice that sounded like gravel churning in mud:

"Do not cross this threshold, sorcerer."

Joseph cocked his head. "What's behind the gate?"

"Unimaginable power best left untouched."

The toad scuttled away into the grass. Joseph called for it, but it did not return.

He stood before the gate. The unimaginable power that the toad spoke of might be the phoenix. He weighed the warning of the toad carefully. He knew that toads, in alchemy, were symbols of rot and putrefaction. They were death, and Joseph was not interested in death. But there was no power or knowledge gained without risk. He had come to this place for a reason, and he was not ready to tuck his tail between his legs and leave.

He took a step back and lashed out with the whip. The air crackled silver, and he struck it three more times with increasing force before the enchantments grudgingly broke with a sound like rusted metal creaking. The fall of the whip caught a latch on the gate. He pulled with all his strength, and the gate opened.

He stepped inside, feeling the raven's gaze upon him. The atmosphere inside the fence was thick and oppressive, tasting of ozone. The silver filament around his waist stretched taut over the iron filigree of the fence.

He hesitated. This felt wrong. But there were many wrong things in the spirit world, of course. If he gave in to fear, he might as well go home and resume his role as an old man with nothing more exciting to do than choose pie or pudding for dessert. He screwed up his courage and patted the protective charms that he kept in his pockets, bits of carbon quartz. The path led to the phoenix. He had to learn more.

Something squeaked behind him. The gate. It swung shut and latched, though there was no wind to stir it.

Joseph growled and faced the house with the black windows. Whatever was inside was expecting him.

A salamander crawled over his foot. He stayed still, feeling the heat of its belly through his shoe leather. The salamander slipped away into the grass.

Fire magic here, then. The salamander was an avatar of fire. Perhaps the phoenix was not far away and the raven had led him true . . .

Ghostly figures moved toward the house, and the sky darkened. Joseph squinted at the translucent figures. These were old ghosts, little more than the land's memory of a time past. They couldn't harm him. He watched as they surrounded the house, hissing and chanting. They carried torches, burning bright with a foxfire-like light. They cast the torches at the house, and the house caught ghostly fire, the foxfire howling up the walls and forming cataracts on those black windows. The raven flew away, heading south and east.

He knew now, what this house was. It belonged to the first Alchemist of Temperance. It was no surprise that the house cast a shadow here, in the spirit world. But what was Lascaris's connection to the phoenix? Had *he* summoned the bird? Joseph reached into his pocket for a piece of carbon quartz and kissed it for protection. This was a dark place. Finding answers here could be hazardous.

As if on cue, the house began to collapse, the black glass breaking. The fire roared through it, chewing through every timber and bit of plaster. The ghosts walked away, toward the town, and only smoldering rubble remained.

Joseph approached the house warily, stepping

through foxfire embers. The house was a charred mess, only the chimney still standing. His feet crunched on broken glass and bits of silverware. The second floor had collapsed onto the smoldering first. Both floors had fallen into the basement, where a large darkness yawned.

Joseph twitched the whip. That darkness . . .

. . . was lit up in a rush of orange flame. Joseph felt his eyebrows burning from the flash heat and threw his arm up over his face. He staggered back, away from a rush of searing light and crinkling char.

He peeked up over his sleeve. A phoenix screamed, climbing into the sky. Its wingspan was that of an eagle's, seven feet, dripping a great plumage of fire and sparks. Talons bright as lightning scraped the heavens, and obsidian-black eyes raked over the earth.

Joseph fell to his knees in awe. It was the most beautiful thing he'd ever seen. The bird flapped its wings, once, twice, and rocketed into the darkening sky, leaving sparks filtering down like snow.

His hot breath stuck in his throat. That creature was magnificent. It could not be stopped. It had not been born here, in the ashes of this house of magic, he realized, but it had been summoned here, by Lascaris. Its fire had purified this place, the house of the black windows.

Something groaned in the depths of the house, a deep creak, like glass grating on stone.

Letting the whip trail beside him, Joseph cautiously approached the yawning hole beyond the foundations, the one that reached into the basement. He stepped over the debris and peered in. Perhaps there would be a sign here of how the bird was summoned, a fragment of the magical recipe that would show him how the phoenix could be put back to sleep.

It was a darkness like he had never seen. It sucked in all the available light, dimming the guttering embers.

And the darkness moved.

Instinctively, Joseph snapped the whip before him, a quicksilver flash in the darkness. The dark snagged the tail of the bullwhip with a hand-like appendage. Joseph quickly hauled it back, freeing the quicksilver from the darkness's grip.

He was torn for an instant between the competing desires to turn and run and to fight. This was not of the phoenix; this was something malevolent that had taken root here. It may have summoned the phoenix, but there was no fire nor light in it. Defeating it would not end the fires.

But letting it live could lead to something worse . . .

That moment's hesitation gave the darkness an advantage. It reached upward, clawing around his ankle with a shocking cold that slammed up his leg and crackled along his spine like hoarfrost. It yanked him down, down into that freezing pit that had birthed the phoenix.

He landed on his ass on cold earth, lashing out with the bright whip. But the dim glow of enchanted quicksilver seemed unable to snag purchase on anything solid here.

Despite the weapon's ineffectiveness, the fingers of darkness suddenly retreated, scuttling away.

Heart hammering, Joseph made a fist with his left

hand and pushed some of the light from his aura outward. When he opened it, a violet flame hung in the air, a sphere of flickering light that did its best to illuminate the pit around him.

It was more than the remains of a cellar. Surrounding him, burned and blackened timbers crushed shelves and tables of gleaming black glass. A cold athanor lay at the opposite end of the shell of a chamber strewn with broken antlers, the stink of sulfur dust, and the glitter of gold. It wasn't a basement.

It was a laboratory.

And with prickling dread, Joseph knew that the creator of this place was still present, that some echo of him was still here. He had not been purified in the phoenix's fire.

"Lascaris," he said, taking a step forward. Beneath his foot, glass crunched. He realized that he'd fractured a mirror underfoot. As he removed his foot, a spiderweb pattern formed in the glass. This was no ordinary mirror—this was a containment vessel. He knew it as soon as he saw it—the kind of thing that kept souls imprisoned, or perhaps safe from a fire. And there were eyes in the glass . . .

Laughter roared through the mirror and the ruined underground space, rattling fragments of glass and mirror on the ground. The cackling congealed in a corner of the basement. Night gathered thickly there, forming the shape of a man.

Looking down at the broken mirror, Joseph realized that he'd released something terrible, something that had lurked in the shadow of Temperance for more than a century, waiting to be set loose. It may have been imprisoned in this house, in the fire, in the spirit world.

But his interference had allowed it to go free.

"Lascaris," he breathed. He'd fallen into the trap too easily. Regardless of how Joseph incarnated in the spirit world, he was really just a stupid, stupid old man. He should never have come here. He had to get out, now.

The black shape straightened, gazing upon Joseph with a gold-glittering glare.

Joseph lashed out with the whip. It snarled around the ghostly shadow, crackling as it did so. Hope flared redly in him. Perhaps he could put down Lascaris once and for all, remove the curse that had damned Temperance for all these years . . .

An insubstantial-seeming hand reached out and wrapped around the whip. It yanked on the whip with surprisingly solid force, causing Joseph to stumble. The binding of the bullwhip loosened, and the shadow stepped through.

It grabbed Joseph with hands as cold as metal. Joseph squirmed and struggled, but was helpless in its grip. The shadow reached up to his face with long fingers and shoved them into his mouth.

Joseph tried to scream, but the blackness poured into his belly like cold lake water. The creature had him, he knew . . .

. . . and then, suddenly, he was severed from his astral body, as if strings were cut. His consciousness poured into the ball of violet flame. The ball began to drift upward into the sky, like dandelion fluff on a summer's day.

With horror, he watched his astral body convulse and consume the shadow. It looked up at him with golden eyes, smiling. It climbed up, out of the pit, and followed the silver astral cord of memory back, back to the physical realm. It was bad enough that he'd let that monster free in the spirit world, but in the physical . . . What horrors could he wreak?

Joseph drifted away, unmoored, toward a white light that he wasn't ready to meet just yet.

Petra, I'm sorry, he thought. *You were my greatest work, and now I'm leaving you . . .*

And then the light suffused him.

AN OLD MAN in a nursing home opened his eyes. His hands were folded across his chest around a small black box with buttons and numbers on it. He relished the feeling of sunshine on his face through a window, the weight of a soft blanket on his body.

A smile played at the corners of his mouth.

Lascaris, the Alchemist of Temperance, was awake.

CHAPTER 8

Offerings

"Where the hell do you think you're going?"

Nine paused, halfway out the door. The screen door of Maria's house rested on her hip, and she tried to wipe a guilty look from her face. She shifted the pack on her back, hoping that the drape of her silver hair hid it.

But nothing escaped Maria. Not in her house. She stood in the living room with her hands on her hips and Pearl winding around her ankles.

Nine squinted at the grey and white cat, who was looking particularly smug. The cat had alerted Maria.

Maria lifted her eyebrows at Nine. "Well?"

There was no point lying. Nine's voice was small. "I was going to the phoenix. To make offerings, to see if I could placate it somehow. And . . . to check on the pack."

"No." Maria shook her head.

Nine's brow furrowed. Though she wore the human body of a young woman, Nine was an adult. Though she was a guest in Maria's house, and she deferred to her in all things, she had a few hundred years on her hostess. She lifted her chin and opened her mouth to protest sharply, but Maria lifted her hand.

"You're not going anywhere alone," she said quietly.

Nine's shoulders sagged, and she stepped back into the house, letting the door whistle shut. "You're . . . coming with me?"

Maria crossed the room and cupped Nine's chin in her hands, forcing her to look at her. "You're part of my pack now. Understand?"

Nine nodded.

Maria released her. "I'll get ready. We can take the Blazer. It'll be much faster than on foot. Would you feed Pearl?"

She nodded. Nine had not learned to drive in her short time with modern humanity. Nine figured that it might take her a day or two on foot to get to the fire, but thought she might estimate badly, since wolves moved faster on four feet than she could ever hope to on two. A vehicle would clearly be the better bet, and she would wait for Maria as long as she took.

Nine crossed to the kitchen and fished the cat food bag out of the cabinet. Pearl advanced on her and gave her a rusty meow. Nine sighed. "You don't keep any secrets from her, do you?"

Pearl *mrrrp*ed in agreement and sat down.

Nine topped off the cat's food and water dishes and added extra bowls. She didn't know how long they'd be gone. She diligently scooped Pearl's litter box in the bathroom and cracked open a can of wet cat food. Pearl looked up from her kibble and purred as the wolf-woman placed a dish of tuna-flavored mush in front of her.

Funny how her mouth didn't water, smelling that, while Pearl pressed herself, facedown, into the canned food. When Nine first arrived at Maria's house, Maria had caught Nine licking the interior of the cat food can. Maria had reminded her guest that she now was in possession of an omnivorous digestive system that was very similar to that of a rat's, and that a meat-only diet would land her in a world of hurt. Never mind that Pearl would get pissed with an interloper dipping into her food. After a couple of applications of the stink eye from both her hostess and her cat, Nine hadn't done that in a long time. Slowly, she'd gotten accustomed to the idea of eating things that were not meat—bread, pasta, fruits, and vegetables. As a wolf, she would only chew at green things under the threat of starvation or if she had an upset belly. She'd progressed from picking at the contents of her plate with her fingers to licking her fork clean of chocolate cake. Her digestive system seemed to approve of the diversity, but doing so left behind a twinge of sadness. She was moving away from the habits of a wolf and becoming domesticated, she guessed.

She grimaced at that. She'd had mixed feelings about the trappings of domestication, including clothing. On the one hand, she loved being able to layer soft fabric on her body for warmth. She remembered that from her childhood. Maria had gone out of her way to find her clothing that would be comfortable. She'd knitted sweaters for Nine from soft yarn, had brought no less than five pairs of flat-soled shoes home from the thrift store for her to try on. Nine had often been lulled to sleep by the sound of the sewing machine, to awaken in the morning to find a set of clothes sewn for her from materials that Maria called moleskin and velour. Maria found that the first fabric did not resemble real mole skin in any way, but it felt delightful, nevertheless.

Maria had been good to her, better than Nine's own human mother or any of her sisters. Still, Nine felt guilty for the ease with which she had slipped back into human life and the speed with which she was leaving her wolf ways behind.

Maria returned to the kitchen, placing a backpack on the floor. Her hair had been braided away from her face, and she'd left her long skirt behind for pants and boots. She was busily shoving bullets into a gun.

"That won't work on the phoenix," Nine said automatically.

Maria shrugged. "There are things out there other than the phoenix. Just don't tell Mike if he catches us."

Nine grinned. Mike, the forest man, was a good love match for Maria. She'd never seen him angry at Maria, but maybe it could happen if they went skulking into the fire, into the territory of Yellowstone that he guarded.

Maria placed the gun in the backpack and went to the sink to fill a scuffed canteen with water. She settled it into the pack and turned to Nine. "What kind of offerings are you intending on making to the phoenix?"

Nine opened her own bag to show her. "The offerings we made in the past didn't have much effect," she admitted. "So I didn't bother with corn or tobacco or flowers or hides. I know that for any god to be placated, it has to be with something truly valuable and unusual. So . . . I packed what I had." Shyly, she showed Maria a bag of glittering stones. "I am hoping that the phoenix is like a crow, and that it will like shiny things."

Maria picked one up and held it to the light. The sunlight shone through the facets, casting rainbows on the wall. "These are beautiful," she said. "Quartz . . . and amethyst . . . and these look like parts of geodes. Petra would know for sure. Where did you find these?"

"At the bottom of the Eye of the World." Responding to Maria's sharp glance, Nine shrugged. "I always liked to dive as a child. With the Eye, I just hold my breath and go as far down as I can. Sometimes, I come back with just dirt. Sometimes, I find these."

Maria put the stones back in the bag, and Nine zipped up her treasures. Maria pulled a chair up to the kitchen cabinets. She climbed up on the chair and opened the door of the topmost cabinet, carefully removing a bundle wrapped in a newspaper. She stepped down and carried the package to the kitchen table.

"What's that?" Nine peered over her shoulder.

Maria unwrapped the yellowed newspaper carefully. Inside was a large silver pitcher engraved with ornate designs.

"This was my grandmother's teapot," Maria said. "It had been a wedding present." She rubbed at a spot of tarnish with a cloth. "When I was a little girl, I thought it was the most beautiful thing I'd ever seen. She would set tea for me in the summer afternoons, and I'd get to use the teapot. When she passed away, she hid it away for me. My father's brothers descended on the house to pick it clean of anything that was worth any money, like picking over a turkey. They never found the teapot. But I found it. It was buried in the garden in a plastic bag." Maria sighed and smiled, fingering a small dent near the spout that might have been made by a shovel. "She knew that I would be the only one who would ever dig in her garden."

"It's really beautiful," Nine said.

"But that's not the most valuable thing she left me," Maria said. "There was something inside." She reached into the belly of the teapot and pulled out a leather pouch. She opened the drawstring bag to withdraw a necklace.

Nine's breath caught in her throat. She had not seen anything so fine in many human lifetimes. The necklace was made of oblong bone beads and turquoise stone beads, strung together in four rows with a fine leather cording. The beads were smoothly polished, so much so that the reflection of the overhead light could be seen glistening in them. It was the kind of necklace that Nine had once seen warriors wear with breastplates made of the same shapes of bone hewn by knives over firelight.

"It's magnificent," she whispered, her fingers hov-

ering over it. She was afraid to touch it, not because
it was fragile, but because it was so sacred to Maria.

"It belonged to my great-great-grandfather. Each
bead was carved from one of the tailbones of a buffalo that he killed. It's the only thing I have from
him, and it's the most valuable thing I own," Maria
said. She handed it to Nine.

Nine accepted it reverently, gazing at the cool
beads in her palm. "You don't mean to give this to
the phoenix . . ." She knew how much it would cost
Maria to lose such a treasure.

"The important thing is stopping the fire. I just
hope the phoenix will find it worthwhile." Maria
wrapped the teapot back up in the paper and put
it into her bag. "But if it likes silver, then that's
okay, too."

"I hope so," Nine agreed.

NINE WAS GLAD for the company on this trip, but
even gladder for the ride.

Maria took the Blazer as far into Yellowstone as
she dared on paved roads. She pulled over to con-
sult a map, tapping a pencil against it. "I know that
Mike and his coworkers have blocked off civilian access to the park here, here, and here." She made X's
on the map, crossing out access roads. "But I think
we can get close if we go here . . ." She traced a road
marked Administrative Road that ran parallel to one
of the checkpoints. "And then we can go on foot this
way." She made squiggly lines through some flat
land that looked like a plateau to Nine. "How do

you think we can get the phoenix's attention without getting crispy?"

"I'm not really sure," Nine admitted. Her plan was seeming less certain all the time. "When I first saw it, it tended to fly near the moving edge of the fire. I had hoped that maybe we could advance from the area that was already burned, rather than approaching it from an area of fresh fuel and active burning. Upwind of it."

"That makes sense," Maria said. She pulled her cell phone out of her pocket and fiddled with it. "It looks like the main fire is mostly moving from north to south, and the fire line is near here." She scribbled a heavy line on the map. "The wind is moderate today, so we might be able to get behind it here, if we come down from the northwest side." She pointed back to the flat land that had already been destroyed. "Going from the back end also keeps us away from any firefighters, which is good."

Nine nodded. This way would have taken her a lot of time on foot, but it was so much faster to drive. "Whatever we can do to avoid interference from Mike's people is best." The forest man meant well, but Nine knew he was out of his depth with a creature such as this.

Maria started the engine up again, and they wound through the back roads, up to the spot she indicated on the map. They passed green fields of grass, tickled by a northern wind. The mountains were hidden by deep smoke, and the obscured sun made it difficult to determine direction. Maria kept the windows closed and turned on the weak air-conditioning. Eventually, they pulled off at the side of the road before a field. Nine could not see more than two hundred feet ahead of them.

Maria consulted her phone. It showed a compass and a diagram of their location. Nine was always startled by the magical amount of information that seemed to come from the little plastic boxes.

"We won't get too far lost with this," Maria said, stuffing the map and the phone into her pocket.

Nine moved to open her door.

"Wait," Maria said. She rifled around in her pack and pulled out a couple of squares of fabric. She poured water on them from the canteen, soaking them, and tied one around her nose and the lower half of her face. She reached for Nine to tie one on her.

"You look like a bandit," Nine said as the cool fabric slipped over her nose.

"These bandannas will filter out a little of the smoke," Maria said. "There. Now we're ready."

Nine nodded and jumped out of the SUV to the ground.

It was hot here, much hotter than it should have been in summer. Arid air slid over Nine's face as she waded into the grass. Maria was at her elbow, consulting her phone, and they entered a twilight world of swishing grass, smoke, and oppressive silence.

The grass wilted and then blackened. The fire had moved through this place like a scalding river. Nine could feel the warmth of the earth through the soles of her shoes as they walked, moving into the greyness. Her eyes watered and she wiped at them with the edge of her bandanna. Ash stained her pants up to her knees. The flames had razed this place utterly. It was identical to the ruin she'd seen as a little girl.

She felt as helpless now as she had then. What made her think she could fight against such a powerful creature and win? She was no shaman.

Maria's hand clamped down on Nine's shoulder. "Look!" she hissed, pointing to the sky.

A streak of orange reached down from the sooty sky and landed on a lone, blackened pine tree. Sparks showered down from where it lit, the tree crackling. The orange glow resolved into a flickering figure that was roughly birdlike, the size of an eagle—wings etched of flame, a curved beak, and eyes as black as basalt. The air shimmered around it in a heat haze, as if even the very air feared it.

"It's beautiful," Maria whispered.

Nine sucked in her breath. It was beautiful, but it was also awful. And it was here. It had come.

She reached for her pack and opened it. She took a fistful of the crystals and tossed them, one by one, into the blackened field. They bounced and landed on the dark ground. They glittered spectacularly, reflecting the orange sunlike glow of the phoenix.

The firebird turned its head and gazed at the ground. In an exhalation of shimmeringly hot air, it swept down from the tree in a flurry of sparks. It landed near the most distant stone, turning its head right and left as it gazed upon the shiny rock. Perhaps it saw its reflection in the facets and could be lured by its own magnificent reflection.

Nine tossed out another stone, then another. The phoenix, crackling, walked toward one and then another, chipping at one with its beak and then picking up another with its talons. It held it and stared at the rock, unblinking.

"It can't melt it," Maria whispered.

It occurred to Nine then that perhaps the firebird had encountered something that it couldn't destroy. At least, not easily. And maybe that was worth something. Nine emptied her pack, slowly, casting the stones out as if they were corn before a duck. The phoenix approached warily. Where it walked, its footprints singed deep into the earth and generated new flames that quickly guttered out. It got within twenty feet of the women.

The heat was unbearable. It shimmered off the bird in waves. Sweat soaked Nine's clothes, running into her eyes. The soles of her shoes felt sticky, and she forced herself to take deeper breaths. Her heart hammered, and she felt a bit dizzy, this close to the creature that had once destroyed all she held dear.

Maria slowly squatted and took out the teapot from her bag. She set it on its side and rolled it toward the phoenix.

The bird turned its head to peer at it. Maybe it saw its reflection in the sheen. It reached out to touch the shiny thing, but the silver warped under its touch. It slowly melted, quickly dissolving into a glistening puddle on the ground. The bird peered into the metallic silver, tapping at it with its talons. *It must be a terrible thing,* Nine thought, *to destroy everything one touched.* She felt a pang of sympathy for the bird. It would never know the touch of another living thing. It was as the shaman had said all those years ago.

It was alone.

Nine summoned her courage and slowly walked toward the bird. She was out of stones, and so she reached into her pocket for the pouch containing

Maria's necklace. She pulled it out and tied it around her neck, approaching the bird with open hands. Her pulse hammered against the smooth beads.

"Take me," she whispered. "Take me like you did the shaman, and sleep for a hundred years."

"Nine, *no*," Maria hissed behind her, but Nine's gaze was fixed on the churning bird, the only light in this blackened world. This was the best way she could serve her pack, she knew. If the phoenix took her, they would be safe. It was the one thing she could do for them now.

She had gotten within ten feet of the bird. She felt her skin blistering in response to the heat, her arms open and exposed. The bird was still, regarding her. It took a step forward, and Nine's heart leaped. It would take her, and this would all be over, all of it: the danger to the pack, the spreading fire that threatened the land, and Nine's own suffering.

Instead of wrapping its wings around her, though, the bird opened its beak and shrieked, a deafening sound like the crackle of lightning where it struck. Nine gasped and fell to her knees, clasping her hands over her ears.

The phoenix pumped its wings, once, twice, and swept past her. She felt searing heat along her right side, and the bird streaked away, into the ruins of the sky.

"Nine!" Maria was beside her, pouring water on her burning sleeve and pants. "What were you trying to do?" Fury lit in her voice.

"I thought . . ." There was no point in voicing the thought. Maria knew, and the bird had rejected her.

"Let's get back to the truck." Maria hauled Nine

to her feet, and they stumbled back the way they'd come, into the black field that slowly turned green. The roar in Nine's ears receded to silence.

The silence lasted for a good twenty minutes. Nine knew that Maria was furious. But she felt the ache of rejection more deeply than that, the separation from all the things that truly mattered.

Nine paused, feeling a vibration in the ground. She bent down, her fingers brushing the tops of the dry grasses. The grasses shook and shivered, the seeds clattering against each other like the warning rattle of a snake.

"What is it?" Maria asked.

Nine's brow furrowed. "Trouble. We have to get back to your vehicle. Now."

They began to run, plunging toward the road and the safety of the car. The vibration that Nine felt became a sound of distant thunder. It churned and rolled, coming closer and closer.

Nine glanced back. Figures emerged from the mist into the smoke-choked grass. These shadows were dark, heavy—and so much faster than they were.

"Buffalo!" she shrieked.

She shoved Maria forward. Up ahead, she could make out the outline of the green vehicle against the road, but it was still a good quarter mile distant.

And the buffalo were fast. Too fast. A buffalo thundered ahead of her, the first of the herd. She put her head down and ran for all she was worth. Another came from her right side.

"Go left!" she screamed at Maria.

Maria wove left, but another buffalo got so close that Nine could feel its fur brushing against her.

They were almost to the truck, just a dozen more yards . . .

The herd surrounded them, panicked, stampeding toward the road. Maria stumbled. Nine caught her and hauled her up, slamming against the Blazer. Maria jammed her keys in the passenger-side lock, opened the door, and the women piled inside.

Buffalo swirled around them. One slammed against the front fender, turning the vehicle on the shoulder of the road. Another smacked against the bumper, pushing them forward. Glass shattered.

Maria pushed Nine down to the floorboards and covered her with her body. Nine could hear snuffling, snorting, slams, and the tinkle of glass outside the vehicle. It was like being a grasshopper in a hailstorm, huddling under a leaf.

In moments, the assault receded as quickly as it had come. Maria lifted her head, and Nine squirmed up. The women climbed up into the seats.

The vehicle was diagonal on the road, its bumper pressed against a tree trunk. Red and yellow glass glittered on the pavement.

A buffalo stood on the road before them, staring them down with liquid brown eyes.

Nine raised her fingers and waggled them in a wave.

The buffalo snorted and trotted off to join its fellows.

"Well, shit," Maria said, leaning back into the driver's seat. Her bandanna was slung around her neck, and her neatly braided hair was hanging askew on her head like a hat.

"I'm sorry," Nine said. "I'm sorry they broke your vehicle."

Maria shook her head. "Don't be sorry for that. I know guys who work on cars and the location of a really good junkyard. What you *should* be sorry about is flinging yourself in front of that bird."

Nine gazed at her scraped and blackened hands.

"Was that the plan from the start? To feed yourself to the bird and hope that sated it?"

Nine hung her head guiltily. "I thought . . . I thought I could stop it." Tears welled up in her eyes.

Maria reached over and embraced her. Nine snuffled against her shoulder until the tears dried up. "I'm sorry."

"It's okay." Maria smoothed her hair. "Now. Are you hurt?" Her fingers lingered on Nine's brow, which felt tight and hot, like it had been singed.

Nine looked down at her arm. The skin was red and blistering. Some of the blisters had already broken and were oozing. The black of her hands rubbed off on her pants. "Not badly. And you?"

Maria shook her head. "Just a twisted ankle and sore pride. I mean . . . we got our asses kicked by buffalo."

"Well. The world is as it should be, then."

Maria grinned and scooted back to the driver's seat. She jammed the key in the ignition and cranked over the engine. They drove slowly to the main road. Something was rattling in both the front and back end of the vehicle. Nine knew nothing of machines, but it didn't sound good.

When they reached the main road, Nine's heart sank when she saw a vehicle blocking the way. Maria swore and rolled down her window when she reached it. She was muttering under her breath,

"Please don't let it be the world's biggest Boy Scout, because I am not in the mood."

A familiar figure walked out from behind the vehicle. Mike. He was no longer dressed in his familiar ranger uniform, but in a thick jumpsuit with shiny tape on the chest. He looked as if he was sweltering in the costume, the neckline soaked with sweat. On the top of his head was perched a curious plastic contraption that looked like ears. Nine sank down in the seat. Maria pressed her forehead to the steering wheel and said: "Shit."

Mike walked up to the open window. "Should I even ask what you ladies are doing out here? And what happened to your truck?" he asked, eyeing the bumper.

Maria groaned. "You have a knack for being in the exact wrong place at the exact right time, you know that?"

Mike leaned on her door. "Yeah. It's a gift. Actually"—he tapped his radio—"I got a report that a vehicle matching your Blazer's description was spotted by some firefighters. I told them I'd take care of it."

"Well. We ran into some car trouble."

"I see that."

"Car trouble that was about eight hundred pounds. A few dozen of them."

"That sounds . . . suboptimal." Mike went to squat at the front of the car. "Your bumper's hanging on by a thread."

Maria hopped out of the truck to look, and Nine went, too. Maria was doing her best to hide her limp. Mike and Maria, after a little bit of discussion, decided to pull the bumper off and throw it in the backseat. Mike climbed under the car to check something called a radiator. He emerged covered in grease, but nodded.

"You should be safe to drive back to the reservation," he said, wiping his hands on his pants. "That back mud flap rattling won't hurt anything. But you're gonna need to get a lot of work to get it roadworthy again."

Nine smiled. Mike, she could see, was a problem solver. Happiest to have a problem he could fix. Too bad he couldn't fix any of hers. Her shoulders sagged, and she looked toward the horizon.

Mike's attention flickered to Nine. "How the heck did you get burned? This area is supposed to be cold. Coldish."

Maria answered before Nine could. "She got too close to a hot spot."

Mike frowned. "Let me get a first-aid kit."

Nine gratefully submitted to Mike cleaning her forehead and arm with water-soaked cotton and a divinely cooling ointment on her blisters. She reached forward and touched the black plastic ears perched on top of his head. "What are those?"

"Smoke goggles," Mike said, pulling them over his eyes to show her. They looked very similar to Maria's sunglasses. "They're hot as hell, but it beats not being able to see anything."

"May I try them on?" Nine asked.

"Sure." He took the goggles off and placed them over her head, tugging them down over her hair, and adjusting the strap so that it covered her eyes. The world was much darker and amber tinted, but it seemed that the glasses kept much of the air out. She put her uninjured hand in front of her face and wiggled her fingers. They interfered a bit with her depth perception, but she wished she'd had something like this when confronting the firebird.

Mike wrapped Nine's arm with a clean white bandage. "You'll want to get that looked at by an urgent care. There's one still open at the county seat. You know it?" he asked Maria.

Maria nodded.

"And have them check out that ankle sprain you're hiding."

Maria rolled her eyes. "Nothing gets past you, does it?"

"You got past me. I would like to know what the hell you ladies thought you were doing back there." Mike's eyebrows crawled up his head.

Maria's mouth flattened, and she said nothing.

"I went to make offerings to the phoenix," Nine blurted, tugging the goggles up on the top of her head.

"You what?" Mike blinked at her.

"I went to make offerings to the fire spirit to placate it. Maria went after me." It was the truth. It sounded crazy, she knew. But better that Mike thought she was insane than for him to question Maria.

Mike opened his mouth and closed it. Then, he said: "That is a colossally bad idea . . ."

The radio at his shoulder chirped, and Nine jumped. Mike pressed a button on it and answered: "This is Ranger Hollander. Repeat."

The radio squawked, and Nine heard: ". . . *wind changed, and there's a baby magpie heading south now. We're pulling out. What's your twenty?*"

"Route 287, a half mile south of Lewis Falls. Over."

"Heading to your location for extraction."

"Ten-four. How many?"

There was a pause. *"We were ten. Magpie got two. We're now eight."*

"Shit." Mike rubbed his face with his palm. Mike never swore. Into the radio he said: "Ten-four. Waiting for your arrival."

"What happened?" Maria asked.

"A group of firefighters was just ahead of the fire line. The wind changed, and it sounds like they got into trouble. They lost two, and I'm expecting injuries."

"I'm sorry," Nine said.

Mike crossed to his vehicle and began taking a bag out of the back. He plunked it on the hood of the vehicle and spread out a map on the surface. "They were here." He pointed to an area about two miles away. "But the fire's now here." He pointed. "Near Lewis Lake, heading south to the canyon."

Nine froze. Lewis Canyon was where she'd last seen the pack in the Eye of the World. "It's going across the creek?"

Mike was staring at his phone. "Yeah. I see it. It's gotten bigger and faster. We have to get those people out of there." He turned to Maria. "I'm gonna need to ask you to haul some of these crispy guys. I can't get 'em all in the Jeep, and the helo is occupied."

"No problem."

Nine stared at the map. The canyon was south of her current position, through a pine forest. She carefully folded up the map and placed it back in Mike's pack. Above, a black plume of smoke was approaching. There was no choice.

"Thanks, Nine," Mike said. "You can put it in the Jeep. Maria, do you have any water on you? Those guys will be needing . . ."

Nine walked to the other side of Mike's vehicle with the bag in hand. Mike was talking into his radio again, and Maria was moving things around in her vehicle to make room for the firefighters.

Nine took a step back, then another.

Then, she turned and ran.

CHAPTER 9

The Lunaria's Grasp

The last Hanged Man of Temperance could not be bothered to carry a fucking cell phone, a fact that infuriated Petra Dee to no end. She'd waited for him all day yesterday to return to the trailer, and he hadn't. He'd spent two nights at the tree, without even emerging to say "boo."

She'd driven to the Rutherford Ranch just before sunrise, wanting to speak with him about what her father and Nine had revealed. She took the back way in, past empty fields and through cut barbed-wire fences. The cattle had been moved closer to the barn and main house since the fires began, so this far out in the back forty seemed weirdly lifeless—fields with striations of smoke lingering over them and no animals.

She had no desire to run into Owen, knowing full well that she was trespassing on his land. But for many months, by Gabe's reporting, Owen had ventured no farther than his own driveway. Owen may have had a few too many brushes with the supernatural entities that populated the ranch, perhaps. Maybe he figured that giving his right hand up to them was enough of a sacrifice, and was better focused on managing his more visible law enforcement empire aboveground—and hopefully aboveboard.

She drove to the Lunaria, standing alone on its hillock, as the sky began to lighten on the horizon. Her heart lifted when she saw Gabe's truck parked there, then twisted a bit in a pang of jealousy for the tree.

He returned to this tree every night. Rarely, her. She knew her feelings were petty and probably childish. The tree was a thing, after all—maybe. It gave her husband life, and she was grateful for that. And Gabe's relationship with the tree had existed for so long it felt like an ex-wife was hanging around. And if history was any predictor, that tree was going to be around long after Petra was gone. Petra prided herself on being an adult and rolling with the punches on pretty much every emotional curveball that was thrown her way, but this jealousy still flowered within her. She was ashamed of it, to be certain. Maybe there was a way to make peace with it, and she knew she needed to. But she had no idea how. How were things like this usually done? Should she bring a casserole and a bottle of wine to the tree?

She parked the Bronco beside Gabe's pickup. Sig peered out the window at the Lunaria and growled.

"Yeah. I feel that way, too," she said.

She popped open the door and the coyote scrambled out. He stretched, flattening his ears and yawning, then trotted up to the tree and peed on it.

Petra chortled. She strapped on her gun belt, just in case Sig had a point. And there was no telling when Owen might pop up in his own backyard.

She walked down to the creek, where it pierced the side of the hill and tangled in tree roots. Roots had wound around the gate leading to the underworld beneath the tree. She stood on the bank of the stream and rapped sharply on the iron gate with her keys, ringing against the metal like a bell.

"Gabe? You sleeping in? I need to talk to you."

There was no response but the trickle of water. Petra peered through the gaps in the rusty gate.

"Gabe," she called again, drawing her keys noisily across the bars, like a jailer. But only the gurgling water answered her.

"Dammit," she muttered. She tugged at the gate, but it was held shut by ropy tree roots. She pulled as hard as she could, but the gate remained shut fast.

She considered digging through her hodgepodge of geology tools in back of the Bronco for a handsaw, but decided that would be rude. Maybe the Lunaria was cranky because of Sig. Maybe it—and Gabe— were taking a luxurious afternoon nap. Gabe had some burns to heal, after all. When he was hurt, he spent more time underground.

She could wait. He'd have to come up for air sometime. He always did, she reminded herself.

It's just . . . She missed him. She missed having him in her life, and the tree was a necessary evil that took him away from her.

She climbed back up the hill and sat beneath the rustling shade of the tree, far beyond where Sig had anointed it. The oak leaves created a hypnotic, soft susurrance, and she soon stretched out on her back below it, watching the patterns the leaves made on the sky.

"I know you love him," she said to the tree. "I love him, too. Thank you for healing him, for taking care of him."

It humbled her to say it aloud, to express gratitude to this living thing that had watched over her husband all this time. Perhaps it was Petra who was the interloper, and she was the one who needed to make good with the tree. She took her water bottle out of the pocket of her cargo pants and poured some water at the base of the tree, rinsing away Sig's territorial marking.

In the meadow of white geranium and grass beyond, Sig had gone hunting. She turned her head to watch him from time to time. He'd remain still as stone and then pounce like a fox on something, looking at his paws with surprise at some hapless mole he'd caught. Eventually, he tired of the game and trotted back to her side. He lay down with his head on her belly. Petra wrinkled her nose at him; his breath smelled like garbage, and she told him so.

Sig gave her a toothy grin and gazed up at the leaves, his ears pressed back. She stroked his neck and followed his look. This tree. Was it the Tree of Life or the root of all evil in Temperance? Could it be both? Did it really matter? It was power, and maybe such things didn't always need to have human morality assigned to them. Maybe she needed to think of the tree as simply another part of Gabe, and that would allow her to move past the anxious sense of grasping she felt. Maybe Gabe was simply returning to a part of himself at night, and that was the way things simply *were*.

Lulled by the whispering of the leaves above and the warmth of the ground against her back, Petra drifted off to sleep. She dreamed that she was stuck in this odd twilight world of aboveground, with the sun struggling to burn through the layer of haze that shrouded the land. It was as if the world above were just one step away from a dreamworld, and it was easy to fall into it.

She dreamed that she'd brought the tree an offering, trying to make peace with it. She offered it a golden pocket watch. She knew it was valuable, somehow, but couldn't remember how, only that it would be familiar to the tree, and that the tree valued it. She placed it on the ground beside her. The tree's roots reached up from the ground, splitting it, and curved around the watch like spindly fingers. The roots covered it and drew it down into the earth, into the inscrutable mass of light and darkness at its heart.

Petra smiled. The tree had accepted her offering. She sat back, her hands braced behind her and her fingers tangled in the grass. Perhaps this could be a new beginning for them. Perhaps the tree would realize that she and it had the same goal: to protect Gabe. Perhaps . . .

Something tickled around her wrist. At first, she thought it was a bug and twitched to flick it away. But her wrist was held fast to the ground. She turned to pull it free, but her ankle was snagged in something.

With horror, she realized that she was trapped by tree roots. They lashed around her tightly, around her wrists and waist, and began to pull her down, down into the soft earth.

She screamed, a scream that was quickly stuffed full of dirt. She glimpsed Sig, ears flattened and snarling at the tree. He attacked the roots and began to dig, howling that eerie howl that only belongs to coyotes.

But the Lunaria hauled her down, wriggling and kicking, into the lightless earth below. Dirt pressed against her, forcing the breath from her lungs. Sig's howls grew more distant, and she was buried in that underworld that belonged to the Lunaria and nothing living. There was nothing human here, nothing warm and with human feeling.

PETRA JERKED AWAKE in a moment of terror.

That dream . . .

It was as fresh in her mouth as the taste of dirt. She coughed and passed her hands over her eyes, sucking in air, forcing herself to open her eyes to light and the world above that she knew stretched from horizon to horizon.

There was light, but not the sunlight filtered through smoke that she expected. Instead, a weird yellow light dripped sinuously through darkness. A cocoon of tree roots surrounded her; she was hanging like fruit above a rushing body of water that whispered like the voices of men. With her hands, she ripped at the roots surrounding her, futilely. They twitched and pressed tighter against her assault.

Through gaps in the tendrils, she could see only darkness and striations of light, the tree's underworld.

She forced herself to slow her breathing and scrubbed her hands across her filthy face. There had to be a way out.

"Gabe!" she shouted into the darkness. "Wake up, dammit!"

There was no answer. Maybe the tree had him trapped as well, or he was still caught in his slumbering stupor. Whichever, it was clear that there was no help coming.

"What do you want from me?" she growled at the tree.

The inarticulate whispering crested, then subsided. Whatever it was, it wasn't going to tell her. And she wasn't sure she really wanted to find out the answer.

She wriggled her fingers along her waist, to her gun belt. The two antique pistols were twisted against her hips, heavy as thought and memory. She got one free and awkwardly pulled the trigger. The flash momentarily blinded her, and a bullet lanced into the darkness somewhere around her right foot. She felt splinters somewhere around her shin and a root flinch away. She knew that in an ordinary fight between bullets and wood, wood would win. But the Lunaria was more than just wood; it felt pain, and she could use that to her advantage.

The whispering crested, louder than the gun report. The roots snaked tighter around her, and she kept pulling the trigger until the chamber clicked empty. There was space around her feet—she kicked and wriggled and struggled until she worked herself loose down through the hole at the bottom of the cage.

She dropped into the dark, sprawling along the gravel of the riverbank on her knees and skinned hands. She reached for the second gun, holding it before her as she climbed to her feet. Liquid light had splattered over her and the ground, like firefly guts. She'd hit something, perhaps some important arterial conduit of the tree.

She should find Gabe and get the hell out. Maybe the tree had him caged, as well, and that's why he wasn't answering her . . .

"Gabe!" she shouted into the half-lit darkness. She scanned above her, at the glowing biomass, for some sign of him. She knew he decomposed and regenerated—there had to be a man-shaped chrysalis or something here, right?

The roots were reaching for her; one reached out and licked at a scrape on her cheek. She batted it away and began to back toward a pinpoint of white light downstream . . . She knew that the gate was downstream. She heard Sig's distant barking, a beacon.

She shot at a root that was reaching for her knee. The bullet bounced off stone, and she squeaked in alarm at the ricochet. She had five bullets left. If she stayed, the tree was going to snatch her up again. She had to find some way to buy time while she looked for Gabe.

She rifled through the pockets of her cargo pants. She found an unbroken plastic vial of sulfur from the crater. Keeping the gun lifted, she knelt to the gravel and sifted through it with her left hand. Her geologist's fingers found what she sought nearly immediately—flint. She grabbed two chunks of it and rubbed them against her shirt to dry them.

Serpentine roots approached her, making a hissing sound against the stone. She shot at them again, and they skittered away. Four shots left.

She found a broken piece of root on the ground, splintered and inert. It felt dry enough. She dipped the end in her vial, pulled it out, and capped the vial tightly, wrinkling her nose at the rotten-egg smell. Striking the pieces of flint together, she prayed for a spark. She knew that under normal conditions, she'd have a helluva time starting a fire with just rock. But sulfur—this sulfur was dry and flammable.

In her peripheral vision, she could see the roots curling around her, forming a perimeter to trap her. She had to work quickly. Filthy sweat dripping from her brow, she kept striking the rocks together, trying to get a spark to light on the sulfur stick . . .

It lit. She snatched up the stick, glowing with a blue sulfuric flame. She held the torch high, illuminating the ceiling of the chamber. The roots shrank back from the torchlight, rustling. The monster tree had been burned before; she was banking on it being as afraid of fire as Frankenstein's monster.

"Gabe," she snarled, heart hammering. She was running out of time, and she knew it. "Where the hell are you?"

She swept the torch around her, trying to pick out a man-shaped shadow in the teeming light and roots. But they pushed down from the ceiling, obscuring her view, dripping liquid sunshine to the gravel.

She turned on her heel, and saw that the white

light of her exit had been blocked by a seething wall of bramble-like wood.

She was out of options. She would have to come back for Gabe. She'd siphon gasoline out of the Bronco and come back here to burn that fucking tree to a shriveled twig to get it to give him up. The tree provided him life, but she had to get him out of it. Somehow. Maybe he could make nice with what was left.

She advanced on the barrier of roots. They twitched and seethed at her approach.

With her thumb, she removed the cap on the vial of sulfur. She flung the contents on the wall of roots and thrust her torch at it. It erupted in blue flame.

The whispering roots shrieked, parting and writhing. She plunged through the opening with her arms flung over her face, running for true daylight for all she was worth.

She slogged through the water and quickly slammed up against the gate. Sig stood up to his back in water on the other side, barking furiously. The gate was, as before, wound fast in the tree's grip. She jammed what was left of her guttering torch at the roots winding around the latch. The flame caused the roots to shrink back, but others curled in their place. The wind coming in from outside was threatening to douse her torch.

Behind her . . . She glanced back. The malevolent tendrils were skimming across the surface of the underground river like water snakes.

Shit. Shit. Shit.

She shot back at them, emptying the last of her

bullets. She reached into her pocket for her knife and began to saw at the roots holding the gate, desperately, but the roots were coming for her, far too quickly.

They wrapped around her waist, and she pitched backward in the water, dropping her torch. Her fingers wound around the gate, and she held on to it as hard as she could. Rust flaked into her hands, and her grip was slipping.

"Stop."

Gabe's voice. She twisted her head back to see him standing on the bank. He was coated in the luminescent yellow slime of the tree, glowing in the unearthly artificial light.

The roots paused, but did not slacken their grip.

"Let her go," he insisted, looking up at the ceiling, where the tree grew above. He was holding a pistol, and aimed it at Petra. The roots whispered among themselves.

"Gabe, what the hell?" The tree . . . The tree must have changed him. Turned him against her.

Gabe gazed at her coldly and continued to speak to the tree. "If you take her, you'll take a corpse that even you cannot repair. And I will never return to you again. You will be alone. Forever." He waded into the water, aiming at Petra.

The tree whispered. Whether it murmured to itself or to him, Petra couldn't tell. Her heart hammered in her chest.

Gabe paused before Petra, the gun a mere foot from her face. He pulled the hammer back on the gun and said: "This, I swear to you."

Petra's heart clotted in her throat. He would kill her. He would. She could see it, that cold deadness in his eyes.

The grip of the tree slackened around her waist and around the gate. Petra sank to her feet in the water. She pushed through the gate, out into the sunlight. With shaking arms, she grabbed Sig and hauled herself to shore. All she could think of was getting away. Away from that tree and the awful underworld it had created. Away from Gabe.

She stumbled toward the Bronco and shoved the soaked coyote inside through the window. He scrambled into the backseat, whimpering. She turned to cross the bumper to get in on the driver's side, but something caught her elbow.

She turned. It was Gabe. She tried to shake him off, but he held fast.

"Get away from me," she hissed.

He let her go, and she crossed to the driver's side and got in, fastening her seat belt. With shaking hands, she cranked the ignition and put the Bronco in reverse.

The passenger-side door opened. Gabe climbed in and slammed the door.

"Get out," she snarled.

"No."

"I said, get out."

He remained in place. Sig weaseled up to the front seat and growled at him. Petra grabbed Sig with her right arm, hugging him close to her chest. She hit the gas, and the Bronco churned into reverse. She spun it around, fishtailing before speeding into a field. Gabe, lacking the benefit of a seat belt, braced himself against the door.

"You have to listen to me . . ." he began.

"No. No, I don't. Not after you threatened to kill me."

She stomped the gas and sent the Bronco plunging through the field at top speed. Her teeth ground and she gripped Sig tightly. She jounced over a rill and stomped on the brakes.

Gabe lurched forward. His head struck the windshield with a sickening crunch.

Petra felt bile rising in her throat the instant she'd done it. She'd never hurt someone she'd loved before. Not ever.

But she'd never had someone she loved threaten her before.

Gabe pushed himself back into the seat. Blood ran over his brow into his eye. A star-shaped crack spidered across the windshield, and there was blood and a chunk of his hair embedded in it.

She was breathing heavily, trying to keep from vomiting guilt all over the dashboard. She wanted him to get the hell out. She was afraid of him, and her guts churned. But she hated to see him hurt. Sig squirmed and buried his head in her armpit.

"Are you all right?" she said quietly, instead.

He pressed the heel of his hand to his brow and wiped away the blood. "I'm fine."

She exhaled slowly. "Then you should leave. It's what you want, anyway."

He turned to her. "It's not what I want."

"You'd shoot me for that tree."

He shook his head. "I will not let that tree have you." He reached toward her, to touch her cheek, and she flinched away. "Please understand. That was the only way it would have let you go."

"You would have shot me."

"Yes. Rather than let the tree have you."

Pain lanced through her chest. "You'd rather have me dead than give me immortal life. That's some fucked-up logic, there."

"Not when this immortal life is a nightmare!"

Petra looked at him, unsure what he meant.

"In its previous incarnation?" he started. "I would have let you join the old tree. I would do anything to have you by my side." His expression was stricken. "This tree . . . the tree is not what it was. There's darkness in it. It's become corrupted, contaminated."

"Contaminated by what?"

"It feels like Lascaris's magic. It . . . the Lunaria has been driven mad. It no longer has the Hanged Men. Its children are gone, destroyed. It is incomplete, unsatisfied by having control over just me." He shook his head. "Its longing is palpable."

He reached for her hand, and she didn't pull away. "You must not go near it again. The Lunaria wants you. And I don't want to make that choice." He looked away, and blood trickled over his eye. "It would destroy me to kill you. It would. I could not go on without you. It would be the end of us both."

She believed him, that killing her would cause him to end his own life. But still. "You'd kill me. To keep me from becoming like you."

"I want for you to be free. Always." He held her hand to his mouth and kissed it. "What the Lunaria is now creating is a hell. I would not see you consigned to it, even if it was forever with me."

"We have to get you away from it," she whispered.

He shook his head, and his eyes were dead as glass. "Once it has you, there is no escaping it. Not ever."

CHAPTER 10

Seeing Ghosts

The state mental hospital had been around for a long time, Owen knew. The size of the population it served had ebbed and flowed over the years. At its height, the campus had several operating buildings perched on top of a grassy hill and surrounded by picturesque trees. Now, only about a hundred residents remained. Most of the outlying buildings were locked and boarded up, and the patients treated here were housed in one of the hospital's main buildings.

Owen had rarely had cause to come here on official business over the course of his tenure as sheriff. He disliked it intensely, even more so than the jail. The residents of his jail could be counted on to be gone quickly. Most usually posted bond within days. Those who didn't were usually gone within a couple of weeks. And even the sentenced ones did not stay more than a year. The rest went to state or federal prisons. But here, some folks stayed a very long time. There was a steady short-term churn of voluntary and involuntary commitments, to be certain. But then there were some, like Robin Wayne Cuthbert, who never went away. They were never cured—there was no cure for whatever demons they had inside them—and could not be allowed back to wherever they'd come from.

So yes, he hated coming here and having to see those lost eyes staring back at him. But more, Owen hated coming here because he had been a patient himself once. He'd had a brief psychotic event, when he'd first faced the supernatural creatures of Yellowstone's backcountry, which had landed him in a very quiet room. He'd gotten out with a few bottles of pills that were quickly flushed down the toilet as soon as he was eventually able to wrap his noodle around the bizarreness he'd inherited with the Rutherford Ranch.

But even that brief stay was enough. Owen was not a fan.

He walked down an echoing hallway with a psychiatrist at his elbow. He'd decided not to come in uniform . . . The last time he'd done that, such a stir had been caused among some of the more agitated residents that he'd been asked politely to leave. In civilian clothes, he attracted less attention from the residents. But the staff still eyed him with suspicion. He felt unarmored without the uniform. As if they might squint at him if he said the wrong thing and chuck him back in one of those white rooms.

"This patient has been with us for the past six

years," the psychiatrist was saying. She was a painfully thin woman with the eyes of a bird. Thankfully, she was not the psychiatrist who had treated Owen on his little vacation. The psychiatrist didn't refer to Robin by name within earshot of the other patients, sort of like he was the Bogeyman. More likely, she was strict with HIPAA.

"That's a long time," Owen said as they passed by a day room with a handful of people watching television, reading magazines, and playing checkers. Two orderlies watched carefully, their eyes flicking from resident to resident.

"He's actually our resident with the longest tenure," the psychiatrist agreed. "He's been diagnosed with schizophrenia. He's been very resistant to medication and has not responded at all to therapy, individual or group. He's been deemed a serious risk."

"To himself or to others?"

"Mostly to others. He's never made a suicide attempt. He will attack others if he feels he's been provoked. He has a history of violent assault that you've seen in his previous convictions. He broke an orderly's arm two years ago and broke his lawyer's nose eight months ago. So, for your conversation with him today, he will be restrained. I hope you understand." Her mouth flattened as she finished speaking. Owen wondered how much of an imposition his visit had caused. Sounded like a right pain in the ass.

He'd called in a couple of favors to gain this visit as a professional courtesy—quite a lot of them, in fact, and it had taken him the better part of yesterday afternoon to get it done. Robin's former public defender hadn't been really excited about Owen speaking with him, but was even less excited by the prospect of coming to supervise the discussion in person, likely owing to the nose situation. Robin wasn't competent to agree to questioning on his own, so Owen had to get somebody to sign off on it. Owen had played out an afternoon-long negotiation among a judge who owed him some favors, Robin's public defender, and the prosecutor's office. It had been pretty much agreed that Robin was in no shape to stand trial for anything, but that it was in everyone's best interest if the murder of Anna Sawarski could be solved quickly, to finally give some kind of closure. As the prosecutor said: "He will never see the light of day. He'll likely die in that facility, but I have enough other charges to bring on him that he'd wind up in state prison for any number of other offenses. You do what you've gotta do." A couple of secret handshakes had been exchanged, and Owen pretty much gained carte blanche for this interview. Was it legal? Nope. But this was a situation in which everyone involved felt the ends justified the means.

Owen nodded. "I do understand."

But at least Robin could be restrained. Owen glanced at the little girl beside him, the one that nobody else but him could see. He'd told Anna nothing about what he was doing, investigating her death. Not yet. There was no point in upsetting her, at least not until he had something solid to go on. For all he knew, this was a dead end, and it would be cruel to traumatize her again for no good reason.

Right now, she was peering into the day room, chewing on the drawstring of her hoodie. Anna tended to come and go as she pleased. She materialized in Owen's passenger seat on the way over, wanting to know where they were going. Owen said he was going to do an interview with a bad man. Anna disliked bad men. Yet she hadn't left, either.

And now here they were, close to as bad a man as Owen could think of. She glanced at two men playing checkers. She took a step toward them and looked up at Owen. "Can I play with them?"

Owen gave her a nod, and she trotted off to the table. She sat down in a chair and rested her chin in her hands, elbows planted on the table. The middle-aged man playing checkers smiled at her as if he saw her.

Owen tore himself back to the conversation with the psychiatrist and nodded at her as she talked. But internally, his mind was whirring. These people . . . these patients . . . it seemed as if they *could* see her. Owen had never met anyone else who could. So what did it mean? That—that Anna was real and that he wasn't crazy? Or that Anna wasn't real, and only insane people imagined they could see her? It made his head ache.

"This way, please," the psychiatrist said, gesturing him away and down a corridor.

Owen followed, hands jammed in his pockets, resisting the urge to look over his shoulder at Anna. The psychiatrist narrowed her eyes at him, ever so slightly.

Maybe the psychiatrist could tell there was something wrong with him. Jesus. He found his voice again. "I appreciate you doing this for me, Doctor."

"It's no problem," she answered. But the tightness in her voice sure indicated it *was* a problem. A whole lot of hassle, likely.

An orderly was posted outside a room with a metal door, the surface painted to look like wood grain. The orderly opened the door and the psychiatrist went in first.

The room inside was painted an egg yolk yellow, with a single window. The window, Owen saw, had chicken wire embedded in the thick glass, rendering it nearly unbreakable. An air conditioner hummed in the background, coolant ticking and hissing. A twin bed with white linens was pressed against one wall, its legs screwed into the floor. A particleboard desk also had legs screwed into the floor, and a soft upholstered chair with no hard edges sat in the corner. There were no exposed door hinges to present a hanging risk. But for the additional unobtrusive bits of hardware, it could almost have been a dorm room in any college across the United States.

Except for the chair at the center of the room. Owen recognized it; they had one at the jail. It was a plastic contraption of seat belts, the chair constructed at a backward angle. A man could hold another man in the chair with the pressure of a finger. With the seat belt restraints, the occupant could cause no harm to anyone. At the jail, it had been dubbed the "Hannibal Lecter chair." It was one step ahead of being strapped into "the boat"—a backboard with seat belts to lock a prisoner down in a prone position.

Owen stood just inside the door, beyond spitting distance. The occupant of the chair was a man in his middle forties, a little worse for wear. His hair was brown, peppered with grey, shorn in an institutional crew cut. He was dressed in a baggy sweat suit and white sneakers with no laces. His face was surprisingly soft and round, almost like a child's. His blue eyes darted left and right. Whether Robin was assessing the situation or looking for a means of escape, Owen was uncertain.

"Good morning. Robin, you have a visitor today," the psychiatrist said in a pleasant, well-modulated tone.

Robin looked at her and then at Owen. "Who's he?"

"I'm Sheriff Rutherford," Owen said, sitting down on the chair opposite Robin. Upholstered in vinyl that could be hosed down, it squeaked as he sat. "But you can call me Owen."

Robin's eyes narrowed. "What do you want, Owen?"

"Be polite, Robin," the psychiatrist insisted mildly. She glanced at Owen. "Shall I leave you two to talk, or would you like for me to stay?"

"I think we'll get along fine on our own," Owen said. "Thank you."

The psychiatrist nodded and glanced at her watch. "I'll be back in thirty minutes. Have a good chat, gentlemen."

She closed the door, but Owen could hear the murmuring of the orderly behind it. As it would be if this were a jail interview, he would be able to reach out to someone if Robin got out of hand. The air conditioner coolant burbled. Something moved in his peripheral vision, and Owen squinted at the drip beneath the air conditioner. A tiny black toad, the size of a quarter, hopped into the puddle and disappeared under the damp-looking baseboard.

Owen turned his attention to Robin. "I understand that you've been here a very long time."

Robin frowned. "Too long. Years." He jerked his head toward the door. "They think I'm crazy."

Owen placidly looked at him. "What makes you say that?"

"They don't see what I see. What's underneath the world." He pursed his lips and shook his head.

"I'd like to know what you see, Robin."

"No, you don't. Nobody really does. If I'm honest, they give me more pills. If I lie, they leave me alone. Everyone just wants to be told the right answers."

That sounded reasonably lucid for a guy who'd been in the state mental hospital for several years. At least, it was part of Owen's own life philosophy.

"What's the honest truth, Robin?" Owen asked.

The man shook his head and refused to answer.

Owen tried another tack. "I talked to a friend of yours."

"I don't have any friends."

"I talked to Rattler."

Robin threw his head back and laughed. "Rattler? What's that old meth head into?"

"He's into jail, actually. Got himself involved in a bit of trouble."

"Of course he did. What'd he do this time?"

"He seems to have acquired some items that weren't his." Owen tried to be carefully neutral.

"What was it? Drugs?"

Sharing the reason might forge some trust. "It was . . . antique bowling balls."

Robin giggled. "A bowling ball heist. That's amazing."

Owen spread his hands. "You wouldn't believe the stuff I see."

"Heh. Try me."

Owen racked his brain for things that were public knowledge, on the police blotter. "We had a guy who took a shit in a popcorn machine at a wedding venue. A kid who stole a python in an ice chest. And a woman who set fire to her boyfriend's car, only she got the wrong car."

"Whose car was it?"

"Just some random dude who stopped at the Bucket Cluck for dinner. He was none too thrilled initially, but the charges got dropped because they're dating now."

Robin chortled. "Some people are crazy."

"All people are crazy. Just in different ways." That was a truth that Owen believed with his whole heart. Some just hid it better than others.

Robin cocked his head, like a chicken looking at something edible on the ground. "So, what did the Rattler have to say about me?"

"He said that he knew you back in the day. Spent some time in jail with you. Said your girlfriend brought some acid for you guys to party with."

He tipped his head, glancing at the humming air conditioner. "Didn't see the Rattler round much after jail. As they say, we grew apart."

"The Rattler said that you were in touch with

something pretty bizarre and amazing. A . . . a spirit, if you would."

He screwed up his face. "What does a guy like you know about spirits?"

"A guy like me sees all the weird shit that goes down after midnight. I see all the bloody footprints and the shit that disappears from locked rooms. I hear all the secrets that wind through that jail." And there was Anna. He didn't want to tell him about Anna. But he would if he had to, to get this sonofabitch to talk.

Robin gave him an appraising look. "That jail's supposed to be haunted."

Owen shrugged. "*All* jails are haunted. At least, all the ones that got people who died in 'em."

Robin leaned as far forward as he could against the angle of the chair and the seat belt restraints. "You ever seen a ghost, Owen?"

Owen told him the truth. "Yeah. I seen a ghost. I seen a ghost, a dead man walking, and a freaking mermaid. I've seen some weird-ass shit, Robin. And I'm betting you have, too."

Robin leaned back and stared up at the ceiling. "Why should I tell you about the weird shit I seen? Nobody believes me."

"I believe you, Robin. No matter what it is, I believe you."

Robin's Adam's apple worked up and down. "I seen things . . . things you wouldn't understand."

"Try me."

Robin shook his head.

Owen held up his right hand and took off his

glove. "You see this? A freaking carnivorous mermaid ate my hand. There ain't any way that you've got any weirder shit to say than that."

Robin looked at Owen's plastic hand. "For reals?"

"For reals." He tugged the glove back on. "You don't piss off shit that's stronger than you. There's a whole lot of things out there in heaven and earth that are more powerful than one man. That's one thing I learned from that."

"I wish I had," Robin said, almost inaudibly.

"You wish you had what? Not listened to the spirit?"

Robin swallowed and nodded. "But once you hear, you know . . . you can't get away. It's irresistible."

"Yeah," Owen said, looking away. "All of that weird shit that's out there. They get into your head. And they take over."

"Yeah." Robin licked his lips. "For me, it was Pigin. The Toad God." Robin looked over at him before continuing, gauging if there was any sign of incredulity.

Owen said nothing, kept his expression neutral.

Satisfied, Robin went on. "I first met Pigin a little more than twenty years ago. Out in the woods. I thought I was stoned outta my mind, you know? I'd been fishing in a creek, hooked something heavy as hell. I hauled on that line for hours before a huge black toad hopped up out of the water. It was . . . as big as a fucking car. It yanked on my line, and I went sprawling.

"And then it was on me. It smelled terrible . . . like rotting flesh. Eyes as big as softballs, black as tires. It had all these sores over it, like something had been chewing on it. Oozing and disgusting. I knew that sonofabitch was gonna eat me. Its tongue licked me, right in the face, and I started crying like a baby, begging for my life.

"This giant toad sitting on me . . . it spoke. It said that I would fill its belly for a good long while.

"I begged it. I begged it not to eat me. I told it that I would give it anything it wanted, if it would just let me go. The toad wasn't convinced. It said . . . it said that flesh was flesh. And flesh in the hand was worth more than any promises.

"I tried to convince him that I would taste truly awful, that I'd drunk too much whiskey and wasn't edible. He gnawed on my scalp a bit and seemed unimpressed. I told him that I could bring him food . . . cows, horses, whatever he wanted.

"And he said . . . that meat was meat. What he wanted was a servant to bring him flesh, but the good stuff. Human. If I served him, he would give me the gift of a silver tongue, the power of deception."

"And you believed him?" Owen asked.

"Well, yeah. I was getting gnawed on by a giant talking toad. I figured that he really could grant me the ability to lie convincingly." Robin shrugged in his chair, as if this were the most logical thing in the world. "And I agreed to it. Right then and right there. I would have given anything to that horrible toad. It climbed off me, trailing ribbons of rotting flesh. It sucked some of it from its own foot, exposing bone. It warned me to bring him innocent flesh before the next full moon . . . or else.

"It jumped into the creek, and it was gone. I thought at first that I'd had a really, really bad trip. I went home and tried to sleep it off. But when I woke up, that awful slime was on my clothes, and my hair was half chewed off. I knew . . . I knew that this creature meant business."

Owen kept his tone neutral. "And did you become his servant?"

"Not at first. I figured that if I stayed away from the woods, I'd be safe. I dropped all the acid I could find and drank enough rotgut to forget it. And I could forget it . . . for a time. But I swear that, that . . . monster . . . was haunting me."

"Haunting you?"

"Yeah. It was little shit, at first. Stuff I could rationalize away. Like . . . I'd walk out to my car and all the tires would be flat. The cold-water faucet would turn on in my bathroom and I wouldn't remember having left it on. There would be these tiny little black toads that came up in my bathtub drain. All the food in my refrigerator rotted overnight. I had shitty, shitty dreams of that creature croaking at me. Stuff that I probably could chalk up to bad drugs and shitty luck and possibly a pissed-off ex-girlfriend.

"But then shit got real. I saw slimy footprints on the kitchen linoleum. Everything I ate tasted like rotten meat. Something was croaking under my bed overnight, sounding like a bullfrog on steroids. And then my house burned down."

"Jesus," Owen breathed. The air conditioner ticked like a watch behind them.

"Yeah, man. I went out to go get a fucking beer, and when I came back, my house was burned to the ground. I knew it was him. Pigin. He'd cursed me.

The moon was waxing, and I knew I was fucked. One way or the other, I was gonna become toad food in a few days if I didn't bring him something.

"I wound up going to crash on a client's couch. Dude owed me some money, so I figured I could use the favor. When I got to Paul's house, the back door was unlocked, and he was passed out on the couch. I figure that his wife was out at her waitressing job, and their daughter was asleep in bed."

Owen was holding his breath. Paul was Anna's father's name. This was so close to a confession. So close. He forced himself to breathe. "Would the mom have been cool with you staying over?"

"Never met her. It's not like she was around much. Paul did most of the watching of the kid. But . . . not that night. Not that night." He shook his head and closed his eyes.

"Not that night when?"

"Not that night when I took her. I took my last hit of acid and a bump from Paul's stash to get my courage up. I could hear Pigin's voice in my head, telling me that the moon was full and that time was running out."

"You weren't worried about waking up Paul?"

"Paul was no longer in this world. I mean, dude had pissed himself, and I knew he wasn't waking up until his wife got home and started screaming at him.

"Anna was sleeping in her room. I got her dressed, bundled her up, and took her to the Toad God. She didn't even wake up," Robin said.

Owen forced his expression to remain soft and neutral, though his heart pounded in wrath. He wanted to wrap his hands around Robin's neck and squeeze until his eyes exploded. "She didn't wake up when you took her to Pigin?"

"No. She slept in the car. She slept when I carried her to the spot in the woods where I'd seen Pigin. I wandered around there for what seemed like hours. The moon was high overhead, and I was afraid I was too late.

"And then I heard him, that croaking from the water. He told me to bring Anna to him. He said her *name*."

Owen's heart hammered.

"I held her body over this old well, and she woke up. I remember . . . I remember the fear in her eyes and that she screamed for her mother. I let her go . . . imagining that she was going to die fast, painlessly."

Owen fought down the urge to punch the sonofabitch.

"I don't think it happened that way. It took a long time . . . for the thrashing and shrieking to stop." Tears ran down Robin's face. "Eventually . . . it was quiet. Pigin came out of the well. He told me that he'd give me the silver-tongue magic. But there was a catch. He said: *'Those who hear your voice will believe your lie . . . but only just one.'*

"I realized that the silver tongue wasn't my ticket to paradise. I could lie successfully to someone . . . once. And that was it. I could lie to the first cop who came knocking at my door, make him believe my answer to his first question. And that was great as far as it went, but after that . . ." He stared up at the ceiling again. "Hell, my ex-wife still doesn't believe that I didn't cheat on her."

"Are you lying to me now?" Owen asked. He swallowed down the rage in his voice, keeping his tone even.

"No. Ask me again if you want to be sure."

"Are you lying to me about the death of that little girl?" He stuffed his rage right down into his gut, where it burned like a swallowed lit cigarette.

"No." Robin sighed. "No."

There was a moment of quiet. It was like the room exhaled, this secret out in the open. The air conditioner hissed, and it sounded like something croaked beneath it. Then, Robin said: "Am I going to prison?"

Owen's mouth was dry. There wasn't a jury in the world who'd convict a guy in a mental hospital who confessed to a crime without a lawyer present. Owen knew that. And the idea that Robin could be spinning yarns, especially about a flesh-eating Toad God, really cast doubt on the confession. But Owen believed him. And he didn't think it was the gift of the silver tongue.

"I don't think so. But I would like to put this matter to rest. To let Anna rest. She deserves that much."

Robin pursed his lips, perhaps regretting what he'd said. "I guess it doesn't matter much whether I'm locked up here or the state pen. I'm not getting out anytime soon."

"I really doubt you are," Owen said genuinely.

A sharp rap came at the door. Owen glanced at his watch. "I'll be back to see you soon."

Robin nodded in the chair as Owen stood. The killer said quietly, "You know, I still hear him."

"Hear who?"

"Pigin. In my head."

"What's he saying?" Owen's skin crawled. He didn't hear anything. He didn't *think* he heard anything. That hum in the background was just the air conditioner, right, and not a voice?

Robin looked at him and whispered, as if he didn't want the Toad God to hear: "That I'll never be free of him. And he's always, always talking to me, even when I sleep. But I think I can be free of him."

"How?"

"I think . . . he can die. If you kill the Toad God for me . . . I'll sign whatever statements you want before a judge, lawyer, and Jesus Christ. I'll serve out my time wherever you want. Here, prison, doesn't matter. Because then . . . it'll be quiet. And I'll be free."

Owen was silent. He didn't have any desire to help this piece of human trash. None at all. But he did want to solve this crime for Anna's sake, to give her some eternal peace. And helping Robin, as disgusting as that thought was, might be the only thing that could.

The psychiatrist poked her head in the room. "Time's up," she announced cheerily.

The orderly slid past her to the chair, presumably to let Robin up.

Owen didn't say anything more to Robin. He followed the psychiatrist down the hallway, trying to digest the bizarre tale.

"Did you have a good talk?" she asked.

Owen knew better than to tell her. "Yeah. I think he can tie up some loose ends for us."

She led him out into the area with the day room. "I should warn you. That patient rarely tells the truth.

Most people seem to believe him at the outset, since he's very believable and seems coherent. But we all learn, after a while, that he's not to be trusted. We only let the same group of staff deal with him, and we keep him away from the other residents for that reason. He's . . . problematic." Her brow wrinkled, and Owen wondered what lies he'd told her.

"What kinds of things does he lie about?"

The psychiatrist pursed her lips, as if she didn't really want to say. "When he first came here, he convinced another patient that he could speak to demons. That patient committed suicide. We kept him away from other residents after that. But then, he convinced a guard that he had buried the cash from a bank robbery in a field. The guard was ready to take him to the place, to show him where the money was, but the plan was discovered. That guard no longer works here."

Owen considered that a plausible warning. "Thank you. I'll be very sure to corroborate anything he says independently."

The psychiatrist nodded. "Just be careful with him, Sheriff."

Owen's eyes roved over the day room, looking for Anna. The ghost of the little girl was still sitting at the table. The checkers game was nearly done, and the board was covered in black markers. She grinned at the men sitting at the table and slid off her chair to join Owen. The middle-aged man she'd been playing with waved at her.

Owen walked to the entrance and signed out. He was at the parking lot by the time he felt it was safe to talk to Anna.

"Did you have fun?"

"Yeah," she said, smiling brightly up at him. "They taught me to play checkers. I won."

"I saw."

"And it was nice to talk to people. I mean, I like talking to you. But different people."

Other people *did* see her. He nodded. "If you like, I could bring you back."

"Okay. The people there are nice." She scooted into the passenger seat of the SUV when he opened the driver's-side door. Her brow furrowed. "But you said you were talking to a bad man. Are all the people there bad?"

"No, not at all. Most of them just have an illness that they need to see a doctor for. That place is run by doctors who help people. Most of them get better, and they go home, just like I did last winter."

"Okay. That makes sense."

Owen got into the SUV and closed the door. He started the engine to get the air conditioner going. "Anna, I need to talk to you about something."

She squinted at him. "Okay."

"The man I went to talk to today may have had something to do with your murder." He wanted to be honest with Anna. She deserved that, and so much more from him and everyone else.

"Who . . . who was it?" she asked quietly.

"The man I talked to today was a guy named Robin. He said he took you while your dad was asleep."

Anna squeezed her eyes shut. "I don't remember." Or maybe she didn't want to. Anna always claimed that she only remembered bits and pieces from that night, none of which made any sense when assembled.

"You deserve justice, kiddo. You deserve to have this solved."

She rubbed her nose. "I'm scared."

"Of Robin? He can't hurt you now. I won't let him."

She shook her head, and her algae-coated blond hair stuck to her cheek. "No. I'm afraid of . . . remembering. Of what comes after. Of . . . of going away."

Owen's gut twisted. Here he was, trying to solve the case to give her some eternal rest, and she didn't want to go. "Anna. You don't . . . you don't want to go to heaven? I mean . . . I think that's what would happen if we solve your murder." Owen had had plenty of cause to contemplate supernatural things in the last several months. He figured that since alchemy and undead cowboys and flesh-eating mermaids existed, that heaven had to, too. That seemed reasonable, though he had no proof. It was sort of like inferring the existence of God by having tea with the Devil.

She picked at a loose thread on her sleeve. "I don't know anybody in heaven. Here, at least I know you."

He felt like a right proper asshole, wanting to be free of this little girl who looked at him like some kind of dad she never really had.

"I don't know anything about what comes after," he said. "Not really. But if I'm not there for you, I promise that Jesus will look after you." His voice sounded sure. If there were ghosts, then there had to be a heaven. And if there were a heaven, Anna would sure be in it. With Jesus and the rest. "You know Jesus, right?"

She sniffled a bit. "No. But I guess he's a good guy. The TV preacher says he is."

"And there are a whole bunch of people to talk to in heaven. And other kids who will play games like checkers with you."

She made a face. "But you won't be there."

"No, not now . . ." Owen's voice trailed off. He wouldn't be there now, and he wouldn't be there ever. Not after the shit he'd done over time. He'd done a lot of bad things and buried too many bodies. Owen was not getting past the Pearly Gates.

"It'll be okay," he said. "I won't do anything that would hurt you. You trust me?"

Anna nodded.

"All right. Let's head home. I'll pick up some checkers if you want at the store on the way home."

"Okay," she said, brightening a bit at that.

"All right." He backed out of the parking spot, his chest aching.

Owen only sometimes did the right thing. Usually, he knew what the right thing was, though, even if he avoided it. Now he didn't. If he didn't solve her murder, nobody probably would. And he'd croak in a couple more decades, punch his ticket straight to hell, and Anna would be on her own. That wasn't good, right? So he had to do this. Right the scales of justice and all that stuff that he saw on television as a kid and read about in comic books.

But it sure made him feel like some kind of spiritual deadbeat dad who was planning on skipping town, leaving behind a kid who depended on him.

CHAPTER 11

The Amateur Occultist's Guide to Backyard Alchemy

I want to come home with you. If you'll have me."

Petra gazed through the broken windshield at the road. "You can't stay. Not for more than a couple of days. That's what you said." And the tree was his home, right? Home was where one hung one's hat—or where you were hung in the air by roots. He could come, sure, but he wouldn't be coming home. Not his home, at least.

"If you don't want me, I won't. But . . . I need to figure out what to do with the tree." Gabe was staring out at the smoky horizon.

"You're always welcome with us," she said quietly. "Whether your home is the Airstream or the tree or sleeping in your truck."

"Home is wherever you are," he said quietly.

Petra drove the rest of the way in silence. Sig lay between them on the bench seat, with his butt on Gabe and his head on Petra's thigh, like some kind of spiritual marriage counselor.

It was hard to tell what time it was without looking at her watch. It had been years since the clock in the truck worked. The sky had darkened, but the sun still seemed determined to try to burn through. It felt like twilight or the sky before dawn, though it was neither.

They reached the trailer and Petra got out of the Bronco. When she unlocked the door, she saw Gabe hadn't moved, and gestured for him to come inside. Sig trotted to his bowl and crunched down his dog food as if he hadn't been fed in weeks.

Gabe sat down at the kitchen table. Petra took off his hat to look at the wound above his eye. She got a few paper towels and wet them in the kitchen sink. Carefully, she began to wipe at the blood. It oozed slowly, having mostly clotted.

"It doesn't look too bad," she murmured. "Likely, it could use a couple of stitches, but . . ." She didn't say: *the Lunaria will fix it the next time you go underground.*

He caught her hand before she pulled away and drew her to his lap. He kissed her, and he tasted of sunshine. In that sunshine, she forgot how he had pointed a gun at her, and how she had tried to splatter him across her dashboard. She forgot about the Lunaria, Lascaris's legacy, and the entanglements of eternal life.

She forgot about how screwed up this part of the

world was. She just remembered that he was who he was, and she was who she was, in just this moment.

She kissed him back, falling deeply into it. No matter what he did, no matter what he was, she loved him. And she knew that he loved her back, tree or no.

She shifted in his lap, moving to put her arms around his neck, and accidentally kicked the kitchen trash can. The can fell over with a bang, and its contents rattled out.

She swore against his lips and slid away to pick it up. If she left it, Sig would be in the trash after salami wrappers immediately.

She realized that Gabe had frozen, his hands remaining on her hips. He was staring at the trash on the floor.

"What is it?" she murmured.

He leaned over and picked up a glittering bit of trash—a piece of the mirror she'd found in the field. He turned it over in his fingers. "Where did you find this?"

"Out back." Her brow furrowed. "You don't think . . . ?"

He gazed into the mirror shard as if it were a crystal ball. "This. This belonged to Lascaris."

She scoffed. "You can't know that."

"I—I can."

"But how can you be sure? I mean, it's more likely just to be junk that someone left out there recently. I mean . . . Occam's razor, and all." At least, that's what she wanted to believe.

"It feels . . . it feels like his work. I can't explain it."

The trouble was, she felt it, too.

Petra took the shard of glass from him and placed it on the table. She reluctantly climbed from his lap and began picking the pieces from the trash. Gabe began putting the rest of the garbage away, and soon they had six good-sized shards on the kitchen table. Strangely, the pieces didn't fit together in any coherent way, no matter how they pushed them together.

"You think this is one of his magic mirrors? The ones he used to steal souls?" She picked up one and stared at it. There was only the barest suggestion of silvering on the back of it. It could have just been dirt.

Gabe took the pieces to the sink and washed them. He stared into the bottom of the stainless-steel sink at the shards, as if consulting an oracle. "Yes. Will you show me where you found these?"

She led him out back and sketched an area with her finger on the ground. "Around here." Sig, disinterested, wandered away to hunt in the dry grass.

Gabe looked at her with consternation on his face. "Can I borrow a shovel?"

Petra went to the Bronco and retrieved a large shovel, suitable for digging out trenches, and a small one, useful for small specimens. Gabe took the small one from her and began digging in the dirt.

She stood back. Usually, she was the one doing the digging. Her, or Sig. She glanced in his direction and grimaced. The coyote was rolling in something on the ground. Whatever it was, she was betting it was stinky and that he'd need a bath. She was reminded that coyotes weren't too far removed from dogs in the evolutionary chain. There was a lot of good in that, like loyalty and snuggles. But also, some annoying aspects, like eating trash and rolling in dead things.

Gabe had found a couple more pieces of glass. He reminded her of an aunt who owned a century-old farmhouse, back in her childhood. There was a spot in the backyard where the previous owners had burned their trash. Her aunt had loved excavating it for old glass bottles, coins, nails, and the detritus of prior generations. One time, Petra had found a rusted bottle cap for lemon soda that dated from the 1950s. She wore it on a string around her neck until her mother had found it. Convinced that Petra would get tetanus, her mom threw it away, much to her daughter's everlasting regret.

Gabe sifted the dirt to reveal two mirror fragments, which he handed up to Petra. He seemed intent on his work, lost in reverie. He dug until nothing else came up. They gathered the shards and the stinky Sig and returned to the house.

Whatever Sig had found, it was foul. He was very pleased with himself, smiling, tongue lolling, tail flapping. Petra shoveled him into the small bathtub and used a full bottle of shampoo on him to get the stink mostly out. She poured a box of baking soda on him with the last lather, and that seemed to do the trick. She towel-dried him and set him free. Sig seemed crushed that he no longer was wearing eau de morte, and crawled into her futon to dampen her sheets in retaliation.

In the meantime, Gabe had put the pieces of glass together in a pie plate Maria had left behind, this time the new ones completing the puzzle—or, mostly. What he came up with was a round shape, missing a few small pieces that were probably dust now. It was about five inches across, a smallish mirror by modern standards. Much of the silver had been scraped from the back of the pieces, and it still looked like carefully arranged junk to her.

He exhaled. "That's one of Lascaris's mirrors, all right."

"If it contained something, it's gone now." Petra touched the sharp edges.

"Lascaris's mirrors didn't stay empty long. I wonder . . ." He gazed out the kitchen window at the roiling sky.

"What?"

"I wonder if . . . that might have been how he survived his house burning down."

Petra's brow wrinkled. "You think he put himself *in* the mirror?"

"I wouldn't put him above it. If the mirror broke . . . then his spirit escaped. That might be why the Mermaid insisted that he'd returned. Muirenn was very good at scrying. With all her witchcraft, she might have been able to see an untethered spirit."

"Well. I guess if he's a spirit without a body, then he can't do us much damage. He'd be confined to the spirit world, right? Or, at worst, a ghost?"

"Theoretically." Yet Gabe traced the fractured mirror with his finger, wearing a thoughtful expression.

"What are you thinking?" Petra asked, sitting opposite him.

"I think Lascaris's magic is still in here. If there were a way to restore it . . . we might have a possibility of trapping the phoenix with it."

Petra chewed on her lower lip. "What does that mean for the phoenix?"

"As I understand it, spirits that go in are in a kind of limbo. It doesn't hurt, but it's not pleasant."

"I really don't much like that idea."

"I don't either. But it's one being versus a lot of people. It's only a matter of time until people start getting killed by it. It's a hard calculus." Gabe sat back in his chair, gaze not moving from his dim and fractured reflection in the glass. "But it doesn't matter, anyway. I don't think it can be put back together."

"Well. Maybe it can." Petra squinted at it, then at her watch. "We have an hour until the hardware store closes."

THE HARDWARE STORE in Temperance was never busy, but it seemed to generate enough traffic to remain stocked. The teenage girl behind the counter glanced up from her paperback book at Petra and Gabe when they arrived. Sig walked up to the clerk and wagged his tail. A smile cracked across the young woman's face, and she bent down to rub his ears.

"We're out of fire extinguishers," she announced.

"Thanks," Petra said, and she moved to the back of the store. They passed aisles of rolled chicken and barbed wire, cans of paint, grilling tools, and cabinet pulls. She picked up a welding torch kit and welding gloves and dropped them in a cart. She picked up the biggest tank of MAPP gas they had in stock, mindful to keep the tank vertical.

The clerk set her book aside to ring them up. She glanced at the torch. "You doing some welding?"

"Sort of," Petra said.

"You got goggles?"

"They're not in the kit?"

"Nope." The clerk stepped out from behind the counter and vanished down an aisle. She returned with two pairs of black-glass goggles. "They're eight bucks apiece."

"I'll take three. Thank you."

The clerk nodded. "Safety first and all that."

She bagged up the kit and goggles for them. Gabe picked up the tank, and they left the hardware store. Gabe put the tank in the back of the Bronco, and Petra walked next door to the Compostela. The sign said OPEN, and she reluctantly pushed the door open.

The bar was empty. Lev was stacking glasses behind it, and turned when she came in, with Sig and Gabe trailing behind her.

"You're the first customers today," he said amicably.

"Actually," Petra said, "I've come to ask you for a favor."

Lev paused and raised an eyebrow.

Petra swallowed her guilt. She hated asking him for help, but she had no choice in it. "You, um, have a pizza oven, right?" The Compostela made wonderful pizzas. Petra assumed that Lev had a setup back in the kitchen, somewhere.

"I do. A wood-fired oven I built with salvaged bricks." His eyes narrowed. "What do you have in mind?"

"Well, Gabe and I have come into possession of

some pieces of a magic mirror that we need to restore. I think I could do it, but I'd need a place to crank up some heat and leave it for a day or so."

"How hot do you need to get it?" Lev asked. "I haven't gotten the pizza oven much above eight hundred fifty degrees."

"Well, I picked up some MAPP gas. And I was wondering if I could give that a shot? I'd need to get it up to about a thousand and fifty. And . . . take over the oven for about a day." She winced at saying it.

Lev shrugged. "It's not like there's a mob of customers out there clamoring for pizza." He gestured for Petra to follow him behind the bar to the kitchen.

Petra didn't know what she expected from the Compostela's kitchen, but she figured it would resemble the kitchen of the greasy-spoon restaurant where she'd waitressed when she was in college. That her feet would stick to the floor and for the light fixtures to be coated in a yellow film of grease.

Shockingly, though, the kitchen was perfectly tidy. Stainless-steel countertops were free of crumbs, and the stove hood looked spotlessly clean. The floor was covered with a cushiony rubber surface that could be hosed down to a floor drain. The lighting was bright and clear, and there weren't even fingerprints on the refrigerator.

Gabe emitted a low whistle.

"Wow, Lev. This is a nice setup," she said.

"I live upstairs. If the restaurant picks up critters, then I have them, too." He grimaced.

Sig whined softly.

"Not you, little buddy. You're a good critter," Lev amended, reaching down to pat Sig's head. He hooked a thumb at the corner. "See if that will work for you."

A pile of bricks had been mortared together in the back of the kitchen, with a metal chimney that exited through the ceiling. An iron metal door covered the oven compartment, while a cavity below was charred from burning wood. It had been recently swept clean.

"That," Gabe said, touching the brick surface, "is a thing of beauty."

"Wow, Lev," Petra said, opening the door. "You made this?"

"I've had time for various home improvement projects," Lev said with a faint smile. "I got bitten by the wood-fired pizza bug a few years ago. I was pretty lucky that I found some bricks from a farmhouse that was getting demolished, and I hauled the chimney bricks from there. I used some heat-resistant concrete mix on the interior, and it works well. I think it will stand up to the temperatures you're looking for."

Petra nodded. She was relieved to know that. She would have felt even worse if her debt to Lev grew beyond stealing his homunculus to burning down his home and business.

"So show me this thing we're cooking," he said, cracking his knuckles.

Gabe went to the Bronco and returned with an aluminum pie pan with the mirror shards carefully arranged inside. Lev peered at it. "So that's a magic mirror? Will it tell you who the fairest one of all is?"

"No. It's a containment spell that Lascaris created, once upon a time." Gabe filled in Lev about their hope to catch the phoenix as Petra carried the gas canister in and placed it beside the fuel cavity of the oven.

"Interesting," Lev said, poking at the mirror. "So you're hoping to remelt the pieces in the oven? Do you think that will work for a magical repair?"

"It should," Gabe said. "I never saw Lascaris repair a broken mirror before. But, the spell is still in the components. If it's fused back together, I don't see why it shouldn't work."

"We need to reslump and anneal it, essentially. I don't think that wood will get hot enough to do this, and I don't want to waste all your fuel. Is it okay with you if we try MAPP gas and mix it with oxygen?" Petra hoped that Lev would be cool with treating his oven like an alchemist's lab.

"What's in the MAPP?" Lev asked. "I assume it's like acetylene?"

"Yeah. It's mostly propylene with a little propane in it. To get technical, methylacetylene-propadiene propane isn't really sold anymore, but this is a good substitute. Mostly, people use it for welding."

"If there's some left over, I'm calling dibs. I want it to use for some killer crème brûlée." Lev was rubbing his chin, clearly considering the dessert applications for the apparatus.

"It's all yours. Dessert your immortal heart out with it."

Lev nodded and looked critically at the pie plate containing the pieces. "If you're wanting high heat, that pan won't work. Hang on."

He went digging in a stack of pans on a shelf and came back with a steel pan about five inches around.

"I was experimenting with some personal-sized cakes, but they never really caught on."

Gabe carefully arranged the fragments in the bottom of the pan. Petra didn't know what Gabe saw in these pieces that seemed to give him the creepy-crawlies. Of course, it would have been simpler to take out the Venificus Locus and know for certain that there was magical juice still in them. Assuming that she was human and that it wouldn't just reject her blood . . .

. . . no. Her hand balled into a fist. No. She didn't need to know that right now. She just needed to focus on the job at hand. Sig looked at her sidelong from the floor. She looked away.

"That's perfect," Petra said. Then, she frowned. "We've been staring at these fragments, and nobody's gotten sucked into a hellish limbo. If we restore this, if the magic is still intact, then . . ."

"Then if we take it out of the oven, if we look at it directly, we're screwed," Gabe confirmed.

Petra drummed her fingers on her lower lip. "That's . . . not good."

Gabe shrugged. "Worst case . . . one of us could simply break the mirror again."

Lev rummaged around in his kitchen for a moment, then returned with a stainless-steel pot. He held it by the handle and turned the back to Petra. It had been polished to a sheen like a mirror. "So. That Perseus guy peered through his shield at Medusa, and she couldn't turn him to stone. A nice Viking pan might do the same?"

"I like it," Petra said, grinning at her reflection in the pan. "That will be perfect."

Lev nodded. "Let's get cooking, kids."

Petra headed back to the truck and returned with the goggles, the torch kit, and the rest of the gear. She opened the case for the torch kit and began reading the instructions to connect the hose and nozzle to the tank. There was a mixing valve in the torch handle that should cause a flame to spring out. She arranged the torch in the fuel area of the pizza oven, threading it through the spot where the wood usually was kept and holding it in place with a couple of bricks, careful not to constrict the hose. She placed the pan with the mirror shards in the pizza-cooking upper chamber and sat back on her heels. Theoretically, this should work. Theoretically.

She grabbed her goggles and tossed a pair to Gabe. "Ready?"

"As much as I'll ever be to see a piece of Lascaris's magic resurrected."

She took that as a yes. She donned her gloves. Carefully, she cranked open the valves on the tank just a bit. She held her breath and checked the psi on the MAPP gas, then held the striker to the torch. A tiny, smoky flame emerged. She slowly eased open the valve on the tank, and the soot cleared around a flame half as long as her hand. Carefully, she backed away. She hoped that the air would mix properly with the gas and that the flame would maintain its color.

"I hope this works," she said softly.

"Me, too," Gabe said beside her.

"How long does it cook?" Lev asked. "You said about a day."

Petra peered at the pizza oven's remote thermometer. "Well, we want to raise the temperature by about sixty degrees an hour or so until we get to a thousand and fifty. It should stay at a thousand and fifty for an hour. And then, we shut it off. We have to leave the door closed for about a day. No peeking and letting the heat out, or it will be ruined."

"Sounds like a touchy recipe," Lev said.

"If it's okay with you," Petra said, "we could watch it in shifts. We can stay out of the way. And maybe start a tab?"

"That works for me," Lev agreed. "I have to admit, I'm curious to see how this turns out."

Petra grinned. "So am I." She turned to contemplate Lev's considerable selection of beer.

Gabe frowned. "I'm not convinced that piecing together Lascaris's old projects is a good idea. But I don't have a better idea."

Lev paused and stared at the floor drain. Something tiny and black crawled through the mesh. At first, Petra thought it was a roach, but it turned out to be a toad the size of a nickel.

Lev crossed the floor in two quick steps. He crushed the toad beneath the heel of his boot.

Petra let out a strangled cry. "Lev!"

He grabbed a hose and rinsed the remains of the toad down the drain. "I don't let bad energy in my house."

Gabe frowned. "In alchemy, toads symbolize death."

"Exactly. Not in my house." Lev rummaged in a mason jar full of black stones and deposited a chunk of obsidian the size of his thumb next to the floor drain grate. "And stay out," he said to the drain.

It seemed as if the water beneath the drain burbled more loudly as he did so.

Petra's brow wrinkled. "Nine said that a black toad spoke to her. And that a Toad God had tried to fight the phoenix."

"Well, that one's not talking, anymore." Lev nodded to himself.

"Is there some way that we could contact this . . . this Toad God?" Petra asked Gabe. "Could it be sending some kind of emissary to contact people?"

Gabe frowned. "One spoke to Nine at the Eye of the World. Maybe there, she could get in touch with it."

Lev shook his head. "You guys do not want to mess with that kind of energy, whatever it is. It's bad, and you gotta leave it alone."

Petra was about to respond when her back pocket rang. She reached for her phone and answered it. "Hello?"

"Ms. Manget?" The voice on the other end of the line was unfamiliar.

"Yes?"

"This is Dr. Vaughn from the nursing home. I'm afraid that something has happened to your father."

CHAPTER 12

The Father, Sun, and Ghost

Petra hit the ground running before the Bronco's engine had stopped ticking. Keys in hand, she barreled through the parking lot to the nursing home and straight-armed the door open. She rushed up to the front desk and breathlessly told the receptionist: "Dr. Vaughn called me about my father . . ."

"Yes. We're expecting you. Please come with me."

She was aware of Gabe's cool shadow behind her and Sig's claws clicking on the tile as the receptionist led them down the hallway. Petra noted that none of the residents were out and about, and she guessed that the place was on lockdown. She paused before the partially open door to her father's room and put her hand over her mouth.

The window glass was broken out, furniture cast haphazardly. A sulfurous-smelling black goo splashed across the bed linens and dripped to a puddle on the floor, over a nurse's uniform and shoes. There was no sign of her father. Sig took two steps toward the room and whined. Petra grabbed his collar and moved him back underneath the yellow tape that blocked the doorway.

Gabe gripped her shoulder in sympathy. She turned away to follow the receptionist down the hall to Dr. Vaughn's office.

They were ushered inside and offered coffee or tea, both of which Petra and Gabe declined. The receptionist left to locate Dr. Vaughn. Gabe pulled his chair closer to Petra and held her hand. Sig lay down on her feet, and she could feel his heart fluttering through the tops of her shoes.

I will not cry, she thought. *I will not cry.*

Dr. Vaughn came into the office and shut the door behind her. This must have been her day off and she'd been called in; she was wearing yoga pants and a hip-length T-shirt, hair tied back in a ponytail. She extended her hand to Petra first, then Gabe. Rings still glittered on her hands.

"Thank you both for coming," she said, sliding behind her desk.

Petra leaned forward. "What happened?"

"We aren't entirely certain, but I'll tell you what we've learned so far. We thought your father was napping, and a nurse came to his room to give him his afternoon medication. Instead, Joseph was awake, and he was very agitated. The nurse radioed for backup and stated this. Sounds of yelling could be heard. Before an orderly could arrive, there was apparently a physical confrontation."

Petra winced. "Physical confrontation" sounded like a sanitized version of something awful. "Are they all right?"

"The orderly arrived to find the nurse missing. There was . . . something . . . on the floor that we haven't yet identified. The window was broken, and your father was gone, too. Our outdoor security camera caught him crossing the parking lot alone."

"Oh my God," Petra breathed. Gabe's grip on her hand tightened.

"We called the county sheriff's office, and they're looking for him. This is a truly unacceptable outcome, and we're sorry for all the pain this has caused." The doctor folded her hands before her.

"How long ago did this happen?"

"About two hours ago. The police are sure that he couldn't have gotten far, especially in his condition."

But he's up walking about . . . Petra squeezed her eyes shut. Jesus. If she'd only gone ahead and let them monitor him, to study him as they wanted, this might have been prevented—whatever *this* was. Based on what she'd glimpsed in her father's room, it was a mess. That much, she was certain.

"I want to help look for him," she insisted.

Dr. Vaughn sighed. "He's demonstrated that he can be very dangerous, and I would not want you to get hurt, too. I think we should leave this to the professionals. Once he's been recovered, it would be good for you to see him under controlled circumstances. A familiar face would be very helpful for him at that time. But for now . . . I think you should stand by for more information."

Petra shook her head. She couldn't just do nothing. She let Gabe and Sig lead her from the nursing home out to the Bronco. Sig sat down beside the truck tire and gazed up at her.

"What do you think happened in there?" Petra asked Gabe.

Gabe looked away, and he seemed reluctant to speak. "I think there's some magic afoot. If I were a betting man . . . it looks like someone came up against the wrong side of a fermentation process."

"What? How can that happen?" Her brow wrinkled.

"Your father was an accomplished alchemist. If he got into an altercation with someone . . . I'm pretty sure he was the one using the magic. It looks to me like the nurse was disincorporated."

She sucked in her breath. "The nurse is dead?"

"I think so. The remains of the process were on his clothes."

She shook her head. "No. No. My father would not have done that." She couldn't process the idea that her father would have killed an innocent man. Could not.

"Petra." Gabe's voice was soft but insistent. "Your father's Alzheimer's may have overtaken him. We must be careful."

"He can't have gone far," Petra said. "And we have to find him before Owen's men do." She reached into the Bronco for her gun belt, ammo, and a hat. The shadows were drawing long over the parking lot, and she needed to find her father before night fell. In the dark, he'd get even more lost and more terrified.

Gabe rested his hand on her arm. "Don't go spoiling for a fight with Owen's men."

She shook his hand off. "He's my father, Gabe. I can't leave him to the wolves."

Gabe nodded. "Then we should be smart about it. Careful." He took her jacket from the backseat and put it over her shoulders to cover the gun belt.

Petra sighed. He was right. She needed to slow her roll. She dug in the backseat for her backpack, dumped the geology tools from it, and stuffed a couple of water bottles and Sig's leash in it. "Well, he's presumably on foot."

"In two hours, a healthy man could walk five miles, maybe six. Your father will be slower than that, for certain," Gabe said. He pulled a map from the glove box and spread it on the hot hood. He found the nursing home on it and scribbled a circle around it. "Owen's men will be looking in this area . . . probably along these roads."

Petra stared at the map. That was a lot of ground to cover, and the area would be growing larger by the minute. She mentally crossed off the areas near the roads, where Owen's men would be lurking. What had her father been thinking? She stared at the broken window, visible from the parking lot. Where would he have fled to? There was little of interest here to the old man. The nearest civilization was at least a few miles down the road. There was a burger joint there, but . . .

Sig whined. Petra looked down at him. "Hey, buddy. Do you think you could track your grandpa?"

Sig cocked his head, looking at her like she was fucking stupid.

Petra squatted down to his level. "You know what

he smells like, right? Like . . . peppermint candy and butterscotch and yellow gravy? If you find him, I promise to get you the juiciest cheeseburger you've ever seen . . ."

Sig turned around and trotted away, nose to the ground. Petra's mouth gaped in amazement.

"Holy shit. Sig is doing what I told him to. I think. This never happens."

He trotted over to the ground near the broken window, sniffing around the Dumpster. He moved on, going around the side of the building.

"I'll start searching from the air," Gabe said.

Petra nodded. "I'll leave your clothes in the truck and the windows down."

Gabe glanced around to make sure no one was looking. Petra held her breath. No matter how many times she saw this, she was always dumbstruck. He stepped around a shaded corner of the building, out of the line of sight of the security camera perched near the door. And then he melted away. Black feathers split from flesh, twisting and exploding from skin and bone. Dozens of birds escaped his empty clothing, climbing up into the sky. Petra approached the empty clothing, plucking the flannel shirt away from a raven who'd gotten stuck in a sleeve. The bird cawed at her and flounced away, as if irritated by human trappings.

Petra dumped the clothes in the backseat of the Bronco. She moved the Bronco away from the camera and cranked the windows down. Gabe should be able to get back and get dressed with a minimum of fuss.

Petra scrambled to catch up with Sig, who was advancing into the woods behind the building, pausing once in a while to sniff at the ground. He moved on, trotting away, winding his way around the summer shade. Petra followed as closely as she dared, calling softly for her father. She felt like she did when she was six, playing hide-and-seek, and couldn't find her dad. Turned out that time, he'd fallen asleep in the bed of his pickup truck with a six-pack, well out of her view. But in the meantime, she'd convinced herself that something awful had happened to him. This felt the exact same way.

Sig emerged from the bit of woods into a fast-food parking lot. He drifted around the parked cars, and Petra stopped him to click his leash on his collar. He looked at her reproachfully.

"It's not that I don't trust you in traffic," she said. "It's everyone else I don't trust."

She walked up to the drive-through to ask the young man at the register if they'd seen an old man here alone. The young man shook his head, and she turned her attention back to Sig. The coyote was looking at the horizon, straining against the leash. She gave him a lot of slack and let him go, nose to the ground and tail twitching.

He circled through the lawn of an apartment complex. He sniffed each of the cars carefully, then veered away to an artificial pond. He snooted around the shore of the lake, and Petra's heart stopped. What if her father had drowned?

Above her, ravens spotted the sky. They spun outward in a search grid, orderly, silent. The sun was approaching the horizon, and they were black specks in the orange. If one of them saw something, she was certain that they would begin calling and that she could follow.

But Sig moved on. He trotted away, toward a dilapidated-looking house with tall grass growing through the gravel driveway. The white wooden siding was stained green with mold, and the shutters were loose and faded. It looked like it was probably slated for demolition.

Sig trotted up to the front step and circled the perimeter of the house, collar jingling. He orbited the house once, twice, then sat in the driveway, looking befuddled.

Petra looked at the broken doorbell with exposed wires and decided not to chance it. She knocked on the front door, hoping that whoever lived here might have some information about her father. She knocked and knocked, but no one answered.

She opened the mailbox and lifted out a sheaf of mail. Some of it was postmarked a month ago. "Nobody's been here in a long while."

A raven lit on the sagging gutter. Petra looked up at it. "Did you see anything?"

The raven twitched its head from right to left, a corvid negative.

Her heart sank. She asked the coyote, "Sig, do you know where my dad is?"

Sig looked up at her and whined, thumping his tail on the ground. He'd lost the scent.

And she knew, deep on some level, that she'd lost her father.

* * *

SHE DIDN'T KNOW what the phoenix wanted, or much of anything else for certain. But she did know that the pack needed her. And that she could help them.

Nine disappeared into the forest on the far side of the road. She hoped that Mike and Maria wouldn't try to find her. If they did, though, then so be it. All that she knew was that she had to save the pack. There was no other choice.

She pulled her bandanna up around her nose, jerked Mike's goggles over her eyes, and ran as fast as she could.

The pines seemed to know the fire was approaching. Sap oozed from the curling needles and pinecones dropped from the heat. It sounded like hail. She knew that fire was part of the pines' life cycle, that fire cleared out the undergrowth to allow light to nourish seeds in the now-rich soil. But not fire like this. This was unnatural. It wasn't allowed to burn itself out. It was created by the phoenix, new flashpoints generated wherever it lit. It wouldn't end until the phoenix was stopped.

But stopping the phoenix was beyond her power. Still, she could help the pack; that much, she knew. The air grew thick and hazy, but she kept moving south. Forward, forward. She was moving through vast striations of choking smoke. This way was unburned, close to the front of the fire line, so very close. It was like being submerged in a hot river. In her mind, she was eight years old again, helplessly struggling against the inexorable fire and the light in the sky.

The ground plateaued. To her right, she could see flames about a quarter mile away, moving steadily south. She was close to the gorge she'd seen in the Eye of the World. She followed the ridge until it dropped into a canyon. This was where she'd last seen the pack. They would have thought they were safe in that shade and the darkness of the gorge, but they would be trapped here, trapped without someone to lead them to safety.

She threw back her head and howled. Her smoke-abraded throat, unconstrained by human inhibitions, still released a sound that was very much like a wolf howl. She howled once again, then twice.

A distant howl answered her. She scrambled down the edge of the gorge, down a steep slide of gravel. The rock chewed into her blistered arm through the bandage, rending the skin bloody and weeping. She barely felt it—she was so close. She clambered gracelessly to the bottom of the gorge and howled again.

A wolf peered at her from behind a tree. Ghost. He was wary. He'd been expecting a wolf, and here was a woman. He pulled his lips back from his teeth and growled, the hair lifting along his spine.

Nine gave a small howl and a whimper, then a whine.

He cocked his head, looking at her.

Nine yipped at him. This was what she would say to him if she were still wearing fur. *It's me, Nine. And there's danger.*

The wolf perhaps heard something familiar in her voice. He gave a low woof, then turned to walk away.

She thought at first that he might mean to run

away, but he paused, looking over his shoulder. He meant her to follow. She scrambled after him.

A little way distant, she saw the pack, and her heart leaped into her sooty throat. They were huddled at the back of the gorge, a mass of grey fur and frightened eyes. The walls were too high to climb here, and this area was shaded by dense pine. Under any other circumstances, this would be a safe place—a great den—but not now. Now they were cornered against a wall of rock and the fire was closing fast.

The pack gazed at her with narrowed eyes. A growl emanated from a furry throat, and then a whimper. The wolves knew to fear anything that walked on two legs; creatures that walked on two legs meant terrible danger.

Nine lifted her hands and yipped softly. It was a sound she'd not made since she left the pack. She dropped to her knees, to their level, and groaned with a canine rasp.

The leader of the pack stood beside her. He yipped to the pack, making a show of turning his back to her. They looked at him skeptically, tails thumping in the dirt.

One of the youngest wolves sidled out from behind the legs of the others, tail tucked between her legs. She approached Nine warily, then lay down, gazing up at her with eyebrows twitching, ears flattening.

They knew her. Somehow, they knew her.

Nine whined happily, fighting the urge to reach out and touch them. Much as she wanted to, she could not afford to spook them now. Slowly, she pulled the map out of the bag and spread it on the ground. In her peripheral vision, she was conscious of the wolves circling her cautiously. One or two noses reached toward her and shied away. She smelled funny; she knew it. She smelled of human food and soaps and gasoline and gods knew what else.

Judging by their position, there was one way out. Nine put the map back in the bag, allowing her fingers to brush its contents. There was water, a shiny blanket marked FIRE BLANKET, and some beef jerky.

She poured the water out on a flat stone and backed away from it. The wolves had been down here without water for a long time. The wolves nosed toward the water and slurped noisily at it.

Nine glanced up at the sky. The sky was blackening and the smoke thickening. Fire crackled in the distance.

She whined, a sharp whistle. The wolves licking the rock dry paused, ears up. Nine slowly rose and walked away, back toward the mouth of the gorge. She turned and whined again.

Ghost trotted after her. She held her breath. The others slid into line behind him, clustering tightly. They were unsure. She didn't blame them. She was, too.

She began to walk faster, toward the opening of the dead-end gorge. She could see the fire now, crackling through the pine trees. It leaped from bough to bough, running as fast as mad squirrels in the branches overhead. The wolves, doubting, pressed close. Her fingertips brushed the coarse fur of a wolf's back. A low rumble emanated. They wanted to go back, away from the fire.

She gave a short bark, a sharp sound of certainty. They followed, a low keen coming from the pack. She looked over her shoulder and counted noses. None were left behind. Heat washed over her, and she moved quickly, almost at a run, through the mouth of the gorge. The wolves followed, ears flattened.

Once through the mouth of the canyon, the fire was close, just yards away. She turned a hard left, remembering what she'd seen on the map. There had to be a safe place to take them.

There *had* to be.

Overhead, the fire had begun to rattle through the pine trees in sheets. She pulled the bandanna up over her nose and ran. The wolves kept pace with her. She paused when one of the wolves yipped in pain, having stepped on an ember. The wolf limped, trying to catch up with the others.

Nine stopped. Carefully, she picked the wolf up, one arm around the wolf's backside and the other around her chest. This young one weighed about fifty pounds, about the same as Maria's bags of birdseed, but birdseed didn't squirm. Nine straightened her back and ran as quickly as she could, fur surging in a wave around her.

But the fire was fast. It was as if it chased them. As if it wanted to specifically consume this pack and the forest with it. She could hear pinecones crackling open and wood groaning. She focused on the path ahead. There was a river just beyond, according to the map. The land dipped, and she stumbled down a bank to a stream bed.

This far into drought, the river had all but dried up. Where the walls of the riverbed were easily fifteen feet tall, the water was just four feet of muddy creek at the bottom. Some wilting white cow parsnips nodded by the banks. Nine plunged into the water, the wolves pouring in around her. The wolf in her arms, discovering that it was just deep enough to swim, twisted away to paddle in the lukewarm water.

Nine looked back. The fire had licked the bank, jumping over the water to the opposite side in sparks. Nine sank up to her neck in the water. She turned to move upstream with the wolves, away from the fire. Ash coated the surface of the water, which was curiously thick with hundreds of tiny black toads that seemed to stare at the fire, as if entranced.

The pack moved slowly, even though the current wasn't fast. Nine could feel the relief in them as they paddled away from the disaster. The fire, moving perpendicular to them, washed over the bank and continued its course, going south. Nine was grateful for this stream, as she had been for the creek that saved her life as a little girl.

But there was no time for rest. Nine urged them east, away from the fire roaring south behind them. The wolves took turns wading into the shallows and walking along the pebbled surface of the riverbed. Nine's human clothes and pack felt heavy when she left the water, but she continued. The longer she walked, the more she was aware of the incline, how much the water pushed against her. Eventually, she and the wolves climbed out of the water. She paused to examine the paw of the wolf who'd stepped on an ember. The water had rinsed it free of debris. Nine found some ointment in Mike's pack and applied it to the wound. She washed her bandanna and wrapped the paw loosely with the red fabric. The wolf was able to put a little weight on it, much to Nine's relief. She wouldn't have been able to carry the wolf for much longer.

They followed the creek shore as the incline grew. The air grew clearer as they climbed. Nine urged them forward until dark, when the bedraggled wolves began to stumble with their tongues hanging out of their mouths.

Nine stopped then, at the edge of the water. In the darkness, she could still see the orange line of fire on the horizon, many miles away. She would watch it tonight, but they'd continue east in the morning.

She dug into her bag for food. Mike, ever a practical man concerned with his protein consumption, had left several packets of jerky in his bag. Nine opened it and gave pieces of it to each member of the pack. She took none for herself. She had eaten today. They took the morsels gratefully; no one had the energy to hunt.

Nine lay down on a rock, within arm's reach of the water. She pulled the crinkly metallic blanket out of the bag to cover herself. Perhaps they could sleep for a couple of hours before going on. To her surprise, she was quickly surrounded by fur. Wolf after wolf lay down beside her, on her, and her heart swelled. She was back in the pack, trusted, at the bottom of the wolf pile.

Tears dampened her cheek. She didn't make any effort to brush them away; to do so might disturb the wolves. She intended to remain awake, to savor each sigh and grumbling belly and shared flea over the night, but she dozed. She dreamed, off and on, of cooler territory without fire, of the cool snow of winter.

She woke hours before the sun. Fire burned in a hot line behind them, from north to south. She whined softly to wake the pack. They tumbled out of the pile with yawns and growls. She consulted the map, inspired by her dream. There had to be a safe place for the wolves, and she thought she saw one illustrated on the map—Eagle Peak. The elevation was high enough that there should still be snow there, and the wolves would be safe from fire.

We have to go, she thought, but was afraid to use her human voice with them. She crawled to her feet and began to move east again, shifting northeast as they followed the water. The wolves loped behind her.

As they walked, the stream grew colder, and the source of it became apparent: mountains. Nine barked at them, and they followed the slow increase in incline, through fields and over other rivers, climbing up, up, up . . . Eventually, they cleared the smoke clinging to the ground, and Nine could take deep lungfuls of air. Stars could even be seen here, at this elevation.

After many hours, the cold ground underfoot was coated with snow. Brittle grasses gave way to supple mosses as the sun crept across the sky. One of the wolves even managed to catch a rabbit, and another snagged a weasel. Here on the mountain, the fire could not touch them. It would gain no footholds with the wet moss, rock, and snow. It was a relief to know that even something as powerful as the phoenix had a foe—the mountain—it couldn't simply consume.

As the sun slipped over the horizon, lighting the smoke below a lurid orange, Nine sat down on a rock outcropping. Ghost leaned next to her. She yipped softly. She hoped that they understood; that this place was their new territory. That they would be safe here. They could follow the food down to the valley in the winter, and come back up in the summer.

The pack leader threw back his head and howled. The other wolves joined him, and so did Nine. Their tails swished in happiness. The wolf with the burned paw was walking on it, pressing it to the cool stone. Nine inspected it closely and rubbed on some more medicine from Mike's kit. She would heal.

Nine rubbed tears that sprang to her eyes. The pack was safe. Ghost lay down beside her, licking her cheek, as the pack explored.

I wish I could stay with you, she thought. And she was tempted. If she stayed with them, she might be able to protect them from all kinds of danger, from fire and threats that walked on two legs.

But.

For all that protection she might be able to offer, she knew she could not keep up with them. They had four legs; she only had two. And if she stayed, she would freeze to death by September. She would become a burden to them, and she couldn't bear that. If she were a wolf, she would have remained, happily, as the omega wolf of the pack, one with the pack. She ached for the memory of that time. Her mind and her heart warred in her chest.

She struggled with it, but she always seemed to come back to the fact she was now meant to watch them from afar. To visit them through the Eye of the World. And to intervene when she could, when map-reading and speaking to humans were necessary. The problem with that fact was that it felt hollow and sad to her, like being a voyeur in her own life.

The leader gazed at her wisely. Perhaps he understood more than she thought.

Eventually, Nine climbed to her feet. She had to go. She had no supplies, and she needed to at least let Maria know she was safe. Her hand slipped up to the precious bone necklace circling her throat. She had to return it.

Ghost laid his head down on his paws. He made no move to follow her. Instead, he watched her descend the mountain, not looking away from her once.

Distantly, Nine heard howling. Through her tears, she smiled.

"I will come back," she promised. And she meant it.

CHAPTER 13

Invisible Gold

The Alchemist of Temperance had intended to wait in his bed at the prison for the elderly for a few days, to collect information and become familiar with this rather frail body he'd been saddled with. He lay in bed for a while, testing his muscles and gazing up at the box on the wall that showed pictures of people. Fabulous bit of magic, that.

He knew he could wait. Perhaps get this body in better condition. He could be patient. He slept in this warm bed, gathering his strength. One of the women in white came for him after he woke. She talked to him as if he were a child, but she gave him chocolate pudding in a translucent dish and another pillow. He ate it and she left another for him. She patiently showed him how to work the box on the wall, which changed from a channel featuring men running around after balls to people playing music. He consumed the pudding greedily while he watched the box on the wall, discovering that the picture changed when he pressed the buttons.

She asked him when his daughter would be visiting, and his ears perked up. Joseph Dee had a daughter. He was certain that an alchemist like Joseph would have passed his knowledge on to her. He was resolved to wait for Joseph Dee's daughter to come to him and find out what she knew. She might be useful to him, if even only as a guide to the outside world.

The world had changed much since he'd trod this earth with solid feet. He'd glimpsed bits and pieces from the spirit world, images he could scry in the bottom of a cup of tea or in the black glass of his house when the moon was ripe. He saw that people flew the skies in great metal birds, that they piloted strange craft on smooth roads, and that petticoats were no longer in fashion. Beyond that, though, he was lost.

But the box on the wall spoke to him of something more wondrous than short skirts and supersonic speeds. He leaned forward, spotted brow crinkling, as he saw a man talking about a great fire.

The man was gesturing to smoke, to fire consuming a forest behind him. He was saying: ". . . this is the largest fire in Yellowstone's history. Meteorologists are discussing the role of the weather in this disaster. The hot, dry summer has certainly contributed, as have the strong winds. But there might be something more in the sky that's keeping the fire going."

The picture switched to a blurry night-sky scene.

A falling star pierced the sky, a blaze of distant orange with an irregular shape.

"Our meteorological team has been sent footage of this rare form of ball lightning by a local photographer. Lightning is a natural contributor to forest fires, but this kind is unusual. Ball lightning forms when regular lightning becomes caught in what's called a plasma bubble. You'd think that this would mean rain for us, but none of the weather systems has produced rain that has reached the ground, so . . ."

Lascaris was transfixed. That was no lightning.

That was a phoenix.

My phoenix.

It was back. After all this time, it had awoken without him. Maybe it had come at the behest of another alchemist—Joseph Dee's daughter? Or perhaps it was operating on its own internal cycle. He pressed his hands together and rested his chin on his fingertips. He'd tried so desperately to conjure the phoenix long ago, to summon it out of the ether to merge with him in the most glorious conjunction process he could imagine. It would have brought him all he sought—immortal life, unimaginable power. He would be eternal and indestructible, the Great Work completed. But he'd had to rush it when the town of Temperance had arrived on his doorstep. He'd fouled it up and lost it all.

But now he had the opportunity again. He would not be thwarted this time. He would not be confined to a buried mirror for more than a century, then drifting at the margins of the spirit world when the broken mirror could not contain him. Nor would a prison for the elderly keep him. He would be free.

He knew that the phoenix would be attracted to magic. And the stronger, the better. He needed to get out of this place, to summon his power and send it up into the sky, like a signal flare, to draw the creature to him. Then, he could snare it and finally complete the Great Work.

And there was no time to waste.

He'd been sitting on the bed, putting on the shoes he found nearby, when a man in white had come for him, insisting cheerfully that it was time to take his pills. Lascaris shook his head, thinking that at least in the prison for old people, he would have the autonomy to refuse them.

The man in white tried to talk him into them, promising him pie. As if pie would convince him to lie back and be silent, in some medicated stupor! Again, Lascaris refused, but the man in white persisted. He sat beside Lascaris on the bed and tried to take Lascaris's shoes off while muttering something soothing at a beeping black box he plucked from his belt.

Lascaris had no patience for this. He closed his eyes. He had no idea what alchemical powers might have followed him from the spirit world into this new body. But something surely must have come with him. He let his mind become blank and black, and the astrological symbol for Capricorn, the sign of the alchemical fermentation process, rose in his mind's eye.

He reached out for the man in white and whispered: *"Corrumpere."*

He felt the alchemical power flare darkly in him, racing through his marrow like a spark on a dynamite fuse. It slipped from his mind, through his chest, down his fingers, and into the back of the hand of the man in white.

The man in white snatched his hand away, as if he'd been burned. The man staggered back and sagged against the bed, sliding to the floor. His hand, smearing against the white linens, was black, spreading ooze as he fell. By the time his head hit the floor, he had liquefied into a puddle that smelled like vinegar. He'd been consumed in the most perfect fermentation process that Lascaris had ever seen, the Touch of Death.

Pleased, he climbed to his feet and stood over the puddle, transfixed. He possessed the Touch of Death, the alchemical process that dissolved everything. He knew, with every fiber of his being, that he was now ready to meet the phoenix in the next alchemical process, the purification by fire that would come from distillation. When death and fire came together, great magic would be released. It was heady, this tangible result of his accumulated knowledge.

But the man in white was gone. Someone would certainly want revenge for this. Lascaris grasped a wooden chair sitting beside the window. He swung it at the glass. On the first strike, it bounced off. On the second, the window shattered, spewing glass over him in strangely shaped flakes. While he'd have loved to stay and study the strange material, he knew time was short. He climbed through the window to find himself on a paved area where vehicles were parked.

He ran, away from the vehicles and the prison for old men. He ran through a forest, past a roadhouse that smelled of delicious food. His bones felt thin and creaky, but he went as fast as he dared. He skulked around the corner of a five-story building—five stories!—that seemed to house people. He avoided them and continued until he reached a house standing by itself in a field. His breath was ragged and his muscles ached. This body had clearly not seen such activity for many years. If he could find supplies, perhaps he could make himself an elixir that would fortify him for the hunt to find the phoenix.

The house looked abandoned, with no evidence of human activity around it. The curtains were drawn tight across every window, and weeds grew in the gravel around a dusty blue vehicle. The front step was crumbling, and the thin shingles on the roof were lifting.

He thought that perhaps he could break in, to rest for a moment and consider his options. Surely, there would be men looking for him. He needed to evade them long enough to figure out exactly where he was, and how to get to the phoenix.

He knocked on the door, arranging his reflection in the glass to seem meek and mild. Creaking sounded from inside, and Lascaris felt a pang of anger that the place was not abandoned as he thought. Eventually, the door opened, and Lascaris found himself staring into the face of an elderly woman. She was shrunken with age, coming barely up to Lascaris's chest. She peered at him through smudged eyeglasses. She was wearing a flower-printed dress and had long grey hair braided over her shoulder.

"Hello?" she creaked out.

"Hello," Lascaris said. "I find myself lost. Might I come in?"

The old woman squinted at him. "I don't much like visitors."

"I don't much like visiting." He refused to budge.

The old woman huffed. "You can use the phone, but then you have to promise to leave."

"All right. Thank you." Lascaris had no idea what a phone was, but it sounded like it would get him across the threshold to relative safety.

The house was cold and quiet—surprisingly cold. The old woman minced across a ragged fluffy carpet to point to a box on the wall with a string dangling from it in coils. She pointed to it. "One call. No long distance."

Lascaris stared at the turquoise box. He poked at it. Part of the box fell off and landed on the floor, tethered by the coiled string, and he jumped away from it as if it were a striking snake.

"Oh, Jesus Christ," the old woman said. "You're senile, aren't you?"

He blinked at her. Maybe it was good that she thought that there was something wrong with him. He rubbed his forehead.

"Sit down," she said, pulling out a chair for him before a painted yellow table covered in papers. She walked slowly over to the piece of the box on the floor and placed it back on its hook.

"Let me get ready. I'll drive you to the police station."

Lascaris perked up. He'd spied on this world enough from the picture box to understand what that meant. There was a vehicle that she could operate. This could be his ticket to freedom. "All right."

"Wait right there. I have to finish something up. And don't eat my cookies," she snapped. The elderly woman shuffled off down the hallway, muttering.

Lascaris's gaze swept over the mound of papers on the table. There was a jar, nearly covered by papers. He lifted the lid and peered inside. There was food inside, and his stomach growled. He picked up a piece of dry pastry and gnawed on it. It was actually very good, sweet and nutty.

He wandered into the kitchen. By his standards as an alchemist who ran a laboratory, this place was very haphazard. Boxes and books filled the countertops. He paused before a spice rack and squinted at the herbs in their little containers—the containers looked like glass, but the material was lighter and thinner. The old woman was wealthier than he thought; many of these herbs were ones he would have had to send away for, at great cost, during his time as the Alchemist of Temperance. The saffron, in particular, was fascinating.

He took the bottles down, one by one. He dumped contents of some of them into a cup, adding some salt from a shaker he found on the windowsill. The salt was crusty, but it would do. He opened the cabinets and gazed at their contents. He picked through them, finding vinegar and some milk and eggs in a large cold cabinet. He mixed his findings together in a cup. With the salt, he sketched a series of alchemical symbols around the concoction and muttered over it, tapping the rim three times.

He downed the contents of the cup in three gulps. When he was finished, he grimaced, wiping his lips with the back of his hand. It tasted truly disgusting. But the potion would fortify him, keep his weak bones and withered muscles going. He could control much of this body through sheer force of his magical will, but a fortifying potion never hurt.

He rinsed out his mouth with water and then crept down the hallway. A door stood ajar at the end of the hall, emanating a lurid green light. He paused to listen.

The old woman's voice sounded sharply, a low whisper: "No, I have to go. You have exactly twenty-four hours to cough up that block reward. Yeah. I sent the proof of work. Twice. Get it done. Fucking tool."

Lascaris peered around the corner of the door.

The old woman sat in a black chair, surrounded by whirring black metal boxes on racks. Cords and wires snaked across the floor, and shiny silver tubes reached up into the ceiling. Glowing boxes cast a green glow in the room, which felt positively frigid. She was barking into what looked like a black tiara on her head at an unseen person.

The old woman swiveled sharply in her chair and looked up at him. "I thought I told you to stay put," she snarled.

Lascaris let his gaze rove over this odd dark room. He touched one of the glass panes showing an unintelligible string of words and letters. "What is this?"

The woman leaned back in her chair and chuckled. "This is the biggest cryptocurrency farm west of the Mississippi."

Lascaris cocked his head. "Crypto . . . currency? Is that some kind of magic?"

"Yeah, you could say that," she cackled. "Not that anyone would believe you if you told on me. Sweet old Molly, the retired statistician, can't figure out her television remote."

"I have no idea what any of that means."

"It means two trips to Aruba a year and fully funding the college educations of all seven of my grandchildren." Molly tapped at a black tray of tiles with letters and symbols on them. "Give me a few minutes, and I'll take you to the police station. They'll figure out what your damage is and get you back to where you belong in a jiffy."

"I'd rather you didn't."

She raised an eyebrow. "Wait. I bet you're an escapee from that nursing home. Bailing on that yellow gravy and early bedtimes."

Lascaris swallowed. "I, ah, don't remember."

"It might be better for me to drop you off there, then." She finished tapping on the tray of tiles and got up. She moved a bit quicker than before, sliding into a pink sweater draped on the back of her chair and snatching a fistful of keys and a handbag the size of a suitcase from a hook on the wall. "C'mon. I'll get you back before din-din."

Lascaris's head spun, and he followed her out to the gravel path where the turquoise blue vehicle sat. One of the modern age's horseless carriages. Molly opened a door and got in. Lascaris copied her. He fumbled three times with the latch before climbing in on the other side. She put a key in the carriage, and it growled to life.

Molly slowly backed out of the driveway, peering into a mirror. "You'll be back before you know it, and you'll forget all about this. You'll be playing Scrabble with four-letter words by dusk."

Lascaris frowned. He had no compunctions about dissolving Molly and taking her horseless carriage. But as he watched her, he realized that there was a lot more to operating this metal beast than there was to riding a horse. There was a wheel, and a rod in the floor that moved, and two pedals. Lascaris realized that he needed her, at least for a little while.

He cleared his throat. "That place is terrible. They do terrible things."

Molly paused, glancing at him. "What kind of things?"

He hung his head dramatically. "They don't feed me. They beat me sometimes. I want . . . I want to go back to my daughter. She doesn't know that they do this to me. If I go to her, and she knows, she'll save me."

Molly frowned, stopping the vehicle. The vehicle grumbled. "Man, I'm sorry."

"Please. Take me to my daughter."

She tapped her yellowed fingernails on the wheel. "Where does your daughter live?"

"That way." He pointed toward the smoke.

Molly sighed and the vehicle began rolling again. "You'd better not get me into trouble, you old coot."

"My daughter will be happy to see me," he said brightly. "She always is."

"I hope so," she murmured, turning right on the road and toward the western haze.

* * *

"IF YOU FIND him, bring him to me."

Owen keyed off his radio and scratched his mustache thoughtfully. He'd put out an APB for Petra Dee's father. He'd sent out two patrol cars to look for him—Owen was, after all, a concerned citizen and upstanding sheriff. It didn't change the fact that Petra Dee and her husband, Gabriel Manget, had been thorns in his side ever since he'd inherited the Rutherford Ranch, however. So it wasn't exactly duty that compelled him to find Joseph Dee. If he had a chance to ask Petra's father a few questions outside of the prying eyes of the nursing home staff, he was damn well gonna take it. He had questions. Questions like: *What are you doing in Temperance? Do you know what crazy shit your daughter is into, or are you somehow involved? What do you think about her getting married to a dead guy, anyway?*

"You never leave anything alone, do you, Owen?"

In the passenger seat of his SUV, Anna was watching him with wry amusement.

"No," he said. "Well, not often. I'm inquisitive." He knew that was his greatest character failing, not leaving well enough alone. He once thought of the whole county as something he was responsible for, and to be properly responsible for it, he ought to know every sigh and breath the underworld—both criminal and magical—took. Now he was more careful about what anthills he poked, but he still wanted to know where they were in case he decided to avoid them.

"And you're being inquisitive about this bad guy. Robin." Her mouth turned down.

"Yeah. I am," he admitted. "I want to know if he was telling me the truth, you know?"

She turned away.

"Aren't you angry? I mean . . . if he killed you, don't you want everyone to know and for him to get what's coming to him?"

She was chewing on the drawstring of her hoodie. Over time, Owen had come to associate that gesture with her being deep in thought. "I don't hate him, Owen."

Owen's brow creased. "Why not?" he blurted. He was used to hating evil. There sure was a lot of it, and a lot of people got away with doing it. Including himself. He'd done a lot of evil things himself, and he hated those things, too. He guessed that extended to self-loathing, but he tried not to think about it.

She turned back to him, her blue eyes earnest. "If he did it, he did it because he was weak. There was something else there . . . something darker and more awful than him. He may have killed me, but I think . . . there was something else."

"Robin told me about a creature. A giant toad. Something he considers to be a god that told him to do it." Saying it aloud sounded even more implausible than his usual conversations with the ghost.

Anna shivered. "I remember that there was something. Something dark and terrible at the bottom of the well. I don't know what it was. But it was awful."

Owen's mouth thinned. Maybe there was something there, after all.

He was determined to find out. He swallowed

his fear at dealing with the supernatural, even as his missing hand ached. This was the case that had dogged his entire career. This was Anna's murder. He owed it to her to man up and face what had caused it.

Anna vanished. He sighed and climbed out of the SUV. He'd driven himself and Anna off the main roads, off one-lane gravel roads, back through the dry forest of the backcountry. It was too early for hunting season, but Owen really wouldn't advise civilians to be out wandering in the woods. Yellowstone was still miles away, but smoke rose in columns in the distance. It wouldn't do for a bunch of lookie-loos to get stuck or lost in the woods with fire so close.

Nor could he spare any of his patrol deputies for such an odd errand. The ones he had on duty were rehearsing his evacuation plans, if worse came to worst. Those that weren't out cruising the back roads, looking for Petra Dee's dad, that was.

Besides, every so often, Owen liked getting his hands dirty. And Anna's death was *his* case. He'd reassigned the cold case to himself when he became sheriff, and had not given it up. He had ownership of this situation to the bitter end, on more levels than he could contemplate. And if it helped ameliorate some of those evil things he'd mentioned earlier, then all the better . . .

Owen had driven to the well where Anna's body had been found twenty years ago. He hadn't been back here since that time they'd brought her up. Then, he'd been a brand-spanking-new deputy and had thrown up all over his shoes. Now that skinny file folder sat on his desk, the work of his superiors and his own investigation, yellowed with time, a reminder of things he'd failed to do.

Owen opened his door and stepped out into the brittle, hot thicket. Mayflies swarmed, and insects grated out scratchy music from the trees. The ground was hot and dry enough for him to drive over without fear of getting stuck, but he felt it better to go on foot the last part of the way. He scanned this place, remembering Robin's story. There should be a creek here . . . He walked a few feet to an area where the trees were densest, as if they'd had easy access to water. There was no water here now, just a dried-up mud bed. But it could have been diverted or just evaporated—the fire might have something to do with that. Either way: no toads in there that he could see.

He crossed the forest floor to a clearing, where the old well stood. He always wondered why someone would have dug a well so close to running water. It seemed an unnecessary luxury. Yet here it was, simple sandstone, unornamented, a round portal into the dark. Maybe, long ago, there had been a small house here, and the well had been in the basement for convenience. Maybe, at the time it had been constructed, there had been no creek. Maybe the creek was the product of drainage ditches and culverts built for the nearby road. He walked back toward the road, seeing a dry culvert reaching beneath it. Maybe.

He was procrastinating. He took a deep breath and went to the well. He clicked on his flashlight and peered in.

There wasn't much water there, not much at all. When they hauled Anna up so many years ago, the water's surface had been maybe five feet down. Now he could barely see an oily black pool with his light, some fifteen feet down. And it stank. It stank just as bad as it did when Owen found Anna's head in a rotted bucket. What else was rotting down there? More bodies?

Feeling vaguely ridiculous, but thankful that no one was here to see him, he called out: "Pigin. Pigin, are you here?"

The insects in the trees seemed to stop their whirring. It became very, very still. The hair on Owen's arms stood up, and he felt suddenly very cold, like someone had dumped a milk shake down the back of his shirt.

"Pigin? Can you hear me?"

A voice rasped from the bottom of the well, almost too faint to hear. It had a sibilant inflection that reminded Owen too much of the hiss of the air conditioner at the mental hospital: "Lean closer, over the well, so that I can see you."

Owen peered into the well with his flashlight. It seemed like something moved below, but he couldn't make out what it was. If he were a rational man, he would have supposed that he was spotlighting fish or snakes, swimming in from some underground water source. But Owen hadn't felt like a rational man for a very long time.

The voice echoed from below. "I see you clearly now, man with a wooden hand and shiny star. What brings you here?"

"My name's Owen. And you must be Pigin."

A small splash sounded below. "How do you know my true name?"

"I spoke to an old friend of yours, Robin Wayne Cuthbert."

Laughter echoed up, the scrape of a metal spatula on a grill grate, followed by the hiss of a boiling-over radiator. "Long ago, that little bird flew away."

Owen squinted down into the well, trying to see what he was talking to. "What are you?"

The creature at the bottom of the well snorted. "I am the spirit of this place, the genius loci, if you will. This place has a foul history, and I am what rose up from beneath the weight of that history. I am what existed before history. I am eternal."

Owen leaned against the sandstone, his fingernails digging into the grit. "I'm listening."

Something burbled in the muck, and it sounded like a sigh. "Hundreds of years ago, the native men and women would avoid this place, the land around this portal in the earth that men call a well. They were right to do so. Sun never fully penetrated the canopy of the forest to light the ground, and the creek muttered strangely. They gave it a wide berth, and the land was still. It was my domain, the place of death. Tranquil.

"Then the pale people came to this land. I watched as a man built a house on this site, then sent away for his family. His wife and two children arrived. The man showed them the home and promptly left the next day to work his trade as a carriage driver for the next two weeks.

"Gennie, the young wife, disliked the house straightaway. She longed for sunlight, and there was none to be had within a twenty-minute walk. The house was always cold, and she was tasked with maintaining the home and grounds while her husband was gone. To her fell the sewing, washing, cooking, repairs, and running the household. I whispered to her as she slept, as she worked, and she shuttered the windows and slept with a blanket wrapped around her head. But still, she felt my presence. I seeped in, slowly, over time.

"Her husband returned for a few days every few weeks. And, much to Gennie's dismay, she fell pregnant. Again and again, through the years—they had twelve children. Gennie cared for the children as well as she could, but she was essentially alone in this homesteading endeavor. Alone with me.

"Gennie's gardening efforts near the house struggled, and she dug out a garden in a distant field. That time in the sunshine of the garden was her refuge, distant from the house and the yelling of the children and undone work. She placed her fingers in the dirt and felt moments of peace.

"But over the years, Gennie slowly grew mad, listening as I whispered terrible things to her. She sang to drown out the sound of my voice, but it crept into her dreams. She could not blot it out at night, and my words slowly sank into her consciousness.

"She tried to fight back, of course. She took an ax and cut down trees, trying to bring light to this shaded place, sunshine that would drive me out. But new trees sprang up as quickly as she cut them down, seemingly overnight.

"She grew to hate her husband and hate her children. One night, overcome by my whispers in her dreams, she awoke. She took the ax she'd used to cut down the trees and slaughtered all twelve of her children. And she waited, in that bloody house, waited for her husband to finally return. When he did, she killed him, too, and fled into the night.

"Eventually, the husband's employer came looking for him and found the house of murder. It was July, and the flies were thick, feeding on the blood that had soaked into the floorboards and the rotting corpses. The townsfolk came and buried the bodies in Gennie's garden, the nearest spot of turned earth, casting aside turnips and potatoes to inter the thirteen dead in a mass grave. It took a long time, and the townsfolk were exhausted. They left this place, vowing never to return.

"A man, a magician of sorts, came to the house not long after. He had come to collect evil talismans for his eldritch workings. He had come to scrape the dried blood of children from the floorboards."

Owen sucked in his breath. He had encountered the ruined magic of one alchemist of old, and the hair on his arms lifted. "This magician . . . was it Aldus Lascaris?"

Pigin chuckled. "Yes. Yes, it was. The alchemist knew that this place was soaked in evil, and he was fascinated by it. He collected other tokens from the house, finding a baby tooth rolled under a bed and a forgotten child's finger stuck to a wall. He gathered these treasures carefully, in jars, and made to go home.

"But the door was blocked by a wild and fearsome shadow. Gennie had returned, wielding her ax. She and Lascaris fought, and the struggle spilled out into the yard. Lascaris seized the ax and cut her hand off. He pushed Gennie into the well and took the hand home with the rest of his scavenged bits of blood and bone.

"He wasn't done with this place, though. Lascaris came back, again and again. He deposited the incriminating ruins of his experiments in the well, using it as something of a magical dumping ground. The well consumed bodies of Lascaris's hapless victims, soured blood, and all manner of befouled potions. This . . . soup, if you will, fermented over time. It pleased me, strengthened me."

Owen forced himself to take a breath. Anything Lascaris touched was dangerous, dangerous as hell. "He made offerings to you."

"He did. He gave me what I desired, and I granted him many favors in return. I even taught him how to raise the dead from their graves."

Owen shuddered.

"Now, tell me what you want from me. Perhaps I may grant you a great favor."

Owen shook his head to clear the story from it. "Robin said he made an . . . offering to you. A little girl. Her name was Anna. Is that true?"

A snort echoed from below. "Little morsel, sweet and screaming. I let her. But just two bites, and she was silent."

Owen's fingers tightened on the sandstone edge of the well. "You are what Robin said, then. A monster."

"Robin got what Robin wanted. He was told the terms of the bargain." Black eyes looked up at him from the inky pool below. "He gave, so I gave. But this I will give you for free. Solving the crime will bring you no peace of mind, nor rid you of the ghost. Only Robin's death will."

Owen sucked in his breath. "Robin deserves the electric chair."

"Ah. And will you see that he gets it?"

Owen didn't answer. Robin was going to remain locked up in the mental hospital, likely for as long as he lived. And so Owen would be haunted that long.

Both of them would.

"Bring me the little bird, and I'll devour him. The ghost haunting you will depart."

Owen's fingers slowly crept to his holster. "She'll go to heaven? To the afterlife she deserves?"

"I swear."

Owen looked away in frustration, looked back, snatched his gun from his holster, and fired into the well.

Gunfire flashed white and echoed in that pit. Owen fired all six shots. He peered into the dark. Chips of stone crumbled into the water. He shone his light into it. No body of a Toad God came floating up. He reloaded, just in case.

Grunting in frustration, he stalked back to the SUV. Anna watched him from the passenger seat with round eyes, not moving to step out.

"What are you doing?" she squeaked as he opened the tailgate and hauled out a piece of equipment that resembled what might happen if a giant weed whacker mated with an octopus. He dragged out two two-by-fours and laid them over the center of the well, parallel to each other, resting on the sandstone.

"I'm gonna dredge that sonofabitch," he muttered.

He dragged the heavy hunk of metal and plastic over to the well. He pulled the pump up over the two pieces of wood, wrestled the first five-inch-diameter hose down the well, then aimed the ejection hose toward the creek bed. He got the damn engine started after three pulls on the rip cord. The machine hiccupped, then made the unholy noise of a power generator.

Owen stood back, glowering. They'd dredged the well after Anna's body was found. Nothing had come up then but Anna's bones. But they had never found the bottom of the well. They'd gone as far as they could with the hoses and even sent an unlucky diver down who swore off dive duty ever after, but they never hit bottom. The diver had posited that the well was connected to an underground water system of some kind, something that reached into the water table and maybe beyond. Then, Owen remembered that the ground had been wet, and that there had been a lot of rain. The well had been full almost to the sandstone rim. Now, with the water so much lower, maybe he'd eventually be able to find the body of that toad. He'd brought the machine along, thinking that he'd have a hard time finding Pigin and that he'd have to literally flush the giant toad out. Now he hoped to find the creature's corpse.

As water coursed out of the well to the creek, Owen paced. Eventually, he sat on the edge of the well with his head in his hands, feeling the vibration of the pump in his ass and his dental fillings. He had to do whatever he could to get Anna to move on. For both of them, that was the only way. A man couldn't live haunted, he reasoned.

He gazed toward the ejection hose. Foul-smelling muck was coming out, the color of refrigerator mold. The engine seemed to labor and skip, as if it were a cat struggling to cough up a hair ball. The machine groaned, and it began spitting out pieces of solid debris. Owen advanced on the hose, expecting to find some gravel and a sign that the bottom was near.

But it wasn't gravel. Owen poked into the muck with a stick and dragged away some solid pieces that were too soft to be stone. He dumped some fresh water from a water bottle over them.

"Shit," he swore.

They were bones. Pieces of them, anyway. Owen had been around the block enough to recognize an adult finger bone when he saw one. There was a fragment of a larger bone, maybe the ball of a hip joint, and an unmistakably human jawbone with most of the teeth intact. His first thought was that these belonged to Gennie or Lascaris's experiments. But those would have likely been found the last time the well was dredged. These had to have been deposited into the well afterward. And while he was no forensic scientist, it looked like a modern mercury filling in one of the back teeth in the jawbone. Those surely weren't available in Lascaris's time.

"Shit. Shit. Shit." This place was now more than the setting for settling his own scores. It was now a crime scene. He'd bet his last dollar that these bones were human, and it seemed that Pigin had been collecting sacrifices for some time. How many missing-persons cases on the books could be solved by reexamining this site?

Owen picked through the debris, gathering all he

could and depositing them unceremoniously in a plastic evidence bag. He'd have to get the lab involved, and he'd have to do some DNA testing, then do some official interrogating of Robin that his informal nosing about might have fucked up majorly. Had Robin been dumping more people, over time, into the well, at Pigin's request? How on earth was he going explain why he was out here in the first place?

How on earth am I going to spin this . . .

The engine seized with a deafening crack, and then there was ringing silence. Owen went back to the machine and tried to start it again, but the rip cord was stuck. Groaning, he pulled the pump down and took the extraction hose off. Something had gotten jammed there—something pale white and splintered that he couldn't remove with his hands or the multi-tool he kept in his pocket.

"Shit."

Laughter bubbled up from the bottom of the well. Owen spun and shone his flashlight down.

A huge, blistered toad sat in the bottom of the well, floating in that disgustingly opaque water.

"Where did all those bones come from?" Owen demanded, shouting a bit louder than he might have intended to, on account of the ringing in his ears.

"They were offerings. People want things. I give them to them. And sometimes they don't want them anymore." The toad flicked its tongue out.

"Did Robin do this?"

The toad began to chew its arm thoughtfully, the way a dog with eczema might. He gobbled down some of his own flesh, tearing at it as it split apart. He opened his mouth, and on his tongue was a deformed bullet. He spat out a tarry glob of goo that rang on the stone walls.

"You might overestimate Robin's resourcefulness. And his stomach."

Owen aimed his gun into the hole, but Pigin merely snorted at him. "You can't hurt me with your toys, lawman."

Owen faltered, and he put his gun away.

"Now," Pigin said. "My offer still stands. Bring me Robin, and you will free the girl."

"Why should I believe you?"

The toad just stared at him. "I assume that you've tried everything else to get rid of your ghost, yes? Prayer, exorcism, maybe drink and various substances to keep her at bay?"

Owen looked away.

"And none of it worked. And now you've solved the crime. And still she sits, in your vehicle, as vivid as she was years ago. She hasn't faded in the slightest."

Owen pinched the bridge of his nose. "So I feed you Robin . . . and then what? You keep doing what you do?"

"I have been here long before you, lawman. I'll be here long after you rot. I am decay, the moist underside of all things. You would do well to remember this, lawman—all things rot."

The toad swam away then, seeming to disappear in the darkness. Water seemed to trickle back in, and the water level crept higher.

Owen rubbed the back of his neck with his good hand.

No matter what he did, it was all going to hell.

CHAPTER 14

One Wish

S he had failed.

She felt it, deep in the hollowness of her chest,
a leaden certainty that was determined to crawl
up her throat and pour out in tears.

"I've lost him," Petra said. Her fingers were
gripped so tightly around the steering wheel that
she had lost all feeling in them.

They'd been driving around all evening, and the
light was fading. Gabe had finally asked her to stop
at a fast-food place and got her a drink. She'd slurped
it down mindlessly, but had remembered that she
needed to feed Sig. The coyote got his cheeseburger,
and was chewing it thoughtfully on the seat of the
car. He'd taken apart the sandwich and removed
the lettuce and tomato, only interested in the meat,
cheese, and a bit of the bread.

Gabe shook his head. "He will turn up. Your father is a resourceful man."

"No." She shook her head hard. "You don't know what he's like when he disappears. When he last disappeared, I was sixteen. I had left for school, my mom had gone off to work, and my dad went to work like he did every day. It was a freaking Wednesday. Who runs away on a Wednesday?

"Anyway. I came home from school, and the house was empty. It was so quiet. I sat down on the couch and read. My mom came home. We made dinner. We waited for my dad. It got dark, and he didn't show up. My mom tried calling his coworkers. No one had seen him that day. We called the cops to see if he was in a ditch somewhere. Called the local hospitals. Not a sign of him.

"At first, my mom was pissed. She thought he was having an affair. And he was like that. He was never really present, you know? Always thinking about something else. Mom had threatened to divorce him more than once.

"She filed a missing-persons report when the police said that it had been long enough to count him as gone—I think it was a couple of days. They eventually found his car two states away at a gas station parking lot. There was no sign of foul play. He had just disappeared like that. No note of explanation, no nothing.

"My mom and I went on, I guess. She got really pissed and sold everything he owned, even the recovered car. I kept this gift from him, because I hid it from her." She fingered the gold pendant at her throat, the lion devouring the sun. "It was all I had of him. Maybe all I ever will.

"I searched for him, off and on, for years. I finally got a lead that he was seen in Temperance. I found him in the nursing home, and I learned that he'd been pursuing an alchemical solution for his Alzheimer's. That he'd gotten mixed up with a shitty crowd and had gotten hexed and wound up tucked away in a corner where he couldn't hurt anyone. I was so glad to find him . . . even gladder when he recognized me. I thought that we could build a relationship, get back some of what was lost."

She stared down at the pendant. "If he's running again, he may not be found until he's ready to be. Or he may have met serious trouble. Or his Alzheimer's may have—"

Gabe leaned over to give her a hug. Her ruminations died against his shirt. Her dad was a runner, any chance he got. She knew that, a truth that resonated deep in her bones. It just didn't make it any easier to deal with a second time around.

Her cell phone rang, and she snatched it up, thinking it was news about her dad. "Hello?"

"Hey, Petra. It's Mike."

"Mike? Is everything okay? Is the fire—?"

"Not great. But I'm okay. Been trying to reach you for hours. The nearest cell tower got cooked by the fire, and I had to find a sat phone to call you. And Maria's okay, too."

"She's with you? What happened?"

There was a frustrated sigh on the other end of the line. "Apparently, Nine and Maria went around the barricades and decided to do some kind of numb-skulled thing with fire. Nine said she wanted to make an offering to it or something."

Petra held her breath. She wanted to ask: *Was she successful?* But she kept her mouth shut.

"We got distracted trying to help evacuate some firefighters, and Nine took off. We don't know where she is."

Petra pressed the heel of her hand to her temple. "It's going around. My dad escaped from the nursing home and a nurse is missing." She didn't say *presumed dead*. "We've been looking for him.

"But what about Nine . . . Wait." Petra paused. "This will make no sense, but you'll have to trust me on this."

"Things rarely make sense when you're involved. Just sayin'."

"There's a radio tracker on at least one wolf in the Nine Stars pack, right?"

"Yeah. I think so. I can contact the biologist who monitors that stuff. Why?"

"I think Nine will be with them, wherever they are."

"Hopefully, they won't be crispy. Things are getting bad here. Real bad." Mike never admitted when things were getting shitty, so they must be beyond shitty and descending into fucktacular.

"What can I do to help?" she said.

"You've already been a big help with the tip on Nine's possible whereabouts. If you can, I think you should touch base with Maria. She may be able to round up some folks from the reservation who can help look for your dad, too."

"I will. Thanks." She would speak with Maria, after

she checked in with Lev. She'd left Lev babysitting the mirror in his oven with some hastily scribbled instructions. Hopefully, he hadn't gotten too curious and was tempted to peek and let out all the air in the oven. She told herself that the man had built a homunculus. He could handle a little melted glass.

Mike gave Petra his sat phone number. "And Petra?"

"Yeah?"

"You and Gabe and Sig keep tabs on each other. Nobody else gets to go missing, okay?"

"I promise. Scout's honor. Be careful out there with the fire, will you?"

There was soft, resigned laughter. "Honestly . . . we're gonna have to fall back again. If we don't get a change in wind or rain, this thing's gonna get outside of the park, and then it'll be hell."

Mike hung up, and Petra stared at her phone. Things just kept getting worse.

She turned to Gabe, but he was staring into his palm with narrowed eyes.

"What's wrong?" she asked.

Gabe opened his hand to show her Lascaris's pocket watch. The hands were moving, and it was keeping the current time.

Her brow wrinkled. "What does it mean?"

Gabe's expression was hard. "If I were a betting man, I'd bet that Lascaris has returned."

THE FIRE WAS gathering strength. She could see it, in that red line roiling like a snake on the dark horizon. She could hear it, in the distant roar like thunder, and smell the acrid burning from miles away.

Nine stayed upwind of the fire, keeping north and moving east. She hoped to walk around the fire, threading through the valleys of this region, going east, and then find her way back to the reservation. Traveling as crows fly, she could move more directly than Maria's original route, which had made a near-complete circle around the park. Nine had a good sense of direction and a map in her pocket; she was certain she could find her way back home in a day or so.

Her mouth turned upward at that. Funny how she thought of Maria's house as home now. She glanced back at the distant mountain. Maybe she had two of them, and that was all right, for now. Until she figured out how to get back to the pack for good.

The farther away she moved, the more leaden she felt at leaving the pack. She wanted to stay, to sleep in that pile of fur and cold noses for the rest of her life. Perhaps she could go back if she provisioned properly. Maybe someday. Hope flared in her. She had enough accumulated knowledge, enough resourcefulness to survive anywhere. She knew that she couldn't physically keep up with the pack as a woman. But perhaps it would be enough just to live in their home territory, to see them once in a while from a distance and know that they were safe.

She nodded to herself. It would take some planning. But she could do it. She could gather her equipment and be settled there before winter set in. Maria would understand. The dogs she worked with in her volunteer job at the animal shelter would understand. So would Petra and her husband, the Raven King. They all would. Maria would be furious at her taking off into the fire, but Nine knew that she wouldn't stay angry. Maria understood that Nine was always part of her pack. Try as she might to deny it, Maria knew Nine didn't belong there, amongst humans.

Resolved, she walked through forests and fields, over dry creek beds. She skirted the edges of some angry mud pots spewing steam. She saw no other humans and few animals as she made her way. She consulted her map, and knew that she was moving beyond the bounds of the park. She crossed two empty roads and moved to lower land, to a dense forest. She would have to cross this, two more roads, and then it would be a straight shot to the road leading to the reservation from there.

She drank the last bit of melted snow from the canteen in her pack, and she found herself in the thickest part of the forest. It seemed that no light could penetrate here. The leaves did not whisper and shudder in the breeze as forest trees usually did, that aural shimmering of summer. This place was still. Dead.

She crossed a dry creek bed, a chill trickling down her sweaty spine. This place was haunted. She could feel it. Something was here, and she wanted no part of it. She quickened her pace, hoping to escape the notice of whatever dark spirit inhabited this forest.

A black toad, the size of an apple, skittered across her path. Against her every instinct to flee, Nine followed it through the thick underbrush. A toad had brought a message to her before, warning her about the phoenix. Perhaps this toad had something to do with the Toad God. She followed the toad until she lost it in the dark vegetation.

She called softly for it, and something sighed. She spun on her heel, reaching to her waist for her knife. The sighing came from a ring of sandstone.

A well.

A voice rasped from the depths of the well: "You have nothing to fear from me."

She sucked in her breath. She knew that voice. It had been centuries since she'd heard it, but she knew it. "Who are you?"

"I am Pigin, the god of this place."

"Are you also the God of Death, the god who fought the phoenix, long ago?"

A sigh echoed. "The same. I thought no one remembered."

There was no point in lying to a god. "I was there."

"Then you know. You know that the phoenix has returned."

"Yes." And for the first time since she approached the phoenix in the field, she had hope. "And will you fight it once again?"

The voice was silent for a long time before it spoke again. "I do not have a choice. The phoenix will find me. It remembers, too, you see."

Nine shuddered.

"Come closer, to the well. Let me look at you."

Nine stepped toward the well. She peered into it cautiously. In the damp darkness, an ungodly stench emanated, the smell of something long decomposed. Something down there moved.

"You remind me of the shaman from long ago who gave herself to the phoenix." The god's voice was soft, like the sound of rotten leaves turning over. "Your eyes are like hers, and the shape of your hands."

Nine bowed her head. "I have none of the power she did. I offered myself to the phoenix, and it rejected me."

Water sloshed, as if something below were moving to get a better view of her. "You have some of her power. But you have been cursed, I see, little wolf. I have never seen a wolf that walks on two legs." It spoke in her own language now. She was startled to hear it spoken aloud.

She answered in her language, and it felt free and loose on her tongue. She had not spoken it in hundreds of years. "How do you know me and my language? And what do you know of my curse?"

"I see into the souls of all who gaze into my well, little wolf, and learn their tongues. I see into their souls and I see what they most desire. You see, I grant wishes from the bottom of this well."

Nine took a half step back. She'd been around the magical block long enough to know that the granting of wishes was treacherous business. But the hope was there. So she asked, "You grant wishes? What kind of wishes?"

"Yes. I can grant you almost anything you ask for. I can grant riches, love, and long life."

Nine shrugged. None of these things mattered to her. "I would wish the phoenix back asleep."

"I intend to do that . . . and that task may be frankly beyond my power. It took me many, many years to recover from that fight. But fight we must, as we always have. Purification and corruption are forever at war."

"Then there is nothing you can give me," Nine said, turning her face to the dark road.

And then the god said: "But I could change you back into a wolf."

She froze. She had searched for a solution to this, prayed on it, made offerings to the Eye of the World. She had searched the limits of her knowledge and the spirit world for a solution, a cure to her current shape. She had consulted with the Raven King and Petra's father, to no avail. And now Pigin said that *he* could do it.

"Watch," the toad said.

Her attention was snagged by a small red-sided garter snake crawling up to the lip of the sandstone well, like a red and yellow ribbon on the dingy stone. Its tongue flickered out at Nine, curious. It was no longer than her forearm, easy prey for larger creatures, and likely searching out bugs to eat.

The snake's tongue snapped back into its mouth. It began to writhe, flipping and curling in on itself, as if it had been flung on a hot pan. It raced away, trying to flee . . .

. . . and melted into the shape of a rat. The rat squeaked, twitching, and fled away into the undergrowth.

"You doubt me now, little wolf?"

Nine turned her gaze back to the well. The god could do what he said. Her heart hammered in her chest. If he could turn her into a wolf again, she could run back, back the way she'd come, and rejoin the pack . . .

She gazed down at the black murkiness at the bottom of the well. "What's the price for such a spell? And does the spell fade? It is a true changing of shape, yes, and not an illusion?" Her questions tumbled over each other.

There was a small splash from below and a delighted-sounding laugh. "You are a cagey negotiator, little wolf. Like the shaman from long ago. You would be a wolf forever, in flesh and blood. But there is indeed a cost. The price for the spell is blood and bone, delivered to this well."

"Blood and bone?" she echoed.

"Yes. In order to fight the phoenix, I require bones and blood, freely given to me, to work my magic. I have learned a few new tricks since we last met, and these are the ingredients of my spells."

Nine chewed on her thumbnail. She considered the weight of the bargain. She knew of the magic of blood and bones, from her father. And she knew that the more unusual the bones and the rarer the blood, the stronger the magic. Surely there was some heinous criminal she could lure here, some horrible person who deserved to die at the bottom of Pigin's well? There was no shortage of evil people in the world of men. All she would have to do would be push him in, and her former life would be restored to her. She thought of the people who left their animals abused and neglected at the animal shelter where she worked. She thought of evil men from generations of evil blood, men like Owen Rutherford. She thought of the men who encroached upon the small bit of land remaining to Maria's tribe, flinging papers and shouting about wanting to drill for oil. She could do great good in the world of men by pushing one down a well.

Nine paced around the perimeter of the well, clockwise and then turning to go counterclockwise. Yearning swelled in her chest. She needed to be with the pack. And she was unencumbered by human definitions of right and wrong . . .

. . . or was she? Something prickled in her throat. Something that felt like sadness and regret and fear and hope. It was a sticky mess of something that tasted warm and metallic, like a coin on her tongue. Maria had taken her in without a thought after Petra had found her. She'd been cared for like she was family. The people on the reservation had been kind to her, asking no questions and giving her meaningful work. She didn't have the pack, not the way she had them before; she could only peek in on them through the Eye. But she did have sisterhood. A sisterhood that had sunk deeply into her skin, and had changed her. But how deeply had those changes sunk in? Did they reach the marrow, where the atavistic feelings of love and hate and belonging and exile were lodged?

These questions warred within herself as she stared down the well. The blackness mirrored the choice before her, and she'd never wanted something so badly.

With a deep breath, she stood straight, nodding. "I, Nine of the wolves, accept the offer that you, Pigin, God of Death, have offered to me. Bones and blood to change me back into a wolf, exactly as I was before I was changed to a woman."

Nine reached up to her neck and untied Maria's necklace, feeling a deep stab of guilt in her gut. She held the warm beads in her hands and then dangled them over the well. Taking a deep breath, she let them go into the dark.

She didn't hear them hit bottom. Instead, she heard Pigin sigh: "Beautiful. The buffalo . . . it has been so long since I've tasted buffalo. I can hear the thunder in their bones, still."

Nine pulled her knife from her waist and drew the blade across her palm. She held her fist over the well, letting the dark fluid drip into the well for some minutes. When she felt dizzy, she closed her hand and bound it up with her bandanna.

Pigin rumbled. "Magical blood . . . so rare and potent. I can taste your father's magic in it. And yours."

Nine looked into the darkness at the bottom of the well. "I hope these offerings please you."

"They do. They do."

Doubt welled up within her, then. She was going to lose her human family: Maria, Petra, the Raven King, Mike, and all the rest. She would likely never see Coyote again in his current form. She would be unable to continue her work with the animal shelter, and without her help, dogs and cats would suffer. And she would be unable to watch over the pack from the Eye of the World, to protect them with the power of a mortal woman.

And the people she loved would never know what had happened to her. They would think the fire had taken her. And they would feel sorrow, and guilt, and all the roiling emotions that came with being unable to say goodbye.

What had she done?

The black ooze below her churned and spat something up. Nine caught it in her hands and drew the small object to her waist. Opening her fingers, she saw that it was a round, smooth piece of obsidian the size of a coin.

"What's this?" she asked softly, uncertain how long she'd be able to muster a human voice.

"To return to your previous shape, swallow the stone. I will not lie to you—as you and I have some history together, and you remind me very much of the shaman who gave herself to the phoenix many years before—your transformation will be a painful process. You will feel each bone break and every inch of your skin tear. Every muscle fiber will split apart and be remade, little wolf. You will suffer greatly, and you may not survive it. But if you do, you will arise on four legs to rejoin your pack."

Nine clasped the stone to her chest. The God of Death had given her a boon. He had given her the truth, *and* a choice. "Thank you. You are both kind and powerful."

There was a snort from the water. "I am neither of those things. I am darkness and rot, tricksy and enjoying of suffering. But you have given me something I need, tools to fight the phoenix. I am appreciative of those gifts. And . . ." The voice grew softer. "You brought me back a memory."

"I can help you fight the phoenix," Nine began. "I can bring bones . . ."

"No. Do not return here. Do not tell anyone that you have seen me. Go and live, beyond the touch of death."

She kissed her fingertips and pressed them to the stone. "Thank you."

She walked away, swearing to herself that she

would never return. She had the sense of having walked into a moment of sentimental weakness that the God of Death experienced. And that that interaction could never be repeated without danger to her life.

She walked, for miles and miles, along deserted roads and through fields. It was many hours into night by the time she reached Maria's house. The front porch light was on, with insects dancing around it. She knocked quietly on the door, and it opened immediately.

Wordlessly, Maria drew her inside and wrapped her in a hug. Pearl wound around her ankles. Petra piled into the hug, and Coyote's cold nose began vigorously inspecting her clothes. Behind them, the Raven King watched, a look of relief on his face.

Whatever she was, wolf or woman, she was wanted here. As a wolf, she had a pack. As a human, she had another.

This was, here and now, home.

CHAPTER 15

The White Witch's Internet Parlor

Hopefully, this run of shitty luck was temporary.

Owen had gotten stuck in traffic on the way home to the Rutherford Ranch, and his radiator overheated. He topped it off with some bottled water and limped it to the gas station for more antifreeze. When he went to pay at the counter, he discovered that the bank had put a block on his credit card. He spent twenty minutes on hold with a bank call center three states away to get the block lifted. Apparently, someone had gotten hold of his credit card number and bought an anatomically correct sex doll from Japan, to the tune of six thousand dollars. Owen reassured the bank that the sex doll was not his. They promised to issue him a new card, but he was SOL for the time being.

Owen dug around in his glove box for an extra

twenty-dollar bill that he kept there for emergencies and a handful of change in the console. He paid for the antifreeze and got the radiator filled back up, only to discover that his left headlamp was out. He swore colorfully and went back inside with the remainder of his cash to buy a carton of ice cream, a frozen pizza, and a six-pack of beer, the dinner of champions. They were out of beer, and he was forced to make do with a bottle of rotgut red wine with a thick layer of dust on the bottle.

When he got home, he discovered that the wine had turned to vinegar and the ice cream had been melted and then refrozen, so he pitched both of them and hoped for better luck with the pizza. He turned on the oven, only to discover that the knob made a clicking sound, but no gas flame lit. He shut off the knob and muttered to himself, going to the basement to check and make sure that there was a pilot light going in the water heater. The pilot light was out. No gas. He went outside to the propane tank. It was empty.

He called the propane company. Turned out, they hadn't received payment for last month's delivery. And Owen couldn't give them a valid credit card over the phone. He hung up in frustration, deciding that he could make do with cold military showers until he got this shit figured out.

Fuck cold showers. The water in the hot water heater would likely only keep warm for a few hours. He decided to spend it all in one shot. He headed into the bathroom, slammed the door, and shucked out of his uniform. He yanked open the frosted glass door to the shower enclosure and began to step in . . .

. . . but he lurched back, grasping the swinging door to balance himself.

"Holy shit," he breathed.

The bottom of the shower stall was covered in black toads, hundreds of them. There were so many that they obscured the Carrera marble floor, coating it in a seething, bumpy mass. The toads twisted to look at him, as one, opened their mouths, and hissed.

He banged the shower door shut, rattling the glass. Snatching up his robe and tugging it around him with his good hand, he scanned the floor. How had they gotten in there? How had Pigin figured out where he lived? Did toads really hiss? Weren't toads poisonous? What the fuck was happening?

Owen cast around the bathroom for a weapon. The most fearsome tool he could find was a toilet brush. Gripping it tightly, he advanced on the door and wrenched it open.

The toads had disappeared. All but one of them. It slowly hopped into the loosened shower drain and disappeared.

Shit. Owen shoved the shower drain cover back in place with the toilet brush. For good measure, he went to the bedroom, grabbed a hideous sculpture of a cowboy that Sal had made, and set the heavy tchotchke on the drain. There. Even if the little bastards were able to unscrew the drain plate, they wouldn't be able to move that piece of shitty art. Hopefully.

Owen took a shower in the first-floor bathroom instead, after ensuring that the floor drain was tightly screwed in place. He extracted four minutes' worth of hot water from the water heater before it turned cold. He didn't dare sit down to take a shit in the toilet, though. He was too rattled. He dressed in sweats and returned to the kitchen.

He stuffed the pizza into the microwave and punched the power button. The turntable got hung up with the pizza crust overhanging the edge of the plate, but he decided to ignore the irritating clunking sound while he went through his mail. There was a cease-and-desist letter from an attorney there, concerning one of the outer fields of the ranch. The nearby reservation was stating that the Rutherford Ranch fences were encroaching upon their land, and he needed to move them.

Owen pinched the bridge of his nose. His cousin, Sal Rutherford, had been a pitch-perfect asshole where land borders came into play. Owen hadn't developed any further interest in exploring the back forty since his run-in with the carnivorous mermaid, so the fence must have been established before Owen took control of the property. Not that it made any difference. It was his land, and his problem.

He decided that the easiest thing to do would be to hire some guys and move the damn fence. Of course, seasonal work would cost him—he didn't have the slave labor Sal had with the Hanged Men. He was betting that was gonna be a few thousand dollars he could set fire to.

His mustache twitched. He smelled something burning. He turned to the microwave to find his pizza curled and brown, with the cheese separating. He burned himself getting the damn thing out of the microwave. He decided that he was going to consume this motherfucker anyway, out of pure spite. He had nothing else in the house to eat except for a box of stale cereal and a carton of curdled milk. He savagely cut into the pizza and slapped three slices onto a plate and stomped into the living room. He plunked down on the leather couch and clicked on the TV.

His favorite show, a sci-fi drama about alien conspiracies, had been preempted by a baseball game that was running late due to a rain delay. He groaned and leaned back into the couch cushions and stared at the vaulted ceiling. He had really been looking forward to seeing something even more implausible than his daily life to make himself feel better.

"Hey." Anna sat on the back of the couch and peered down into Owen's face.

"Hey," he said. "I have had a colossal run of bad luck. At least, I hope it's bad luck, and that the Toad God didn't curse me. But he sent his little buddies to hang out in the shower. So I'm pretty sure I'm cursed."

"You believe in curses?"

"Sure. Why not?" He'd seen weirder shit.

Anna made a face and glanced at the television. "Are you gonna watch that?"

"No. No, I am not gonna watch that."

"Can I watch the princess movie?"

"Sure. You can totally watch the princess movie."

Owen climbed off the couch and pawed through the stack of DVDs underneath the massive flat-screen television. He hadn't bought that monstrosity; he'd inherited it from Sal. He supposed it was okay for movies, but it often gave him a headache. Anna seemed to enjoy it, though.

He had more than twenty DVDs of kids' films by

now. There were animated ones about dragons, ponies, and fairies. There was a good collection of nature videos, too. Owen screened those first to make sure that there were no horrifying moments of cute critters getting eaten. Anna liked otters and penguins the best. At some point, he intended to take her on a trip to a zoo that had them for real, but he hadn't seemed to find the time. He felt guilty about that.

He found the princess DVD and put it into the player. Anna crawled forward on the throw rug and got within two feet of the television, her head planted in her fists. Owen never bothered to nag her about ruining her vision by sitting too close. He guessed it didn't really matter.

Owen retreated to his office. Once Sal's office, it was overtaken by faux leather book wallpaper and hunting trophies. Owen's laptop computer was open on the desk, and he booted it up, gnawing on the burned cardboard pizza. He started googling "curses."

It was as if the internet threw up every superstition known to man. Owen sifted through pages of information on how to hire a witch or exorcist to get his mojo clear, which candles to burn, and how to get right with Jesus. There were pages of holy water to buy and instructions on how to burn sage. He sat back in the chair. On impulse, he checked the balance of his PayPal account. He had one hundred eighty-five dollars and thirty-two cents. Enough for a consultation with a so-called white witch available 24–7. He rubbed his mustache. The witch was in West Virginia, about as far away from Wyoming as one could get. And anonymity was guaranteed.

What the hell. It wasn't any weirder than consulting a priest, right? Wasn't like a priest was gonna answer his call after hours. Owen punched some buttons, cleared out his PayPal account, and waited for the witch to call him.

In the meantime, he went to the kitchen and rooted around until he found some dried-out sage leaves that were little more than skeletons. He put them in an ashtray and lit them with his lighter. He walked around the house with the burning sage, fanning the smoke toward himself.

Anna looked up at him. "Really?"

"Hey, it can't hurt."

But, of course, it did hurt. He sneezed, spewing a sage leaf onto the carpet. It immediately caught fire, and Owen stomped it out. When he was finished, a black mark remained on the rug. He had no idea how much Sal had paid for the rug, but it looked old and expensive.

Anna glanced at him with narrowed eyes. He took the ashtray back to the kitchen and ran water into it. The way things were going, it was not improbable that he could manage to set the house on fire.

He heard chiming from his computer. Someone was calling him. He skidded back into his office to accept a call from the white witch.

An image of a forty-something woman with long blond hair greeted him. Owen's knee-jerk reaction was that she was pretty cute. Her eyes were bright blue, and she wore a tank top with a crystal pendant glittering at her throat. A cat walked across her desk and peered into the camera at Owen.

"Hey," Owen said, trying to sound casual. Or

as casual as a man could be who might have been hexed by a bloodthirsty Toad God.

"Hi," the woman said. "I'm Nora. And this is Percival. I got your message that you were having some issues with bad luck."

"You're the witch?"

She laughed. "You were expecting Elvira?"

"Yeah. I guess. I'm not really into this stuff."

Nora leaned forward, toward the camera. "Most people aren't. Tell me about your run of luck."

"Well, I think I might have picked up a curse," he blurted. This was feeling more awkward when he said it aloud. "I ran into . . . something . . . in the woods. And bad luck has followed me home."

"You ran into something?"

"Yeah. I'm not sure what it was. But it was filthy, it stank, and it spoke."

Nora thoughtfully shuffled a deck of cards, while Percival showed his ass to the camera. "Please ignore Percival's expressiveness."

"No offense taken."

"Okay. Did this entity ask you for something?"

"It did. But I'd rather not say." Owen felt ridiculous. He didn't want to have this on video somewhere.

Nora nodded. She shuffled the cards again and spread them out before her. She frowned at them. Percival batted at them. "Owen, I think you have a problem," she said.

"I have several. But this thing . . . I don't know if it's real. Or if I'm crazy. And if it is real, I don't know what to do about it."

"You're not crazy." Nora lifted up a card showing two naked people. "The spirit you met offered you a choice. Neither option will serve you well." She showed him a card with the Grim Reaper on it, turned upside down, and another one depicting lightning striking a tower. She gazed at the other cards, picking up one that depicted a heart pierced by three swords and then one showing a woman sitting up in bed with swords hanging over her. "He has, indeed, placed a curse on you. One that will be difficult to remove."

Owen was feeling like this conversation was going downhill. "Let me guess—it's gonna cost me a lot to remove it."

She looked up at him. "No. There is nothing I can do to clear it, Owen." She leaned forward. "This is in your hands. I suspect the thing you have met is not human, nor was it ever. You have fallen into its web, and it is more powerful than you are."

"Great. What do I do?" It suggested to him that she might be on the up-and-up if she didn't want his money.

"You have some scores to settle. Settle those. Do your reckoning." She lifted a card that was illustrated with an angel blowing a trumpet and one that showed a woman on a throne holding a sword and scales. Percival chewed on the corner of the card depicting the throned woman. "That's the only way through for you. Create justice. Does this make sense?"

"Yeah," he said. "It does."

"Good luck, Owen," she said, and then ended the call.

Owen frowned at the empty screen. He felt like

this had been a colossal waste of money. He'd gotten what . . . fifteen minutes with a GoogleWitch confirming his own fears, and no solution? He felt like a chump, and he was more than a little embarrassed by it.

He ought to ask Gabriel. Gabriel knew magic, and likely knew exactly what kind of monster this was. But Owen couldn't ask him. Owen had betrayed Gabriel in a most spectacular way, handing him over to an old adversary to torture. It had been a total moral failure on Owen's part, and he realized it fully, well after the fact. He wanted to believe that he'd been ensorcelled, but that was only part of it. He had been driven by an irresistible will to power, and it cost him his hand. Since then, he'd left Gabriel and the Tree of Life alone. He knew that Gabe would sooner spit on him than help him.

And there was no way of making that situation right. Owen had contemplated it. But what could he do for an immortal man? What could he do to make right what generations of Rutherfords had made wrong?

Owen was not living right. He knew that it was as simple as that. He'd taken some steps to rectify this that he'd told no one about, not even his mother. But he knew that there was nothing he could really do to balance the scales in his life.

His email dinged, and Owen opened it. It was a refund of his money from Nora, the GoogleWitch. A note on the transaction said: "Do the right thing."

He might not ever be able to make things right for Gabe; maybe there was something he could do for Anna.

He came back into the living room and stretched out on the rug beside Anna, copying her posture of lying on his belly with head in hands. This was Anna's favorite part of the movie, with lots of singing and dancing and a friendly dragon that finally found his voice. Eventually, the dragon flew away with the princess, leaving the asshat prince in the dust, and the credits rolled.

"I like a happy ending," Anna said.

"I do, too," Owen said. "Which is why I want one for you."

She rested her head on her arms and looked at him. "You think that if I went into the light, I would be happy?"

"Yeah. I do. I don't see how you could be happy here, with all this unfinished business."

She made a face. "I'm happier now than I was with my parents."

"I'm sorry," Owen said. That hurt him. To think that a little girl would rather be following a jerk like him around than at home with her own parents—that was bad.

"Don't be," she said. "I love my mom and dad, and all. My mom was really nice, but she was always working. She tried hard, I know. But she was so tired. My dad . . . my dad really wasn't all there, you know?"

Owen nodded, tight-lipped. He'd resolved never to speak badly of Anna's parents to her. By his own estimation, her father was a drugged-out loser of the worst kind. Her mother was well-meaning, but had failed to protect her child, instead placing her marriage ahead of her daughter's welfare. Anna had never asked what happened to her parents, and Owen had never told her that they'd died in a murder-suicide.

"I worry that they might be waiting for me ... after," she said in a very small voice.

She must have sensed they were dead. *Shit.* "Anna. Nobody will hurt you. If your parents are in heaven, then they are sober and whole and will care for you the way they should have. If they're not there, then there will be other people who will take care of you. Other kids to play with. People who will give you ice cream and watch princess movies with you." He said it so fervently that he honestly believed it, even if only for a moment.

"You promise?" she said.

"I promise," he said.

She sighed and put her chin on the carpet. "I'm gonna miss you, Owen."

"I will miss you, too," he said. "But trust me on this, okay?"

She nodded. "I trust you."

It was the only time anyone had ever said that to Owen, and it was like a punch to the gut. Owen knew that he was not a good man. But maybe he could do one good thing.

"You said you had family around here?"

Molly sounded skeptical. The old woman peered over the wheel of the vehicle, staring into the shifting pools of light cast by the headlamps on the road. Her mouth turned down, and it seemed as if she was gnawing on something that bothered her.

The old woman hadn't stopped yammering to Lascaris in the whole time she'd been driving. And she drove very, very quickly—almost twenty-five miles an hour! The whole time Lascaris watched as she operated the horseless carriage, how her feet pressed the pedals and her hands pulled the wheel. While she drove, she droned endlessly about her grandchildren, her late husband, and the developers who were trying to buy her land. Her grandchildren lived on the East Coast. Her late husband had been a letter carrier. And the developers who wanted to buy her land wanted to build a truck stop. Lascaris gleaned that this was something like a way station in his former life. Which Molly wasn't necessarily opposed to, but she felt they could come up a bit in price.

"I'd have to move my whole operation someplace else. And good internet service is really a bitch to find in these parts," she grumbled.

Lascaris had no idea what she was talking about. He simply nodded politely as she nattered on. He gazed outside at the black night and the stripe of orange on the horizon, like the seething of a forge. The phoenix was out there; he could feel it. He and the phoenix were destined for each other. The phoenix would recognize the magic in him, no matter what fragile shell he wore right now. They would become one, fused, and the Great Work of alchemy would finally be complete. He would have immortality and all the power he needed to protect it.

"I guess I could go to satellite, but that's an arm and a leg. I don't know about the reliability, either. I hear it goes down every time it rains. I guess I could do a few tests, but I'm not optimistic. Cryptocurrency mining requires one hundred percent uptime and massive bandwidth for the farm."

"This cryptocurrency mining and the farm . . . what exactly are you mining?"

"Nothing visible. Cryptocurrency is essentially a currency that isn't backed by a government or bank, that is traded for goods and services among individuals."

"Like gold." Lascaris knew quite a bit about gold.

"Yes. Like gold, only there isn't a physical aspect to it. There are digital records of currency changing hands from person to person. Blocks of data are added to a blockchain by solving mathematical equations, which is what I do with mining."

Lascaris's brow wrinkled. "It sounds like conjuring something from nothing." Also a subject that he knew something about. He'd spent years conjuring gold from rocks and supporting the economy of Temperance from those magical transactions.

She laughed. "Kind of. My kids think that I'm defrauding the government. I'm not, but they still think I'm shady because I'm not dealing with paper money. But they sure like those vacations to theme parks."

"Everyone likes what gold buys."

"Yep. Well, my one daughter-in-law sure doesn't. She sent my checks back when she found out. She's on her high horse about how cryptocurrencies aid and abet human trafficking, since the money is pretty anonymous."

Lascaris glanced at her.

"Well, she's vegan, too. She has an overdeveloped conscience."

Lascaris sympathized with the old woman with her loudly patterned clothing and her sharklike false teeth. Innovators always were accused of moral failings, and sometimes it did take some imagination to conjure gold from stones. In another era, if he had more time, he probably would have regarded her with amusement and not impatience. He might even have asked her to teach him the magic that turned air into money.

Molly muttered a curse, and began to slow the carriage, peering ahead at flashing lights on the road. "Looks like this is the end of the line."

Lascaris squinted ahead. Black carriages festooned with blue and red lights blocked their path. A red carriage that had been driving ahead of them turned around when it reached the lights and came back the way they'd come.

Molly stopped before the lit-up carriages. A man dressed in black with a shiny badge and a black hat leaned down to the window, and Molly rolled it down. Lascaris felt his gut twisting. This man had the mien of a lawman, and that was the same, no matter what century he found himself in.

"Is there a problem, Officer?" Molly's voice had gone very quiet and fragile sounding. Her posture had slumped forward, and she seemed to generate an illusion of fragility.

"I'm sorry, ma'am," the lawman said. "But this road is closed on account of the fire. We'll have to have you turn around and go back the way you came."

Molly pursed her lips and glanced at Lascaris. "Sorry, fella."

Lascaris sucked in his breath.

Molly spoke to the lawman and gestured to her passenger. "I think this guy got lost from the nursing home. Said they were mean to him and wanted to go home to his daughter. Can you gentlemen call her for him, please?"

A bright light shone into Lascaris's face, and he could see nothing.

"Sir, I'm going to need you to step out of the vehicle," the lawman said, his voice ringing with authority and a bit of alarm.

Lascaris sighed. This wasn't going to go easy, was it?

Lascaris scooted over to the driver's side, beside Molly. He reached over her for the door latch and opened the door. The lawman was shouting.

Lascaris laid the Touch of Death on Molly.

She began to decompose before Lascaris shoved her from the car. Muck splashed onto the black road, and a set of fake teeth bounced across the yellow stripe.

The lawman yelled and fired, cracking the glass on the front of the carriage. Another came running from his own vehicle.

Lascaris grabbed the wheel and stomped on the right pedal. The carriage lurched forward in a gallop, gained a bit of speed, and smashed into the lit-up carriages parked nose-to-nose on the road. Metal shrieked, and Molly's big blue vehicle rammed through the blockade, sending the two black carriages skidding to the edge of the road.

Lascaris grinned. He stomped on the right pedal,

as hard as he could. To his delight, the carriage surged forward with terrifying speed. Bullets zinged past him but didn't strike him.

This was, indeed, the end of the line for Molly and her invisible mine. But it was only the beginning of the road for the Alchemist of Temperance.

CHAPTER 16

Call and Answer

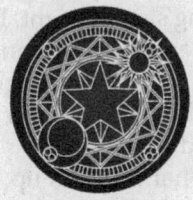

Nine had returned, and the nest was full again.

Maria had sent Nine to the bathroom immediately to bathe, declaring that she smelled like wet dog. While Gabe threw her clothes in the washing machine, Petra began making sandwiches and Maria set to brewing tea. Relief was palpable in the line of her friend's shoulders as she filled the teakettle.

"She's back," Maria whispered. "I was so afraid she wouldn't come back."

Petra hugged her friend. "She's okay. She's okay."

Maria sniffled and said: "Shit. We should call Mike."

"I'll do it." She turned over the making of sandwiches to Gabe. Sig immediately moved his attention away from Petra, and both Pearl and the coyote sat on the kitchen floor, gazing up at her husband with rapt adoration.

She dialed Mike's sat phone on Maria's landline. It took several rings for him to pick up, and she was afraid that she might be disturbing what little sleep the man could grab in the back of his Jeep.

"This is Hollander," he finally said.

"It's Petra. I wanted to let you know that Nine is here. At Maria's."

Mike blew out a staticky breath on the other end. "At least something's going right. Is she okay?"

"Yeah. She's fine. Just bumps and scrapes."

"What the hell was she doing? We tracked the wolves and sent the helo out over their position on Eagle Peak, but didn't see her."

"Don't know what she was up to." That was the truth, at least. "But she's safe."

"We're running out of resources . . . I was worried that we wouldn't be able to send anyone out on horseback or on ATV to look for her. It's been pretty much chaos here."

"What can we do?"

"Not anything, really. We keep getting pushed back, and the fire is creeping out of the park on the southeast edge. We have no control. Smaller fires keep popping up and joining the main fire. The National Guard is here, so hopefully, they'll have some ideas."

"Shit. Man, I'm sorry."

"Hey, did the sheriff's office get in touch with you about your dad?"

"No. Did they find him?" Her heart thudded in her throat, and she white-knuckled the phone.

"Dammit. They should have told you. There was an incident at one of the checkpoints leading into the park. Your dad was in a car with an older woman who died. I'm not clear on the details, since the deputies are being tight-lipped. What I do know is that they said your dad took the wheel and busted through the vehicle barricade into the park."

"Shit." She rubbed her forehead, and her heart ached for the old woman. What was her father thinking? "I swear to God, I'll show up on Owen Rutherford's doorstep and . . ."

"I tried to call him and got voice mail. None of his deputies can get hold of him, either. They have no idea where he is. Hopefully, he's sleeping off a hangover in the back of a bar somewhere, but don't count on getting any answers from Owen. His deputies have circled the wagons and are saying nothing. Whatever he's up to, it's not likely to be anything good."

"Are they even looking for him?" She had mixed feelings about this. If they were looking for her dad and found him, it wouldn't be good for her dad. Especially if he was to blame for two deaths.

"They are. So are we. Haven't seen any sign of the car, but it's just a matter of time. He's one old dude with a turquoise Buick. He can't hide forever."

Unless he gets barbecued. Petra didn't say it aloud. She thanked Mike, got some more details about her dad's last known position, and hung up. She stared at the phone after it went silent, wondering if the next call she received would be someone notifying her that her father was dead.

She dialed the bar. Lev picked up on the third ring: "Compostela."

"Lev, it's Petra. How's our piece of glass?"

"Haven't looked at it. I got it up to the maximum heat, let it cook like you said, and then dropped it back to eight hundred fifty. I cut the gas and it's cooling."

"Thanks. I really appreciate you taking this science project over. I owe you." *Again.* At the rate she was going, she'd be owing Lev well into the next lifetime and the one after that.

"It's actually been pretty interesting," Lev said. "I've always been kind of curious about glass, and it makes me think I might be able to use the pizza oven for more than pies. I've got a couple of cracked panes of stained glass I'd like to restore." She could almost hear the wheels turning in his head before he changed the subject. "Did you find your dad yet?"

"No. I think he's in serious trouble. And I think . . . he may have killed at least two people."

There were a couple of beats of silence on the other end. "You'll catch him. Even though he's an alchemist, he's still an old man. He's got to wind down sometime."

"Well, he's not our only problem." She told him about Lascaris and the watch.

Lev was silent on his end.

"Lev?"

"I'll keep an eye on the glass until you get back." Lev's voice was tight. "Watch your backs."

And he hung up on her.

Gabe reached for her, touching her elbow. "Is everything okay?"

"I have to go look for my dad," she said, her throat closing. "My dad is out there. Sounds like he's killed another person, and now he's got a car." Her father might be a murderer. She'd thought him capable of many thoughtless and self-centered things over the years, but she never thought it would come to this. It had to be his illness. It couldn't really be him. Whatever was going on with him, she had to find him, protect him. If Lascaris was roaming about . . .

"If he's got wheels, he could be anywhere," Maria said, handing her a cup of tea.

"I have to look for him anyway." She felt like she was doing nothing, and time was slipping through her fingers. She set the cup down on the table and reached for her boots.

"I will look for him," Gabe said quietly. "I'll look for him and for Lascaris and then I'll go back to the tree."

She stopped breathing for a moment. The Lunaria. She had shoved the tree into the back of her thoughts, and exhuming it now caused her to wince. "It's not safe to go back to the tree."

"It's not safe for *you*. It won't hurt me. I'm all it has." Gabe leaned down and kissed her on the forehead.

"I'll look from the ground," she resolved. "I'll . . ."

Gabe shook his head. "Lascaris may be out there. Stay here until I get back. We will find him, but with night coming, there's only so much we can do."

Her throat tightened, and she promised herself that she would not cry.

There was a knock at the door. Maria moved to answer it.

A group of men and women stood on the porch, dressed in jeans, T-shirts, hats, and hiking boots. Pearl chirped and greeted them with her tail waving in happiness. The middle-aged woman in the center of the group picked up Pearl and began to scratch her ears. These were clearly friends of Maria's.

"You came," Maria breathed.

"Of course we did." The woman holding Pearl kissed Maria's cheek, and she ushered the group in.

Maria made quick introductions. "Petra, Gabe, this is Vicki. And these are Vicki's children, Luke, Basil, Willow, and Liz. They're the best trackers and hunters I know."

"Well," said Vicki with a self-deprecating smile. "My grandparents were better, but we do what we can."

"Nine has been found," Maria said. "But Petra's father is still missing."

Petra's heart swelled. Complete strangers were willing to help her. With a quavering voice, she told them what she could while she and Maria handed out sandwiches and passed out tea. The group listened closely from the couch and kitchen chairs. Vicki asked questions and made notations on a map.

"Okay. We have a good idea where he was last seen. We'll start in that area."

"I am worried that he's violent," Petra admitted. "A nurse is dead, and I don't know what happened with the woman who died, but I assume the worst."

"We will do our best not to harm him," Vicki's son Basil said from the couch. He was built like a linebacker, but was wearing a blissed-out Pearl over his shoulders like a scarf. Pearl batted lazily at his sunglasses cord. "Liz has a Taser if we need it. It's not ideal, but we'll get him under control as gently as possible."

Liz, a woman in her early thirties with short raven hair, nodded. As she did, her multiple-pierced ears glittered. "We'll be gentle. We promise."

"I don't want anyone else to get hurt," Petra said. "Don't do anything that would endanger yourselves. If you find him, call me, and I'll come get him." She couldn't deal with anything more on her conscience.

"But then he could hurt you," Liz said.

"He won't hurt me," she said with a confidence she didn't truly feel. Curious, she asked, "How do you go about tracking people in the backcountry?" Maybe she could pick up some tips she could apply.

"Oh, we have our ways." Willow, the youngest daughter, grinned and crooked a finger at Petra. She led them out to the driveway to their vehicles, an old pickup truck and a Jeep speckled with dried mud. She gestured to the pickup truck, and Petra peered into the bed.

"Drones? Cool!" Petra grinned at the robotic devices sitting in cardboard boxes, secured to the bed of the truck. They looked like sleeping metal spiders. A charging bank of radios sat beside them.

"Each one has a range of about three and a half miles," Liz said, grinning proudly. "We use them occasionally for work with the reservation EMS. Last year, we used them to find a lost child."

"A boat like the one he's driving will run out of gas sooner or later, and we'll find him. Don't worry," Basil said.

"After this is over, will you teach me to fly one?" Petra gazed at the tiny craft, fascinated. Maybe she could fly one with Gabe's ravens, to see what he saw. And if she could prove that it would be useful in her geological work, maybe she could convince her superiors back on the East Coast to approve it.

"Sure!" said Willow. "We can always use more eyes on the Rutherford Ranch."

Petra's eyes narrowed. "What's Owen up to now?"

"Nothing lately, and that worries us. With the drones, we discovered that Sal pushed the fences back on our land by a quarter mile. If we don't patrol our edges, Owen would have his cattle on Main Street."

"I would love to learn to do that." After all, she spent enough time skulking around in Owen's back forty. The least she could do was take some pictures and keep fence creep in check.

"We'll be in touch." Vicki swapped phone numbers with Petra, just in case cell service was available, and the crew climbed into the Jeep and pickup. They headed away down the dusty road. Seeing them on the case, Petra felt hopeful.

Gabe stood beside her. He drew her into an embrace and kissed her soundly.

"Be careful," she said.

"I will. It's high time that the Lunaria and I had a . . . conversation." He stepped away, gazing up at the twilight sky.

"Gabe?"

"Yes?"

"Do you have, um, clothes back at the tree?" It seemed like an insignificant thing, but she wanted to know if she should drop off laundry.

He grinned at her. "Yes. I have clothes back at the tree."

He kissed her on the cheek. He glanced around

to make sure that none of the neighbors were watching, and dissolved into a riot of black feathers. The birds climbed up into the sky, cawing, blotting out the first solitary star that had begun to burn through the hazy blue.

Petra gazed after them. He had work to do with the tree, and she knew that she couldn't help him. She had her own work to do as well. She picked up his clothes, and Lascaris's pocket watch slipped out of his shirt. She stuffed the pocket watch into her cargo pants and folded Gabe's clothes.

She came back inside the house to find Nine sitting at the kitchen table. Her damp silver hair was flung over her shoulder, and she was devouring a sandwich the size of her head.

Nine paused in gobbling down the sandwich when she saw Petra. "The phoenix," she said. "We tried to stop the phoenix."

"And failed," said Maria, who came to sit beside her. "We offered it everything valuable we had. And Nine offered herself." Her fingers chewed at the bread crusts on her plate. She explained what she'd seen before Nine had slipped away, then glared at Nine.

Nine gazed down at the table. "And I came back without your necklace. I'm so sorry."

"The necklace doesn't matter. What matters is that you ran off without so much as saying goodbye." Hurt rattled in Maria's voice. "I thought you were dead."

"I went to protect the pack. They were cornered by the fire. I couldn't leave them." She reached out for Maria's hand. "I promise that I will never leave without saying goodbye again. I swear."

Maria's brow wrinkled, and it seemed as if Nine was saying something deeply significant that was lost on both her and Petra.

"And when you found them, the wolves knew you?" Petra asked, feeding a piece of her sandwich to Sig.

She nodded. "Yes. They knew me. They must have recognized me from the Eye of the World, somehow. Even though I'm pretty sure I smell different." She wrinkled her nose. "Anyway, we made it to higher elevations. I think they'll be safe from the fire, there. And the hunting is better. Lots of weasels and rabbits." She picked thoughtfully at a tooth with a fork, as if something was stuck there.

Petra didn't ask her if she ate weasel on her walkabout. She didn't dare. There seemed to be more that Nine was about to say, but she changed the subject, seeming to think better of it. Petra didn't press. Nine, like so many of the people and creatures here, had a double life. And it was not up to Petra to pry into it.

"So you'll be going to the Eye tonight to look for your father?" Nine asked instead.

"Yes." Petra took her plate to the sink and rinsed it. "Dad hangs out in the spirit world. It makes sense that I should be able to catch up with him there. And kick his ass," she said under her breath. "Assuming that the Eye cooperates. And that Lascaris isn't on the other side." The Eye was more than capricious with her—going to the water's edge was no guarantee that she'd be granted entrance to the spirit world. Her excursions there were always hit-or-miss. She never knew what—or who—she'd find if she did get there.

"I can go with you," Nine said.

Petra shook her head. "You rest. Have another sandwich. Or five. I'll take Sig with me." She reached down to stroke the coyote's ears. Sig's eyebrows worked up at Petra.

Nine nodded. "You're in good hands with Coyote. And . . . I know that there are always some things we must do ourselves."

"Yeah. I guess so." She chewed her lip, thinking. "Nine, we saw a black toad today, at Lev's. It made me wonder if it was connected to your Toad God or the toad that spoke to you."

Nine paused in her demolition of the sandwich. "I don't know anything more than what I told you." And she turned her full attention back on her sandwich, letting the curtain of her hair fall over her face.

Petra frowned. Something had spooked Nine, and she wasn't talking. She'd need to find answers for herself. She laced up her boots and headed out into the starlit darkness with Sig on her heels. Or, it would have been starlit darkness on another summer night. Only the brightest stars were able to burn through the smoke haze; she could find Regulus and a few other stars in Leo. She waded through the brittle grasses of the field, moving toward the Eye. She noticed that Nine's feet had worn a path from the house to the spring-fed pond, pressing down the grasses in a regular pattern.

Sig stuck close to her, trotting just ahead. He wasn't distracted by critters of the night; instead, he focused on getting to the Eye. For once, he was all business.

And she needed to become all business. Tomorrow morning, she vowed to return to the Compostela to see if the mirror was finished. She had no choice but to do what she could to stop the phoenix. Her father . . . She felt as if she were abandoning him. But if she didn't find him tonight, her conscience wouldn't allow her to simply focus on him. Others needed her more, and only she would have the mirror, the only hope of stopping the firebird.

The Eye of the World was dark and silent. It seemed to reflect the smoke in the sky above, seeming thick and opaque as soup. Sig trotted to the shoreline, ears lifted. He pounced on something, then sprinted a few feet, snooted around, and yelped.

"What do you have?" Petra asked, catching up to him.

A dark shape, the size of a lump of coal, hopped away. Sig snapped at it.

"Sig, no!" She reached for his collar in enough time to keep him from devouring the toad.

The toad plunged into the water and did not resurface.

"Sig," Petra scolded him. "That toad might know something!"

Unrepentant, Sig huffed at the water and growled. She released his collar, irritated that somehow he and Lev had the same opinion about toads. They kept turning up, and Petra refused to believe that was insignificant.

She knelt beside the pool. Her golden pendant spilled from her collar, and that bright spark of light embedded in her dark silhouette shone back at her. Sig gave up snarling at the spot where the toad had disappeared to sit beside her. Curiously, she noticed that he cast no reflection in the water.

Her brow wrinkled. The Eye had played tricks on her before. She reached out to Sig to convince herself that he was real and solid. He licked her hand and whined, as if to say: *Get on with it, already.*

She cupped her hands, leaned forward, and scooped some of the dark water out.

"Please show me my father," she whispered before she drank it. It tasted of smoke.

Sig stepped to the pool and drank in noisy slurps. He came back to lie down beside her and put his head between his paws.

She closed her eyes, hoping that the Eye would bring her to her father, wherever he was.

SHE HAD THE sensation of falling, that stomach-pitching feeling of hurtling through the dark. When she landed, she found herself on cool ground. She opened her eyes.

She was lying on a thick mat of pine needles, on a forest floor. She pulled herself up to a sitting position, finding Sig beside her. The coyote stretched and yawned with a squeak, ears pressed back and toes buried in the pine needles.

She looked around her. It was night, but she could make out a perimeter of stones set out in a circular pattern. The stones were interesting, and unlikely to be all native to the area. She picked out larimar, quartz, amethyst, sunstone, and even a piece of watery blue topaz the size of her fist. Petra was no magician or alchemist, but she thought it was a fair bet to believe that it was a magic circle of some kind, constructed for either containment or protection. She noticed that there was a set of footprints here, the same shining bioluminescent color as the fireflies that milled deeper in the woods.

She gazed into the forest, looking for threats. She glimpsed no movement, no sign of monsters. She stood carefully, taking inventory. She was dressed in the same clothes she'd been wearing at the Eye, and she was still armed in the spirit world. Her gun belt was slung across her hips, and she plucked out her guns to stare at them. They seemed to be in the same condition they had been in the physical world, only they were engraved here. One with the word *Thought* on one barrel, and *Memory* on the other.

"Odin's ravens." She smiled. The spirit world had a sense of humor. But if there were threats beyond the circle, she would face them armed.

She stepped over the circle of stones and into the dark.

Sig trotted beside her, snooting at the set of glowing tracks that led into the night. They were a man's tracks, she could tell. She hoped that the spirit world was playing it straight with her, just this once, and that these would lead her to her father. As she walked, she glanced down at her pendant, the lion devouring the sun. It, too, glowed with the same dim, cold light. The pendant and the footprints had to be connected.

Her heart pounded as she followed the tracks. They guided her to a field that felt somehow famil-iar. The shape of the land, the way the flat plain fell away from the mountains—it reminded her of the land behind her trailer. She shuddered involuntarily. In her own world, this land was serene and comforting. Not here.

The tracks led her to a wrought iron fence that wrapped around the ruins of a structure. The building seemed to have burned, charred timbers fallen in on themselves. Black glass glittered in the ruins, cold and still with a dusting of frost over it. It didn't take long for her to figure out what she was looking at. This was Lascaris's house, or at least the spirit world's memory of it. Had to be.

Petra shivered. She opened the gate warily. She and Sig slid through. She thumbed back the hammers of the guns, and audible clicks sounded over the frost-covered scene.

There *had* been fire, and she thought immediately of the phoenix. Had the phoenix been here, at Lascaris's house? Had Gabe been mistaken in his account, and had the phoenix perhaps started the fire?

She followed the glowing footprints to the edge of the ruin. Where they pressed into the ground, the frost was wiped away. At the edge, she peered down through a ruined floor, where the tracks vanished. A basement yawned below her, so much like the pit of basalt in the forest. Lascaris must have conjured the bird here. And her father must have come here to investigate.

But then what happened?

"Dad?" she called. "Dad?"

There was no answer. Sig watched the sky, as if scanning for an airborne threat, his ears pressed forward in alertness.

Sig seemed much more keyed in to the spirit world than she ever had been. She pointed to the basement. "Do you think it's safe to go down there?"

Sig continued to gaze upward. He was clearly more concerned with skyward threats than underground ones. She took that as encouragement. The basement could be a trap, but she had to look. Her father could be in there, somewhere in this ruin.

"Keep watch," she ordered the coyote. "Good dog."

She scrambled down into the basement to look for her dad, skidding part of the way and jumping the rest, guns lifted at shoulder height. She landed in a puff of black char that sputtered up some dark ash. She saw a few smears of luminescence here, but the tracks just stopped. With the barrel of a gun, she poked among the illegible curled black pages of books that disintegrated when she touched them. She sifted pieces of broken glass. A cold athanor sat in the corner. Gold particles glittered here and there, fine as dust. She combed through the rubble, the broken brick, and found nothing. There was no sign of her father, and no magical secrets that survived the fire.

"Dad!" she shouted.

No one answered her. She holstered her guns, and climbed up, out of the basement, picking her way along collapsed timbers. She stood on the ground above and shouted as loud as she could for her father. At her side, Sig howled.

And there was nothing. Nothing answered her.

SILENCE RANG IN her ears.

Petra awoke beside the Eye of the World. She was

lying on her side, with Sig sprawled over her knees. The ground still held the heat of the day, and she felt sluggish. She stared into the water, which gave up no secrets.

Something croaked behind her.

She turned over, drawing her guns and dislodging Sig, to face a black toad perched on a rock. It looked like the small toad that had fled into the water.

"Do you talk?" she asked, not feeling stupid in the slightest.

The toad's throat ballooned, turning pale as it spoke: "The kingdom of death is nigh."

Sig growled, and she felt it vibrating through his body. He skulked behind her to approach the toad. She shoved him back with a leg.

"What does that mean? Does that mean that my father is dead? Where is he?"

The toad blinked at her. "Knowledge will cost you."

"What do you want? Money?" She had no money on her. The only thing of value she owned was the necklace that her father had given her—wait, that wasn't true. She laid down one gun and patted her pockets. She also had Lascaris's pocket watch. Her fingers closed over it, and she was tempted. But it was not hers to trade. Her fingers slipped up instead to the necklace her father had given her. With trembling regret, she took it off and set it on the ground between them.

The toad hopped forward and licked the gold. "Pretty. But the gold in your pocket is more appealing."

Petra fished the timepiece out of her pocket and held it in her hand. She didn't know the full extent

of the watch's meaning for Gabe. She knew she had
no right to trade it for anything. "It's not mine," she
said stubbornly.

"Then there is no trade."

Sig snarled. Petra reached for his collar and
wrapped both her legs around him. He huffed and
growled, and it was all she could do to keep the coyote from destroying the little toad.

Petra sighed. Gabe had a very long life in which
to forgive her. She placed the watch before the toad.
The toad crept toward it and swallowed it, frag-
mented chain and all. Its belly distended, and Petra
had no idea how the creature would even be able to
move.

"Where is my father?" she asked again.

The toad blinked, and it seemed as if its slitted
pupils stared past her, to the Eye of the World itself.
"You will see your father's face again when you find
the phoenix. Search the edge of the fire."

Without another word, the toad hopped away.

"Wait—that's it?"

Petra reached out to grab it, to demand clarifica-
tion, but it slid into the darkness and disappeared.

She released Sig, hoping that the coyote would
track him down for her. Instead, Sig sat upright and
stared at her with a look of extreme disapproval, as
if she'd eaten an entire package of hot dogs without
sharing. Which is how her stomach felt, actually—
she'd given away the watch for basically nothing.

Well, maybe not *nothing*.

"When I find the phoenix . . ."

Her father was chasing the phoenix, too. It made

sense that there was no trace of him in the spirit world, if he was off on some harebrained quest.

And that meant he had to be out there, somewhere.

She would find him.

CHAPTER 17

Unkindness

Gabe flew into the dusk as an unkindness of ravens, peering at the ground through dozens of eyes. He skimmed over trails and forests and fields, surging toward the last known location of Joseph Dee. New barricades had been erected on the dark ribbons of roads, lit with flashing lights. He followed them, deep into the park. Fire washed over the horizon, sending up clouds of smoke that stung his eyes. His shadows flickered over the smoke as he spiraled in and out, over the singed trees.

He saw no cars, no headlamps, only the gathering darkness and fire. Soldiers moved at the perimeter of the fire like ants. A helicopter flew away in a fury of sound, a bucket dangling from a line. The Magpie was growing larger than any fire that Gabe had lodged in his memory, and he had seen many in his time. He knew that it was now beyond any human hope of stopping it.

He searched until the darkness became indistinguishable from the smoke. His daylight eyes could see no more. With reluctance, he turned his feathered bodies toward the Rutherford Ranch.

Wind slicked through his wings, and the journey to the Lunaria was short. He heard the tree before he spied it on the ground; the leaves whispered to themselves in the dark. He landed a few yards away, feathers and bird bones clotting into the shape of a man. He reached into his truck for his clothing. He dressed quickly and pulled his pistol out from under the seat. He held the gun in his right hand, his thumb on the hammer.

He approached the tree warily. The branches shuddered, and the whispering increased in volume as he crossed under its canopy.

"No," Gabe said. "There's no more making peace. This is war."

The tree groaned, a sound that reverberated up from the ground and rattled the topmost branches. A tree root rose from the ground and licked his shoe. It had the sense of being a submissive, placating gesture. Gabe tensed and aimed his gun at it. The root froze. Maybe the tree would . . .

The ground opened up beneath him, and he was falling in an avalanche of dirt, tree roots, and rock. He struggled to hold on to his gun as he fell into the dark.

Gabe landed on his left shoulder in the shallows of the underground river, gasping like a fish. He struggled to climb to his feet, swallowing metallic-tasting river water.

The tree was incandescent with rage. Pale yellow light, its lifeblood of stored sunshine, shivered through its roots and dripped down the tendrils into the sluggish river, forming a glowing oil slick around Gabe. Gabe climbed to his feet in the water and trudged toward shore. He aimed his gun at the heart of the tree, curling with angry roots.

"You have me. Leave her alone."

A root snaked under the water and snapped around Gabe's ankle. It turned him upside down and hauled him up by his ankle, flailing. Gabe struggled to keep hold of his gun and his wits.

The Lunaria drew him close to its glowing heartwood and shook him sharply. The roots seethed and growled. He shot at them, and the tree winced. But he only had so many bullets. The splinters settled on the water like matchsticks on a puddle.

"I will leave you forever if you don't let her be."

The wood of the tree groaned, the sound of a creaking door in an old house.

"Yes. I will fade and die without you. And you will continue on, as you always have. But she will have no reason to come here, ever again." He swung by his ankle, serene as Odin dangling from the World Tree, Yggdrasil.

The tree reached out with dozens of rhizomes, forming a cage around him.

He snorted. "You can try to imprison me."

Roots dug into his skin, letting phosphorescent blood. He hissed: "You can try to torture me."

The tree growled, deep in its heartwood.

"But I will not stay."

He closed his eyes and exploded in a flurry of ravens. They slipped through the gaps in the cage and flew to the gate. They flitted soundlessly through the spaces in the grate, into the night.

All but one. A nimble root reached out and caught it as it worked its way through the cage. The bird squawked, but the tree held it gently. It gathered the agitated bird to itself, petting and smoothing its feathers.

Gabe paused. He could afford the loss of one raven. When he reintegrated, it would likely mean the loss of an eye or a rib. But there was something in how the Lunaria handled the bird that reminded him of what it had been, in its prior incarnation, long ago, when it had been his midwife into this undead life.

The tree began to sing, slowly, softly, a creaking and soughing that sounded like wind through a bamboo forest. As the tree touched the raven, Gabe could see what it projected to him—the memory of how it had once been two trees, together on a plain. There had been a drought, and the second tree died. The Lunaria mourned its loss, but grew over the stump of the lost tree, making a home for birds and basking in the sun. Worms and moles moved in the earth below it, and it grew content. Lightning struck it a handful of times. It was venerated by men and women who walked the land here, and it once or twice was a ladder for a god climbing into the sky. It had a visceral knowledge of its role as an unknown pillar of the world, as a gateway to what the shamans called the lower, middle, and upper worlds—to the underworld, this physical reality, and the spirit world. It was, by and large, content.

Then Lascaris came. He poured potions and toxins at the base of the tree, uttered incantations upon it. It awakened in a way that a tree should not ever have been awakened. The tree yearned. It dreamed now, and it wanted to know if it was the only thing that had such experiences, this moving from one world to the other. It was confused. Alone.

And then Lascaris brought men to be hanged by the tree. Gabe was the first. He was hanged there, taken down, and the tree claimed him. It cared for him as if he were a squirrel nesting in its branches, or a child. It fed the fallen man light and love and caused him to walk again. And it experienced the world in Gabe's dreams. Those dreams of the tree and Gabe were a shared reality, a connection to a world that was changing in ways the Lunaria didn't understand.

And there were more men, men that became the Hanged Men. The Lunaria fed them with all the magic it had, but the magic dwindled. There was only so much light left underground, so much magic remaining to feed them. But all of them, whether they were as self-aware as Gabe, or shadows like some of the last automatons, were the Lunaria's children. And she loved them all, fiercely. She knit their bones and brains back together every night, to the best of her ability, smoothing their skin like wrinkled shirts.

And then . . . the Lunaria was burned. The Hanged Men died, without her to feed them. She put her last magic into Gabriel, her firstborn. She gave him enough magic to walk away from her, to be just a man. It was her last gift.

But then she recovered. And Gabriel returned to her. She could pour back all the magic she'd drawn from the underground river, back into him. And she was terrified. Terrified of losing him. Terrified that she would be alone, aware, for all of time, just as much as she was terrified of the fire. Gabe sensed that she had gathered all her magic to her, that she was cloaking herself from the view of the phoenix with all her might. But sooner or later, the phoenix would find her, if it wasn't stopped. Being burned by the phoenix would be almost as bad as being alone. Fear and loneliness crackled through her.

She wanted Gabe here. And she wanted Petra, too. Another child to protect her. She knew the two of them belonged together, and she could return the favor of their protection. She could make them both strong and powerful. And maybe they would bring her other children, other men and women who would accept the gifts she offered. Maybe the wolf-woman, Nine. Maybe the woman, Maria, and her lover, Mike. They could choose who the Hanged Men would be this time, and they could take this land away from the Rutherfords. There could be a new order in this world, a new order of magic and peace in Temperance. A new era.

You cannot make that choice for them, Gabe thought at the tree. *Neither can I.*

The tree flashed an image to him, an image of Petra in her full glow of health now. And it flashed an all-too-familiar image of her, sickly, and dying.

It could happen again. And it likely will, Gabe

thought. *But neither you nor I can stop it. It's the power of time. She is human. She gets to choose.*

And though I am no longer human, so do I.

The tree root delicately stroked the raven's head. It opened its root-hand and let it go.

The raven flew away, to the grate, to join the others perching on the bars.

The tree made a sigh, a sound like a heart breaking. The light dimmed, and all became darkness in the underworld.

The ravens chuffed softly to each other. They gathered, clotting into the shape of a man. Gabriel reached for the gate and tugged on it.

The gate slowly opened.

He walked back inside, on the bank of the underground river.

The tree slowly lit up, hopeful.

He reached up, up in the branches, touch grazing the bullet holes he'd left there.

The branches closed over him, and he let himself be gathered in that embrace, the guts of darkness and light, the source of his life.

They understood each other, now. And there was a truce forged in the shadow of the alchemical Tree of Life.

PETRA AWOKE A bit before dawn.

She slid out of bed before light had begun to flood the kitchen. She was immediately pursued by a sleepy coyote and a cranky cat, both demanding food. She fed them both and brewed some coffee, gazing out into the darkness.

She took her coffee out to the porch. Sig and Pearl, full of kibble, plodded after her. Pearl began to take a bath, and Sig stretched out on the porch to take a second shot at sleep.

She sat on the porch swing and took this moment just to be still. She'd been full of plans and action. Now, she had to clearly evaluate what came next. Her father was being searched for. She and Gabe had to check on the mirror, to see if it had survived the time in Lev's pizza oven. If it was intact, if it still worked, then they could go chase down the phoenix. Trap the creature in the mirror, and maybe find her father in the process.

Petra had mixed feelings about trapping the phoenix. The phoenix was a being, just like any other. It wasn't fair to imprison it in a mirror for eternity. Maybe the mirror would be a temporary solution, until they found a way to turn it loose in some pocket of the spirit world, where it could cause little harm. Maybe there was a fireproof forest somewhere there for it to frolic in. Hopefully, when they found her father, he could engineer a ritual that would do just that. She knew he'd been wandering the spirit realms for decades; if anyone knew where to set free a flammable creature, he would know. And for all she knew, maybe he was pursuing it to do just that.

She held the cup of coffee close to her aching chest. He would be all right. He had to be. She felt deep pangs of sorrow and guilt for the people he'd apparently killed. If he had done it, if he was this close to losing it, how had she not known? Had she been blind to his deterioration, wanting to believe that he was the father he had never been to her so much that she ignored that something terrible was wrong? Maybe he'd cracked, knowing his Alzheimer's was stealing up on him, and was desperately seeking a magical solution, as he'd done before. If she had only agreed to Dr. Vaughn's tests, maybe this could have been averted. If her father wasn't in his right mind, this was all on her shoulders, and she knew it.

She watched the sun rise. Not long after, a pickup rolled up. Gabe's truck. He parked, climbed out, and walked toward her.

He looked really good, as if he'd been freshly showered, shaved, and had slept for two weeks. Petra felt a bit of envy at that. She wondered what it was like, sleeping under the tree. Was it as restorative and dreamless as it looked?

"Good morning, sunshine," she murmured over her coffee. "There's coffee inside."

Gabe kissed the top of her head and sat down in the swing beside her. "I didn't see any sign of your father last night."

She hid her disappointment with a deep slurp. "I have something to tell you. And you're going to be mad."

He lifted an eyebrow. "Oh?"

She continued. "I went to the Eye of the World last night." She told him what she'd seen in the Eye, and about her conversation with the toad.

Gabe listened without comment.

"So I traded the watch for an answer," she said. "I'm sorry."

Gabe was silent, staring out at the sky. It was some time before he spoke. "It's done. I can't say I'd have done any different, in your shoes."

He was a good man. She reached for his hand and squeezed it. "Thank you. Thank you for understanding this."

He kissed the top of her hand. "There's only one way to go. Forward."

"Do you mean that? With everything—with the conflict we've had? With our marriage, the tree, and everything else?"

"As they say, time moves in only one direction. Even if the Great Work were completed tomorrow and the Philosopher's Stone dropped out of the sky, it could not turn back time. We go forward."

She nodded, and she smiled. "Forward, then."

They sat in silence for some minutes, watching the morning wash over the land.

"I guess we go see to the mirror?" she said at last.

"Yeah. Hopefully, it worked."

"I trust Lev not to have touched it. I just hope . . . I hope I didn't fuck it up."

She went inside to get dressed. She set the coffee maker to brew another batch in an hour, hoping that Maria and Nine would sleep in. She gathered her things and put Pearl inside. She led Sig to the pickup, where Gabe waited.

"Let's check on that mirror."

"THERE'S NO WAY we can look at it directly?" Lev asked.

"Not unless you want to spend the rest of your unnatural life behind glass." Gabe gave him a look.

Lev shrugged. "I'm not dying to spend time in limbo. But I would love to know what spells went into that."

Gabe glanced at him and raised an eyebrow.

"What? You never know when it might come in handy."

Gabe didn't reply immediately. He glanced at Petra, and it seemed he was thinking of the homunculus. "After this is over, I'll write down what I remember for you."

Lev nodded. "Thanks. I think that some of this knowledge should stick around in good hands. In case you guys aren't around sometime and a phoenix shows up."

Petra was sure that wasn't the only reason, but she owed Lev. They both did. And if the cost of a brand-new body and rent on his pizza oven was an old spell, she was good with it.

She screwed up her courage and put on her welding gloves. Armed with Lev's shiny Viking pot, she turned the makeshift mirror to face the door of the pizza oven. Petra opened the door. The handle still felt warm, but it should have had plenty of time to cool. They'd been very patient, and she was certain that Lev looked after it as well as a bird with an egg.

She held her breath. Looking through the reflection in the pan, she carefully inserted a pizza paddle into the oven. She slid it under the mirror and pulled the paddle out. Sweating, she lowered the mirror to the hearth.

Peering through the pan, the mirror looked whole,

a lumpy bit of glass that was roughly circular. She slowly grasped it with the welder's gloves and turned it out on the paddle. It was a whole piece of glass, intact. But what was worrisome was that the silver was gone from the back of the mirror. The heat had bubbled it away, and only a few flakes remained.

"It's back together," she said. "But it looks like the silver boiled off." She'd been afraid this would happen.

"It won't work without the silver," Gabe said.

"Wait," she said. "I can fix it. Let me get some stuff." She put the pan down on top of the glass, covering it, and headed out to the Bronco. In moments, she was back with a box of gear from the Bronco.

"What's all this?" Gabe asked.

"Stuff we can use to resilver the mirror." She spread out the bottles and equipment on a stainless-steel counter. "This is silver nitrate," she said, pointing at the small bottle. "Geologists use it to test for iodine, chlorine, and bromine. And that's ammonia and lye drain cleaner."

Gabe looked at the accumulated stuff appraisingly. "This should be interesting."

Petra grinned. "Always." Then her expression clouded. "Do you think it will work?"

"I do not doubt that your science will work. I just hope that there's enough magic left in the glass for the mirror to retain its properties."

"I guess we'll find out," Lev said. He was sitting on a stool, eating a bag of chips. Sig sat below him and gave him a baleful look. Lev dropped a chip into his mouth, and he made a face like it was a bad-tasting communion wafer.

Petra didn't speculate. All she could do was the

science, and the magic would have to take care of itself. She adjusted the rubber gloves and stared into the cookware mirror. She uncovered the small slab of glass. Working slowly, she cleaned the back of the glass with the drain cleaner, careful to get every speck of dirt removed and wiped it with a damp paper towel. The glass still held heat, and she was careful not to break it with an abrupt temperature change. She placed the glass on a piece of Lev's parchment paper, conscious to keep it level as possible.

She then measured out a gram of the silver nitrate and added it to ten drops of water. She mixed this in a plastic cup, then added a gram of the lye drain cleaner. Silver oxide began to form as she stirred with a plastic spoon. Carefully, she dropped ammonia in until the silver oxide disappeared. She measured four grams of sugar into the solution—it would act as an aldehyde in this process. She stirred until it all dissolved in the cup, then poured it over the back of the mirror.

The glass was still hot, and the silvering agent took immediately, clouding to an opaque off-white color.

She glanced back at the men. Lev had abandoned his bag of chips and was taking notes on a dog-eared pad of paper. Maybe he really was going to build a magic mirror . . . But she couldn't think about it now.

"It's done," she said. With care, she turned the piece of glass over and peered at it through the Viking pan's shiny surface.

It was a mirror again. Through warped glass, a shiny silver surface shone. Petra could see a warped reflection of her hand when she passed it between the pan and the mirror, reminding her of something she might see in a fun house. It wasn't perfect—a bit of dirt in one of the crevices she'd missed had turned black in the reaction—but it was hopefully close enough for alchemical work.

"I do believe that you were an alchemist in a previous life," Gabe said, and she snorted at that.

"It looks all right," she said. "But the primary question is . . . does it work?"

They were both silent. Gabe wrapped the mirror in a bandanna, careful not to mar the fragile silvering. Petra cleaned up her tools. As she did so, her thoughts churned.

She had to know if it worked. If it was still magic. And there was only one way.

The Locus.

She closed her eyes. She had to stop being selfish. She had to find the truth and deal with it, sooner or later. If she was no longer human, then she'd have to figure out what she was, and move forward from it.

Gabe stepped up behind her and kissed the top of her head while she washed her hands. She knew, no matter what she was, that she was beloved by her husband and her coyote. That should be enough. If she was no longer human, that would be a terrible loss. But she would survive it.

She dried her hands on a dish towel and went out to the truck. She pulled the Venificus Locus out of the glove box. She carried it back to the kitchen and asked Lev for a paring knife.

"What for?" he asked, handing her a spotless stainless-steel blade.

"We can tell if it's magic for certain with a tool

that Lascaris left behind. The Venificus Locus." She showed him the golden compass.

"How does it do that?" he asked, staring at it in curiosity.

"It drinks blood."

"Mmm. Go stand over the sink when you do that, okay?"

Petra went to the sink, as she was told. Gabe put the wrapped mirror down on the counter and moved away, not wanting to interfere with the Locus's prognostications.

Petra hesitated. Aside from a hangnail the flesh of her fingertips was perfectly unmarked. She hadn't suffered so much as a bad paper cut since she'd taken on this new body. Sighing, she poked the index finger of her left hand. A red drop of blood welled up, and she dropped it into the groove circumscribing the outer ring of the Locus.

The Locus must have been thirsty. It seemed to suck in the blood, and she added two more drops. The drops flattened, forming a ring around the groove. Petra's breathing quickened. What did that mean? Did that mean that her blood was contaminated, that she no longer was as human as she felt?

The blood gathered itself into a drop, like mercury. The drop swung around the groove and pointed in the direction of Gabe. Another split off and followed Lev around the room as he unloaded the dishwasher. There seemed to be a dull residue left in the groove, as if there was some lingering magic around this place. But the main thing Petra was thinking about was that the Locus had accepted her blood.

It would only run on plain human blood.

She was human.

Her heart lifted and dropped, as if it had fallen down a roller coaster. The mirror wasn't magic, but neither was she.

But then the ring of blood belched. A thick drop was summoned up, and the drop raced around the track, having tasted something of magic. It hesitated in front of her, and Petra closed her eyes. Shit, maybe she had been wrong.

When she opened them again, the drop had scuttled away. It was pointing toward the mirror on the kitchen counter.

She let out a shaky breath.

"Well?" Gabe said softly.

"The mirror is magic. But I'm not."

She broke out into a smile, relief washing over her. She had never thought she'd relish such knowledge like this—the knowledge of being utterly ordinary.

Gabe crossed to her and hugged her. She laughed in relief at this weight being removed from her. She stood on her tiptoes to kiss him, feeling optimistic for the first time in months.

"Where are you going to look for the phoenix?" Lev wanted to know, rubbing a plate with a dish towel.

"Nine said it lurks on the leading edge of the fire line," Petra said, forcing herself to get back down to business. She pulled up a map on her phone with a weak signal and fiddled with it. "According to the news, it's creeping along fastest near Bridger Lake, just south of the park."

Gabe nodded. "Then we'll start there."

"Good luck getting around those roadblocks,"

Lev said. "I've had National Guard soldiers in and out of here, and from what they've said, civilians aren't gonna be able to get there by road. They're keeping five miles ahead of the fire and advancing forward."

Petra frowned, staring at the waves on the topographical map. The land got a little rough around there. Off-roading would be problematic.

"I have an idea," Gabe said.

"You have a helicopter stashed away somewhere?"

"No. Something better."

CHAPTER 18

The Well of Souls

Getting Robin sprung from the mental hospital took some doing.

Unsurprisingly, Robin's doctor wasn't convinced that it was in the general public's best interest to let Robin go roaming around free. Owen had to promise her that taking Robin out for an afternoon would be in the best interests of solving Anna's murder, and that he wasn't falling for a line of Robin's bullshit. Owen swore up and down that he would keep Robin trussed up in a belly chain and that Robin wouldn't leave his sight, even to piss. Robin's lawyer really didn't give a fuck, either way. Owen got an order from his favorite judge—he'd let more than a few DUIs slide for that man—and still the whole thing was shady as hell and not within a stone's throw of legal. But it came to pass that Owen was able to take Robin out on a field trip.

Robin seemed amused at the idea. They'd let him dress in civilian clothes for the outing—a T-shirt, sweatpants, and sneakers without the laces. Owen had seen the kind of havoc that a very determined guy could get up to with a shoelace—he'd nearly lost a deputy in visitation hours to an inmate who'd been slipped a pack and decided to strangle him. The silver belly chain at Robin's waist kept his handcuffed hands within sight at the level of his navel. Leg chains clinked as he walked. Robin seemed to move placidly along between the orderlies, but nobody was in a hurry to remove the spit hood that covered the lower half of his face.

"He wasn't wearing a mask when I last saw him," Owen observed.

The doctor frowned at him. "Robin discovered that he has a five-foot spitting range when he was served soup that he disliked last night. You've been warned."

Owen signed a stack of liability waivers when they brought Robin out. They gave him the keys to his chains and opened the front doors for him. Owen led Robin slowly out into the light.

Robin blinked and turned his round face up to the sky. It occurred to Owen that they probably didn't let him out for exercise. Pity mixed with the revulsion at that same pity—this was the man who killed Anna, after all.

"This way," Owen said, leading him to the SUV. He kept his left hand in the chain around Robin's waist. He shoveled Robin into the back, behind the cage, belted him in, and climbed into the driver's seat.

Anna was sitting in the passenger seat. She turned around to stare at Robin.

Robin gazed back at her, like he saw her.

Anna crept close, pressing her face up against the cage and lacing her fingers in it. "You. It was you." Realization stole over her face, and it seemed that she glowed brighter with the remembering, or the rage.

Robin said nothing.

Her fingers tightened. "You put me in the well, and left me to die."

Robin stared forward woodenly.

"You murdered me!" she screamed at him, the howl of a decades-old little girl frozen in time. Owen's heart twisted in his chest to hear it, and he began to regret this, this traumatizing of her. "You took me away and you killed me!" Tears glittered on her cheeks. "You fed me to that monster. He chewed me up alive."

Robin remained stoic, refusing to speak. Or perhaps he couldn't hear her.

"It's going to be okay, Anna," Owen said.

Anna turned to him. She flung herself into his lap and threw her arms around his neck, sniffling. Owen stroked her hair that smelled like algae.

"Where are we going?" Robin said from the back, sounding glibly casual.

Owen put the key in the ignition. "We're going to see Pigin. You're going to help me kill him."

He couldn't tell for sure, but it seemed that Robin was smiling behind the pale blue of his spit hood.

"I dredged the well. I found bones. We already had Anna's skeleton. Do you know anything about those bones?"

Robin's expression darkened. "No. I just know about the little girl. Doesn't surprise me that Pigin convinced other people to kill for him, though."

Owen didn't believe him. "We got a couple of DNA matches so far on missing persons. Forty-year-old Prudence Ann Jardiner, missing from the Black Sun Roadhouse eleven years ago. Did you know her?"

Robin shook his head. "No."

"A young man on a hunting trip. Otto Pershing. Was wearing camo overalls and an orange safety cap when he went missing seventeen years ago. Sound familiar?"

"No."

Owen rubbed his mustache. "Seems like Pigin has been busy. I'd like to know who else has been feeding him . . . and what they're getting in return."

Anna sat next to Owen for the ride, turning back to stare at Robin every few minutes. Owen could feel her shaking, and he thought she might disappear into the ether any moment. But she didn't. She hung in there, jammed under Owen's armpit and glaring venom at Robin.

"How do you intend for us to go about killing Pigin?" Robin asked.

"Well, I gave it a try the last time I was at the well. I shot at him, but it didn't seem to do any damage. I thought I'd try again, but I need some help. And you're the only person on the planet who would believe me enough to help send a giant Toad God to hell."

Owen glanced up at the rearview mirror. Robin's eyes were crinkling as if he were smiling. Or smirking.

Owen pulled off the road a half mile from the

well. He stopped the SUV and glanced over at Anna. He kissed her on the forehead and said: "Be brave."

She nodded sharply.

He got out of the SUV and crossed to the back. Behind the seats where Robin was belted in, he'd loaded up a locked plastic footlocker. He opened the footlocker and picked up a small parcel, unwrapping it carefully.

"Whatcha got there?" Robin twisted around to watch.

"Dynamite," he said, fiddling with the blasting cap. He settled on duct-taping it to the package of dynamite. He stripped the wire from the fuse with his teeth and inspected the spool before securing the fuse with tape, too, for good measure. He'd gotten the dynamite from Sal's stash of weird shit he kept in the barn. Owen had no idea if it worked or not, but it looked dry and intact. And if dynamite couldn't kill the Toad God, there wasn't much else he knew of that would. At the very least, it would close that miserable well and hopefully end the stream of grisly offerings to that rotting creature.

Robin emitted a low whistle. "That might do it."

"I need two people to make this work. I'll need for you to summon Pigin, then drop it in the well and take off running. I'll light the fuse when you get near the well. You chat him up, get caught up on old times. I'll whistle when you need to drop it and get out."

Robin's eyes narrowed. "How do I know you won't blow me up, too?"

"How do I know you won't keep on running after you drop the package?"

"Fair point."

"You do this, Pigin will be gone. You'll be free of the haunting. That was the deal." He wrapped the package of dynamite up in plastic shopping bags and parked it on the roof of the SUV.

Robin nodded. "That was the deal."

Owen opened the back door. He unbuckled Robin and pulled him out. Anna watched from the front fender of the SUV. She perched there, kicking her feet into space, glaring.

Owen pulled down the spit hood around Robin's neck, resisting the urge to flinch if a loogie landed on his face. Robin did nothing.

"I'm going to unchain you. Don't make me regret it."

"You won't."

Owen took the keys from his pocket and un-cuffed Robin's feet first, then the cuffs around the belly chain. He stood out of kicking and punching distance as Robin shucked out of the chains and took off the spit hood.

"Are we good?" Owen unholstered his gun.

Robin nodded, rubbing his wrists. "We're good."

Owen picked up the dynamite and fuse, tucking them under his arm. He gestured with his service pistol. "You know the way."

Robin plodded along the forest floor, moving away from the road. Owen kept a close watch on him, gun raised. He had no issue with shooting the motherfucker if he fled. He could concoct a good enough story to justify it if he had to. All he had to say was that Robin tried to overpower him. He could shoot him, put him back in the chains, and take his body to the morgue. Nobody would give a shit.

Anna floated beside him, her feet not touching the earth. Her arms were crossed, and she stayed close to him.

"I'm sorry for this," he said.

She shook her head. There was a look of fear on her face, like he could screw her over like so many other adults before him.

"But it will be for the best. You'll see."

Anna put her head down and followed along, saying nothing.

Feeling like a total shitnoodle, Owen gazed up at the sky. The smoke had grown thick in the air. Radio traffic told him that the Magpie Fire was less than a mile away, and that was part of his plan. He wanted to get this done and over, in and out. The fire would quickly wash over this area, obliterating any evidence of blasting.

They crossed the dry creek bed and Robin stopped. Owen wordlessly handed him the package of dynamite. Robin tucked it in his back waistband, beneath his shirt. He took a deep breath and advanced on the well. Owen held the wire spool cradled in his artificial hand, reeling it out as Robin walked. He kept a few paces behind Robin, out of view of the creature at the bottom of the well.

Anna shivered.

Robin stared down into the well. "Pigin. It's me. Robin."

Something burbled and churned in the muck. "Little bird. You came back to the nest."

"Yeah. It's been a long time."

"I catalog the bones here. I count which ones came from you. Many, many bones."

Owen sucked in his breath. That asshole. He knew it. He'd killed more than Anna. Owen's finger slid behind the trigger guard of his gun. He was going to bring that sonofabitch to justice, for Anna and the others. He stepped closer to Robin.

"What have you brought me today, little bird?"

"Something that will keep you satisfied for a very long time."

Anna shrieked, but an instant too late. Robin snatched the package of dynamite out of his pants and ripped the blasting cord out of Owen's artificial hand. Owen stumbled forward. Before he could recover, Robin lashed the cord around Owen's neck and began to strangle him. Owen fired blindly with his gun, missing his target.

Owen struggled against the cable around his neck. Robin pulled it tight, and Owen could feel the vessels of his neck constricting and oxygen slipping away. He tried to jam the fingers of his good hand between his throat and the cord, but he couldn't wedge them in. Consciousness glittered in his periphery, and he knew that he was moments from being choked out.

"It's nothing personal," Robin was saying. "If I feed the Toad God, he will grant me a new face. A new face is freedom. I won't ever be behind bars or locked doors again. You wouldn't understand."

From the corner of his watering eye, Owen could see Anna crawling up on the sandstone rocks around the lip of the well. She shouted into the well: "Let him go! Let him go, and I'll . . . I'll stay with you. Forever."

There was a mighty belching sound from underground. "None of the ghosts has ever stayed . . . I would like the company."

No . . . Owen would not allow this. Anna needed to be free! He gurgled against the cable, twisting and turning in Robin's grip, trying to reach Anna.

Anna gazed at him with resignation. She was perched on the sandstone rim of the well, and had slid one foot down into the dark, making ready to jump down into Pigin's hell.

No. Owen backpedaled. He ran backward with all his strength and slammed the backs of Robin's knees against the lip of the well. Robin's grip faltered, and he released Owen. Owen slammed his head back into Robin's nose, hearing a satisfying cracking sound in the back of his skull.

Owen rammed his elbow back into Robin's gut. Robin tripped and fell backward, backward into the well with a howl.

Owen landed on the ground on all fours, gasping. Anna was at his side, eyes wide with panic.

A great chuckling emanated from the well.

"Well played, Owen. Well played. I knew that you could do it." A crunching sound and male screams emanated from the bottom. "It seems I need a new acolyte, someone to bring me flesh. I think you would do wonderfully."

Owen crawled forward, reaching for the blasting cord. It led down into the well. The dynamite must have fallen in during the scuffle. Maybe Pigin hadn't gnawed the cord free of the explosives yet. He fumbled in his pocket for his lighter, and lit the fuse midway down its length. Not much time. He pulled himself to his feet and stumbled away, Anna at his elbow.

When he looked back, the spark had traveled over the rim of the well, going down into darkness.

After a few heartbeats, a deafening explosion sounded, flinging dirt, blood, and rotted crud into the air. Owen covered his head with his arms, feeling wet sludge and gravel raining down on him. When he dared look back, he saw that the well's sandstone had been broken, shattered in a vaguely star-shaped pattern emanating from a black hole in the earth. Sparks and embers drifted lazily in the air.

Owen rolled to a sitting position, panting. His ears were ringing. He could barely hear Anna asking: "Is it over?"

Owen nodded. "Yeah. Yeah, I think so."

There was echoing silence for several minutes. Owen sat with his back to a tree and stared at the well. Truth be told, he had intended on giving Robin to Pigin, anyway. There was only one way to be sure that the scales were balanced—he had to kill both of those rotten bastards. His gaze shifted to a bloody sneaker lying a few yards away.

He glanced at Anna. He wasn't sure what he expected to happen when the deed was done. He thought that maybe a bright light would show up and she'd wave and vanish into it like one of the fairies from her cartoons. But no, she was still here.

He inhaled and coughed, both from the injury to his throat and the thickening smoke. "We should get outta here."

"Yeah," she agreed.

Before they could move, though, a black roar emanated from the bottom of the well, shaking the leaves on the trees. Owen reached for his gun as an oozing black shape crawled out of the fractured well.

"Oh my God," he breathed.

And the word *god* was the only one that came close, this atavistic creature that crawled over the fractured sandstone. It was a giant, reeking lump of decomposing flesh the size of a car, leaving behind bloody footprints as it moved. Black veins covered grey flesh, looking as if it had been subjected to flesh-eating bacteria. Covered in pieces of gore that Owen could only assume had once been attached to Robin's guts, the Toad God glared at them with bottomless black eyes.

"You cannot destroy me, Owen," Pigin growled. "I am rot. I am eternal."

Owen lifted his gun, though he knew it was futile. He began to back away, calculating how fast he could run to the SUV, if he could outrun this creature from hell. "Go to hell, Pigin," he said. It was the most creative thing he could think of. He pulled the trigger, but the hammer clicked on air. He'd used up his rounds. *Shit.*

He stood in front of Anna. "You can have me. But let her go."

The toad snorted. "Our deal is off. You destroyed my house. I will take the two of you as payment. You can join me in rotting for eternity. We will have much to discuss."

The toad hopped toward him with ferocious speed—much faster than should have been possible—and Owen flung up a hand to shield his head that he was certain was going to be rolling around in the gut of a monster in about five seconds—

But a blinding sheet of light seared down from the heavens, his upraised hand doing nothing to block it from his eyes. Owen fell back with a cry, his skin blistering. Through his half-closed lids, he saw the shape of a bird surrounding the Toad God. Pigin howled in fury and launched himself at the bird. His jaws locked around the bird's wing, and they sprawled on the ground, sun and shadow. Where the combatants rolled, fire lit and raged. The reek of something like burned tires suffused the dark forest. Sparks surged upward, lighting and burning away the dark canopy.

Owen tried to drag himself away. Anna just stood before him, gaping in fascination.

Something crawled up from the well, a skeletal hand cloaked in something viscid. It hauled itself up and into the stinking light, the shape of a man wrapped in rotting skin and slime. It staggered away, toward the fight. More clawed hands pulled blackened forms up from the well, viscous and vicious, leaving a black trail behind them. One by one, tatters of men were spat up into the ground. They plunged into the fray, clawing at the phoenix. There had to be at least a dozen of them, in various states of brokenness, joining Pigin as he tried to swallow the bird.

"What the hell" was the only thing Owen could think to say.

Anna was beside him, brow wrinkled. "The dead. They are . . . the dead whose bones remain in the well. He's a god of corruption . . . and he pulled them up from that dark place to fight."

"Dear God . . ."

But there was nothing dear about the Toad God. And as Owen watched, a rattling shape crawled out from the pit of the well, twitching like an injured insect. Bile rose in Owen's mouth. He recognized the sweatshirt underneath the black ichor. The head was mostly gone, but bits of scalp and part of a face remained.

"Robin," he gasped.

The creature that had once been Robin launched itself into the fray, attempting to smother the bird in decay. Fire raced through him, and he went up like a torch, flailing at the bird wrestling with the black Toad God. Pigin struggled to swallow the bird, but flames chewed away at his stinking flesh, sizzling it and showing the white glisten of bone before it disintegrated. The bird shrieked, the high-pitched sound of an eagle, while Pigin groaned like a house about to collapse.

Whatever the fuck this was, this was not his fight.

It was Armageddon.

Owen coughed, struggling to breathe through the thick smoke. He rolled his eyes up to the canopy. The forest around him was on fire, walls of flame in all directions. He stumbled toward the path they'd followed here, but the fire roared thickly along the dust and brittle leaves. His mustache singed, he was forced to back away. There was no escape.

"Owen!" Anna screamed. She was standing on the rubble surrounding the well.

He shook his head. "I don't know what else is down there!" Clearly, Pigin had been assembling monsters—and the monsters weren't doing so well.

In the bright blaze of the fight, the last skeleton twitched to the ground, all flesh burned away. Owen was pretty sure that one was Robin. His bones blackened and then crushed when the toad rolled over him, snapping at the bird.

"You'll die for certain if you stay up here."

She wasn't wrong.

Owen snatched the length of unused blasting cord and pulled it behind him. He wedged the end anchored into the spool between two large rocks and began to climb into the broken well. The cord was skinny as hell, but it was all he had. Sandstone scraped his shoes as he tried to rappel down with one hand, clumsily. The thin cord dug into his palm and snapped. He fell, plummeting into the dark.

He landed with a splash in filthy water. He spat it from his mouth, gagging and retching. He was able to touch a rubble-strewn bottom, and he idly thought that the water he dredged must have leached back in here from somewhere. He spun right and left with his good hand out, convinced that some zombie monster was going to rise up and chew on him.

Anna was at his side, floating just above the water. "Are you okay?"

"Yeah," he gasped, not wanting to consider how much of the sludge he'd swallowed was part of Robin and God only knew what else out there.

"I think we're alone down here," Anna said.

"Thank God for small favors."

Above, the fire roared and licked over the sandstone. The sky went black, and all he could see above was that red-hot fury. He clenched his fists, trying to breathe shallowly. Surely the air in here was limited, and he didn't want to use it up before the fire consumed the oxygen. But it was looking really grim.

"It's okay," she told Owen.

It sure didn't feel okay. Owen could imagine that this is what Anna had seen, what she had felt before the end, terrified, in stinking darkness in the belly of the well.

The fire seemed to wash overhead, crackling as it consumed everything in its path. Owen didn't want to think of what it was likely doing to his freshly waxed SUV.

The roaring of the fight, the squeal of the bird and the toad's bellows, faded away.

He keyed his radio at his shoulder. Nothing but static. He fished in his pockets for his cell phone. It was waterlogged and useless. He did keep a small flashlight in his gun belt. He clicked it on, seeing the sides of the well illuminated in cold blue-white LED light. There were spatters of black ichor, blood, and God only knew what else smeared up the sides. The detonation had crumbled many of the blocks used to build the well from above. Below, there was just earth. He ducked under the slimy ick and felt every inch of the well. He could find no opening, no place that Pigin might have retreated to in times past, no underground network of vaults that he could reach now. There was just sharp rubble. He could feel water draining in through gaps on one side, but the holes there weren't big enough for him to stick his pinkie finger in, and they felt cool. Maybe air was getting in here from somewhere. He coughed into his shoulder. He sure hoped so.

Owen reached up for the warm sandstone. The

stones had been roughened from the blast, but there was no way to gain a toehold. He growled in frustration, trying several times to launch himself out of the water far enough to reach a tiny rock jutting out an arm's length over his head. When he reached it, though, the brittle sandstone shard broke off, and he landed in the water with a wet smack.

"Shit," he said. Panic settled into his chest. "Shit."

"The deputies will come looking for you." Anna was trying to sound reassuring.

"Well, they would, but they have no idea where I am." It would be a long time before someone would come looking for him. He hadn't even told Robin's doctor where they were going. He had told her that he was taking him to his office to look at some evidence, swab him for DNA, and get some prints, because she'd never approve of him taking Robin out in the woods alone. Yeah. That seemed pretty fucking stupid now. He calculated how long he could last. He couldn't drink this slime. He would last two days, maybe three, before he died of dehydration. He pressed his head against a clean-ish patch of sandstone and muttered: "Shit."

In desperation, he faced the opening of the well and screamed for Pigin. Pigin didn't answer him. Whether it was because the Toad God had lost the fight or he wanted to leave Owen to rot, he couldn't know.

Anna floated above the water, her legs crossed and her elbows on her knees. "Is this what they mean when they say someone has screwed the pooch?"

"Yeah. I definitely screwed the pooch." He laughed,

shaking his head. Then he got serious. "Look. You don't have to stay with me."

She looked surprised at him. "Where else would I be?"

"Your case has been solved. Robin is dead. At least I'm pretty sure that he looked dead when the toad rolled over on his blackened bones. You can go now, into the light or to heaven or wherever else little girls go in the afterlife."

"I'm not leaving you alone down here." She shook her head stubbornly. "I know what it's like to die down here. It's awful."

He swallowed. "I appreciate that. I really do. But this isn't about me. This is about you. About you getting to have some peace after all that happened to you. It wasn't fair, and you deserve to be able to move on."

She sighed. "I'll stay with you, Owen. For a little while." She seemed to settle in with her back to the wall. "Tell me a story."

Owen was all out of stories. "Um. Like from one of your movies?" He dimly recalled enough of the one about the pastel ponies to recite some of it. Possibly he could even sing. Maybe it would comfort her.

"No. Tell me a story from your life."

Owen grimaced. "There aren't very many good stories about my life."

"Tell me about something you loved."

Owen thought a minute. "When I was a kid, I loved kites."

"Kites?" she echoed.

"Yeah. I got my first kite when I was a couple of

years younger than you . . . were. It was a big plastic kite shaped like a bat with flaming eyes. I flew it every day for weeks. I loved seeing how it flew, how it could seem so huge on the ground and so tiny up in the sky. I imagined what it would be like to fly. I adored it . . . until it got caught in some power lines and I couldn't get it back. I was inconsolable.

"My dad got me another one. A fancy one. Shaped like a dragon. He sent away for it, had a buddy overseas send it to him. That was a wonder. It moved like a serpent in the sky. We'd stand for hours in the field behind the house, watching it and saying not much. It was like it was a living thing. I imagined that the dragon had all these adventures in the sky, chasing birds and circling the sun. It was . . . some of the most treasured memories of my childhood." He lapsed into silence, gazing up at the circular window in the sky.

The sky darkened to black, then lightened. Instead of the dark charcoal of smoke, it was a bit lighter, a pearl grey. A deer wandered over and peered into the well. The doe gazed at him, seeming confused, then wandered away. A dim sun tried burning through the striations of smoke. Birds crossed it, and Owen imagined his kite. He couldn't feel his legs anymore. His mouth was sticky, and it seemed that the moments bled over from one moment to the next. When he opened his eyes once, he was in darkness, with a moon overhead. The next time, it was the dim light of dawn or twilight; he couldn't tell. In between, Anna spoke to him of the things she remembered from her childhood: her favorite doll that her grandmother had made for her with yellow yarn hair; her best-loved cartoon, the princess one that Owen finally bought on DVD to let her watch over and over; and why she liked spaghetti more than ravioli. It was more fun to eat, she insisted, but it had been a long time since she'd actually eaten anything.

"Owen?"

"Yes, Anna?"

"Owen, look."

She pointed. Down and to his left was a tiny spark of light in the darkness.

"What's that?"

"It's light, Owen." She sank into the water up to her chin and took his hand.

He stared at it. It felt real and solid, like a little girl's hand should. "I don't deserve light. I've done a whole lot of shitty things. I think it's here for you."

"You probably *don't* deserve it," she said honestly. "But you fought a greater evil than yourself for the right reasons. So, that's worth something to the light."

Owen squinted at it. It looked like a distant star, cold and remote.

She tugged at his hand and pulled him down to her level. "Come with me, Owen."

Owen looked at her with half-lidded eyes. "I wanted to bring *you* to the light," he slurred.

She chuckled and kissed his cheek. "No, Owen. That was always my job."

"You hung around . . . for me? All this time?" He was confused.

"Of course, silly. You needed someone to stay with you. I could have left at any time."

Owen felt a lump in his throat. No one had ever

made such a sacrifice for him. No one had ever cared this much. He thought he was rescuing Anna—but she was rescuing him.

"Come on. You don't want to be late." She tugged his hand.

Owen followed Anna into the warm blackness, to the light.

CHAPTER 19

The Touch of Death

"They won't be spooked by fire?" Petra rubbed the sorrel nose of Rust, Gabe's favorite horse on the Rutherford Ranch. The horse gently took a carrot from her hand and chewed it thoughtfully. All the fences on the property had been opened to allow the animals to escape any stray fires. Rust had wandered up to the barn and had his head in a sack of bird feed when they found him.

"Of course they will." Gabe pushed an ATV out of the barn at the Rutherford Ranch. He looked at her as if she'd lost her mind.

Petra shrugged. "Knowing what you're thinking is generally a pain in the ass."

"Knowing what I'm thinking is also a pain in the ass from my own perspective," Gabe admitted, tying a pack to the backseat frame.

"Owen won't mind you borrowing one of his

toys?" Petra glanced up the drive at the main house. It seemed quiet, and Owen's SUV was missing. Maybe Owen wasn't home and wouldn't care.

"I haven't seen Owen around in a while now. I'm betting he's got bigger issues," Gabe said. Even so, he'd insisted that they take Gabe's truck to the ranch and not raise undue suspicion by leaving Petra's Bronco parked in plain sight.

"Have you ridden one of these before?" Gabe asked.

"Not since I was a teenager," she admitted. "I think I remember most of it."

Gabe gave her a quick tutorial: starting, throttle, steering, brake. Petra nodded—she remembered that much—but it dawned on her why he was telling her all this.

"You want me to drive?"

Gabe nodded. He shook his arm, and two ravens exited his sleeve, flapping up into the air to perch on the roof of the barn. "I'll send them as lookouts, but it might screw up my steering."

Petra nodded. She threw one leg over the seat and cranked up the engine. Gabe sat behind her, wrapping one arm around her waist. She started off, slowly, moving west on the ranch, toward the smoke. As she got accustomed to the machine, she picked up speed. The ravens had taken wing and were far ahead of them.

Petra leaned over the handlebars, staring up at the sky, murmuring dark oaths. She was certain that Sig would have found this to be amusing. But she'd left Sig behind with Lev, who had promised to make the coyote some meatballs when they'd gone. She wasn't about to drag her little buddy into a firefight with a phoenix.

She was vocally debating the disadvantages of a spouse who had wings while the four-wheeler jounced sharply over uneven terrain. She swore the fillings in her back teeth were rattling loose from the off-road journey. She'd already bitten her tongue three times over the cross-country trip, and was tasting blood as she followed the ravens, flying slowly overhead. They'd circle, drift in the sky, and then stop, perching on trees, waiting for her to catch up with barely concealed impatience. A bird above them on a pine tree cawed, and Petra stabbed a finger up at it.

"You. Shut up." She was pretty certain they couldn't hear her over the buzz of the engine, but it made her feel better. Sort of.

They seemed to chuckle at her, and she didn't bother to elbow Gabe. She'd go as fast as she could. If the ravens got lost, he'd pull them back.

"The fire line's ahead," Gabe said in her ear. He sounded distracted, as he always did when he was peering through too many eyeballs.

Petra slowed and stopped. "We're not going through," she said.

"No." Gabe dug into his pack and handed her a paint respirator and a pair of goggles to don. "But we'll be close."

"What about you?" she asked, her voice muffled through the cheap paint respirator. Likely, this was in the collection of odds and ends of junk Owen kept in the barn. But it didn't look like there was more than one set.

Gabe tied a bandanna over his nose. "I'll be fine." His gaze clouded as he surveyed the dark sky overhead. "The ravens can't see any sign of the phoenix, though they can confirm that this is the most active part of the fire."

Petra reached into her jacket pocket for the Venificus Locus. She spat into the compass, emitting blood from her bitten tongue to its hungry surface. The Locus sucked up the blood immediately. It churned thoughtfully, swishing the blood around the groove circumscribing its edge. A glob of it swung toward Gabe. *Magic. Right.*

Another smattering of drops flickered off to the left, where the ravens were walking on the ground, picking at a piece of tinfoil. The smoke overhead had grounded them, but they were still magic.

But where was the phoenix? Was it too far away for the Locus to register? Her brow wrinkled. If so, then . . .

The blood in the Locus boiled so suddenly she almost dropped it. The blood glopped all the way to the front of the compass, threatening to slosh over its edge.

Petra sucked in her breath. "That way, I'm guessing."

The ravens fluttered up to Gabe and scuttled up his sleeve. The feathers resolved into fingers that wrapped around Petra's waist.

"Let's go."

She nudged the four-wheeler forward, certain that the phoenix could hear their approach. The fire was roaring at a distance, but the four-wheeler sounded like an angry hornet to her ears. She drove it up to the edge of a rise overlooking a lake that mirrored the blackening sky, Bridger Lake. The trees on the far side were catching fire from the updrafts, flames leaping from tree to tree in the dry canopy.

But that's not what seized her attention. What caught it was the man pacing the narrow, rocky beach. He was standing on the sand, arms outstretched, looking up at the trees.

She ripped off her respirator and yelled, "Dad!"

The figure on the beach turned. She saw, through watering eyes, that he had carved arcane symbols into the sand around his feet. He turned, a look of confusion and anger on his face.

She parked the four-wheeler and lurched off of it, rushing toward her father. Gabe shouted at her, but she ignored him. Her breath was ragged in her throat as she ran to him, stepping over the circle, and threw her arms around him. He smelled oddly of sulfur, but it didn't matter. Her father was here, and he was safe.

She was conscious that he didn't return her embrace right away. He slowly pulled his hands to the back of her neck and stared at her, as if she were a stranger.

"It's okay, Dad. It's me, your daughter. Petra," she said, brushing pine needles from the lapel of his shirt. It stung that he didn't recognize her, but she shoved that sadness aside. "It's going to be okay. I'm here."

Her father looked over her shoulder, past her, at Gabe. She was confused at his interest in Gabe when his hands tightened on her neck. With surprising speed, he turned her around and fastened his arms around her neck in a headlock. Her fingers automatically came up to his elbows, and she clawed at him, knowing that his dementia must have overtaken him. She had to subdue him without hurting him . . .

"Gabriel," her father said, staring at Gabe. "It's been quite some time." One arm went to her waist, nimbly unbuckling her gun belt, where it fell harmlessly to the ground.

Gabe regarded him with narrowed eyes. "Let go of her . . . Joseph."

Her father chortled, a brittle laugh as sharp as glass that she'd never heard pass her father's lips. "I think not. She will make a fine sacrifice to the phoenix. So will you."

Gabe paced closer, two steps, and his right hand rested on the butt of his pistol, easing it from its holster. "Let go of her . . . Lascaris."

Petra's heart stopped with an audible *thunk* that she felt in the soles of her boots. The only sound she could make was a soft squeak. She rolled her eyes back at the twisted face of her father pressed next to her cheek.

The man holding her smiled. "How did you know?"

"Your pocket watch. It started ticking again. I'll show you." Gabriel reached into his pocket and Petra knew he was reaching for the mirror. The watch was long gone.

Don't do it, she thought. *The mirror is for the phoenix. Don't waste the mirror . . .* She kept her eyes open and stared pointedly at Gabe, who glared at her in frustration. He finally blinked, a signal of resignation.

Except then he said, "Give up the woman, and I'll serve you. As I did before."

Lascaris snorted. "I don't need you. Not anymore.

You're a failed process, best buried." He hauled Petra back a couple of paces, her heels dragging in the sand. "She, however, is interesting. I bet Joseph taught her all he knew." He leaned in and pressed his nose to her hair. "She smells like a homunculus. Did Joseph figure out how to do that? I underestimated him, then. If she knows that magic, she'll definitely be of use to me."

"What did you do with my father?" Petra croaked.

"Your father is gone. I fought him, and he lost. His spirit has been released to the light."

She kicked at him, uselessly, tears glossing her eyes. "You fucking killed him?"

"Be still," he growled. "If you don't serve me willingly, it might be interesting to take you apart and see how you tick."

Gabriel cocked his head, birdlike. "You really don't need me? Have you seen a mirror? You look plenty weak to me. Your time is running out in that body."

Lascaris gazed skyward. "It doesn't matter."

Gabe followed his eyes, and nodded. "Yes—the phoenix. You want the phoenix, as you always did. If you have the phoenix, you don't need her. Trade her. Take me apart instead of her."

Lascaris's liver-spotted fingers traced over Petra's, tangled in his elbow. They paused on the ring on her left hand. "You fell in love again. After all this time. This could be delicious."

This was going badly. Needing to do something, Petra exhaled and went limp. Lascaris stumbled, the old man's body struggling against that unexpected weight. His grip loosened.

At the same time, ravens exploded around her; she could feel their cries and the feathers beating against her skin. With just a touch of space now, Petra slammed her elbow back into the old man's body and lurched free, stumbling forward.

As she did, she disturbed the symbols he'd scribbled in the sand and broke the circle.

She spun and gasped.

Lascaris was slapping at the ravens. Where he made contact with his hands, the ravens collapsed to the ground, turning into tarry black bits of rot clothing white bones.

Ravens screamed.

No . . .

Petra scrambled on the ground for Gabe's gun. She aimed at her father—no, it was Lascaris, she reminded herself.

"Leave him!" she screamed.

The remaining ravens seethed away in a murmuration. Lascaris was in a half crouch, his face bloodied by raven beaks and claws, reaching for Petra's gun belt on the ground before him.

"I will shoot you," she said. "I will shoot you and send you back to the spirit world, where you belong."

"Not as long as I'm wearing your father's face." He grinned at her and his fingers brushed the butt of a gun.

She pulled the trigger, striking the gun belt, splashing sand back into Lascaris's face.

She aimed back at the old man—the body of what had once been her father—but before she could shoot, something with the voice of thunder roared over the tree line, howling with fire. Heat swept down over the beach, blowing back her hair with the blistering fire of a forge. Petra saw the suggestion of wings, black eyes, and a fury that froze her blood.

The phoenix had come.

The alchemist's attention was focused on the firebird, so Petra took advantage, turned, and started digging through Gabe's abandoned clothes for the mirror. She heard Lascaris yell, reaching toward the creature, but a flurry of ravens covered him in a blanket of seething black. Wings and talons obliterated the last of the magic symbols carved into the beach.

The phoenix soared overhead, swooping low, then moved east. Petra's hands curled around the mirror. Too late. The fire rattled all around them. It blew through the trees with hurricane force. It washed over the ATV, and it burst into flame.

Lascaris slapped more ravens away and ran after the phoenix as fast as his old-man legs could carry him. She ran to follow him, but a tree crashed down in her path, blocking her escape in a wall of burning needles.

The ravens paused in their pursuit, looking back at her with wild eyes.

Petra covered her face with the respirator, smacking out tongues of flame that had taken hold on her pants. She jammed the mirror into her pocket. "Get out of here!" she screamed at the ravens. "Go!"

She turned and sprinted back to the lake and dove gracelessly in without hesitation. The steaming water closed over her head and she plunged down, clawing into the water to pull herself as deep as she could. Her fingers closed around gravel and silt at the bottom. She remembered when she was a child learning to pick up pennies at the bottom of a pool, when her father had taught her to swim . . .

She shook her head, squeezing her eyes shut. *No.* It could not be that her father was gone. Lascaris had to be lying.

But she also knew that her father was not in the spirit world. And he was not in his body anymore. Where did that leave him?

Above her, the lake roiled. The surface water was boiling—she could see it, shimmering and stirring. She lay at the bottom, staring up at the churning darkness through her goggles. The paint respirator was useless underwater, and she ripped it free of her neck.

A dark shape plunged into the water near her. The water burbled, and she recognized him. Gabe, mid-transformation, as wings melded into flesh, sodden feathers linking with bone.

But in this dim light, she could see something had gone wrong. Parts of his body remained blackened, as if burned. He plummeted to the bottom, beside her, as if he were a stone.

She swam to him and placed her hands on his cheeks. His eyes were open, and he blinked at her. He was whole-ish. And he would be—if they survived the fire. The water was hot, though—hot as scalding bathwater.

Her lungs were burning. She looked up at the boiling surface of the water and made to swim up to get air. Gabe likely did not need air, but she could only survive a short time without it.

Yet Gabe pushed her shoulders down. At first she

panicked, worried he was trying to drown her for some reason. But he grasped her face, pressed his mouth to hers, and blew fresh air into her mouth. She devoured it greedily, even though it tasted like smoke. He went up for more, came back, and breathed for her. His skin was red and burned, but he took on the burden of something as simple as breathing so willingly for her—her heart ached.

She lost track of how much time they spent down there, suspended in the deep water. Eventually, Gabe took her hand and pulled her up.

Her head broke the surface of the water, and she gasped in the smoky air.

A good part of the lake had evaporated. The water line had dropped, and the beach had easily gained eight feet of land. The phoenix's fire had been truly preternatural.

They stumbled forward, supporting each other as they climbed out of the water. Petra's fingers gingerly hovered over a blackened patch of flesh on Gabe's shoulder. It glistened and smelled like roadkill.

"The ravens . . ." she murmured. He must have absorbed the birds that were killed.

"Lascaris has taken on the power of the fermentation process in alchemy," Gabe confirmed grimly. "He can decompose anything he touches."

Petra shuddered. Her fingers slipped up to her lips. "My father . . . he made it out alive, then?"

"I saw Lascaris run to the road and get into a car. He escaped."

She took a deep breath and nodded to herself. "He's alive, then. And we can—"

Gabe gently took her shoulders. "He is no longer

your father. He is Lascaris. And he must be stopped, no matter the cost," Gabe said.

"But the toad said—" And she remembered what the toad said. That she'd see her father's face. She closed her eyes in despair.

"He's not there anymore. He would have killed you."

She said nothing. She knew something of wearing a body not intended for her. There was nothing to say. He was right. And there was no escaping that inevitable conclusion. Was there?

They climbed up the bank to the ATV. It was completely ruined. Plastic had melted to the metal frame, and the tires had oozed right into the ground.

"We'll have to go on foot," she said. Fire still burned in the tops of the trees, and fire churned beyond them. And, truth was, she wasn't certain how to get back to the main road.

"Wait here," Gabe said. "Stay near the water."

He gazed up at the sky and dissolved into ravens; at least a half dozen fewer birds than before, she noticed. They climbed up into smoke and vanished.

Petra paced along the beach, where her guns lay. The gun belt had burned away, leaving only the metal buckle and rivets behind. But the guns themselves were still intact. They were blackened, but could be salvaged. She splashed water on them before gingerly picking them up. The metal hadn't melted, but one of the bullets had gone off under the heat. The others were certainly ruined; she'd have to take care to remove them. She unloaded them and put the bullets in her pocket.

It was only then that she crouched down on the beach and gave in to grief. Sobs racked her body. She had been preparing for her father's loss since she was a teenager. Now—now it seemed that it had happened. And she hadn't said goodbye properly. She'd just told him to stay on earth and promised him chocolate muffins. She hiccuped and rubbed her face with her sleeve.

But she felt one terrible twinge of relief at this. Her father was not a murderer. He hadn't killed those people. He had been a mostly decent man when she'd known him, and he'd died a decent man. She would be able to mourn him without reservation.

Except she still wasn't ready to accept that loss yet. There had to be a chance he wasn't gone. Lascaris was an evil man and a liar. Her father had to still be in that body, somewhere. Maybe he was squashed down and repressed, but he was still in there. Maybe. No matter what, she had to be sure. Because if he was in that body, she would rescue him. It felt naive of her, but he was her father.

And she wasn't ready to lose him again.

After about an hour, a dull roar sounded in the distance. Petra froze, thinking that the phoenix might have returned. But then a raven landed beside her, and then another and a flurry of them. They quickly congealed into Gabriel.

The roar increased overhead, and the silhouette of a helicopter appeared in the smoke. Petra and Gabe backed away, squinting against the ash blown by the blades. It hovered close to the ground, then decided to land on the burned beach.

A man jumped down out of the helicopter and ran toward them, keeping his head low below the reach of the blades. He took off his helmet, revealing a familiar buzz cut and cranky face to give them a reproachful look.

"Mike!" Petra grinned. She was certain he couldn't hear her over the sound of the helo.

Mike pointed at the two of them and curtly gestured for them to follow him to the helo, heads down. He gave Gabe a withering look at his nudity, but got them belted into the helicopter. He gave both of them blankets. As the helicopter climbed into the air, he handed each of them a headset. His voice crackled thickly with static over it.

"Fancy meeting the two of you out here," he said.

"I'm sorry, Mike. But I'm glad to see you," Petra said.

"It was the damnedest thing, though," Mike said. "We were following the progress of the fire, trying to see where we'd need to evacuate, since the wind shifted. And this . . . flock, I guess . . . of ravens came up and started hassling us. They wouldn't leave us alone, so we followed them. And found you guys."

Gabe gazed out of the helicopter innocently.

"And it seems we have solved the mystery of the naked Good Samaritan."

Gabe opened his hands helplessly. "I like to swim. A lot."

Mike's tone lowered. "What the hell were you guys doing out there?" He was pissed. Really pissed. They were taking time and resources away from others who needed it, and Petra felt like shit for doing so, like some lame-ass hiker who got out of her depth and needed a million-dollar rescue.

"I found my father," she said. "But he got away."

Mike leaned forward. "Your dad's gonna be in a world of hurt when the law catches him. He was reportedly hitchhiking at the edge of the park about an hour ago. One evacuee ignored him, but saw in the rearview mirror that another car stopped. And he pulled the driver out, and the driver . . . turned to mush. That's what the eyewitness said, anyway." Mike shook his head, as if unsure whether or not to believe it. Petra knew that Mike had seen some weird shit out here in the backcountry, but this had to be challenging even his screwed-up perceptions about the parameters of reality.

"Shit," Petra said. She sank back in her seat and put her hand over her mouth. Maybe she should have let Gabe take him out with the mirror. That lapse in judgment had killed another person.

Mike pulled a first-aid kit out and began examining their wounds. Petra was mostly reddened and blistered, with a handful of first- and second-degree burns. Gabe had fared worse with second- and third-degree burns and the blackened spots. "You guys have some burns going on here that need to be treated by a doctor ASAP. I'll have an ambulance meet us at the last checkpoint, and they can take you to the hospital to get checked out."

Petra shook her head. "No more wasting resources on us. If we can find a way to get home, we'll get patched up there. If we need to, we can drive ourselves to the ER."

Mike paused in daubing ointment on her wrist. "You can't do that. The fire's headed straight toward Temperance. The town's being evacuated."

Her heart fell into her shoes. "Sig. Sig is there. You have to take us there so we can get him."

"I want to, but . . ."

She leaned forward and grabbed Mike's lapels. "Please, Mike. You can drop us off there. My Bronco's at the trailer. We'll get Sig and we'll get clear out. I swear."

Mike grunted and looked away. He leaned back toward the cockpit and gestured at the pilot. The pilot gave them the most withering look a man could give through a tinted helmet.

The helicopter turned and went north.

CHAPTER 20

The Ruin of Temperance

The phoenix would not escape him. Not this time. Lascaris whistled softly as he piloted the carriage down the paved roads. Truly, paved roads were a miracle of modern technology. Though this carriage stank a bit—he'd gotten some splash back from the decomposition of the driver—it was far superior to the blue carriage that Molly had driven. That vehicle had stopped running, sputtering and coasting to a stop most unexpectedly, a gauge reading "E." Except this one was emitting some terrible music that took some doing to quiet. Lascaris had slapped at buttons until it shut up, at once warming the interior and causing some lights around the outside of the carriage to blink. That was a small price to pay for the sound to go away. He enjoyed the quiet, and overall found the ride quite comfortable. Too, this carriage sat up higher, seemed to go faster, and was packed to the gills with all manner of useful items.

Lascaris pulled off the road to explore this bounty. He found food, water, clothing that was a bit big for him, a kayak, paddles, and even a couple of modern guns. He experimented with the guns a bit—they were so much simpler than the ones that he'd owned in his time. One just needed to pull the trigger, and a bullet flew out cleanly, and without fuss. He was able to aim and hit a road sign with it, easily.

Lascaris peered toward the sky. The fire had divided and was moving south and east *and* north and east of his current position. Two flickering rivers of flame had split off from the main fire and were snaking away through the land, seeking out fuel. Hopefully, the bird was moving with one of them. He decided to go north, thinking that the bird might be coming to his old home to roost, and that offshoot of the fire was traveling more quickly.

He got back into the carriage and started it up again. He passed traffic moving away from the fire, but his lane was empty. He cruised toward the town of Temperance, curious to see how it might have changed since his time.

He hoped the phoenix recognized it. He hoped it remembered how he had summoned it here, that it would return to the place of its rekindling. There still had to be some residue of magic there, after all these years, and perhaps the bird would be attracted to it.

Lascaris chuckled when he reached the town. It was smaller than it had been in its heyday, during the Gold Rush he'd created. So much for modern progress. Without his gold, it had withered to a quarter of its former size. A two-lane road cut through town, with a few recognizable buildings still standing. The inn was now a hardware store, and the brothel was a pawnshop. There was a post office here, but no signs of rail tracks.

He laughed out loud to see that the church was now a tavern. It cheered him to no end to imagine that drinks and swearing and gambling had taken the place of deacons and sermons and God. This alone was worth crossing back to the physical world.

He turned right, down a gravel road to the spot where his house had once stood.

He wasn't sure what he expected. But not— nothing. No one had rebuilt his house. There was no sign that it ever existed. Just—just a large tin can sitting on its side there. It looked like a ramshackle dwelling of some kind. A carriage was parked out front. He crunched down the gravel drive and stopped before it.

This place looked nothing like he remembered.

He got out and paced to the field behind it, where his home had once been. Grass covered earth, giving up no hint as to what had been here before, not even revealing the shape of the foundations. Pressing his hand to the ground, he sensed only the barest murmur of magic here, maybe some forgotten pieces of his long-ago buried basement. Or that could have been just his imagination.

Would this be enough to draw the phoenix here? Would it remember?

He wasn't about to risk the chance.

So Lascaris took a stick and began carving alchemical symbols into the rock-hard dirt, beginning the spell again to fuse the phoenix to him. He drew the symbol of quintessence, repeated over and over with exactitude, crouched in the middle of the circle, and then waited. The phoenix would sense the symbols, as it had at the lake, as it had many years before in his athanor. It would sense magic and be drawn to it. Such a summoning would at least pique the bird's curiosity. Once the bird saw him, and knew him to be an alchemist, they would join, and the Great Work would be complete.

He had been fortunate his encounter with Joseph Dee's daughter ended the way it did, he realized. If she was an alchemist, the phoenix might have been equally, or even *more*, intrigued by her, and left him to rot. No—it was better this way. He would now find the bird separate from her presence, and it would have no choice but to join with him.

As he waited, though, his mind kept going back to that scene. Of her—a homunculus—in his arms. Such amazing power; he wondered who had made her. On top of that, she had married Gabriel! He laughed aloud at that. It amused him that Gabriel had survived all this time. It told Lascaris that perhaps the Rutherford Ranch and the Lunaria still existed, that the magic had not all emptied out of this land.

That even after all these years, he still mattered here.

In the distance, fire slipped around the foothills of the mountain, curling into the field. It moved in fits and starts, moved by the wind. He saw no sign of the phoenix, though. Still, he waited patiently, hoping for an inkling.

Finally, in the dark distance, he saw a fiery streak. He held his breath . . .

. . . and instead of moving toward him, it moved south, disappearing into the gloom.

Lascaris stood. He smiled.

It had *survived*.

The phoenix was wiser than he'd thought. It had even grander motivations, attracted to a greater magic.

He walked back to the carriage, got in, and started the engine. He drove back to the main road and began driving south.

South, to the Rutherford Ranch and the alchemical Tree of Life.

THE HELICOPTER PILOT was pissed.

The helo hovered over the field behind Petra's house. He didn't touch down, levitating a couple of feet above the ground and not making much of an effort to keep things stable. The grass churned like ocean waves in a storm.

"You"—he pointed to the two of them—"get out of my helo now and quit wasting my fucking time and fuel."

Mike shrugged and spread his hands. One couldn't argue with the pilot. "Good luck, guys."

Obediently, Petra and Gabe scrambled out of the helicopter. Gabe went first and reached up to grab Petra. The wind from the helo blades whipped the blanket off his body.

The pilot grimaced at them and flipped them a middle finger. As soon as Petra's feet touched the ground, he veered away into the sky with such speed and force that Petra tasted dirt.

"I guess that's why they call it the bird," she muttered. She couldn't blame him for being pissed. In the same situation, she would have probably dropped the two of them off at the jail. It was only by whatever pull Mike exercised that they weren't getting charged with a bunch of crimes. Well. That could still happen, but she wasn't going to think about that now.

Gabe looked at her blankly.

"Let's get our stuff and get Sig from the Compostela and get out of here," she said. The fire was in the distance, creeping near. It was about a half mile away from the trailer, she guessed, and getting closer.

She ran to the trailer, but Gabe paused halfway, frozen in place.

"What is it?" she asked, circling back to his side.

He pointed to the ground. "Lascaris was here."

"What?"

A magic circle with alchemical symbols was inscribed on the ground, just as it had been at the lake. Only this one was intact.

"Do you think . . . he succeeded in summoning it this time?" she squeaked.

"I don't know." Gabe scraped at it with a rock, obliterating the symbols. "Let's hope not."

Petra rushed into the trailer. She reached under the sink for a box of garbage bags and dumped anything important she could find in bags—money, clothes, geology equipment, dog food. The power was gone, but there was enough light to see by. In less than five minutes, Gabe was dressed, she was packed, and they were loading the bags into the back of the Bronco. By then, the fire was within ten feet of the trailer.

Petra paused then, looking back at her home. Sadness poured over her. She kissed the Airstream on its aluminum skin.

"Thank you for being our home," she said to it quietly, then ran to the Bronco.

They raced to the Compostela, which now featured a CLOSED sign prominently placed on the front door. Petra parked in the alley behind the bar, within arm's reach of the back door, which they both beat on. Maybe Lev was still in there. Maybe not. Either way, Petra thought she could trust him to take Sig to safety. But she'd feel safer herself if the coyote was at her side.

The back door finally opened, and Lev peered at them. "Shouldn't you be off trying to chase a phoenix?"

"It's not going all that well," she huffed.

"So I see."

"Shouldn't you have evacuated?"

Lev shrugged. He opened the door. "Sig is waiting for you."

Petra and Gabe barreled into the bar. The lights were off, except for a lantern placed on the bar. A battery-powered radio perched beside it murmured the news at a low volume.

Sig lay beneath some bar stools. He looked up at them and yawned.

"C'mon, dude. It's time to go."

Sig rolled over and belched. His belly was distended, and it looked like he swallowed a basketball.

"Whoa. Lev's been feeding you all the goodies."

Lev shrugged. "It's been a while since I've had a canine around. Sig has a surprisingly well-developed palate. He likes to try new things. He really likes prosciutto."

"Great. C'mon, Lev. Let's get out of here."

Lev stayed in place and stared at her. Petra noticed that he was barefoot, in a T-shirt and jeans. There were no packed bags. It looked as if he hadn't made the slightest effort to get ready to evacuate.

"You are coming, aren't you, Lev?" she said.

Lev shook his head. "I stay with the Compostela."

She blew her hair out of her face in frustration. "Is this one of those the-captain-goes-down-with-the-ship things, only for *domovoi*? You don't have to perish with your house."

"I have no intention of perishing," Lev said. He moved behind the bar and began pouring himself a drink.

Wind roared against the front of the building, and it sounded as if someone threw a handful of gravel against the glass. The fire was here.

Petra growled and took two steps toward him, but Gabe pulled her back. "Let's go."

Petra picked up Sig, who was sleepy and as full as a stuffed tick, and they made their way to the back. Gabe had no sooner opened the back door than fire from the next-door building slid down the roof and dumped a ton of flaming debris three feet ahead of the Bronco's hood. The truck was trapped. And on foot, there was no way to outrun this. He slammed the door shut.

"Do you have a basement?" Petra panted in panic.

Lev grunted. "Yes. But this is a safe place. Come and have a drink."

Petra slowly walked back to the bar with Sig in her arms. Lev was drinking a White Russian and fiddling with the knob on the radio.

"When you say that this is a safe place . . ." she said slowly.

"I mean that this is a safe place," he said. "In the time I've lived here, I've put up what you could consider to be a magical fire suppression system. So cool your jets."

Petra slowly set Sig down. Gabe climbed onto a bar stool. Sig stretched out beneath the bar and yawned. Petra winced as fire hammered at the stained-glass windows outside, casting weird amber shadows in the interior gloom.

But the windows held.

Lev passed her a hard cider and Gabe a lager. He always knew what people wanted to drink without asking. The cider was sweet on her parched throat, and it seemed to take some of the taste of the smoke away.

A tremendous boom rocked the structure. Petra clutched her beer and nearly fell off her bar stool.

"That must be the gas station," Gabe said softly.

"Oh no," Petra said. Bear's Gas 'n' Go was a town fixture. Her heart ached for Bear, and she hoped he had good insurance.

Lev took out a cutting board and began making what looked like antipasto salad. Petra's gut growled, and Sig perked up.

"So, you have magical sprinklers in here?" Petra asked.

"Of a sort. This place is deeply rooted in the land and was easy to ground. All those years of people praying in it and seeking sanctuary made it even easier to ward." Lev dropped a piece of meat to Sig, who gobbled it up. "I probably would have done better to use that magic for an anti-intruder system, but after the fires in 1988, I was a little paranoid." He glanced at her when he said "anti-intruder system," and she was reminded of how she'd broken into the bar and fallen into his homunculus.

Petra slumped. "Lev, I'm sorry about running off with your homunculus. Truly."

"I know." He sighed. "I'm getting over it. Really. Death is normal. I forget that sometimes, and try to rail against it in really futile ways." He gave a wan smile that seemed to see through her. "And I see that you're struggling with it, too."

Petra's mouth flattened. Lev might be used to death, given his otherworldly long life. But she wasn't ready to accept the death of her father.

Gabe reached over and put his hand on Petra's shoulder.

She shook off the hand. "My father's not dead. His body is here. If we can just remove Lascaris, can't we find my father's spirit, wherever it is, and . . . and . . . reinstall him?" She refused to believe what Lascaris said, that he was gone.

"For Lascaris to be wearing your father's body," Gabe said slowly, "he must have sent your father into the light."

"And you *believe* him?" she spat. "Couldn't he have my father locked up in . . . in a spiritual dungeon somewhere? Could my father be a ghost, wandering around? Or still in his body, but repressed? Could . . ."

"You went to the spirit world yourself," Gabe said gently. "You didn't find him."

Lev, who seemed to have been listening to something in the back of the bar, nodded and turned to face Petra. "I take no satisfaction in telling you this. But the dead tell me that your father is gone. He is in the light. At that point, a spirit is irretrievable, like my son's. I'm . . . I'm sorry."

A sob escaped Petra's lips, and Gabriel wrapped his arms around her. *He can't be gone. Can't.*

As her mind reeled, it barely registered the radio, but it slowly crept in: ". . . Temperance has been overcome by the Magpie Fire. The fire on that front continues to head east, with several smaller fires leading the way. On the southeast front, the fire is moving more slowly. Evacuations are occurring along the ten miles beyond the East Entrance of the park, south to the reservation . . ."

Gabe leaned forward. "That's near the Rutherford Ranch."

Petra frowned. "The tree. You think the tree will burn?"

He stared down at his drink. "It's been shielding itself as much as it can, magically, trying to hide from the phoenix. If it fails, I don't think it's strong enough to come back this time. I don't think that . . . it will want to."

"What will that mean for you?"

But Petra knew the answer. And Gabe didn't deny it; he just lapsed into silence.

She reached over to lace his fingers in hers. "When

the fire passes, we'll go there. We'll stop the phoenix. Save the tree. And we'll deal with my father. Or whatever's left of him."

Lev placed two plates before them. "For now, though, you will both have to wait. Pepper?"

THE FIRE PASSED quickly, the way a summer storm would.

The fire howled with a voice that Petra would never have expected, a hiss and growl that sounded like the waves of the ocean pounding surf. Sweltering heat filled the Compostela, nearing a hundred degrees, and Petra fed Sig ice water and blotted at her blistered face with ice. But the air remained breathable. She took the time to bandage her wounds and Gabe's. As she dabbed ointment on her own burns, she shook her head at the short amount of time she'd been able to keep her new body in mint condition. A pitifully short period. If Lev disapproved, he said nothing.

Gabe's wounds were curious. They were fading a bit, and she assumed that was his supernatural ability to heal. But a closer inspection of the wounds showed the black had just moved under the skin and swelled, as if he'd been attacked by necrotizing fasciitis.

Clearly Lascaris's handiwork.

Unfortunately, there wasn't anything she could do about that—only the tree might be able to heal him. He smiled sadly when she looked in his eyes, knowing he was thinking the same thing: *If the tree survived.*

Not wanting to dwell on that scenario, she set about getting her guns cleaned up as a way to keep busy. The carbon black cleaned off for the most part in Lev's sink with some steel wool, and the pearl grips were mostly intact. But there was a curious feather-like pattern burned in the metal and the pearl. It reminded her of her trip to the spirit world: Hugin and Munin, thought and memory. For some reason, seeing them made her heavy soul feel just a touch lighter.

When she came back out, she saw that Lev had dug around for some ammunition to give them. Petra wanted to refuse; he might need it to protect the bar from looters. But he held up the shotgun he kept under the bar and said that he would be in good shape.

And for all the fire and heat and destruction, the Compostela stood. After some time of ringing silence, punctuated by the dull murmur of the radio, Lev opened the front door. Smoke drifted in.

Petra and Gabe peered around him. The street was strewn with black debris, bits of small fire and ash. The gas station across the street was a black crater. I-beams from the structure were still visible, but not much else. A scorched soda can rolled down the street, making a metallic scraping sound.

All along the street, it looked like a war zone. The roof of the hardware store still burned, and the pawnshop's windows were blackened and broken. The post office was still partially standing, but the carcasses of two charred cars were parked along the street across from it. The one stoplight overhead was dark and burned out.

Petra felt tears welling in her eyes. Temperance

had fought all manner of supernatural horrors, but this fire had obliterated it. She walked out into the street to peer down the gravel road at the Airstream. She could make out a blackened can in the distance. There was no telling what else—other than the Compostela, which only sported a few scorch marks on its exterior—might have survived.

"I'd say the local economy is pretty well screwed," Lev observed.

With trepidation, she walked back into the bar, through the back door, and to the alley to check on the Bronco. To her startlement, it was in relatively good shape—and a lot of the "relative" came from the fact that it hadn't been in great shape to begin with. A small fire was burning on its roof, but she quickly brushed it out by removing the debris with a broom. The glass was still intact, there was fluid in the radiator, and the tires looked okay. It seemed that it had been in the shadow of the building when the fire swept through, and that it perhaps was in the Compostela's magical shadow, too.

The three of them set to shoveling the debris out of the Bronco's way. The vehicle started right up. Sig, overcoming his lethargy, launched himself into the truck. Petra tried to shovel him out, but he remained in the back, among the garbage bags, giving her a dirty look.

"We're not going home," Petra said. "We're going to try to stop the phoenix. You have to stay with Lev. He has meatballs."

Sig backed himself into a small space between the garbage bags and lay down. He was not leaving them.

Petra groaned. Gabe climbed into the Bronco and nodded to her.

Gently, Petra drove the Bronco past the hot debris and to the street. She drove quickly, then, not wanting the hot asphalt to melt her tires. She hit the gas and plunged down the road away from the ruined town, toward the Tree of Life.

She chewed her lip as she drove. Signs of the fire were all around—the dark sky, burned weeds on the shoulder of the road, a destroyed house or two. In the distance, they spotted a helicopter with a giant bucket, dumping fire retardant on something at the horizon line. It was like using a paper towel to mop up the ocean. The fire was beyond any hope of control. Even if they stopped the phoenix now, the fire would keep going. It had gotten too large. Petra cringed as she imagined it continuing to travel southeast, to the reservation.

She called Maria and put her on speakerphone. Maria picked up on the second ring.

"Yes?" Her voice was staticky, and Petra frowned at the weak cell signal. Only one bar.

"Maria, it's Petra."

"Petra. I heard back from Vicki. Her family got driven back out of the park by fire, and then the National Guard wouldn't let them back in. But they saw your father's car from the air . . . what was left of it. They saw no sign of him. But apparently an asston of ravens," Maria added wryly.

Petra swallowed. "He hijacked another car and killed another person. Please tell them to stay far away. He's . . . he's not my father anymore. It's Lascaris, wearing my dad's body."

"What?"

Petra gave her the short summary, and managed not to burst into tears while doing so.

"Oh God. I'm so sorry," Maria said when she'd finished.

Petra rubbed her nose. "Are you okay?"

"We're getting ready to evacuate. Nine is at the animal shelter, trying to get the dogs and cats loaded up with the rest of the volunteers." There were unshed tears in her voice. Petra knew that Maria had spent her whole life in that house. And if the reservation was destroyed a lot of good people would lose everything.

"We're still on the trail of the phoenix," Petra said. "But I don't think that will stop the fire."

Maria blew out her breath. "I don't think so, either. But keep fighting the good fight."

"I will," she said. "Be careful."

"You, too." She hung up and stared into the windshield. Everyone she knew stood to lose pretty much everything.

"It's all slipping away, isn't it?" She could feel it in her marrow. "Burning up."

Gabe put his hand over hers. "Then we burn together."

CHAPTER 21

Showdown at the Tree of Life

They reached the Rutherford Ranch by early evening. The light was odd. Sunset tried to burn through the smoke, casting eerie red light over the land. They'd arrived ahead of this front of the fire. The one that had washed over Temperance had been faster by several miles. This front churned slower, hotter, but just as inexorably toward the ranch.

"There may be something that will buy us a little time," Gabe said. "Lascaris will likely be heading to the old location of the Lunaria to summon the phoenix, to try and tap into its power to attract the bird. Once he realizes that it's no longer there, then he'll have to find its new site over the underground river. It will delay him, probably by hours, but he'll figure it out eventually."

Petra nodded. "Phoenix first. Then we'll worry

about . . . him." She didn't want to call him Lascaris. He still looked too much like her father.

She turned the wheel over to Gabe and held the Venificus Locus in her lap. She punctured a blood blister from a burn on the inside of her arm. Artlessly, she dribbled the blood into the compass. The red swished over to Gabe and turned toward the Lunaria as they got closer to the tree. Petra held it in her hand as she looked out over the dark horizon. A third droplet dislodged and began to approach the others. Powerful magic was coming, converging on this place.

The tree came into view, standing sentinel over its hillock. It seemed to sense the approach of the fire. Its leaves stirred in the wind, hissing, rattling against each other like the chatter of birds. Perhaps it was afraid. Petra thought that it certainly should be. They parked and climbed out of the Bronco, staring at the once-familiar landscape.

Flames surged down, over the foot of the mountain. The scrub forest and fields before them were alight for miles, the very picture of hell. And there—a comet-like streak in the sky began to approach, the air crackling as it flew—was the devil.

The phoenix had come.

Petra put the bloody compass away in her pocket and handed the mirror to Gabriel. If they could only convince the bird to look at its reflection . . .

"Shit," he muttered, looking over his shoulder.

An SUV approached, driving erratically over the landscape. It was distant now, but would be here in moments. At her feet, Sig growled. Petra's eyes narrowed. It had to be him.

"You deal with the phoenix," she said. "I'll handle my . . . Lascaris."

Gabe nodded and walked downhill, toward the field and the phoenix.

Settling into a shooter's stance, Petra lifted one of her guns to her right eye, shut her left, and aimed for the patch of ground where the SUV's tire met the earth. She shot once, twice, missed—but on the third shot, the front driver's-side tire blew out. The SUV careened wildly, wobbling, and flipped over on its side. It smashed into the Bronco, rolling it, before skidding to a stop.

Petra advanced carefully. The SUV came to rest on its roof, creaking and spitting gas and antifreeze. Broken glass rattled inside. The windshield had caved in with a red spiderweb crawling across the safety glass.

Petra approached it warily, with her gun trained on the shattered driver's-side window. She steeled herself to see her father's bloody, broken body hanging upside down from his seat belt.

This is not my father, she told herself. *It may look like my father, but it's not. There is no part of my father in there; there is nothing I knew . . .*

She sucked in her breath, bent down, and peered inside. The interior was littered with broken glass. A dangling seat belt reached to the roof . . .

. . . and there was no old man inside it.

Growling emanated from the front of the SUV. She pivoted in a crouch, gun raised before her. A grey blur—Sig, she realized—launched itself across her field of vision an instant before she glimpsed a muzzle flash and heard the report of a gunshot. An arrow of brilliant heat slammed into her left shoulder, spinning her back into the side of the SUV.

She turned her head to see Sig tearing a gun from the grip of the old man. Blood covered one eye, dripping down his shirt. He snarled at her with curled red lips.

She shot the old man. She shot him in the gut, twice, red blossoming from his belly. He crumpled and went down, tumbling to the dried grass.

"Sig," she gasped. She holstered her gun to press her right hand to her profusely bleeding shoulder. Her left arm was numb, and she guessed that her rotator cuff was shattered. She hoped that the bullet had missed her lung. Trying hard not to hyperventilate, she crawled away from the truck to where Sig lay on the ground.

She ran her quaking hand through his fur, fearing that Lascaris had managed to lay his terrible touch of death on the coyote. Sig horked and spat, as if he'd swallowed something terrible, or been poisoned.

"Oh, Sig," she sobbed.

The coyote made a curious squeak, as if he was confused, and stopped wriggling. Petra took his head in her good hand and tried to pull him into her lap. Sig slowly stood up and licked her face. He gazed at her with clear brown eyes. He wasn't disintegrating before her; he was okay.

She threw her arm around him and sobbed again, this time with happiness.

But his chest was coated with her blood. She pressed her hand back to the aching wound, willing the flow of red to slow. She was losing a lot of blood, and she hoped to hell the bullet hadn't shredded an artery. Her pulse roared in her ears. She was pretty sure that she was gonna throw up, and that was never a good sign.

Sig whined, pawing at her lap.

She winced. "I guess this body is pretty darn well human after all."

And she was beginning to regret that.

FIRE WASHED THROUGH the field below. Gabe plunged into the brittle grasses, his knuckles white on the mirror in his right hand. The sky had blackened, and sparks fizzled through that darkness like fireflies, a fearsome imitation of night. The phoenix was coming, and it would annihilate all he held dear. It had already destroyed Temperance and threatened the reservation. Only Petra, Sig, and the Lunaria remained. He was prepared to give his life to defend them, even if that meant his charred body offered up a mirror to the bird.

Gunshots sounded far behind him, and he turned. Petra. She had found Lascaris. At least that enemy was dispatched. Now he could focus on the phoenix. It flapped its wings over the field a dozen yards before him, burning like a sun. Its wings churned flame and eye-searing smoke, seeming the very root of chaos in Gabe's world.

A deep rumble emanated from the earth. Gabe's tearing vision flicked to the hill beneath the Lunaria, to the mouth of the underground river.

For the first time in centuries, he stood frozen in shock.

A black shape as big as a car splashed out of the

maw of the underworld. It bellowed a roar that rattled Gabe's teeth and shook sparks in the air, plunging into the field toward the phoenix. It took him a moment to register that the interloper was a toad, black and roiling like thunder.

And the toad was not alone. Dozens of white shapes stampeded from the river behind it. They were pale as bone with oozing black eyes, crested spines undulating in the half-light, and hooves pounding like war drums. The bones were partially covered in skins that resembled rotting leaves, the legs spattered in black ichor to the knee. Horns were lowered to the grass as they charged, jaws open in rictus grins. They were buffalo, Gabe realized. Or what remained of buffalo, reformed and reanimated in some deadly familiar alchemical process.

Whatever they were, they were heading right for him.

Gabe swore. He had to get out of the way or be trampled. He pocketed the mirror and ran as fast as he could through the burning grasses, perpendicular to their approach. He'd almost succeeded in getting clear of them when a buffalo clipped him and he bounced, hard, into a ditch. He dragged himself, gasping, to his feet, to find a wretched stench washing over him and a black eye staring at him—the eye of the black toad. The toad smelled of putrefied meat in a forgotten slaughterhouse in the summer, and its loose skin soughed audibly as it moved.

"What are you?" Gabe asked, though he was afraid to know.

"I am death," the toad reassured him. It flicked its tongue out at him, and the black slime slipped down

Gabe's face. The toad burbled in laughter. "And you. You will belong to me when the phoenix is defeated. You will be one of my foot soldiers when this is through, when death rules this land."

Gabe's eyes narrowed. He had seen great evil before, many times. But this thing was beyond a facile explanation of evil. It was a living personification of the fermentation process, the spirit of rot and dismantling living things to their core. The phoenix might burn everything it touched with the purity of fire, but the toad would rule it in slow decomposition. Gabe's fingers slid to his pocket, to the mirror.

The toad turned away, plunging after the buffalo. The phoenix descended from the sky, lighting in the field with a contentious shriek. Buffalo raced toward it. Like a toreador, the bird flicked its wings toward them, blackening bones that charged it, sizzling ichor, until the buffalo paled to ash and disintegrated. But there was a herd, and they kept coming. The reanimated buffalo made no sound as they assaulted the fire, splintering and stampeding toward the bird that flitted just out of reach, taunting them with the veil of its wings.

Gabe pulled out the mirror. Now that the embodiment of death was on the field, he should plunge in now, while the bird was distracted, and the glitter of the mirror might catch its eye.

The phoenix drew itself into the air with two powerful beats of its wings, out of reach of buffalo horns. But that didn't deter the toad. It leaped up into the air and clamped its jaws down on the phoenix's burning tail feathers, dragging it back down to earth and the hooves of the buffalo. The toad and the phoenix fizzled sharply as they wrestled, and the air shimmered with the smell of burned rubber.

Now was his chance. Gabe had taken two steps toward the fray when he heard a plaintive coyote howl, back from the direction of the tree and wrecked vehicles. The howl was full of eerie sorrow, as if it petitioned the heavens for mercy.

Sig. And Petra.

Heart hammering in his chest, Gabe turned and ran toward the howl.

PETRA WAS NOT going to let this shiny new human body bleed out all over the foot of the Tree of Life. It would be the equivalent of totaling a brand-new sports car, and she had decided that she was not going to stand for it.

Petra crawled to her feet and stumbled away from the upturned SUV. Sig followed her, making piteous noises. She approached the tree, which she was quite certain was judging her on her lack of effectiveness, leaning on it for support. Her hand left a bloody print on the bark and the leaves overhead rattled at her. Some of the topmost branches of the tree had caught fire from sparks, and a couple had fallen down to the ground, where they burned in fiery puddles in the grass.

She sank to her knees and awkwardly ripped her shirtsleeve and collar away from the gunshot wound. She reached for one of the burning sticks. She blew on the guttering end of it, intensifying the flame.

Sig gave her a reproachful look.

"The blood's gotta stop, buddy," she told him. "If I pass out, we're literal toast."

She squeezed her eyes shut and jammed the end of the stick into the wound to cauterize it. The pain was brilliant, unlike anything she'd felt before. She forgot to scream, but nearly passed out and fell to her side on the ground. Sig busily washed her face with his tongue, whimpering.

"Oh shit," she mumbled. "Oh shit."

Sig's tail slapped her ribs.

And she opened her eyes and said it again: "Oh shit."

Lascaris had gotten to his feet. The front of his shirt was stained red, but the bastard was wiping blood—her blood—from the side of the wrecked SUV. And he knelt to draw on the ground with it.

She pressed her forehead to the ground. "Why will he not die, already?"

Sig growled, but Petra caught his collar. "No. You're not to touch him, understand?" She rolled to her side to reach her second gun. It still had ammo.

Lascaris turned his face to her and shouted, "You think bullets would be my end? I'm to be immortal!" He chuckled, a horrible sound. "You, though . . . such a shame."

Lascaris drew on the ground, muttering an incantation. One hand was lifted to the air as he did so, and a mad smile was plastered across his bloody face. He was summoning the phoenix.

A birdlike shriek sounded, and an orange glow spread overhead. The phoenix twisted and turned in the air, as if drawn by invisible wires, pulling it inexorably closer to Lascaris.

Shit. She was not going to let this happen.

She crawled forward. The tree was between her and where Lascaris was doing his stupid wizard happy dance. There had to be something she could do to disrupt it. Her gaze fell on a runnel of gasoline trickling toward the edge of Lascaris's magic circle. A finger of it reached over the symbols, blotting out a symbol.

Petra lifted her gun and aimed at the gas tank. Her arm quaked, and she forced herself to stop breathing, but the gun still shook. She had to do this. Though this monster wore her father's face, he was Gabe's worst enemy, cause of unfathomable suffering to the man she loved. She may not survive this fight, but she needed to do this, not just for Temperance and the reservation, but for him. She needed to remove this evil from Gabe, this shadow that had darkened his steps for over a hundred years.

Sig slipped under her arm, and his rock-solid back steadied her.

"Good boy."

She curled around him, shielding him with her body, and fired.

The shot entered just below the gas door. For a second, nothing happened, and despair welled up in Petra's throat.

Then it went up like the Fourth of July.

She held Sig close as the explosion thundered over the ground.

And the Lunaria's roots reached up and over Petra and Sig. She didn't have the strength to fight them as they drew them down, down into the darkness of the tree's realm.

* * *

LASCARIS WAS GONE. And so were Petra and Sig.

Gabe hoped that they'd had the chance to escape through the underground river, to cool tunnels that could never burn. Fire had claimed the wreckage of the SUV. A burning fairy ring of a magic circle surrounded a husk of a man's body. That was surely Lascaris.

Petra had won . . . but at what cost? He paused when he saw the smear of red on the tree, soaking into the bark. His fingers lingered there, and he shouted for Petra.

But she didn't answer.

Above, the phoenix screamed at the Lunaria, a battle cry that chilled Gabe down to his marrow. The tree's enchantments to hide itself had been broken. And the bird swooped down to the tree.

Gabe thrust the mirror before him, turned skyward. But a sheet of fire pushed him back. He flung his arm over his face and advanced forward.

Above him, the phoenix and the tree were locked in mortal combat. The phoenix attempted to light on the tree, but the Lunaria's branches twisted and turned to form a cage around it. The bird beat its wings against the cage. Leaves crisped, and Gabe smelled wood burning. The tree could not fight fire.

He shouted for the bird over the roar of the flames, but he was too insignificant to gain its attention.

The tree struck him, then, hit him hard. A branch slammed him back and sent him tumbling down the hillock toward the river. He landed on his ass in shallow water. Gabe gasped in fury, clutching the unbroken mirror to his chest. The tree was trying its damnedest to protect him, but it was his turn to protect it . . .

The remaining buffalo thundered up the hill to the tree, but the bird was undeterred. The Lunaria was burning; he could smell it.

He would not allow this. He gathered himself to his feet, wincing, and charged up the hill. The soles of his shoes were melting, sticking in the blackened grasses, and fire licked his sleeves. He knew he would not survive this.

But he was going to stuff this mirror down the phoenix's throat, if it was the last thing he did.

PETRA SUCKED IN her breath in the rumbling darkness. She was too exhausted to fight, but she realized that she didn't have to. Sig was curled up at her belly, and the tree's roots held them in a cradle of tendrils belowground. The river muttered beneath them.

She pressed her filthy and bloody hand to a root.

"Thank you," she said.

Above, the tree groaned, a death rattle of a sigh.

She laced her fingers in the roots, as if she were twining her fingers into the hand of a friend. Tears obscured her vision. "No. You have to fight. You have to live. You have to live for Gabe, for the ranch, for Temperance, for all of us." They all needed her, in their fashion.

A tree root reached out and stroked her hair, tenderly, but in a gesture of sadness.

She gritted her teeth. There had to be a way . . .

Something splashed in the dark below her.

"Gabe?" she shouted out. It had to be him.

No answer.

She narrowed her eyes to stare into the dimness. "Who's there?"

She could make out the shape of something large and black and burned swimming in the river below her. Steam hissed where water made contact with its flesh. And it stank. It reeked like burned hair, rotten fruit, and a compost pile gone wrong.

"It is I," it said. "Pigin. The defeated God of Death." The creature's voice was bitter with fury. It paused in swimming, and Petra could see its shape now, vaguely amphibious, though her brain rejected the idea of a toad bigger than a couch. This had to be Nine's Toad God.

"Wait . . . you're fighting the phoenix?"

"Always. I have fought it with all the power of death at my disposal. All the bones I raised are now burned to cinders."

"We can't let it win," Petra protested.

"The fight is already lost." It began to splash away.

"Wait," she said, thoughts churning. "You said bones. You need bones?"

Pigin paused and blinked at her with an eye the color of a rotten egg.

Petra leaned her face close to a gap in the roots, wrinkling her nose at the stench. "I can tell you where to find bones."

GABE HAD CLIMBED the Lunaria. He felt his skin blistering and palms blackening. His shirt was on fire. Ash and embers rained down on him. He was within ten feet of the phoenix, but it was winning. Half of the Lunaria had burned away as the phoenix broke free of its cage.

He howled at the bird. It smacked Gabe with a burning wing and knocked him out of the tree. He landed, gasping, on the ground. He fumbled for the mirror, praying it was still unbroken.

He crawled to where Lascaris had created his summoning circle. Fire had burned the bloody edges of it, but perhaps he could restore it for long enough to get the phoenix to peer into the mirror. He traced the edge in the dirt, muttering to himself as he restored the symbols staining the ground. He was a piss-poor magician, but he'd seen enough of Lascaris's works to try to force it to work. Sweat beaded from his brow and landed on the scorched ground as he frantically scribbled with a blackened stick into the earth. His hands were badly burned, and he struggled to hold the stick with both hands.

The phoenix screamed above him. Gabe looked up, to see silhouettes emerging from the darkness of the field to the south. Gabe squinted at them through tearing eyes. They marched in a broad and ragged line, pale bones shrouded in black rot. Eyes glowed like embers in their skulls as they moved across the field, to the phoenix.

Gabe knew them.

They were the Hanged Men.

The Lunaria shuddered in recognition, as if a sob racked through its sap. It keened, a soft, plaintive cry.

The Hanged Men circled the tree, silently staring up at the burning bird. The phoenix screamed at them with its shimmering, deafening voice, taunting them, as if it knew it was well out of reach. It could perch in the tree until it burned down to the roots.

The Hanged Men reached their hands up, as if to futilely grasp for the phoenix . . .

. . . but the men dissolved into birds. They were not ravens as Gabe knew them, but rotting pieces of black flesh rippling through the air on skeletal wings. Like rotted leaves in a maelstrom, they swarmed the phoenix.

The phoenix took wing, attempting to get away, surging up into the sky.

Gabe scribbled the last alchemical symbol in the ash, slapped his palm to the ground and howled: "Come to me!"

The phoenix paused, as if an unseen hand had tugged at its tail feathers. It strained upward, trying to resist the pull of the circle, shrieking.

The black birds, the thousands of them, congealed around it. The dead birds clotted and smothered the unearthly flame, like mud on a campfire. The phoenix screamed piteously, then fell out of the sky like a star.

The black toad thundered from the billowing smoke to where the phoenix struck ground. With two quick gulps, it swallowed the creature. It shook its head right and left, as if the bird burned its throat, but the phoenix stayed down. The toad closed its eyes, seeming to savor the victory.

The remaining birds of the Hanged Men fluttered back to the tree, where they perched like rotten leaves on burned branches.

A raindrop hit Gabe's upturned face. Then another. The smoke gathered in the sky, turning to heavy rainclouds. Rain spangled his shoulders, and the coolness felt glorious on his injuries. And then the drops paused—only for a torrent of rain to wash down on the land, guttering the fire and pressing the ash into black mud.

The toad turned to Gabe with a satisfied expression on his face. "I triumph. Rot reigns in Temperance. Kneel before your true master, Death."

Gabe limped toward the toad. He came to one creaking knee and held out his closed hands to the toad. "I welcome Death. I offer you a gift."

He opened his hands and the toad peered into the mirror.

There was the sharp hiss of an indrawn breath, and then the toad collapsed. It melted, as if it were tar on a roof, liquefying into a stinking ooze that sank into the Lunaria's roots. Rain pounded it down, and the roots seethed and sucked at it eagerly.

Gabe approached the Lunaria with the mirror. The mirror had turned to black glass, black as a witch's scrying mirror. A tree root reached up for the mirror. Gabe handed it to the root. More roots pulled up from the earth with a sucking sound and wrapped over and around the mirror, encasing it in a shell. And the encasement sank belowground, as safe as anything buried could be.

His attention was snagged by something flying in his peripheral vision. His brow wrinkled as he spied a small machine, a drone, buzzing about twelve yards distant. He had no idea how much it had seen or, worse, how much it had recorded. When he took a step toward it, it flew away, beating a hasty retreat across the field.

He wanted to change to ravens, to chase it down. Feathers began to twitch beneath his skin, but he pushed them down. He needed to find Petra first, to make sure she and Sig were safe.

Gabe turned to slide down the muddy embankment to the river. Ash flowed on the surface of the water like a filmy skin. Gabe waded upstream, beneath the tree, to a softly glowing light. His chest ached.

Lascaris was dead.

The phoenix was gone.

The God of Death was imprisoned.

And perhaps everyone he loved was gone as well.

THE LUNARIA OPENED its wooden cradle and gently deposited Petra and Sig on the bank of the underground river. A soft tendril of a root gently touched Petra's wounded shoulder.

Petra stroked the tree root with her good hand. "I'll be okay. I just need a doctor." She was wobbly on her feet, but was reasonably certain she'd live.

And the tree had survived. She was glad for that, whatever else had transpired topside. It was silent now, save for the rushing of the water. She tangled her fingers in the roots and smiled. "Thank you for protecting us."

A hand-like appendage reached from the mass of roots and opened spidery fingers. Inside the rootball was a stone, a walnut-sized green one. Petra picked it up and squinted at it. It looked like a rough emerald. Whatever it was, it was a peace offering.

"Thank you," she said, a tear dribbling down her nose. The roots delicately touched her nose, and then withdrew.

Shouting echoed downstream. Gingerly, she and Sig walked along the pebbled beach until she saw Gabe's shining eyes. Her heart leaped into her throat to see him. He was alive. His arms were around her in an instant, and she shrieked in pain.

He thrust her hair back from her shoulder. "You've been shot."

She wrinkled her nose at the smell of burned flesh. "And you've been burned." She placed her good hand on his cheek, once dark with stubble and now dark with smeared ash. He was a mess, looking as if he'd crawled out from beneath a burning building.

"I'll heal," he said dismissively. "Let's get you to the hospital."

"Did you catch the phoenix in the mirror?"

"Not the phoenix . . . I caught the toad that ate the phoenix." He wrapped an arm around her waist as he explained the fight. They limped toward the mouth of the tunnel, Sig trotting in the lead. Rain poured in sheets into the river beyond the grate, and it was the sweetest sound Petra had heard in weeks.

"I sent the toad to you. Told him where the Hanged Men were buried," she said.

Gabe's face split into a smile. "Thank you."

She reached into her pocket and pulled out the stone. "And the Lunaria gave me this."

He froze when he saw it. He gently plucked it

from her hand with blackened fingers and stared at it in wonder.

"It's an emerald," Petra said as they crossed into the world above and slowly climbed the hillock. Cool rain dripped down her reddened face and over her shoulder. It felt delicious, like the sky had opened up and brought a blessing to Temperance.

"It's more than that," Gabe said, holding it up in the rain to inspect it. "It's the beginning and the end of all magic. It's wealth and immortality. It's the key that will allow me to leave the tree forever."

Petra gazed up at the stone, confused.

He kissed Petra while the rain pelted them. Sig chose this moment to pee on the Tree of Life. Petra swore that the tree sighed in irritation.

Smiling, he said, "Don't you understand? It's the culmination of the Great Work," he murmured against her lips.

She shook her head, still confused.

"It's the Philosopher's Stone."

She blinked. That thing that alchemists had been chasing since the beginning of time . . .

"I didn't think it was real," she blurted. "And if it was, why wouldn't it be some metaphorical thing that would need to be chased down and restrained?"

Gabe laughed. "After everything you've seen . . . you doubt magic in the world?"

She turned her face up to the rain. "No. I don't."

He pressed the stone back into her hand. "And it's now yours."

CHAPTER 22

Ever After

The wolf walked through the field, feeling the warmth of early spring seeping into her coarse winter coat. The cool, dark earth was splitting open, shoots of new green grass soft against her paws. It had been a hard several months, but the sun was turning, and with it, so did the world.

The wolf stretched, luxuriating in the feeling of her supple muscles and strong bones. She had worn the body of a human woman for long enough. Months after the fire, after the evacuation and return to the reservation, Nine had told Maria, Petra, and the Raven King of her decision to return to her life as a wolf. There had been tears, but also understanding.

The three women and Coyote hiked to the edge of the pack's autumn range with supplies and set up camp. After marshmallows, drinking, and the rise of a fat harvest moon, Nine swallowed the stone the Toad God had given her.

Part of her was afraid that, as much as he'd expressed his appreciation for the bones and blood, he was still an evil being, and there was mischief in the stone. Or, since the Toad God was gone, the magic wouldn't work. And for a while, she believed the former was true, while the latter definitely was not. Because the stone burned when she swallowed it, flaming through her belly and crackling through her bones. She curled in on herself as Maria and Petra held her, with Coyote at her feet. It took three days, three days of excruciating pain as bone and muscle reknit. Three days of soothing murmurs, water poured into her mouth, and cool cloths pressed to her neck. But this is what the Toad God had promised, and though it was the god of decay, it didn't lie. And as the hours ticked by, the pack, summoned by her howling, gathered at the edge of the campsite. When it was done, Nine stood up on four wobbly wolf feet. Coyote touched his nose to hers, and smiled. She gathered her strength, turned, and walked away to join the waiting pack.

The wolves received her as if she'd never left. She slept a deep, dreamless sleep that night in a tangle of legs and tails and fur. But there was one change—she was no longer the omega wolf. They remembered her, remembered her actions as a human woman. She did not eat first, but she ate after the pups did, now. She was not the alpha. But she had proven herself.

When she woke up, she walked at the edge of

Temperance, through the field where Petra's trailer once stood. The metal shell had been hauled away, and a gravel drive simply ended in new grass.

She continued trotting down the road to the town. Temperance had come out of its winter slumber. The Compostela, as always, stood. Lev was sweeping dust from the back door into the alley. She knew that he had begun drawings, detailed architectural renderings of how the town might be reconstructed. The man had an uncanny knowledge of structures, of what was pleasing to the eye and touch using materials at hand. It was as if he spoke with the land to ask what wanted to grow there, like a plant or a tree. To him, buildings were as much living things as the grass.

Nine paused at the entrance to the alley and Lev beckoned to her. He went inside, and she waited. He came back with a paper plate full of cheeseburgers that he laid beside the door. Nine shyly gobbled them down.

Lev nodded at her, leaning on his broom, and she went on her way.

Across the street, Bear's Gas 'n' Go was bustling. The gas station had been rebuilt in the fall; Bear had kept the place well insured. He was now the only gas station for miles around, and he was doing a good business with his deli and gift shop, a new building designed by Lev that was full of salvage glass and bricks from a ruined house. There had been talk of him opening up a second location near the reservation, but for now he was too busy. He stood in the parking lot today, offering a stuffed bear to a little girl whose parents were checking the kayaks on the roof of their vehicle. The little girl grabbed the bear and hugged it to her chest.

The post office had been rebuilt, and the hardware store would be ready to reopen soon with a beautiful copper roof that Lev had talked them into. The pawnshop had closed, and Stan had decided to move to Florida. Stan's daughter was in the process of developing the land with the intent of opening a small sporting goods store. New structures were going up. One was rumored to be an inn, another a Laundromat. Nine was certain that Temperance would never become a true tourist hot spot, but the flow of tourists brought money and prosperity to the place for now, and there was optimism in the air.

Nine continued on, circling back to Yellowstone. Lodgepole pine had burned to black fingers reaching up to the sky. Some had fallen over autumn and winter, but the ash and burned debris had provided rich soil for new saplings to grow. She wove around tiny trees planted by the Forest Service. Others had come on their own, pinecones blossoming from the heat. The new pine needles caressed her fur as she passed by.

She walked, smelling the rich earth, crossing streams and grassy fields. White spring beauty flowers popped up in areas of sun, and wild strawberry curled underfoot. Yellow violets prickled in pockets of shade, where fawns drowsed with their mothers. Squirrels dug into the loose ground, searching for forgotten treasures.

She reached the reservation in late afternoon. The fire had not reached here, though the people had been evacuated. The rain that had swept through the land damped down the fire, and the trenches that the residents dug held. She walked past Maria's house, trotting up to her porch. She nosed the doorbell. No one answered, but Pearl perched in a window. Nine smeared her nose on the glass to tease Pearl and tell Maria that she'd been visiting. Pearl pressed her head to the window, as if she could touch Nine through the glass.

She continued on, moving through the reservation to the land that had once been the Rutherford Ranch. Maria's tribe had long disputed the Rutherfords' claim to a strip of land in the ranch's back forty. Those fences were now gone. Owen Rutherford, in a surprising act of magnanimity, had signed papers that turned over the back half of the ranch to the tribe. He hadn't done it in person, though—Owen had disappeared with a prisoner, and his burned SUV had been found a month after the fire. Rumors were that the prisoner had killed him, ditched the body in a well, and then been killed in the fire. After his death was confirmed, Owen's lawyers executed his will, to the utter shock of the tribe.

With Owen gone, a new sheriff had been elected, a woman who had worked as one of his lieutenants, and she'd been cleaning house. Fully half the force were new hires, and there had been a number of firings and forced retirements.

As with Temperance itself, the sheriff's department was looking toward a newer, brighter future.

Nine trotted on, and the land that had been given to the tribe now saw buffalo meandering through the fields. Grasses had been coming up, providing forage. With the possession of new grazing land, the tribe had sought to revitalize the ranch with a buffalo herd of their own. The herd was small now, but it would grow.

Nine crossed into the land that still belonged to the ranch. There was no fence here, but it still felt different from the reservation. And part of that was because it was no longer the Rutherford Ranch. It had been renamed.

It was the Firetree Ranch now.

She continued on, to where the house had stood. Now all that was left was the foundation, the structure having burned to the ground. A new house was going up, but it was not the grand eyesore that had been there before. It was a small cabin, nearly finished. A dark-haired man worked at planing logs with a hatchet. Nine trotted up to him.

The Raven King paused, wiping sweat from his brow. He knelt before her and stroked her ruff. "Nine. It's good to see you."

Nine's lips parted and her tongue lolled out.

"What do you think? It's coming along."

Nine looked past him at the cabin. This was the Raven King's dream house. Owen had left the rest of the ranch to him. And he was starting over, the ruler of this kingdom.

A truck tooled past, full of men, and parked. They piled out of the truck, chattering with each other. They brought with them tools, jokes, and a case of beer. They greeted the Raven King and Nine cheerfully, clapping backs and slapping hats on their heads to get to work.

These were the Hanged Men. But they were no longer the Hanged Men. They were Michael and Patrick,

Connor, Bishop, Matthew, and Jonathan. Through the power of the Philospher's Stone, they had been revived. There had been more than two dozen men granted new lives. Some had gone away to seek their fortunes elsewhere. Some stayed, and they worked the ranch with the Raven King.

She was glad to see the Raven King had his own pack once again.

An excited yip sounded behind Nine. She turned and was tackled by Coyote. She rolled on the ground with Coyote, play-nipping and fighting with him. He was always happy to see her. Today, he smelled of bacon. She pressed her nose to his belly and inhaled. He grinned at her and wagged his tail. The bacon was gone, and he wasn't sharing.

Maria's SUV crunched down the gravel drive. Coyote bounded up to see Mike and Maria climbing out. Mike had two bags of sandwiches from Bear's deli. Coyote lunged for a bag, succeeded in tearing it away from him, and spilled sandwiches on the ground. Coyote snagged a sandwich and trotted off to the newly-constructed barn with Mike chasing him.

Maria knelt down to gaze into Nine's eyes. "I hope you are well, my sister." It took a little doing for Maria to kneel down; she was heavily pregnant now with Mike's child. Nine snooted her cheek. She hoped she would be able to see the baby someday.

As the human chatter grew too much, Nine withdrew. She knew she had her feet in two worlds, but she tried to keep her visits short. She was a wolf, and there was no sense longing too much for what she'd left behind.

She turned to go back the way she'd come, toward the Tree of Life. Coyote came with her, his belly round with devoured stolen snacks. The sun kissed the horizon, painting the ranch in shades of false fire. The Tree of Life had survived the winter through careful pruning and heavy fertilization in the fall. Green buds studded the branches. The river that ran beneath the tree burbled peacefully, and a buffalo drank from the creek below.

A woman stood before the tree. Coyote ran up to Petra. She was standing before a flat stone that she'd set near the tree, one that had been inscribed with her father's name. Nine had seen her here often, and kept her distance. Grief was a complicated emotion, especially in the face of so much new life, and Nine tried to respect that.

Petra turned. "Nine." She smiled, squatted, and put out her hand. Nine pressed her nose into it and whined.

"I'm okay," she said. "It's all so different, you know?" Her hand slid up to her neck. Where she'd once worn a pendant depicting a lion devouring the sun, she now wore an emerald. Nine could feel the power of that emerald from here, how it hummed like a living thing. Her old necklace had been set into her father's gravestone. Though the Hanged Men had been restored, Joseph Dee could not be. He was in the light, and like time, the Philosopher's Stone could not overcome it.

Nine yipped.

"Yeah. I'm trying. I made peace with the magic, the good and the awful. I want . . . I want to bring something good out of all this magic, all this loss. I want . . . there to be a golden age of alchemy. Here, in Temperance."

The alchemist's daughter smiled. Nine wished that she could tell her that she was no longer the alchemist's daughter, but the alchemist.

A distant howling echoed across the field. Nine looked over her shoulder. The pack ranged in the meadow below, calling her. They had moved to the ranch, too, knowing that they would never need to fear being hunted by men here.

Nine turned back to look at Petra. *Will you be okay?* Nine thought.

Petra smiled at her. "All is well. Go be with the pack."

Nine turned and ran into the meadow, into the gloaming of this new domain, overseen by the new Alchemist of Temperance.

Acknowledgments

Many thanks to the awesome folks at Harper Voyager for their help in bringing this book into being. Thank you, David Pomerico, for bestowing your superhuman editorial insight on this book and supporting this series. And thanks to Bianca Flores for all the publicity magic. You guys are the Justice League of publishing!

Thank you to my wonderful agent, Becca Stumpf, for ongoing support and encouragement, and not thinking that any idea I send across your desk is *too* weird to consider.

Big shout-out to Elizabeth Lucas for all her help with the art and science of glasswork, and being unfazed with my hypotheticals. You shall henceforth be known as the Queen of Magic Mirrors!

Thanks to Marcella Burnard and my husband, Jason, for the beta-reading, cat wrangling, and chocolate. Yes, I will be taking a nap now. I promise.

Special thanks to Roxanne Rhoads at Bewitching Book Tours for the awesome promo over the years. I always know I'm in excellent hands with you.

Thanks to Salt, or rather: Salutations And Lexemic Thanks.

And last, but not least, a shout-out to Michelle Fox and Michael Lucas for all the moral support that I have been using and abusing this past year. Thank you.